I0822841

THE SHARP END

BOOK X IN THE RAIDING FORCES SERIES

THE SHARP END

WWII

PHIL WARD

Military Publishers LLC

Notice: This book is a work of fiction. Names, characters, businesses, organizations, places, events, and incidents are either a product of the author's imagination or are used fictitiously. Any resemblance to actual persons, living or dead, events, or locales is entirely coincidental.

Published by Military Publishers LLC

Distributed by Military Publishers LLC
For ordering information Military Publishers LLC at 8871 Tallwood Dr. Austin TX 78759 512.891.6100.

Book Design by Stewart A. Williams

Original cover concept by Greenleaf Book Group LLC

Cataloging-in-Publication data
ISBN 13: 978-0-9968166-6-3

10 11 12 13 14 10 9 8 7 6 5 4 3 2 1

First Edition

DEDICATION

This book is dedicated to Lieutenant General Josiah Bunting III, Superintendent of the Virginia Military Institute, Rhodes Scholar, etc. and he used to write articles for Playboy.

In late 1968, I was in the field on an operation in the Mekong Delta. Upon returning, there were orders to report to the 9th Division Headquarters – Captain Bunting. This could be very good or it could be very bad.

Capt. Bunting turned out to be the Secretary to the Chief of Staff. He conducted an interview that did not seem to go anywhere but covered a lot of ground. Finally, he pulled out a plastic bag and said, "Did you write this?"

Uh-oh, inside was a letter written to the father of one of my men KIA in the Battle of the Plain of Reeds and my signature was on it.

Capt. Bunting said, "Your letter was forwarded to the President of the United States. You're one of us now." And, that's how I became a General Staff officer, an assignment I had not one single qualification to perform.

I did not have the privilege of serving with Capt. Bunting for long. He moved on to be the Operations Officer of one of the Mobile Riverine battalions, but during the time I worked for him he set such a shining ex-ample of work ethic that I have tried to emulate it the rest of my life.

LTG Bunting wrote a novel about his Vietnam experience called *The Lionheads*. Unfortunately, I was killed on page 22.

RANDAL'S RULES FOR RAIDING

RULE 1

The first rule is—There ain't no rules.

RULE 2

Keep it short and simple.

RULE 3

It never hurts to cheat.

RULE 4

Right man, right job.

RULE 5

Plan missions backwards (know how we get home).

RULE 6

It's good to have a Plan B.

RULE 7

Expect the unexpected.

ACRONYMS

ORDERS AND AWARDS

BT- Baronet
CB-Companion of the Bath
CMG- Companion of the Order of St. Michael & St. George
DFC- Distinguished Flying Cross (Royal Air Force)
DSC-Distinguished Service Cross (Royal Navy)
DSO- Distinguished Service Order
GCB- Grand Cross in the Order of the Bath
KCVO- Knight Commander of the Royal Victorian Order
MC- Military Cross
MVO- Member of the Royal Victorian Order
OBE- Order of the Empire
VC- Victoria Cross

MILITARY

AO – Area of Operation
AP – Armor Piercing
AT – Anti Tank
AVG – American Volunteer Group
BAR – Browning Automatic Rifle
BDU – Battle Dress Uniform
BOAC – British Overseas Airways Corporation
CO – Commanding Officer
COW – Coventry Ordnance Works
CP – Command Post
DUKW – A two and a half ton swimming tank
DZ – Drop Zone
GHQME / GHQ – General Headquarters Middle
HE – High Explosive
HUMIT – Human Intelligence
I&R – Intelligence & Reconnaissance (Platoon)
IP – Initial Point
ISSB – Inner Services Security Board
KRRC – King's Royal Rifle Corps
LCT – Landing Craft Tank
LMG – Light Machine Gun
LRDG – Long Range Desert Group
LUP – Laying Up Position
MG – machine gun
NID – Naval Intelligence Division
OKW – Oberkommando der Wehrmacht
OP – Operations (Orders)
PBI – poor bloody infantry
PIR – Parachute Infantry Regiment
PWE – Political Warfare Executive
RAF – Royal Air Force

RFHQ – Raiding Forces Headquarters
RM – Royal Marine
RN – Royal Navy
RNVR – Royal Navy Volunteer Reserve
RNPS – Royal Navy Patrol Service
SDF – Sudan Defense Force
SIGNIT – Signals Intelligence
SIME – Security Intelligence Middle East Command
SIS – Secret Intelligence Service
SOE – Special Operations Executive
TO&E – table of organization and equipment
USN – United States Navy

LIST OF CHARACTERS

Acting Provisional Sub-Lt. Skipper
"Mud Cat" Ray, OBE, RNPS

Acting Provisional Sub-Lt. Skipper
Warthog Finley, OBE, RNPS

Brandy Seaborn, GC
Brig. Raymond J. "R.J." Maunsell
Brig. Stewart Menzies, DSO,
aka "C"

Capt. Reacher
Capt. "Geronimo" Joe McKoy, OBE
Capt. "Pyro" Percy Stirling,
DSO, MC

Capt. Billy Jack Jaxx, MC, SSM
Capt. David Stirling
Capt. Duke Slater
Capt. Hawthorne Merryweather
Capt. Malcom Chatterhorn
Capt. Penelope "Legs" Honeycutt-
Parker, OBE, GM RM

Capt. Peter Fleming
Capt. Roy Kidd, MC
Capt. Roy "Mad Dog" Reupart
Capt. Teasdale Brown-Brown
Col. Bonner Fellers
Col. Dudley Clarke
Col. John Randal, DSO, OBE,
DSC, MC

Cpl. Pettigrew
CWO Hank W. Rawlston
Ens. Teddy Hamilton, OBE aka
"The Great Teddy"

Flanigan
FM Claude Auchinleck
FM Erwin Rommel
FM Sir Archibald Wavell
Frank Polanski
Gen. Douglas McArthur
Guns
His Royal Majesty
King George VI

James B. McGovern, aka
"Earthquake McGoon"

King
Lana Turner
Lovat Scout Lionel Fenwick
Lovat Scout Munro Ferguson
Lt. Jackson
Lt. "Dynamite" Dick Coogan
Lt. Alexandra (Mandy) Paige,
OBE, RM

Lt. Butch "Headhunter" Hoolihan,
DSO, MC, MM, RM

Lt. Clint Hays
Lt. Dan Morgan

LIST OF CHARACTERS

CONTINUED

Lt. Karen Montgomery, RM
Lt. Pamala Plum-Martin, DSO, OBE, DFC, RM
Lt. Randy "Hornblower" Seaborn, OBE, DSC, RN
Lt. Cdr. Ian Fleming, RNVR
Lt. Col. Randolph Johnson
Lt. Col. Valentine Killery
Maj. Mattesion
Maj. A.W. "Sammy" Sansom
Maj. Clive Adair
Maj. Edward Twitterington aka "Twitters the Taster"
Maj. Everard Beauchamp
Maj. Jack Black
Maj. Jack Merritt, DSO, MC, MM
Maj. Jeb Pelham-Davies, DSO, MC
Maj. Sir Terry "Zorro" Stone, KBE, DSO, MC
Maj. Taylor Corrigan, DSO, MC
Maj. The Lady Jane Seaborn, LG, OBE, RM
Maj. Travis McCloud
Maj. Gen. James "Baldie" Taylor, OBE
Masterson
McQueen
Mo
Mr. Jones
Mr. Smith
Pvt. Komansky
Rikke (Rocky) Runborg
Rita Hayworth
Sgt. Frank Hawkins, MM
Sgt. Ned Pompedous
Sgt. Rex Blackburn
Sgt. Tim Authury, MM
Sgt. Maj. Mike "March or Die" Mikkalis, DSM, MM
Skipper Mike "Wino" Muldoon, OBE
Sqn. Ldr. Paddy Wilcox, DSO, OBE, MC, DFC
VAdm. Sir Randolph "Razor" Ransom, VC, KCB, DSO, OBE, DSC
Veronica Paige, OBE
Wg. Cdr. Ronald Gordon aka "Flash Bang

RAIDING FORCES ONGOING OPERATIONS

OPERATION BOMBSHELL. Named after pilot Pamala Plum-Martin—resulted in more than one hundred Luftwaffe an d Re gia Ae ronautica pilots being killed.

OPERATION GOLDEN FLEECE. "Pinch" operations to capture Nazi en-coding/ decoding equipment. Commander Ian Fleming's project.

OPERATION LIMELIGHT. Ice blocks are dropped by parachute, leaving empty chutes when ice melts.

OPERATION RED INDIAN. Cover name for OPERATION GOLDEN FLEECE.

OPERATION SOLID GOLD / SUNDANCE. Hunt down and kill Captain Alfred Seebohm, master of signals intelligence, Rommel's genius radio interceptor and his 621st Radio Intercept Company.

FROGSPAWN. Drop whatever you're doing and carry out the orders you are about to receive. Frogspawn overrides any mission except GOLDEN FLEECE / RED INDIAN.

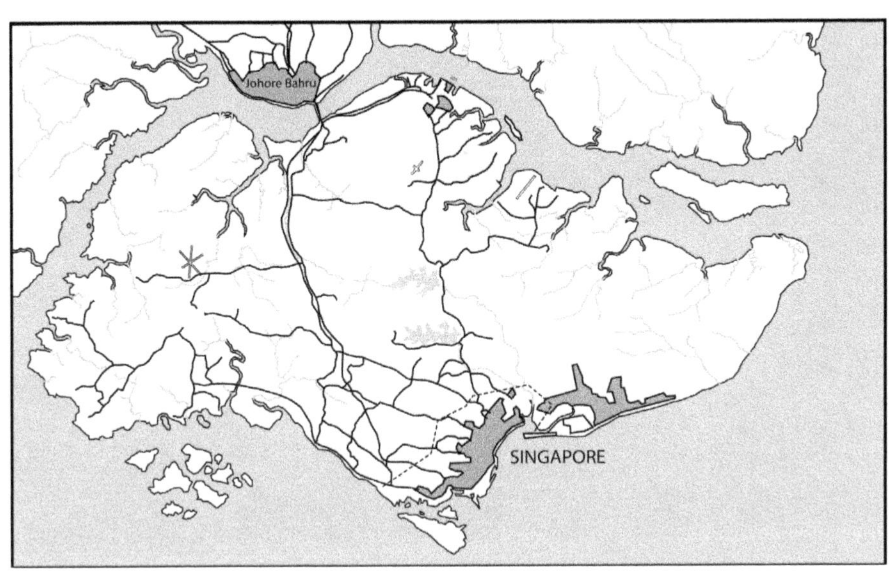
Johore Bahru
SINGAPORE

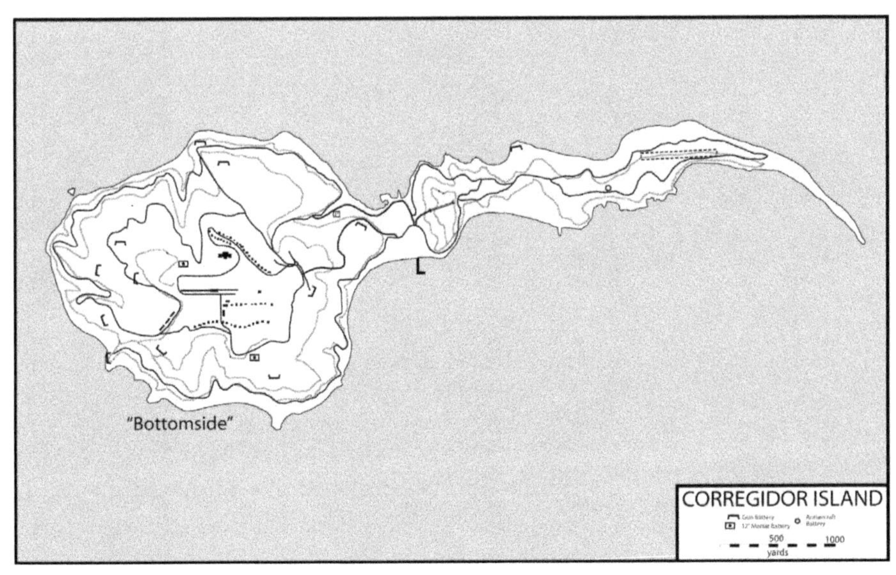
"Bottomside"
CORREGIDOR ISLAND
Gun Battery
12" Mortar Battery
500
1000
yards

CHAPTER ONE

RANGER PATROL

LIEUTENANT COLONEL JOHN RANDAL, DSO, MC, was sitting in his olive-green and pink-colored camouflage gun jeep somewhere in the Libyan Desert. It was pitch-dark, 0220 hours. His navigator, riding in another gun jeep with Sergeant Ned Pompedous, knew exactly where Ranger Patrol was on the map, but all the Raiding Forces commander cared about at the moment was that the patrol's six gun jeeps were hull down on the perimeter of a vast Axis fuel tank farm awaiting his order to attack.

The British Y-Service had intercepted an Afrika Korps message that indicated the Luftwaffe was suffering a critical shortage of aviation fuel. Actually, that was not entirely true. The intercept was a decrypt from Ultra Secret Bletchley Park in England—but Lt. Col. Randal was not cleared to know that.

Not that it mattered where the intelligence came from. The information was dead accurate. Now Ranger Patrol had new marching orders. "Go after Afrika Korps fuel storage depots."

OPERATION CRUSADER was raging. Immediately after the British attack went in, taking the Afrika Korps by surprise, Field Marshal Erwin Rommel flew back to Tripoli from his birthday party in Italy, took charge, counterattacked, and all the smartly tailored staff at General Headquarters Middle East (GHQME/GHQ) watched their predictions for a walkover victory turn to dust before their eyes.

Lt. Col. Randal did not know much about that either. For weeks he had been in the field, deep behind enemy lines, engaged in the risky business of ambushing Axis transport racing down the Via Balbia to reinforce Afrika Korps. Traffic had been so heavy that Ranger Patrol had to resort to attacking *casas di stradas* from standoff range, utilizing its newly acquired 81mm mortar expert. They would roll up at night, emplace the mortar, lay down a barrage on a roadhouse, flee to a preselected laying-up position, then hide and hold up under camouflage netting during daylight.

The tactic worked for laagered enemy convoys as well.

The Raiders called it "shoot and scoot."

The military situation was fluid. No one on either side was quite sure exactly where the front lines were. Opposing tank columns were blundering around the desert churning up giant clouds of dust, endeavoring to run into each other and do battle.

The relief of Tobruk had been a seesaw affair only accomplished after heavy losses in men and tanks. The 7th Armored Division, the vaunted Desert Rats, had attempted to destroy the opposing armor but been decimated by the surprisingly hard-fighting Italian Ariete Armored Division.

That had not been part of the plan.

The question of which side was going to win was in doubt. However, the relief of Tobruk and the initial rough handling of Afrika Korps at the beginning of the battle marked the first time Middle East Command had inflicted a defeat on the Germans—razor-thin though it was.

Field Marshal Rommel took exception with how the outcome was being reported in the press, publicly responding that he was merely executing a tactical withdrawal in order to shorten his lines of communication. The Desert Fox *was* experiencing resupply problems—no matter what he said. That was why he was shortening his lines of communication.

British armor was acting independently again, exactly the way it had in OPERATION BATTLEAX, which had failed miserably and resulted in Field Marshal Archibald Wavell being relieved of command.

The generals fighting OPERATION CRUSADER (now under Field Marshal Claude Auchinleck, who had recently fired the Eighth Army commander in the middle of the battle and taken personal command) had not learned a thing from the BATTLEAX disaster. The British generals thought in terms of tank = horse, and rode to the sound of the guns—but when they arrived, an antitank screen of German 88s shot them to pieces.

The Allied "poor bloody infantry" (PBI) was left on its own, set up in defensive boxes or dug in on one lonely ridgeline or the other.

FM Rommel, realizing that the British infantry had been abandoned, spent a lot of time attempting to locate their defensive boxes in hopes of defeating them in detail. He failed. The fog of war had both sides firmly in its grip.

While the stationary PBI sweated it out, their opposite number—the German infantry—were riding in trucks traveling with Afrika Korps' panzer columns. FM Rommel integrated his infantry, engineers and tanks into powerful, mobile, combined-arms teams that included a substantial component of field artillery—primarily deadly 88mm guns.

In addition, the Desert Fox's armored columns could count on "flying artillery" in the form of Luftwaffe Ju-87 Stuka dive bombers being available on call.

The Royal Air Force (RAF) still refused to fly close air support even though they knew the tactic of flying artillery had worked well for the Nazis from the day they invaded France and drove the British Expeditionary Force out of Europe at Dunkirk. The RAF had its own ideas about the appropriate use of air power. None of them included low level air-to-ground bombing or strafing missions against enemy tanks, trucks or infantry.

Ground combat, the Air Marshals held, was a job for the army.

There was nothing Lt. Col. Randal could do to offset wooden-headed mindsets, fossilized tactics, lack of inter-service cooperation or the confusion of the battle. However, airplanes cannot fly without fuel. And *that*, Raiding Forces could do something about.

While it was easy to criticize the Eighth Army and the RAF, Lt. Col. Randal was aware that his own tactics tonight were nothing to brag about. By necessity, the plan was in keeping with one of Raiding Forces' Rules for Raiding: Keep it Short and Simple. This was not going to be any long-range fire mission followed by a quick getaway. Ranger Patrol had expended all of its 81mm high explosive (HE) mortar rounds.

They were going to have to do it the hard way—up close and personal.

On his command, Ranger Patrol was about to roll out on line and drive through the enemy fuel tank farm, shooting up every storage container it came across. Then the gun jeeps would disappear into the dark and the vastness of the desert.

Hit and run.

The objective was a petroleum storage complex so huge that it was impossible to defend properly. The Italians, who were responsible for Axis fixed installation security, did not even bother. Why should they? The nearest British ground forces were a thousand miles south, more or less, and the Mediterranean Coast too distant for a Commando raid to pose a threat.

An Italian guard post was positioned at the gate to the facility, but Ranger Patrol had no intention of coming in the front door.

"Keep the speed down. Try not to drive too close to the tanks," Lt. Col. Randal ordered ex-Lieutenant Billy Jack Jaxx, MC of the American Volunteer Group (AVG), who was at the wheel of the command gun jeep. "We don't want to be anywhere near one when it blows."

"Roger that, sir," ex-Lt. Jaxx said, sounding semi-bored—"Jack Cool."

"King?"

"Locked and loaded, Chief."

"All right, then," Lt. Col. Randal said, "let's do this . . . move out, Jack."

Ex-Lt. Jaxx revved the engine three times—the signal for the patrol to advance. Then he let out the clutch, and the command jeep rolled through the gap that had been cut in the single strand of rusted barbed wire that the Italians had strung around the installation's perimeter.

When Ranger Patrol rolled out, Waldo Treywick's jeep remained in place while Sergeant Rex Blackburn, formerly the noncommissioned officer-in-charge of the Middle East Command's Officer Training Course's 81mm Mortar Committee, ordered three illumination rounds dropped down the tube of his mortar. He was firing without the aid of sights or the bi-pod. Lovat Scout Lionel Fenwick was holding the tube with his bush hat wrapped around the barrel, moving it slightly left or right as the sergeant stood back and gave adjustments by line-of-sight, eyeballing the objective over the top.

Pinpoint accuracy was not necessary.

On Sgt. Blackburn's command, Lovat Scout Munro Ferguson put three illumination rounds down the tube—one right after the other—as fast as a round cleared the barrel. Three parachute flares cracked open over the objective. They burned stark white, high against the sky, extending over the horizon. An otherworldly glow was cast on the ground below, illuminating a forest of gigantic fuel storage tanks.

Sgt. Blackburn and Scout Fenwick pitched the mortar tube in the back of the gun jeep and jumped aboard. Waldo's AVG driver peeled out to catch up to the rest of the patrol.

Ranger Patrol was spread out on line—fifty yards' spacing between vehicles–driving resolutely toward the giant fuel storage tanks. Overhead, the parachute flares swayed back and forth, creating an umbrella of artificial moonlight and weird shadows as they drifted to the ground.

King was the first to engage. As he fired short, crisp bursts at a distant fuel tank, his pair of Vickers K .303 caliber machine guns (MGs) were making *TSSSS TSSSS TSSSS* sounds because of their high cyclic rate.

Five hundred yards in the distance, King's tracers arched into one of the jumbo-sized storage tanks. The strikes seemed to be swallowed up. Ranger Patrol's Vickers Ks were loaded with tracer, armor-piercing and incendiary rounds. First, liquid fire shot out of the bullet holes. A brilliant flash followed, then came a catastrophic explosion that seemed to erupt from the belly of the earth.

The fireball obliterated the mellow light provided by the swaying parachute flares.

All of Ranger Patrol was in action now. Thirty-five Vickers Ks and a pair of 20mm Oerlikon guns operated by "Guns," the Royal Navy Patrol Service (RNPS) ace, were making a fantastic roar. That many automatic weapons engaging all at once sounded like a monstrous thunderstorm breaking. Fuel tanks were going up, flaming fuel was raining out of the sky, fires were raging—the desert was burning.

As Ranger Patrol rolled closer, Lt. Col. Randal transitioned from his pair of Vickers Ks to his Brixia 45mm shoulder-fired mortar. The weapon was only effective on point-type targets inside 350 yards, and closer was better—it did not have any sights. After launching the first round, Lt. Col.

Randal continued to watch his target while his hands automatically reloaded the stubby firearm.

The little mortar shell plowed into the side of a fuel tank—*CRUUUMP-FLASH—BOOOOOM!*

KAAAAABOOOOM!

Now Ranger Patrol was in among the burning tanks, weaving around them, each jeep acting independently. The depot was an inferno. Tanks were exploding. Flames leaped high into the night. The burning fuel illuminated more storage containers dotting the desert as far as the eye could see.

Sounds were distorted. Colors seemed more brilliant. Lt. Col. Randal was aware of everything around him, all the while continuing to work the Brixia shoulder-fired mortar as fast as he could reload without thinking about what he was doing. Things seemed to be taking place in slow motion.

Ranger Patrol was a superbly trained, highly motivated, battle hardened team of handpicked men who had served together for a long time. Every patrol member was performing to the highest possible standard, executing with precision.

Each man was dialed in, focused on the task at hand—hammering fuel tanks until they exploded. When a primary target began to blaze or blew up, the Raiders shifted their fire to another target and went back to work firing short bursts of six—except for Guns. He triggered shorter bursts of three rounds each on the 20mms—*POCKA, POCKA, POCKA.*

Night turned to day. There seemed no end to the Afrika Korps' installation. It swallowed up the Lilliputian-sized patrol. Fuel tanks were on fire across the desert. Ranger Patrol continued the attack.

More tanks lit off.

Lt. Col. Randal realized he was down to his last few 45mm rounds.

"How's your ammo, King?"

"Final magazine, Chief."

"Jack?"

"Couple left, sir," ex-Lt. Jaxx said. "Lot more of these storage tanks than we counted on."

Lt. Col. Randal retrieved his Very pistol from the side of his seat where it was hanging by a piece of parachute cord. He fired three green flares into the sky: the signal to withdraw. Ranger Patrol needed to move as far away into the Great Sand Sea as fast as they could travel and hide before daylight.

At first light, both the Luftwaffe and the Regia Aeronautica would be out in force searching for them. The Axis Powers air forces had no reservations about flying low-level, ground-attack missions. And they were highly proficient at the task—relentless aerial killers.

At sunrise, Ranger Patrol would transition from being the hunters to the hunted. The life they led was a dangerous game. The patrol had lost one man killed in CRUSADER so far and had evacuated one wounded. A couple of other men with minor injuries were playing hurt.

"Time to go," Lt. Col. Randal said. "Let's get the hell out of Dodge."

CHAPTER TWO

A FEW GOOD MEN

Rommel ain't no military genius," Captain "Geronimo" Joe McKoy said. "Desert Fox—that's a bunch-a' bunk. Sounds like somethin' Hawthorne might cook up when he ain't a-paintin' squirrels orange."

"I can neither confirm nor deny," Captain Hawthorne Merryweather said, "that the Rommel legend is a myth promulgated by Political Warfare Executive for some nefarious reason or not."

"Why do you say that, Captain McKoy?" Lieutenant Colonel John Randal asked.

"Well, John," Capt. McKoy said, "these desert battles all follow pretty much the same pattern. Afrika Korps attacks and drives to Tobruk. Our side counterattacks, and Rommel falls back to around Benghazi. Then Rommel counterattacks. Our boys are callin' it the Benghazi Stakes.

"Ain't no genius to it. Both sides just run outta steam at about the same place every time. Get the supply lines too strung out—two hundred fifty miles or so—and that's all she wrote," Capt. McKoy said. "Dead in the water. Cuts both ways."

The group of officers sitting on the deck of Lt. Col. Randal's apartment at Oasis X were smoking Waldo Treywick's custom-rolled cigars. No one was enjoying himself much.

OPERATION CRUSADER had officially ended on 30 December '41. But it had taken Desert Patrol two weeks longer to get all of its people back to Oasis X from their patrol areas. The fighting along the Via Balbia had turned out to be disastrous for the jeep patrols, just as Lt. Col. Randal had predicted when initially ordered to go after enemy traffic rushing down the highway to the front.

Eighteen men killed, fifty-three wounded—the equivalent of one entire patrol dead, three whole patrols wounded.

Lt. Col. Randal was bitter about the losses. An armored car regiment could have carried out the road interdiction mission as easily as Desert Patrol. Might have taken fewer casualties. Desert Patrol was a high-speed, hit-and-run raiding outfit that specialized in hard intelligence and soft targets.

Raiding Forces had been misused by Middle East Command and paid the price. The losses were irreplaceable—and he could not get equally qualified men to replenish the patrols. A conventional line infantry or tank commander can go to a replacement depot and draw a complement of new troops.

Not so for Lt. Col. Randal.

It took at least six months on patrol for a Raider to be fully qualified.

Lieutenant Westcott Huxley was dead, strafed by a pair of RAF Bristol Beaufighters that refused to call off their attack even after the young 10th Lancer stood on the hood of his jeep waving a British flag in an effort to save his men. Major Sir Terry "Zorro" Stone, KBE, DSO, MC, had been seriously wounded, and his cousin was killed while leading his first patrol. Lieutenant Fraser Llewellyn, seconded from the Long Range Desert Group (LRDG), died in a firefight with a large convoy of German troops on the Via Balbia.

The list went on and on.

Every patrol had seen men killed or wounded with the exception of Lieutenant Roy Kidd's. His Scout Patrol had racked up an amazing score of enemy trucks of various makes and models, plinking them in ones and twos with his scoped .55 Boys Anti-Tank (AT) rifles from long range. Lt. Kidd had brought all of his troops home—a remarkable achievement.

He was in line to be decorated.

"John," Captain the Lady Jane Seaborn, OBE, RM, called from the door to the apartment's living area.

Lt. Col. Randal excused himself and moved inside to where Lady Jane had set up a typewriter on a small table. He paced back and forth, dictating as Lady Jane typed. Tears were streaming down her beautiful face, which did nothing to improve morale.

Lieutenant Mandy Paige, RM, was sitting on the couch sobbing into a handkerchief. Lieutenant Pamala Plum-Martin, OBE, DFC, RM, pale as a sheet, leaned against a wall and stared at him.

It took a long time to compose eighteen letters of condolences. Lt. Col. Randal kept them short and simple but included some personal comment in each one, hoping to make a cold-blooded dispatch seem a little less cold. He knew the bereaved families would most likely read and reread that letter for years to come.

Lt. Col. Randal felt nothing—except an absence of emotion—dead inside. He was not proud of it. Finally, he signed all the letters.

The word was Field Marshal Sir Claude Auchinleck believed Middle East Command had won a victory. Raiding Forces would have taken exception to that idea.

LIEUTENANT COLONEL JOHN RANDAL was putting his pen to the last letter when King announced, "Sgt. Rawlston, Chief."

Even the Merc sounded subdued.

"Give me a report on the status of our vehicles," Lt. Col. Randal ordered.

"You want the long version, Colonel," ex-Sergeant Hank W. Rawlston said, "or the short one?"

"Let's have both," Lt. Col. Randal said.

"We ain't got enough serviceable gun jeeps to put two full patrols in the field, sir," ex-Sgt. Rawlston said. "We can repair some of the damage but it's gonna take shop time. Jeeps is plum wore out—seen hard service. You're gonna need to requisition some replacement vehicles, sir."

Lt. Col. Randal asked, "Would you be better off at Raiding Forces Headquarters, or can you effect repairs here?"

"I think we ought to try to get 'em back home, Colonel," ex-Sgt. Rawlston said. "Ain't gonna be easy. We're gonna have to tow a bunch-a' them jeeps."

"Be prepared to depart at first light, Sergeant," Lt. Col. Randal said. "I'll assign a convoy commander to escort you."

"Yes, sir," ex-Sgt. Rawlston said. "Jeeps with AVG drivers is in the best condition. I don't think our British boys got much drivin' time back home before they joined up. Don't know how to baby 'em. Nothin' against nobody, sir, just my personal observation as your maintenance chief."

"I'll keep that in mind, Sergeant Rawlston," Lt. Col. Randal said. "Good report."

One of Lady Jane's Royal Marines appeared, "Priority message, sir," she said, handing Lt. Col. Randal a flimsy.

UNDERSTAND RAIDING FORCES IS IN NEED OF A FEW GOOD MEN STOP DISPATCH ONE OF YOUR OFFICERS TO FT. BENNING BY FIRST AVAILABLE AIRCRAFT STOP AUTHORIZATION TO RECRUIT FIFTY AIRBORNE QUALIFIED VOLUNTEERS FOR YOUR COMMAND HAS BEEN FORWARDED TO THE POST COMMANDER STOP THESE TROOPS WILL SERVE IN US ARMY UNIFORM AND ARE NOT PART OF THE AMERICAN VOLUNTEER GROUP STOP
JAMES ROOSEVELT, USMCR
OFFICE OF COORDINATOR OF INFORMATION

Lt. Col. Randal stared at the dispatch. He wondered what the implications were. He doubted anyone at Ft. Benning was going to be very happy about losing fifty handpicked paratroopers.

"That's enough out of you, Mandy," Lt. Col. Randal ordered. "Go bring Travis in here."

Lady Jane gave him a look, wiping her own tears. He handed her the flimsy.

"Sorry, John," Lt. Mandy said. "The casualty list is so heartrending . . ."

"Heartbreak's over, ladies," Lt. Col. Randal said. "Is that clear?"

"Agreed," Lady Jane said as she handed the flimsy back, "You are absolutely right—'Keep Calm, Carry On.'"

"You wanted to see me, sir?" ex-Captain Travis McCloud said as he came in from the deck.

Lt. Col. Randal handed him the message. "Pack your bags, Travis. You're going to Benning. Get with Red—work out your travel arrangements most immediate."

"Yes, sir!"

"Mandy," Lt. Col. Randal said, "ask Billy Jack in."

"King, have Desert Patrol fall in at the bottom of the street."

"On the way, Chief."

"Yes, sir?" ex-Lieutenant Billy Jack Jaxx said, walking in from the deck.

"Jack," Lt. Col. Randal said, "Sgt. Rawlston wants to take all the gun jeeps back to RFHQ for overhaul. You're convoy commander. Move out at first light tomorrow."

"Roger that, sir."

"Let me know if you need any other patrol officers to accompany you," Lt. Col. Randal said. "Otherwise, the rest of us will be flying back to Cairo as soon as Pam is ready to take off."

"We can depart any time, John," Lieutenant Pamala Plum-Martin said. "The Hudson has been serviced—all I need to do is a preflight."

"Mandy," Lt. Col. Randal said. "Make sure everyone knows we're taking off in one hour."

"Can do, John."

"Lady Jane," Lt. Col. Randal said, "if you'll come with me."

"Aye, aye, sir."

"On second thought, Jane," Lt. Col. Randal said, "take a moment—repair your makeup. We're not in that big of a hurry."

THE REMNANTS OF DESERT PATROL were waiting at the bottom of the street when Lieutenant Colonel John Randal and Captain the Lady Jane Seaborn arrived. The bearded warriors were in a state of semi-shock. The small group of people present drove home the reality that nearly half their number were dead or wounded.

How could that have happened?

Raiding Forces never suffered losses like this. The unit had lost more men in OPERATION CRUSADER than it suffered in all operations combined since its inception at Seaborn House. Lt. Col. Randal and his officers had always been careful with the lives of the men they commanded, and the troops knew it.

The Raiders did not blame Lt. Col. Randal. They knew he had protested the order to attack the Via Balbia once the battle was full-blown. Nevertheless, this was not a happy crowd.

Someone called, "ATTENTION!"

Immediately Lt. Col. Randal ordered, "As you were—gather around, men."

For a moment he stood and stared at the group with Lady Jane at his side, looking drop-dead gorgeous, as usual. She gave no sign she had been crying—but she was not smiling.

"I'm not going to tell you," Lt. Col. Randal said, "that our people died for King and Empire—we fight for each other in Raiding Forces.

"Anyone who wants to return to their regiment or transfer to any other outfit, I'll make that happen—without prejudice. Those of you who choose to stay on—we've got our work cut out for us. Desert Patrol has to re-equip and recruit and train new men. Then we're going to go get some payback.

"Two weeks' leave," Lt. Col. Randal said. "Come back ready to go full speed . . . and I mean hard.

"That is all."

RECENTLY-PROMOTED BRIGADIER STEWART MENZIES, DSO, aka "C", the Chief of MI-6, the British Secret Intelligence Service (SIS), was in his unofficial office—the billiard room at White's, the exclusive London club. He spent more time there than he did at Broadway, his headquarters. Some thought his choice odd since White's rival, Boodles, was known as the club of choice of the intelligence services.

Commander Ian Fleming, RNVR, was sitting at the table with him in front of the fireplace. The debonair commander served as the personal assistant to Rear Admiral John Godfrey, the director of the Naval Intelligence Division. Cmdr. Fleming was NID's liaison to MI-6 SIS, MI-5 Counter Intelligence, the Inter-Services Security Board (ISSB), Special Operations Executive (SOE), and Political Warfare Executive (PWE). Cmdr. Fleming was also the admiral's intermediary with Prime Minister Winston Churchill.

Brigadier Menzies and Cmdr. Fleming were having a meeting before the meeting.

James "Baldie" Taylor, having flown in from Cairo as requested by "C", was waiting in the foyer. He was not cleared for the subject of the current conversation, which was that the Kriegsmarine was rumored to be in the process of adding a fourth rotor to their Enigma encoding/decoding machine. The sea war, particularly the battle in the Atlantic, was not going well. However, it had been going a lot better ever since Cmdr. Fleming had begun his GOLDEN FLEECE "pinch" operations to capture Nazi encoding/decoding equipment.

Great Britain faced a dangerous situation. With Russia and the United States in the war, the Germans could not win. However, England could *lose* before her two new allies got fully into the fight. U-boats posed the greatest threat. Kriegsmarine submarines were strangling the United Kingdom and were now operating against America and in the process of strangling its sea lanes as well.

The United States Navy (USN) had a lot to learn. Admiral Ernest King, Chief of U.S. Naval Operations, had spurned the Royal Navy's advice to institute a convoy system and was suffering appalling losses in merchant ships as a consequence.

The world's first computers, called "bombes," located at the Ultra Secret Bletchley Park, were able to decode sufficient U-boat traffic so that the combined Allied navies were able to intercept enough of the Nazi submarines to keep Lend Lease shipping running from the U.S.—but just barely.

Without the GOLDEN FLEECE/RED INDIAN missions that targeted codebooks, keys, signal equipment, etc., which gave the bombes at Bletchley Park enough intelligence to break some—but not all—of the Kriegsmarine Enigma messages, it was estimated that it would take one thousand of the best brains in England 1.8 million years to run all the combinations of the current Nazi three-rotor Enigma device.

Everyone cleared for Ultra, from the Prime Minister down, was terrified to learn the news the Kriegsmarine was planning to add a fourth rotor.

Adding another rotor made the number of Enigma combinations incalculable.

So far, Cmdr. Fleming's GOLDEN FLEECE/RED INDIAN missions had been able to pinch the bare minimum of signals intelligence information to allow the boffins at Bletchley Park to penetrate the German Navy's Enigma machine. The priceless product—decrypted German messages—was what Prime Minister Churchill called his "golden eggs".

If the Nazis added a fourth rotor, Bletchley Park would go dark. The problem was solvable, but only if Cmdr. Fleming's GOLDEN FLEECE missions were able to deliver quick results. Bletchley Park needed a lot of help from the GOLDEN FLEECE/RED INDIAN raids if it hoped to crack the four-wheeled machine—brains alone were not going to do it.

To complicate matters, the pinches had to be done discreetly. One of the ironclad rules of intelligence was, "Never let the enemy know what you know or *how* you know it."

The Nazis could never suspect that Cmdr. Fleming was the puppet master pulling the strings when the personnel manning a weather station in the middle of the Great Sand Sea mysteriously disappeared or when a ship equipped with encoding/decoding devices was sunk with the loss of all hands.

Cmdr. Fleming had a problem when he tasked the Royal Navy with capturing enemy ships. Royal Marines, specialists in boarding operations, were only stationed aboard capital ships. That meant boarding parties organized aboard lesser navy vessels were made up on an *ad hoc* basis from the sailors onboard.

He had been horrified to learn that in two recent large-scale Commando raids, staged in Norway as a cover for GOLDEN FLEECE pinches, the sailors assigned to be in the boarding parties had no specialized training. The boarders had been picked at random from the crew and were armed with revolvers, cutlasses and axes—the way it had been done for centuries.

Those raids led to today's meeting. In light of the threat that the Germans were planning to add a fourth rotor to their Enigma machine, Cmdr. Fleming was going to have to step up his pinch efforts. He needed professionals for the job. There he had hit a snag.

His unit of choice for what he called RED INDIAN missions—because the code word GOLDEN FLEECE was classified above Most Secret—was

Strategic Raiding Forces. In the past, Lieutenant Colonel John Randal had executed every RED INDIAN mission assigned his command with alacrity.

Unfortunately, the Raiding Forces detachment at Seaborn House in England had been stripped of Raiders to serve in Desert Patrol and Sea Squadron. All that remained on station was a small team of Raiders performing a highly classified deep reconnaissance mission across the Channel, targeted against elements of the Kriegsmarine's U-boat Command that were using communications other than Enigma.

They were not available for additional assignments.

Brig. Menzies said, "Imperative your GOLDEN FLEECE operations continue unabated. I understand it is your wish to have a unit dedicated to the task. Admiral Godfrey and I have agreed to authorize you absolute top priority to accomplish exactly that objective.

"How do you plan to go about it?"

"My idea, sir," Cmdr. Fleming said, "is to have Colonel Randal expand the Raiding Forces detachment at Seaborn House so that Raiders can be on call when a RED INDIAN target presents itself in this theatre of operations."

"In that case, let us get Baldie in here," 'C' said. "We need to hear his thoughts on how to best accomplish it."

Jim was escorted into the room. He listened as Cmdr. Fleming outlined his desire to use Raiding Forces for GOLDEN FLEECE missions in Europe as well as the Middle East.

"Could be problematic," Jim said. "Now that America has entered the war, it is entirely possible that Colonel Randal will want to serve in the U.S. Army again. Bonner Fellers, the U.S. Military Attaché in Cairo, has already made inquiries about how to arrange a meeting with him."

"Definitely not the news we hoped to hear," Brig. Menzies said. "We want to keep Randal in command of Raiding Forces."

"I understand the U.S. Army Air Force is already actively recruiting American pilots in the Eagle Squadron," Jim said. "Offer a promotion of at least one grade, two in some cases as an incentive to transfer over. You can expect a similar proffer to be made to Randal."

"Possibly we could enlist Lady Jane," Cmdr. Fleming said, "to encourage Colonel Randal to stay on."

"You know better than that," Jim said.

"Quite right—what was I thinking?"

"Raiding Forces took almost fifty percent casualties in CRUSADER," Jim said. "The colonel is more than a little disenchanted with the British High Command at the moment. He was ordered to deploy his gun jeep patrols against Rommel's main supply line once reinforcements started pouring down the Via Balbia.

"The results were exactly what Randal predicted—disastrous."

"As incredible as this sounds, the U.S. does not have a national intelligence service," Brig. Menzies said. "The Yanks intend to create one.

"Colonel 'Wild Bill' Donovan, who is currently heading up the Office of Coordinator of Information, wants the director's job, and we want him to have it—despite the fact that he is a complete intelligence novice.

"Fleming was recently in New York working with our man 'Intrepid,' Bill Stephenson, to lobby President Roosevelt to secure the Donovan appointment."

Cmdr. Fleming said, "Wild Bill and I have conducted extensive discussions on how the U.S. intelligence agency should be structured. As per the brigadier's instructions, I recommended he keep Secret Intelligence and Special Operations under one roof—not allow them to be split up like what happened to us when Special Operations Executive was spun off from MI-6."

Brig. Menzies said, "My intent is for the Americans to participate in Special Operations to their hearts' content, but they are not to be permitted to have any direct involvement with Secret Intelligence. That is to remain a British monopoly—doubly so in Europe.

"To that end," Brig. Menzies said, "I shall propose to Donovan he designate Randal as his SO officer in Middle East Command. The idea being for him to remain in command of Raiding Forces as a joint U.S./U.K. formation if or when he transfers to the U.S. Army. However, we have to keep Randal in British uniform long enough for me to float the idea of Raiding Forces becoming a joint Allied special operation as a bargaining chip with the Yanks."

"Why?" Jim asked.

"Kill two birds with one stone that way—Fleming gets his RED INDIAN Raiders," Brig. Menzies said, "and I keep Donovan out of Secret Intelligence by trading him a Special Operations unit which we will continue to control through back channels—meaning you, Baldie—business as usual."

"Understood, sir," Jim said. "In effect, you are trading Donovan *nothing* for something."

"Very intuitive, James," Brig. Menzies said. "Your assignment is to prevent Randal from rejoining the U.S. Army until such time as we have concluded our negotiations."

"Need to handle Colonel Randal with silk gloves, sir," Jim said. "Should he ever suspect we are playing him, Randal will be back at Ft. Benning commanding a battalion of paratroopers before we know what hit us."

"I have a proposal, gentlemen," Cmdr. Fleming said, tapping a cigarette on his elegant monogrammed sterling silver case. "Why not arrange to promote Randal to full colonel? The U.S. Army will never take him at the grade of brigadier—make him the youngest general officer since their Civil War.

"We checkmate Randal's transfer temporarily while the Americans try to figure out what to tender as an incentive. Which gives you, brigadier, time to cut your deal with Donovan.

"Eventually, in order to induce Randal to transfer, the U.S. Army will have to propose something other than a promotion. We make sure that offer is to remain in command of Raiding Forces—with an invisible chain-of-command that runs through MI-6/NID."

"Should work," Jim said, thinking to himself, *you are not as smart as you think you are, Ian Fleming. Randal will receive a promotion no matter how it turns out—unless that was the commander's plan in the first place.*

Hmmm, possibly there could be more to the sailor than he had given him credit for in the past.

Jim had always judged Fleming to be a man of action who always managed to stay out of it—an appraisal that may have been harsh.

Brig. Menzies said, "I shall ask the Prime Minister to immediately cable Field Marshal Auchinleck to confirm Randal's promotion. At the appropriate time, James, we shall arrange to have you appointed as Donovan's liaison to MI-6, SOE *and* Raiding Forces.

"Perhaps you can prevail on Lady Jane to consent to serve as Wild Bill's social adviser."

"You can count on Lady Seaborn for that service, sir," Jim said. "Any enterprise that champions Randal's cause—consider it done."

"Nicely played, Fleming," Brig. Menzies said. "Splendid."

JAMES "BALDIE" TAYLOR DEPARTED WHITE'S in the club's limousine. He boarded a Vickers Wellington transport en route to Cairo. After a long, miserable flight in an unpressurized cabin, wrapped in more cold-weather gear than an Eskimo, he was met at the RAF airfield by one of his operatives and driven straight to Raiding Forces Headquarters (RFHQ).

Immediately upon arrival, Jim met privately with Lieutenant Colonel John Randal and briefed him on everything that had transpired during the meeting at White's, leaving out only such details as did not pertain to him directly or which he had no need to know.

Lt. Col. Randal said, "I like that plan."

CHAPTER THREE

AUTO GYRO

LIEUTENANT COLONEL JOHN RANDAL was in the third-floor suite at RFHQ that he shared with Captain the Lady Jane Seaborn. The morning had been spent with Lady Jane visiting the Raiding Forces personnel in the hospital. He was not feeling very chipper.

Keeping calm and carrying on in a ward full of his wounded troops was a lot easier said than done—Lady Jane had been magnificent, though she cried in the car on the way home.

Most of the Raiders would make a full recovery, but not all of them, and others would not be coming back to the unit. Operating behind enemy lines for extended periods of time has a way of grinding men down. Nerves go. And it was not always the ones he would have expected.

At best, Desert Patrol was going to be at less than half strength when everyone who was planning to return reported back for duty.

Major Sir Terry "Zorro" Stone had been critically wounded by a burst of MG fire at the very end of an ambush on one of the secondary roads running parallel to the Via Balbia. It was a miracle he was alive. True to form, Sir Terry vowed to be back as the commander of the Lancelot Lancers Yeomanry—his family regiment.

The surgeon, Dr. Stephen Milam, had agreed to increase Maj. Stone's daily quota of female visitors from ten to an even dozen. Which was a good sign that the Errol Flynn look-alike Life Guards officer was on the way to recovery.

Lieutenant Mandy Paige came into the suite, wearing cutoff blue jean shorts and peewee cowgirl boots. She said, "John, I need your help."

"For what?" It paid to take care before agreeing to do something with Lt. Mandy.

"R. J. assigned me an intelligence mission."

Brigadier Raymond J. Maunsell, who liked to be called R. J., was the chief of Security Intelligence Middle East (SIME). However, the lines of his responsibilities were blurry. He also had a role in Colonel Dudley Clarke's A-Force, an involvement with a number of shadowy projects with bad people, and most likely a relationship with MI-6—the British SIS.

"What kind of mission?"

"To run a pseudo agent—a radio game," Lt. Mandy said. "I need you to help me figure out how to go about it."

"The Brigadier tapped you to carry out a classified intelligence operation with no previous experience or instructions?" Lt. Col. Randal asked. "How's that supposed to work?"

"On-the-job training," Lt. Mandy said. "There's not any actual agent—that part's a ruse. My assignment is to create a notional spy residing in Cairo with contacts in Special Forces—that's you, John—and to sell information to the Germans about how Desert Patrol operates so successfully."

"You want me to help you sell information to the Nazis about Desert Patrol?" Lt. Col. Randal asked. "What kind of money are we talking?"

"No, John," Mandy said, "we make up what we tell the Germans . . . it's not going to be true."

"How do you initiate contact?"

"R. J. has a channel to the other side. My job is to create the actor and develop the story line. That's why I need your help."

"Why don't we bring in a real pro?" Lt. Col. Randal said. "No reason to reinvent the wheel."

"Perfect—where do we find one?"

Lt. Mandy had a way of improving his spirits—she always did.

"King," Lt. Col. Randal said, "would you ask Miss Runborg if she would join us."

"On the way, Chief."

"OK," Lt. Col. Randal said. "Help me understand, Mandy. R. J. has a means to contact the other side. You're going to create a profile of a fictitious spy operating out of Cairo with the idea to sell information about Raiding Forces to the Nazis—specifically, Desert Patrol. Have I got that right?"

"Exactly," Lt. Mandy said. "Apparently Rommel is *really* unhappy about all the carnage inflicted by our gun jeep patrols. R. J. says the timing is right to mystify and mislead him about how we go about it."

"I'm all for that," Lt. Col. Randal said. "What do we have to do?"

"There's two types of intelligence, John," Lt. Mandy said. "Human intelligence and signals intelligence.

"The first is human intelligence—meaning secret agents, spies, cloak and dagger operatives, etc. The second is signals intelligence—tap a phone line, break an enemy code—read their mail."

"I see," Lt. Col. Randal said. Meaning he did not.

"My task is to develop the story line of a human intelligence source," Mandy said. "You have to tell me what to say to the Germans."

Rikke Runborg, whose friends called her Rocky, arrived in ballet workout togs and leg warmers. The ice-blond former dancer in the Russian ballet was wearing her trademark ten gold bangles on her left wrist. Rocky had a way of sucking the oxygen out of a room.

"Tell Rocky your story," Lt. Col. Randal said, lighting a cigarette with his old battered U.S. 26th Cavalry Regiment Zippo.

Lady Jane came in from the suite's private pool where she had been sunning in her black, French-cut swimsuit. Lt. Col. Randal noticed his morale had almost returned to normal.

Lady Jane paused to listen to Lt. Mandy.

When she finished explaining, Rocky unleashed a sparkling smile. "Never trust a spy.

"They are deceitful people. Most, the mercenaries who are simply in it for the money—not patriotism or ideology—invent the intelligence they sell their masters."

Lt. Col. Randal had no idea what to make of her answer.

Rocky was a spy—an admitted German agent currently working for Great Britain. Unless she was the Russian master spy Marina Lee, who had been sent to infiltrate the German intelligence apparatus and was then, in turn, ordered by the Abwehr to penetrate the British SIS. Rocky denied being Marina Lee.

MI-5 (Counterintelligence) suspected she could be a triple agent. However, Rocky had sent a message to Field Marshal Erwin Rommel with a false start date for OPERATION CRUSADER. Based on her report, the Desert Fox had flown out of the country to celebrate his birthday and was away from his command post when the British attack kicked off, taking Afrika Korps by surprise.

Rommel's absence at the crucial moment when CRUSADER went in should have exonerated Rocky. However, the Afrika Korps commander had flown back to Libya and counterattacked so quickly with such powerful effect that there was lingering suspicion in some quarters.

Could the Desert Fox's departure from the country be a German ploy designed to cement British intelligence's belief that Rocky had flipped to their side when, in fact, she was still working for the Nazis, all the while reporting—somehow—to the Russians who were her true masters?

The spy versus spy game could be byzantine. And it could also stretch the imagination.

Lt. Col. Randal was having a hard time believing anyone could invent a story convincing enough to fool a national level intelligence agency for any length of time. He had faith in British Intelligence (MI-6) *and* the Abwehr—it being a bad idea to hold your enemy in contempt.

As if reading his mind, Rocky said, "Most spies operating in a foreign country go straight to the nearest public library. They mine the latest newspapers and scientific magazines for stories—it's called 'open source intelligence.' When the spy finds a suitable article with military implications, they edit it, manufacture a credible story, and then send it to their customers."

"Do the spy's handlers realize that?"

"Of course not, John," Rocky said. "Case officers imagine their secret agents spend their time performing fantastic feats of clandestine skullduggery like in the movies—honey traps, sleeping with informants, black bag entries, steaming open envelopes, bribing or blackmailing people into revealing classified information."

"That's what I thought," Lt. Col. Randal said.

"The irony," Rocky said, "is that information obtained from open source stories available to the public at the local library often results in high-grade intelligence. More reliable than human intelligence, even from the trustworthy agents who are not fabricating their reports from whole cloth."

Lt. Col. Randal said, "Really?"

Lady Jane, who had been in MI-6 at the start of the war, having been sent to every school the SIS had in order to keep her occupied—there being no chance she would ever be used as an undercover operative due to being so well known—then transferred to SOE with Section D, where the exact same thing happened, was following every word of Rocky's explanation.

Lt. Mandy was too.

King said, "Rocky's right, Chief—that's the way it works. Not unheard of for a foreign intelligence agent to create an entire fictional network of imaginary sub-agents under his notional control to impress his customer and convince them to buy more information. No way for the employing intelligence service to verify the network—the spy's all alone operating in an enemy country."

"Since I'm not about to tell Desert Patrol's tactics or practices to the other side," Lt. Col. Randal said, "what we need to come up with for Mandy is a true story we can use as a basis to work from—make up the rest?"

"Precisely," Lady Jane said. "Send the Nazis on a fool's errand. I want to play—fun."

"Come on, King," Mandy said. "There are stacks of magazines downstairs for the troops to read. Let's bring some up here . . . look through them for the right article."

"If I'm understanding this right," Lt. Col. Randal said, "the British Secret Service would be better off hiring librarians than recruiting secret agents to penetrate the Third Reich?"

"Exactly," Lady Jane said. "At least that way MI-6 would know the true source of the intelligence—print media written by an accredited reporter. Not the product of some imposter's imagination."

"Most human intelligence is worthless," Rocky said. "Spies are scum."

"That's too bad," Lt. Col. Randal said. "I always liked spy stories."

Thirty minutes later, feeling fairly stupid, Lt. Col. Randal was flipping the pages of a year-old copy of *Popular Science,* looking for who knows what, when he froze. There it was—complete with a photograph: AUTO GYRO—THE THEORY AND HISTORY.

"Here you go, Mandy," Lt. Col. Randal said, handing her the magazine. "Tell the bad guys Desert Patrol is buzzing around the Great Sand Sea in a fleet of Auto Gyros under cover of darkness like a swarm of killer bumble bees.

"That should give 'em something to think about."

"Great story, John!" Lt. Mandy said.

"Agreed," Lady Jane said, looking over her shoulder at the article. "Excellent."

"The Germans will believe you, Mandy," Rocky said. "Nazis are *obsessed* with technology and 'wonder weapons.'"

"Maybe we should look into testing one of these Auto Gyros," King said, "You might be on to something, Chief—could work."

"I can't believe," Lt. Col. Randal said, "that spies do their best work at the public library."

CAPTAIN THE LADY JANE SEABORN stepped out of the shower at her posh Mena House suite, six hundred yards from the Great Pyramid. Lieutenant Colonel John Randal could not help but notice how the white fluffy towel wrapped around her contrasted sharply with her golden tan. Lady Jane sat down in front of a massive, clam-shaped art deco mirror and began putting on her eyeliner.

"Your mission," she said, "is to have Brandy arrive at the Field Marshal's residence at twenty-hundred hours sharp."

"I can do that," Lt. Col. Randal said. He was polishing his Blood's uniform dress boots. There was a two-year waiting period for a pair—provided you were on the client list. He had received his boots a few weeks after Lady Jane had ordered them. According to Major Sir Terry "Zorro" Stone, your father had to put you on the Blood's list the day you were born—provided of course, *he* was on it.

Maj. Stone claimed that Lt. Col. Randal must have replaced Lady Jane's dead husband on the Blood's list in order to get a pair of boots. Only her husband had turned out not to be dead. Now, he was marooned on a semi-arctic island commanding a Royal Navy support depot—under a cloud of suspicion for being the only survivor when the destroyer he commanded had been sunk off Norway.

Lt. Col. Randal wondered what would happen if Commander Mallory Seaborn, RN, decided to order a new pair of boots someday.

"I shall meet you there," Lady Jane said, making eye contact with him in the mirror. "Do not forget that her award is to be a secret."

Brandy Seaborn was finally going to be decorated for captaining the family houseboat to Dunkirk during OPERATION DYNAMO—making five trips to rescue troops. She and Captain Penelope "Legs" Honeycutt-Parker, OBE, RM, were the only all-female crew in the flotilla of private watercraft. Capt. Honeycutt-Parker was to receive a medal too.

Lieutenant Pamala Plum-Martin, Lieutenant Mandy Paige, her mother, Veronica, and Red, the Flying Clipper Girl, were all to be decorated for their actions during the siege of RAF Habbaniya. That was a secret too. The night was going to be full of surprises.

What Lady Jane failed to mention was that Lt. Col. Randal was going to be promoted to full colonel.

That, too, was supposed to be a surprise.

What Lady Jane did not know was that Lt. Col. Randal knew all about his promotion. He also knew Lady Jane was to receive an award for raising her female Royal Marine Detachment—the only one of its kind—in addition to other unnamed services to the crown. And, she was being promoted to major.

Lady Jane had no idea.

Neither Lady Jane nor Lt. Col. Randal were aware that King George VI had arrived in Cairo earlier that morning to congratulate Field Marshal Claude Auchinleck on his recent OPERATION CRUSADER victory and would be conducting the investiture. The King's trip to Egypt might have been influenced by the fact that Lady Jane's award as a Lady Companion of the Most Noble Order of the Garter was conferred at the personal discretion of the Sovereign.

Tonight was a small, private ceremony, a rare event since all the recipients of valor or achievement awards were women. Later in the week,

FM Auchinleck would conduct a ceremony at the hospital for wounded Raiders who were unable to attend the investiture at RFHQ.

It was no problem for Lt. Col. Randal to have Brandy in the Mena House limousine in time for it to arrive at FM Auchinleck's residence at the appointed hour—she was staying in the suite's guest room.

Lady Jane had already departed to oversee the final preparations for the event with Flanigan, her driver/bodyguard, who had been a base policeman at RAF Habbaniya and carried out the same duties for Lt. Col. Randal during that siege.

Lady Jane had a way of appropriating things and people that belonged to or worked for him—she was wearing his old ivory grips on her 1911 Model Colt .38 Super with Raiding Forces carved on them from his days commanding Force N in Abyssinia. And carrying his ivory riding crop that had been converted into an officer's walking-out stick—a long slim blade was concealed inside.

Tonight Brandy was wearing a simple skintight white sheath, and Lt. Col. Randal could not help but notice how it contrasted with *her* golden tan. She did not look old enough to be the mother of a Raiding Forces senior naval officer—even if he was only nineteen.

Brandy and Lt. Col. Randal had been close since the night they met. "Jane is taking this night soooo seriously," Brandy said. "She really loves you, John . . ." Whoops—nearly slipped and mentioned his surprise promotion!

"I don't think so," Lt. Col. Randal said.

"You do not think Jane loves you?"

"No."

Brandy said, "Then why do you suppose Jane followed you halfway around the globe in the middle of a war to serve with Raiding Forces when she could have held any position she desired in England?"

"That's her job," Lt. Col. Randal said. "She's my MI-6 Control."

Brandy started laughing so hard that she found it difficult to speak. "You believe Jane is sleeping with you for the Secret Intelligence Service?

"I love you, John, but you are a total idiot."

"You can't tell anybody," Lt. Col. Randal said. "My IQ is classified."

LIEUTENANT COLONEL JOHN RANDAL was standing in the living room of Field Marshal Claude Auchinleck's residence talking to His Royal Majesty King George VI following the short, private investiture ceremony. The king was the colonel-in-chief of the King's Royal Rifle Corps. The KRRC was Lt. Col. Randal's regiment, though he wore the "Rangers" badge on his uniform by choice because it was the Territorial Regiment he joined when he first entered the British Army. The Rangers had been amalgamated into the KRRC.

"Congratulations, Colonel, always a pleasure to see an officer of the regiment advance," King George said, with the slight stutter he had battled since childhood. He took his role as colonel-in-chief of the KRRC seriously. "'Straordinary evening, thought for a moment Lady Jane was going to have the vapors . . ."

FM Auchinleck's senior aide rushed into the room, made his way straight toward his boss. He whispered in his ear. The Field Marshal turned pale.

"Your Majesty, ladies and gentlemen," FM Auchinleck announced. "I regret I shall have to make my excuses . . . Rommel has launched a full-blooded counterattack at El Agheila."

The announcement was a showstopper.

CHAPTER FOUR

ORDER OF THE GARTER

THE ITALIANS MANAGED TO EVADE the Royal Navy and land a convoy of ships containing a resupply of German Panzer Mark IIIs," James "Baldie" Taylor said. "Afrika Korps had been reduced to an estimated thirty to forty serviceable tanks of all models—mostly Italian—when Rommel pulled back to his defensive positions at El Agheila at the end of OPERATION CRUSADER. As soon as the panzers came ashore, he attacked straightaway—no worrying about logistics, the operational arts, or any of the other preconditions necessary to sustain a major offensive operation. The minute Rommel's tanks arrived, he went over to offense.

"Took us off guard."

Jim was briefing Colonel John Randal in the third-floor suite he shared with Major the Lady Jane Seaborn, LG, OBE, RM, at Raiding Forces Headquarters two hours after the investiture ceremony. The decision had been made for them to go to RFHQ rather than to return to Mena House.

The mood was tense as Jim briefed. Initial reports indicated that Field Marshal Erwin Rommel had caught the British Eighth Army troops spread out, exhausted from the CRUSADER fighting. His new allocation of panzers was cutting through the Allied defenses like a hot knife through butter. Col. Randal knew the first reports from the battlefield are almost never accurate, but he was not questioning the basic appreciation—the Desert Fox was on a rampage.

Jim said, "Auchinleck is scrambling to establish a defensive line that will hold, but the situation is fluid at the moment.

"Place Raiding Forces on alert for immediate deployment."

"With what, General?" Col. Randal said. "We only have enough serviceable gun jeeps for two patrols exclusive of Sea Squadron and barely enough fit men to fill 'em. Besides, Lt. Jaxx won't arrive from Oasis X with our jeeps until later tomorrow.

"My troops haven't had any downtime after over a month's continuous operations behind the lines. They're in no condition to take the field again."

"Point noted—cobble together as many operational patrols as possible. This is an emergency," Jim ordered.

"I have a meeting with Dudley Clarke in an hour. Raiding Forces will be supporting an A-Force mission. Brief you on the details as soon as I return later tonight, Colonel. We would not be having this conversation if the situation was not critical."

"We'll be playing hurt," Col. Randal said. "Every one of our patrols except Roy Kidd's Scout Patrol took casualties. The Regiment is completely out of patrol leaders—Westcott Huxley was KIA, three others wounded. Terry Stone is in critical condition, and Travis McCloud is away in the U.S. at Ft. Benning on a recruiting trip."

"I can take out a patrol," Jim said. "Count on me to accompany you, regardless."

"We may have to take you up on your offer," Col. Randal said. "Raiding Forces was short officers before CRUSADER."

"I say again," Jim said, "this is an *emergency*."

After the general left for his meeting, Col. Randal said, "King, send a message to Lieutenant Hoolihan. Order him to take over command of Duck Patrol. Have Sergeant Major Mikkalis report to me here at RFHQ as soon as possible."

"On the way, Chief."

"While you're at it," Col. Randal said, "issue a recall for all Raiding Forces personnel on leave."

King said, "Probably hanging out in bars all down the coast from Cairo to Alexandria, Chief."

"I don't care if they're in Antarctica," Col. Randal said. "Get 'em back here."

"Roger."

"Find out where Major Merritt is. Have him assemble his Sudan Defense Force Company at a location of his choosing and stand by for orders," Col. Randal ordered.

"Radio Billy Jack, get an ETA for the vehicle convoy to arrive at RFHQ—tell him to step on it."

WALDO TREYWICK CAME IN THE SUITE. "King said I could find you up here, Colonel. Workin' late? Congratulations on gettin' promoted." He took out a pair of his thin, custom-rolled cigars and handed one to Colonel John Randal. They did not light them. Major the Lady Jane Seaborn did not allow cigar smoking in the suite.

"Lady Seaborn got made a 'double' Lady," Waldo said. "Never heard-a' 'at one before."

"It's complicated," Col. Randal said. "Not sure anyone understands the British system of honors, orders and decorations—I don't.

"Where's Captain McKoy?"

"He's at the Gezira," Waldo said. "Joe's havin' dinner with one of the Kit Kat belly dancers before she has to go to work—late shift."

Col. Randal went to the phone on King's desk and rang the Operations Room, "Call the Gezira Club, Stephanie," he said to the Royal Marine on duty. "Have the maître'd' take a phone to Captain McKoy's table—give him my compliments. Ask him to report to my suite at RFHQ as soon as he finishes dinner with the Kit Kat dancer he's having a date with."

"Sir!" The Royal Marine giggled. "Straightaway, Colonel Randal."

King came in. "Captain Corrigan is in Alexandria, Chief—chasing women. I left a message at his hotel for him to call in as soon as he returns. Every other officer not in the hospital is scattered to the four winds—same for the troops.

"The Marines are calling all the contact numbers, but it could be some time before we run down everyone."

Lieutenant Mandy Paige, OBE, RM, strolled in, having changed from her formal dress back into her off-duty uniform of cut-off jeans and pee-wee cowgirl boots. She was walking on air, having received an unexpected

Order of the British Empire (OBE) for her service during the siege of RAF Habbaniya.

Mandy wanted to thank Col. Randal—he had recommended the award.

Before she had a chance, Col. Randal said, "Mandy, reach out to Major Sansom. Have him order the military police to go around to every bar in Cairo and Alexandria and announce a Raiding Forces recall order."

"I'm on it, John."

"Stick around after you talk to Sansom," Col. Randal said. "The general's going to brief us when he arrives. I want you there—we're on alert."

"Roger and wilco!"

Col. Randal walked over and knocked on the door to the bedroom. "Can I come in?"

Lady Jane and Brandy had not changed out of their evening gowns. They were on the bed, laughing and talking like teenagers about whatever it is two beautiful women who have grown up together and like each other talk about when they have both received fantastic surprises earlier in the evening.

Brandy had been the recipient of the highest award for valor that a nonservice member can receive—the George Cross (GC), for captaining the Seaborn family houseboat during OPERATION DYNAMO, the rescue at Dunkirk. The GC was the civilian equivalent of the military's Victoria Cross. She was officially a national heroine.

Col. Randal felt guilty about interrupting them.

"Raiding Forces has been placed on alert," he said. "Jim's conducting a briefing later when he gets back from a meeting with Dudley Clarke at A-Force HQ.

"I'd like both of you to sit in—Parker too if she's available. Who knows what mission Raiding Forces will be tasked with?"

"Absolutely," Lady Jane said. "Confirmed."

"Carry on, ladies," Col. Randal said. "No rush."

JAMES "BALDIE" TAYLOR ARRIVED BACK at RFHQ. He had just left A-Force wherE he had been in conference with Colonel Dudley Clarke who had, himself, recently returned from a meeting with Field Marshal Claude Auchinleck.

The military situation was grim.

Field Marshal Erwin Rommel had counterattacked and was driving hard toward Tobruk. The Afrika Korps had advanced seventy-five miles in less than twenty-four hours. Virtually all of British Eighth Army's tanks had been depleted in OPERATION CRUSADER. (Prime Minister Winston Churchill had shipped the last 350 tanks in England to Field Marshal Auchinleck prior to the operation. There were no replacements to be had.) The Desert Fox's attack had taken Middle East Command by surprise and thrown the Grey Pillars set into a panic.

Unknown to anyone in Middle East Command, FM Auchinleck was in possession of Bletchley Park's Ultra Secret intercepts of Rommel's orders from his boss, Field Marshal Albert "Smiling Al" Kesselring, who had his orders from Oberkommando der Wehrmacht (OKW), who had theirs from the Führer Adolf Hitler—to use the German resupply of tanks to build a "stone wall."

Afrika Korps' mission was to be purely defensive.

The Desert Fox had disobeyed the orders—he attacked immediately, catching both his superiors and his enemy by surprise.

There was no way the Allies were going to be able to stop Afrika Korps in open battle. They simply did not have the armor. In the desert, the side with the most tanks wins.

Col. Clarke did not have a set of rules for A-Force like Raiding Forces, though he was developing one for Deception Operations. But he did subscribe to the doctrine laid down by Captains Fairbairn and Sykes, the inventors of the Commando Fighting Knife, who taught close quarters combat at the Commando Castle: "never fight fair."

He had a plan.

When Colonel John Randal heard it, he said, "*That's* it?"

"Affirmative," Jim said. "All we have—now we need to sell it to your troops. You are the only person in Raiding Forces with the 'Need to Know' the whole story, so what is going to happen is that I am getting ready to stand up in front of your officers in a few minutes and lie."

Col. Randal said, "We sure as hell wouldn't want anyone to know the truth."

Col. Clarke's plan was simple. A-Force was going to try to bluff FM Rommel.

The idea was to deceive the Desert Fox into believing that Eighth Army was luring Afrika Korps into a trap by falling back to the Gazala Line, where a massive British tank army was lying in wait to conduct a double enveloping counterattack against his flanks after the Nazi thrust had spent itself.

Since those were exactly the tactics the Desert Fox favored, he might fall for it.

The hope was to cause FM Rommel to pause long enough for Middle East Command to reconstitute itself with a shipment of M-3 Grant tanks from the United States. The problem with Col. Clarke's plan was that the Grants were not scheduled to arrive for weeks. It was not much of a plan.

There were so few people available at RFHQ that the briefing could be held in the third-floor suite. Those present were: Major the Lady Jane Seaborn, Captain "Geronimo" Joe McKoy, Waldo Treywick, Captain Penelope "Legs" Honeycutt-Parker, Lieutenant Mandy Paige and King.

Lieutenant Pamala Plum-Martin slipped in at the last second.

Col. Randal opened, "Rommel has launched a counterattack at El Agheila. Earlier this evening, an Afrika Korps armored column penetrated Eighth Army lines and is driving on Tobruk. The general will brief on what is expected of Raiding Forces in future. General."

Jim stepped up in front of the small briefing area. "We do not have much information on the tactical situation at the moment. With that said, a plan is already in the works to deal with the incursion. Field Marshal Auchinleck will concentrate a tank force at Tobruk and one other location on the right flank of the German advance. At the appropriate moment, the Desert Rats will fall on Rommel in force after his advance runs out of steam.

"To aid the counterattack, Eighth Army requires the services of Raiding Forces. Our mission is to move to the *extreme* right flank of the Afrika Korps advance and carry out a diversion on the very edge of the Great Sand Sea. A camouflage officer will arrive at RFHQ tomorrow to instruct us in the art of turning jeeps into trucks and trucks into tanks. Our mission is to suddenly appear out of nowhere on the German right in the form of a full-blown armored division of one hundred fifty American Grant tanks.

"We are a distractor," Jim said. "The idea is to trick Rommel into taking his eye off the main object—Tobruk. Having that many tanks suddenly pop up overnight like mushrooms should, as Colonel Randal has been known to say, 'give the bad guys something to think about.'

"What are your questions?"

"When're we a-movin' out, Jim?" Capt. McKoy asked.

"As soon as Lieutenant Jaxx arrives," Jim said. "Take one day to pull as much maintenance on the jeeps as possible, then we are off. Elements of Major Merritt's company will link up with us en route to the objective. I shall be traveling with Colonel Randal's command party."

There were no more questions. The assignment sounded straightforward enough. Even as shot to pieces as Desert Patrol was after CRUSADER, they could handle this assignment.

As the briefing was breaking up, Col. Randal pulled Lady Jane aside.

"The minute we pull out," he said, "put everyone onboard the Hudson and fly straight back to Oasis X—stay there until I tell you different. That means you too, Jane. Understood?"

"Loud and clear," Lady Jane said softly, staring him straight in the eyes. "Do not worry about us."

No fooling her—she knew there was nothing standing between Rommel's point of attack and Cairo—should the Desert Fox choose to go around Tobruk.

COLONEL JOHN RANDAL AND MAJOR the Lady Jane Seaborn were sitting on the steps in the shallow end of the private pool that was exclusively for their suite on the roof of the third floor of RFHQ. They were looking at one million sparkling stars in the Egyptian sky and gazing out at the Mediterranean.

"Not had the opportunity," Lady Jane said, putting her arm around his shoulders. "Terribly thoughtful of you to give the Field Marshal a list of honors to be awarded to all of us before you would accept your promotion. Not many officers would have done such a thing."

"I never heard of the Order of the Garter before tonight, Jane," Col. Randal said. "Don't believe everything people tell you."

"You put your troops before yourself," Lady Jane said. "Many commanders make the claim but never follow through—you are the rare exception."

Wanting to change the subject, Col. Randal said, "Pretty big deal R. J. letting Mandy run her own radio game."

"Possibly what Mandy is doing is more involved than meets the eye," Lady Jane said.

"Really?"

"We know you are not a German agent, John," Lady Jane said. "We are fairly sure I'm not, and King has been through every security check and vetting process MI-5 has—passed with flying colors."

"What's that have to do with Mandy?" Col. Randal asked.

"Do you understand the difference between a secret and . . . a mystery?"

"Maybe you better explain it to me."

"One can always discover a secret," Lady Jane said. "A mystery is what it says it is—a mystery."

Col. Randal said, "I'm not following you . . ."

"Who was present in the room when we developed the storyline for Mandy's radio game?" Lady Jane asked.

"You were," Col. Randal said. "Rocky, Mandy, King—I was there."

"Exactly," Lady Jane said. "Should the Y-Service radio monitoring network intercept a message emanating from the Cairo area debunking our story about helicopters flying out of the Great Sand Sea in support of Raiding Forces, then Mandy will know who sent it."

"Rocky?"

"Very good, John," Lady Jane rewarded him with one of her heart attack smiles. "Rikke Runborg is a mystery—in counterintelligence it never hurts to double, triple check. Even then, it's virtually impossible to ever know for certain where anyone's real loyalties lie."

Col. Randal said, "I can see how that would be."

"For example," Lady Jane said. "Brandy told me that you believe I sleep with you on orders from MI-6."

"True," Col. Randal said. "That's the story, right?"

"Only in the beginning."

Col. Randal wondered if she were joking.

COLONEL JOHN RANDAL SAID, "Jane, do *you* consider yourself one of my troops?"

"Absolutely."

CHAPTER FIVE

ILLUSIONIST

KING PHONED COLONEL JOHN RANDAL from the Raiding Forces' Operations Room. He was laughing. Col. Randal was not sure he had ever heard the Merc laugh before.

"Ensign Hamilton, OBE," King said. "Your new camouflage officer has arrived and is on the way up, Chief."

"Flanigan," Col. Randal called, hanging up the phone. "There's an Ensign Hamilton coming to see me—send him in."

A slim, young—very young—officer wearing silver-rimmed glasses, rank insignia Col. Randal had never seen before, the regimental badges of the Lancelot Lancers Yeomanry and parachute wings, marched in ramrod straight and saluted. Ens. Hamilton had to be the youngest officer ever to be awarded the Order of the British Empire. He looked vaguely familiar.

"Ensign Hamilton reports, sir!"

Col. Randal casually returned the salute, "What's an ensign doing in the Lounge Lizards?"

"It's like a third lieutenant, sir."

"I've never heard of that rank."

"For junior Lancelot Lancer officers, sir."

"Really," Col. Randal said. "Teddy, is that you . . . 'The Great Teddy'?"

"Yes, sir," Ens. Hamilton said. "Good to see you again, Colonel."

"You've grown a foot and gained fifty pounds," Col. Randal said. "What are you doing here in Egypt?"

"Thirty-five pounds, sir—traveled out over the Christmas break to observe camouflage operations at A-Force during OPERATION CRUSADER. The famous magician, Jasper Maskyline, is Colonel Clarke's chief *camoufler.* He was supposed to allow me to be attached to his Magic Gang, but that failed to materialize so I went to the desert with Captain Stykes and helped him build a dummy railroad terminal."

Col. Randal said, "CRUSADER's over—why aren't you back in school?

"Middle East Command has a critical shortage of camouflage officers, sir—only eleven total in theatre, so when the Germans launched their counterattack I was held over by Colonel Clarke to work with Raiding Forces," Ens. Hamilton said.

"Be like old times, sir, back at RAF Habbaniya."

"I don't know," Col. Randal said. "Regulations say an officer can be commissioned at seventeen but can't serve in a combat zone until he's seventeen and a half *with* parental permission.

"You were only fifteen at Habbaniya . . . the numbers don't add up, Ted."

"I falsified my age, sir," Ens. Hamilton said. "My sixteenth birthday came two weeks after the relief of Habbaniya. When I filled out the forms at Eton—added a year."

"You did that . . . ?"

"No one ever checks, including Sandhurst or the Lancelot Lancers, sir—the Duke simply said, 'Welcome to the Regiment.'"

"Well, stud," Col. Randal said, "you were the hero of Habbaniya, but that may not cut it with Lady Jane. I'm sure she will want to hear your story.

"Why don't you march over to the bedroom and knock on her door."

It was not really a question.

Col. Randal took out one of Waldo's thin cigars and stuck it between his teeth. This could prove interesting.

He was not disappointed.

Shortly, from the bedroom came the sound of Major the Lady Jane Seaborn shouting, then a crash followed by the sound of broken glass tinkling—then dead silence. Ens. Hamilton, *aka* "The Great Teddy", marched out of the bedroom, looking grim.

Col. Randal said, "That as bad as it sounded?"

"Lady Seaborn threw her hair brush at me, Colonel," Ens. Hamilton said. "Broke her mirror. I don't think she is very happy with the plan, sir."

"You have to look at it from her perspective, Ted," Col. Randal said. "To Jane you're just a lying son-of-a-bitch."

"Under the best of circumstances, sir, I have trouble concentrating around Lady Seaborn," Ens. Hamiltonaid. "But that message came through loud and clear—hope she does not stay angry at me forever."

"Jane only gets mad when someone she cares about does something stupid that puts them in harm's way—I've been the worst offender," Col. Randal said. "She'll get over it."

Lady Jane came storming out of the bedroom. She was livid. "Flanigan, bring the car around."

Col. Randal heard himself say, "Why don't we talk about this?"

"All right, John," Lady Jane said. "Let's do."

"So, Ted," Col. Randal said, "how old are you, exactly—right now?"

"Sixteen and a half, sir."

"There," Col. Randal said. "Sixteen and a half—only six months short."

"Are we through?" Lady Jane said.

"Ahhh . . . yeah."

"Meet me downstairs at the car, Ensign," Lady Jane ordered.

"Yes, ma'am."

As soon as Ens. Hamilton cleared the door, Lady Jane's green eyes sparkled. She giggled, "Do you know what that little *illusionist* had the nerve to do?

"That would be negative."

"Frogspawned me."

"Ted did that?"

"I was stunned." Lady Jane broke up laughing.

"Yeah," Col. Randal said. "I can see how you would be."

"Dudley Clarke ordered Teddy to say 'Frogspawn' in the event I tried to prevent him taking the field with Desert Patrol," Lady Jane said. "We're off now to try to find some of the supplies he requires to accomplish Desert Patrol's deception mission—hope to be back in time for the briefing."

Col. Randal said, "You're going out again tonight?"

"We have less than forty-eight hours to requisition, assemble and arrange transport for everything before you move out," Lady Jane said. "Challenging."

"True."

"John, you *will* take care of the boy?"

"How would I do that?" Col. Randal said. "Sounds like I'm going to be working for him—has anybody ever Frogspawned you?"

"Not before tonight."

COLONEL JOHN RANDAL AND RIKKE RUNBORG—friends called her "Rocky"—were sitting in the suite's living room. He had two reasons for inviting her there. Neither one of them was quite what it seemed.

"Rocky," Col. Randal said, "as you know, one of my assigned tasks is to be responsible for your security."

"I feel safe," Rocky said, "being under your protection."

"Good," Col. Randal said—her sexy Norwegian accent was hypnotizing. "I realized," he lied, "you don't have a personal weapon—which is an oversight on my part."

Actually, Major the Lady Jane Seaborn had pointed that fact out to him a while back—he had made a practice of giving pistols to the women associated with Raiding Forces for their personal protection—highly embellished pistols so they would carry them. At the time Rocky showed up, Col. Randal was not in a hurry to arm a former—and possibly current—German agent.

Now, Jane's idea was to treat Rocky the same as the other women in the Raiding Forces entourage. He was not exactly sure why.

"Carry this handgun in your purse at all times," Col. Randal said, handing her a profusely engraved Sauer Model 13 pocket pistol with beautiful pearl stocks.

The little gun was a plain vanilla private purchase piece that, while never adopted by the German military, was popular with Nazi plainclothes police and agents of the Abwehr, which made it a fitting choice for Rocky. Lady Jane had taken it to an engraver who did his magic and arranged to have the grips added so it would be on a par with the other women's weapons—all captured from high-ranking enemy officers.

"Thank you, John," Rocky said, admiring the weapon, handling it like a professional. Clearly, she had extensive training on small, concealable handguns. "Does this mean you trust me enough now to allow me to go armed?"

"Yes, it does," Col. Randal said, not wanting to veer off onto the slippery slope of trust—he did not exactly trust Rocky. What he, or more accurately Lady Jane, desired was for her to feel like a full-fledged member of the Raiding Forces team.

"This is the perfect concealed weapon for you, Rocky—Swiss engineering, precision built," Col. Randal said. "Sauer managed to cram a .32 round into a .25 caliber frame. Don't leave home without it."

"An exquisite gift," Rocky said. "I shall sleep with it under my pillow."

"Lucky pistol," Col. Randal said.

Rocky laughed. Big teeth. Golden tan. Hair the color of ice—very likeable.

"On another subject," Col. Randal said, "and we are *not* having this conversation, Rocky—would you clear up a few details about what happened the night Raiding Forces rescued you and Jane's husband, Mallory, from the Vichy French police?"

"Is this for your personal information," Rocky asked, "or has someone made inquiries?"

"I like things to make sense," Col Randal said. "Some events that night don't."

"Nor to me," Rocky said. "What are your questions, John?"

"When our patrol arrived in town, the first thing we did was rescue Mallory from the post office where he was a prisoner," Col. Randal said. "The Commander immediately tried to break away to race to where you were being held. He was a wild man—Sergeant Major Mikkalis had to subdue, handcuff and gag Mallory to restrain him.

"My question to you, Rocky," Col. Randal said, "is, were you and Mallory so close that he was willing to charge a house full of heavily-armed bad guys without a weapon to effect your rescue?"

"No," Rocky said.

"Why'd he do it?"

"While Mallory is beautiful to admire—like a Greek statue," Rocky said, "I was never *emotionally* involved with him. He does not know how to have a true relationship with a woman, even though he is excellent in bed.

"The man loves only himself."

"So," Col. Randal asked, "why were you with him then?"

"My relationship with Mallory was based on two things only. I was in great danger in Norway because of my involvement with the Nazis—the Resistance had issued orders to liquidate me. And, Mallory agreed to take me to England.

"I never revealed my true feelings to him or about my plan to contact the British Secret Service as soon as we arrived. Naturally, Mallory believed I worshiped him."

"I see," Col. Randal said. Which meant that he did not.

"My life has been complicated, John," Rocky said. "I never sought a career in intelligence. All I ever wanted was to be a ballet dancer and later operate my school of dance. . . ."

"Nothing I've heard about Mallory suggests he's a particularly brave individual," Col. Randal said. "His navy career is under a cloud of suspicion for showing cowardice in the face of the enemy.

"Why was he willing to risk his life to attempt your rescue?"

"Mallory may not have been trying to save me—his motive may have been to silence me. Possibly, once Raiding Forces arrived," Rocky said, "he feared I had learned something about his past he did not wish to be made public."

"Did you?"

"No. Mallory was found by fishermen, adrift at sea in a lifeboat," Rocky said. "I met him when he was in the hospital—claiming amnesia."

"Why didn't you identify yourself as an Abwehr agent," Col. Randal asked, "when the police stripped you, tied you in a chair and broke out the burning cigarettes?"

"I tried," Rocky said. "Those swine planned to have their way with me—verify my credentials later. The policemen could always claim to not have believed my story. Spies are not issued identification cards to produce in the event they find themselves in a predicament like mine—being violated by your own side."

Col. Randal said, "That could be a problem."

He had not learned a thing.

"R. J. CALLED, CHIEF," KING SAID from the door as Rikke Runborg left the suite. "En route to RFHQ about fifteen minutes out. The Brigadier requests a private meeting with you, Lady Seaborn, Brandy, 'Legs' Parker and Mandy."

"We'll hold it in here," Colonel John Randal said. "Notify the ladies."

Lieutenant Mandy Paige arrived first. When she came through the door, she immediately leapt on Col. Randal and started kissing him like a happy puppy.

"Mandy, what the hell?"

"I wanted to thank you for my OBE," Lt. Mandy said, kissing him again. "But you have been in meetings ever since I arrived back here from the ceremony—unbelievable, John, love you."

"You earned your medal," Col. Randal said. "Don't scare me like that—have you been drinking?"

"I heard Teddy was here," Lt. Mandy said.

"Not anymore," Col. Randal said. "He's gone shopping with Jane."

"At this time of night?" Lt. Mandy asked. "In Cairo?"

"Roger that—crazy, huh?"

Brandy and Captain Penelope "Legs" Honeycutt-Parker arrived.

Brigadier Raymond J. Maunsell, who liked to be called R. J., walked in right after them. He said, "Congratulations are in order, ladies. Brandy—George Cross, George Medal for you, Parker, and the Order of the British Empire for Mandy . . . impressive, to say the least.

"Is Lady Jane available to sit in?"

"Negative," Col. Randal said. "She's gone shopping with our new camouflage officer."

"In that case," R. J. said, "time is short and I understand Desert Patrol has been alerted for a mission. Expect me to be brief.

"During our initial post-CRUSADER battle assessment," R. J. said as they all took a seat in the living room of the suite, "a fatal defect in the way our forces operate was uncovered—we have to fix it.

"No one not in this room now, with the exceptions of Lady Jane and Jim—who has already been read in on the topic—have a need to know what we discuss tonight unless I sign off on them first. Clear?"

Everyone answered, "Clear!"

R. J. said, "There are two types of intelligence—human and signals. Are you up to speed on the difference, Colonel?

"Mandy explained it to me," Col. Randal said.

Brig. Maunsell commanded SIME (Security Intelligence Middle East). No one knew exactly what SIME did and R. J. was not telling, but it was a cross between MI-6 (British Secret Intelligence Service) and MI-5 (Counterintelligence) with close ties to A-Force (Deception). The chief of SIME was one of the most powerful and mysterious officers in Middle East Command.

Everyone in the room liked R. J.

Lately, the Brigadier had been mentoring Lt. Mandy in the art of counterintelligence. He had always taken an interest in Raiding Forces operations. While R. J. was not an empire builder, he did have his finger in a lot of pies.

"Then you will be aware that human intelligence is practically worthless," R. J. said. "You only have the informant's word for its authenticity.

"Human intelligence can be dangerous because your spy could be a double agent, or the intelligence product he delivers might be misinformation intentionally designed to mislead. Nevertheless, we have to keep mining human intelligence sources because every now and again we come up with a whisper that turns out to be a jewel."

R. J. said, "Signals intelligence is what catches enemy spies and wins battles."

"That's what Mandy said," Col. Randal lit a Player's cigarette with his old battered Zippo.

"All right then, now that we have that laid down, to the main point—what we learned during our analysis of the battle," R. J. said. "Eighth Army radio security is abysmal—practically nonexistent. Commonwealth troops simply do not understand the meaning of operational security.

"MEHQ cannot convince our field commanders to refrain from sending messages in the clear," R. J. said.

"To make matters worse, Afrika Korps has a secret weapon—621 Radio Intercept Company, called 'the Circus,' commanded by Hauptmann Alfred Seebohm. The good captain is a cross between a brilliant radio intercept genius and a psychic.

"Make no mistake, Seebohm is the single most dangerous adversary British Forces faces—he's Rommel's Merlin.

"In CRUSADER, we had every reason to expect a crushing victory," R. J. said. "Seebohm and our poor radio discipline are the primary reasons we failed to achieve little more than a draw after suffering horrendous losses. He was able to provide Rommel signals intelligence about our intentions at practically the same time our field commanders were deciphering the same orders originating from Eighth Army."

"That's not good," Col. Randal said.

"Colonel, you—meaning Raiding Forces—are to put together a special team," R. J. said. "Your mission is to support the team tracking down Unit 621 with the idea to capture Hauptmann Seebohm—failing that, kill him.

"Questions?"

"Is this a RED INDIAN?" Col. Randal asked.

"Negative," R. J. said. "It could turn in to one in the event you stumble across signals equipment, documents, etc., during your quest. But Seebohm is the target.

"Brandy," R. J. said, "I want you and Parker to take charge of the intelligence/reconnaissance element that tracks Seebohm, which means you, Brandy, are in charge of the operation.

"I understand you have already organized a mission Tactical Operations Center here at RFHQ."

"We have," Brandy said.

"Mandy, your role is to be the liaison between Brandy and Parker—whom we shall call Team SUNDANCE—Raiding Forces, and myself.

"Team SUNDANCE and Mandy," Col. Randal said, "will be relocating to Oasis X as soon as Desert Patrol takes the field. Is that a problem?"

"No," R. J. said. "In fact, Brandy, read Mr. Zargo into the SUNDANCE mission as soon as you arrive. He will be an invaluable asset."

"Love to."

Brandy made eye contact with Col. Randal. She winked. They had already had this conversation.

OPERATION SOLID GOLD.

R. J. said, "We are done here."

VERONICA PAIGE WAS WAITING OUTSIDE the door when the meeting broke up.

"You wished to see me, R. J.?"

"I do, but first I should like to congratulate you on a well-deserved OBE, Veronica," R. J. said. "John tells me that at the decisive moment during the siege of RAF Habbaniya you made an independent decision, acted on it on your own initiative and followed up to personally view the results at great risk to yourself, which saved the base from being overrun by tanks—high praise."

"The Colonel was being overly kind," Veronica said.

"Negative," Colonel John Randal said. "Exactly the way it went down."

"We shall make this brief," R. J. said.

"MI-9 is part of Dudley Clarke's portfolio. The colonel has expressed no interest in Escape.

"In the last war, British Secret Intelligence had an unfortunate experience with a female agent. She disobeyed orders, helped a large number of people escape from the Germans instead of maintaining her cover and was subsequently exposed, captured, then publicly executed by firing squad in Paris.

"Ever since, MI-6 has been reluctant to work with female agents, and the SIS refuse to participate directly in escape programs.

"Major Stone has been officially listed as Dudley's officer-in-charge of Escape for the last six months," R. J. said. "Sir Terry made it plain to Dudley he no longer wants to be responsible for MI-9. It's his desire to concentrate full time on commanding his family regiment.

"Veronica, once again that leaves you, the acting chief of MI-9, twisting in the breeze."

"I do not understand," Veronica said, "why no one seems concerned about our prisoners."

"Not quite everyone," R. J. said. "I see things differently. Over thirty thousand of our men are in POW camps here in North Afrika—some of whom are being transferred to Italy—with a few, the most senior officers, being sent to camps in Italy and Germany.

"Every single day we have pilots being shot down and ships sunk and the crews captured, which increases the number of prisoners. Every one of those POWs has eyes and ears and is located behind enemy lines. What MI-9 needs to do is concentrate on finding a way to put all those prisoners to work gathering intelligence or disseminating misinformation.

"The trick will be to develop a method to communicate with the POWs.

"Veronica," R. J. ordered, "starting tonight, you are the permanent Middle East Command Escape Officer. Report directly to me."

"Thank you, R. J. I should like that."

"On paper," R. J. said, "Colonel Clarke still remains the head of MI-9, but he will play no further role in your day-to-day operations except to provide cover as needed for your operations or to use Escape as a source to disseminate A-Force misinformation.

"Any questions?"

Veronica said, "Not at the moment—sure to have many later."

"Colonel, you have always indicated an interest in MI-9," R. J. said. "For administrative purposes, Veronica will be attached to Raiding Forces, which means continuing to operate out of RFHQ. That puts Escape in perfect position for Raiding Forces to execute missions she develops—OK by you?"

"Yes, sir," Col. Randal said. "Veronica and I have a history of working together. She'll get my full support."

"Outstanding," R. J. said. "Now all we have to do is turn MI-9 into a valuable intelligence asset."

Col. Randal walked Brig. Maunsell down to his car.

"Colonel Fellers, the military attaché to the U.S. Embassy in Cairo, has been making inquiries about you," R. J. said. "Claims he knew you—or knew of you—while serving on General MacArthur's staff in Manila."

"Never met the man," Col. Randal said.

"Something to do with a bandit named 'Smiling Jack.' Fellers is leading the effort to return you to U.S. Army uniform," R. J. said. "Your promotion is sure to slow him down, but he's a good man and will rethink.

"To that end," R. J. said, "since it is in the best interests of all concerned for you to remain in command of Raiding Forces, I would like to propose that you allow me to put myself forward to act as your representative in arranging your release from the British Army.

"With your permission, I shall negotiate the terms for your return to the U.S. Army."

"Sir, I don't have any terms," Col. Randal said, "as long as I stay with Raiding Forces."

"Oh," R. J. said, "I believe we can do better than that."

Col. Randal said, "Take your best shot, R. J."

"With pleasure," R. J. said. "One last thing. Priority of missions is: GOLDEN FLEECE/RED INDIAN, SUNDANCE—I hear that mission has been restyled OPERATION SOLID GOLD, and BOMBSHELL in that order."

"Understood, sir," Col. Randal said, realizing that if R. J. knew the designator SOLID GOLD, it meant that Brandy had already briefed him on the mission. The Brigadier had gone to the trouble to come out tonight to establish his command authority, to evaluate in person the principals' response to the structure of the team carrying out the SOLID GOLD mission and to make sure everyone was read in and on the same page.

The chief of SIME was demonstrating superb leadership skills.

"Request permission to include Lieutenant Jaxx on the SOLID GOLD 'Need to Know' list, sir," Col. Randal said. "He'll be my deputy on the team that takes down the 621st.

"Permission granted," R. J. said, climbing into his car.

"By the way, The Great Teddy—I thought the lad was only fifteen years old at Habbaniya. How did he manage to become one of the A-Force camouflage officers?"

Col. Randal said, "It's a long story."

JAMES "BALDIE" TAYLOR ARRIVED BACK at Raiding Forces Headquarters from his hurried meeting with Colonel Dudley Clarke at A-Force. There were only a handful of people at RFHQ to attend his briefing. They assembled in the small briefing area in the suite shared by Colonel John Randal and Major the Lady Jane Seaborn.

Present were Col. Randal, Major Jack Black, Captain "Geronimo" Joe McKoy, Captain Taylor Corrigan, DSO, MC; Captain "Pyro" Percy Stirling, DSO, MC; Captain Hawthorne Merryweather, Captain Penelope "Legs" Honeycutt-Parker; Lieutenant Roy Kidd; Lieutenant Mandy Paige; Brandy Seaborn; and Waldo Treywick. These were all the Raiding Forces leaders who could be located on such short notice. All the others were in hospital or on leave.

At the last minute, Major the Lady Jane Seaborn and Ensign Teddy Hamilton, *aka* "The Great Teddy", arrived with Lieutenant Pamala Plum-Martin, who was still wearing her evening dress.

"As you are all aware, Rommel launched a surprise counterattack from the vicinity of El Agheila," Jim said. "No one saw it coming. Afrika Korps has already advanced over one hundred fifty miles in less than two days."

That was true; almost everything else he was getting ready to say was a lie—to be repeated to their interrogators in the event anyone in the room was captured. Raiding Forces was going to be operating deep behind enemy lines.

"Eighth Army is setting a trap for the Desert Fox along the Gazala Line. Field Marshal Auchinleck is rushing three hundred of the latest model Grant tanks, recently arrived from the U.S., to Tobruk in anticipation of launching a massive counterattack of his own once Rommel's advance runs out of steam. When that happens, Eighth Army has the opportunity to deal Afrika Korps a deathblow," Jim said.

"Desert Patrol will depart RFHQ for a location of its own choosing southeast of Bir Temrid to set up a dummy tank formation that will appear to threaten Rommel's extreme right flank. The idea is to distract the Desert Fox while Eighth Army slams into Afrika Korps—striking out of Tobruk."

FM Auchinleck's trap was a ruse. There were no tanks from the U.S. There was not going to be any strike out of Tobruk. Allied troops were exhausted and materiel spent after CRUSADER. Tank losses had been catastrophic—250 tanks in two days.

The ambush and counterattack was an A-Force deception. Subterfuge was all British Forces was capable of at this point in the desert war.

Col. Clarke had cooked up the plan in about ten minutes before briefing Jim, and then flying off to do a personal reconnaissance of the battle area.

"Raiding Forces' mission is to go out to the desert, set up dummy tanks," Jim said. "Sit this one out—deceiving Rommel."

"Questions?"

No one said a thing.

CHAPTER SIX

BEVERLY HILLS BANK

COLONEL JOHN RANDAL WAS SITTING at a table in the mess hall at RFHQ eating breakfast with two of his troops, Corporal Tim Authury, MM, and Corporal Frank Hawkins, MM. The food was excellent. Major the Lady Jane Seaborn had brought in chefs from the Bradford Hotel in London to cook for the Lancelot Lancers Yeomanry Regiment when it made its epic fighting drive, the longest in history, from Kenya to Addis Ababa. Now, with the Lancers operating as gun jeep patrols, the cooks worked out of RFHQ and Oasis X.

Cpl. Authury had been with Col. Randal in Swamp Fox Force at Calais. Cpl. Hawkins had been in Raiding Forces as part of the original polo-playing intake of volunteers for special service and had been on Col. Randal's personal five-man raid team on OPERATION TOMCAT—the first parachute operation in British Forces history.

"It's about time for you two men to quit slacking off," Col. Randal said.

The corporals froze mid-bite. What had been an enjoyable conversation with their commanding officer came to a screeching halt.

Col. Randal lit a Player's cigarette with his hard-used U.S. 26th Cavalry Regiment Zippo. He studied the two through the blue smoke. "Desert Patrol has to completely re-organize—lot of slots to fill. Time to step up, men—no more free ride for you two."

Cpl. Hawkins looked at Cpl. Authury. Cpl. Authury looked at Cpl. Hawkins. They thought they *had* been stepping up. Both Raiders were recipients of the coveted Military Medal.

Col. Randal reached in his pocket and pitched two pair of sergeant's stripes on the table. "Next time I see you—say in the next five minutes or so—have 'em on."

"SIR!" Both Raiders chorused.

Captain "Geronimo" Joe McKoy strolled over to the table as the two new sergeants were rushing out, nearly knocking over their chairs. He dropped a newspaper on the table. It was a copy of the *Austin American.*

"King thought you might like to take a gander at this," Capt. McKoy said. "Came in today's Royal Mail."

The headline read, GOVERNOR PARDONS UT FOOTBALL STAR—WAR HERO.

> AUSTIN—Today Governor Coke Stevenson signed a pardon for Lieutenant Billy Jack Jaxx, convicted of trespassing at the Tri-Delta Sorority House during a panty raid at UT. Jaxx is best known for running back a kickoff of 102 yards for the Longhorns against Baylor.
>
> Currently, Jaxx is serving out a four-year period of deferred adjudication in lieu of a jail sentence after having volunteered for the U.S. Army Paratroops. Presently his whereabouts are not known other than he is a member of the American Volunteer Group somewhere in Egypt operating behind enemy lines as a member of a hush-hush British Commando unit so secret even its full name is classified.
>
> Lt. Jaxx has been presented the Military Cross, only bestowed for valor, with two bars denoting three separate awards of the medal.
>
> The UT Chapter of the Tri-Delta Sorority petitioned Gov. Stevenson to grant the pardon and have selected Lt. Jaxx to be the recipient of the Delta Delta Delta "ADOPT A SERVICEMAN" program.

There was a photo of the girls in their cut-off blue jeans and peewee cowgirl boots on the manicured lawn of their colonial style sorority house holding a banner that read: "KILL THOSE JAPS BILLY JACK."

Col. Randal said, "Japs?"

"Best-lookin' girls with the richest daddies in the state of Texas," Capt. McKoy said, "ain't real good at geography."

MAJOR JACK MERRITT, DSO, MC, MM, walked in, saw Colonel John Randal sitting with Captain "Geronimo" Joe McKoy and joined the table.

Maj. Merritt was a Raiding Forces lieutenant, acting captain seconded to the Sudan Defense Force (SDF), who commanded a motorized company of Sudanese infantry. The SDF was considered an elite organization. British officers assigned to it served at one grade higher than their rank.

His company was attached to Desert Patrol and spent its days long-hauling supplies to Oasis X and replenishing the hidden emergency supply dumps that Col. Randal had ordered cached every fifteen miles across the Great Sand Sea. The dumps stretched almost to Tripoli.

"My trucks need a complete maintenance stand down, sir," Maj. Merritt said. "If we take the field tomorrow, you'd best have a fleet of recovery vehicles standing by on call—or better yet, take them along with us."

"Don't worry about it, Jack," Col. Randal said. "Schedule your trucks for the shop. The general has arranged for us to have the use of civilian models for the duration of our mission. All we need 'em to do is to haul certain materials to the target. The plan is to camouflage 'em as dummy tanks.

"We're hoping they all get shot up."

"Do you require me to bring my entire company, sir?"

"Negative," Col. Randal said. "A driver, air-defense gunner, and two men for each truck. Send the rest of your troops on a pass—you take leave too."

"Are you certain, sir?" Maj. Merritt asked. "I can be ready . . ."

As a corporal he had been Col. Randal's wingman through all of Raiding Forces training, early pinprick raids, the jump on TOMCAT and was with him on OPERATION LOUNGE LIZARD before being given a field commission. It was said at the time that they could read each other's minds. Maj. Merritt had no desire to let his CO down.

"Like I said, Major," Col. Randal said, "don't worry about it—take some time off."

"Yes, sir," Maj. Merritt said, standing up to leave but still not seeming sure about it.

After he walked away, Capt. McKoy said, "According to the radio yesterday, the Prime Minister stood up in front of Parliament and saluted Field Marshal Rommel—know what he called him?"

"What might that be?"

"A daring and skillful opponent," Capt. McKoy said. "Now why would the man do that?"

"I have no idea," Col. Randal said. "You're not all that impressed with the Desert Fox, are you, Captain?"

"Rommel don't strike me as understanding what's possible with what he's got and what's not," Capt. McKoy said.

"That's real important for the commander of a mobile army who's dependent on his beans and bullets coming from a long way off to know, John."

Col. Randal said, "Yes, it is."

LIEUTENANT RANDY "HORNBLOWER" SEABORN was walking in the RFHQ front door when Colonel John Randal and Captain "Geronimo" Joe McKoy were leaving the mess hall.

"Come on up, Randy," Col. Randal said. "Give me a report on your pinprick raids—you've been out on the sharp end all by yourself for way too long."

"Raiding parties went ashore a total of twenty-three times in the last thirty days, sir," Lt. Seaborn said. "Everyone in Sea Squadron has been pressed to the limit, Colonel—both MAS boats are way past due for engine overhauls. Probably triple the number of hours on their engines the book calls for.

"We barely made it back here, sir."

"Good report, Randy," Col. Randal said. "Get your boats in to be serviced—how long do you think that'll take?"

"A couple of weeks, minimum, sir," Lt. Seaborn said, "possibly longer. When grandfather returns, he can help speed the work."

"Give your crews shore leave," Col. Randal ordered. "You take off too—check on your MAS boats from time to time, Hornblower, but don't overdo it. I want you getting plenty of rest and relaxation while they're in dry dock—no hanging around supervising the work."

"Yes, sir!"

"Lots of good-looking Greek girls in Alexandria," Col. Randal said. "I'll make sure Brandy never goes near there. Not a great place for your mom to turn up."

"Roger," Lt. Seaborn said. "Then I can anticipate you shall have no need of my services during Rommel's current counterattack, Colonel?"

"That's right," Col. Randal said. "Where is your grandfather, anyway? Haven't heard from him."

"London, sir."

"What's the Razor doing there, Randy?"

"Joining White's Club."

CAPTAIN LIONEL CHATTERHORN, formerly of Scotland Yard Special Branch and the elite Vulnerable Points Wing, Field Security Police, was on crutches. Lately, at his request, he had been serving as a patrol leader for Desert Patrol—he had an excellent record as a field commander.

"What's the prognosis, Captain?" Colonel John Randal asked.

"Couple of weeks, sir," Capt. Chatterhorn said. "The doctor says I should be ready for full duty then."

"I don't think so," Col. Randal said.

"Possibly I was mistaken, sir," Capt. Chatterhorn said. "Four weeks."

"I'm returning you to limited duty right now," Col. Randal said. "We never got around to doing that security review for RFHQ. The Razor is setting up an office here, the general is setting up one as well and Veronica Paige is in the process of expanding MI-9. All of those are classified operations. We can't wait any longer."

"My pleasure, Colonel," Capt. Chatterhorn said. "I was afraid you were going to relieve me from commanding my patrol due to my injury."

"Not with your record, Lionel," Col. Randal said. "However, I do want you to take as much time off as possible while you're coming up with our new security plan—spend time in town, relax. That's an order.

"I'll put you back on patrol as soon as you're good to go."

"Thank you, sir."

Walking him to the door, Col. Randal said, "Rumor is Dudley Clarke has a secure site guarded by a tribe of natives who speak no known language. That way a spy can't bribe 'em to find out what's going on at the site. Maybe you ought to get us some of those natives for RFHQ."

"How would we give them orders, sir?" Capt. Chatterhorn asked. "Or, how would they report a security breach?"

"Maybe you could teach 'em English."

"Would that not defeat the purpose, sir?"

"Can't believe one word that comes out of A-Force," Col. Randal said. "Lying is in their job description."

SERGEANT MAJOR MIKE "MARCH OR DIE" Mikkalis, DSM, MM, arrived. He reported straightaway to Colonel John Randal.

"How did you find the experience of being Duck Patrol Leader?" Col. Randal asked.

"You were at your best," Sgt. Maj. Mikkalis said, "the day you dreamed that one up, Colonel. We raided somewhere almost every night.

"Earthquake McGoon would take me up in the Kingfisher float plane. We would select a target. After dark, Warthog would set sail to our release point; Duck Patrol went ashore, mined the road, set up an ambush or shot up a roadhouse, then returned to the *King Duck* to do it all over again the next night somewhere else."

"That's the way to do it," Col. Randal said.

"A DUKW can carry up to a 105 howitzer, but no one was ever going to give Frank Polanski one," Sgt. Maj. Mikkalis said. "So he experimented with captured guns—finally hit on the Cannone da 47/39, called the 'Little Elephant.' Austrian design manufactured by the Italians. Roll up on a roadhouse, reduce it to rubble with four or five high-explosive rounds and go home."

"Was Butch unhappy when I sent him to relieve you from Duck Patrol?" Col. Randal asked. "Turned down the job when I offered it to him before you took command."

"The Headhunter has been raiding out of Lieutenant Seaborn's MAS boats almost all the way to Tripoli—real Commando strike from the sea unannounced and unexpected-like, then disappear-in-the-dark-of-night work, sir. Even had one of his teams stationed on a submarine for a time," Sgt. Maj. Mikkalis said.

"He did not want to give that assignment up, but after a couple of missions to familiarize himself with what we were doing, Lieutenant Hoolihan saw possibilities with the combination of DUKWs, gun jeeps and the Little Elephant, sir."

"I'll go ride with him some night," Col. Randal said. "I'd like to see Frank's cannon in action."

"Why did you pull me off the *King Duck,* sir?" Sgt. Mikkalis asked. "I was beginning to fine-tune my operational rhythm when I received your recall. Should be a lot of thin-skinned vehicles running down the coast road now that Rommel has gone back on the attack—the perfect set-up for Duck Patrol."

"An intake of fifty volunteers from the U.S. is arriving shortly," Col. Randal said. "Mad Dog's wounded—I need you to take charge of training until he's fit for duty."

"Rest easy, Colonel, never give the new troops another thought," Sgt. Maj. Mikkalis said. "Training them will be like a vacation. Life on the *King Duck* is no pleasure cruise; roughest ship I ever sailed on in any weather."

"Warthog Finley loves his LCT," Col. Randal said.

"No one else does, sir."

"Take a couple of weeks off, Sergeant Major," Col. Randal said. "It'll be a while before Travis McCloud gets back here.

"Enjoy yourself."

"You positive you want me to take leave," Sgt. Maj. Mikkalis said, "with the Germans driving on Alexandria, sir?"

"Roger that," Col. Randal said. "Maybe you don't want to go to Alexandria."

"The Headhunter said you recommended it to him," Sgt. Maj. Mikkalis said. "What gives, Colonel?"

"Your mother isn't in Cairo."

KING SAID, "YOU ARE NOT GOING TO BELIEVE THIS, Chief. Lady Seaborn and Ensign Hamilton drove through the gate with a truckload of mannequins aboard one of Major Merritt's 30-cwts. Three more trucks have what appear to be Arab tents stacked in the back. What is this all about?"

Colonel John Randal was studying the map in the suite he shared with Major the Lady Jane Seaborn, memorizing every detail of the proposed Area of Operations (AO) that the remnant of Desert Patrol was going to be operating in. He said, "Illusionists make things disappear *and* appear according to The Great Teddy—what you see in the back of those trucks is an armored brigade of brand new American Grant tanks. The mannequins are the crew—got to use your imagination."

King said, "Things are getting stranger and stranger around here."

"May just be getting warmed up in the weird department," Col. Randal said.

"You and I won't be traveling out with the convoy. We'll jump in and link up later. Why don't you take a few days off, King."

"Negative," the Merc said. "Might miss out on what happens next. Besides, Chief, a major counterattack is in progress—in case you failed to notice."

"At least hit the town in Cairo the next two or three nights," Col. Randal said. "That's an order."

"Can do."

Waldo Treywick came in. "Colonel, got a minute? I could use some advice."

"What kind of advice, Mr. Treywick?"

"Joe says it's time to diversify our portfolio . . ."

"King," Col. Randal ordered. "Take up your post. Don't let anyone other than Lady Jane come in until I finish my meeting with Mr. Treywick."

"Wilco."

"OK," Col. Randal said after the Merc left the room. "I can't imagine any investment advice you'd want from me, but take it from the top."

"You know Joe took them correspondence courses," Waldo said. "'The problem is the solution,' remember?"

"How could I forget?"

"Well," Waldo said, "one business course Joe took said the most important rule of wealth management is to spread out your risk across a number a' different asset classes—real estate bein' one of 'em."

"That makes sense," Col. Randal said.

"Me and Joe got most of our assets tied up in the basement of the U.S. Embassy in downtown Kenya in crates labeled 'Property of the U.S. Marshals Service,'" Waldo said. "And, it bein' gold coins and bars, there's a hitch—private ownership of gold is illegal in the States under current law—the Gold Reserve Act of 1934 to be specific."

"That is a problem," Col. Randal said, accepting one of Waldo's thin, custom-rolled cigars and sticking it between his front teeth.

"Transportin' the crates is gonna be risky too," Waldo said. "We can't insure somethin' we ain't supposed to have, and only a fool would put a load a' uninsured gold on a ship that might get itself sunk by a German submarine."

"Hard," Col. Randal said, "being a millionaire."

"Who'da ever thunk it," Waldo said. "Almost as dangerous as huntin' bad cat. You gotta make a bunch a' decisions, lotta in's, lotta out's, and like your unofficial Roger's Rangers rule says best, 'Don't Forget Nothin'.'"

Col. Randal said, "That is important."

"Like I mentioned to you before, Colonel," Waldo said, "we also got us a vault full-a' precious stones in the Beverly Hills Bank, and we think right now might be a good time to sell a few to get some liquidity so we can diversify.

"Me and Joe like raw land."

"I see," Col. Randal said, which meant he did not have a clue where Waldo was going with this conversation.

"Joe says there's a Jap scare out on the West Coast," Waldo said. "Folks is expectin' to be invaded by the 'Yellow Peril' at any minute. Not too long ago a Nip submarine surfaced in plain view to shell a couple a' targets with its deck gun, which didn't do much for the locals' morale.

"I heard about it," Col. Randal said.

"The way you make money in real estate is to buy low and sell high," Waldo said. "Ever since Pearl Harbor, land values in California along the coastline has done dropped right off the chart—lotsa sellers and ain't no purchasers. Joe's course he took said when that happens it's what you call a 'buyer's market,' which means it's a buyin' signal.

"The best time to invest in land, accordin' to Joe, is 'when the blood runs red in the streets,'" Waldo said. "I don't think he means real blood . . ."

"Sounds like you two have the concept of real estate investing nailed, Mr. Treywick," Col. Randal said. "What's your question?"

"My question is two questions," Waldo said. "Could Joe and I take some leave after we get done fightin' off Rommel in this next scrape so we can go to California to take a look at some property we might want to buy?"

"Sure," Col. Randal said. "Shove off right now if you like. Have a good trip. What's the second question?"

"You know we ain't goin' off leavin' you in the middle of a battle to make money, Colonel," Waldo said. "But after it's done run its course, since you growed up out there, could you recommend some good areas along the California coast we might oughta take a look at?"

Col. Randal said, "Love to."

COLONEL JOHN RANDAL WAS SITTING out by the suite's private pool reading a book. He looked up when Major the Lady Jane Seaborn came out in one of her French cut swimsuits—this one was white. He wondered what his blood pressure was at that exact moment.

"What are you reading, John?"

"*Infantry Attacks*," Col. Randal said. "Captain McKoy checked it out of the Cairo Public Library. He said there were hardly any other names on the card. Hadn't been checked out in over three years."

"Only you would be reading a book on tactics no one else has any interest in," Lady Jane laughed. "Who's the author?"

"Erwin Rommel."

CHAPTER SEVEN

LITTLE BLOODY LATE

LIEUTENANT PAMALA PLUM-MARTIN was in the front seat at the stick of the *King Duck's* 02SU Kingfisher floatplane. Wearing a brightly colored, oversized Hawaiian shirt, Earthquake McGoon was sitting directly behind her in the observer/gunner's seat looking over her shoulder. She was getting a check ride in Raiding Forces' newest airplane—and for once, it really *was* new. With the exception of the Hudson, all their other special operations aircraft were castoffs no one else wanted.

This particular Kingfisher was the personal aircraft of Vice Admiral Sir Randolph "Razor" Ransom, VC, KCB, DSO, OBE, DSC. He had loaned it to Acting Provisional Sub-Lieutenant Skipper Warthog Finley, OBE, RNPS, for use on the Landing Craft Tank (LCT) *King Duck*. Sometime in the near future, the floatplane was going to be reported as "lost at sea," and then the Razor could get a replacement more befitting the Deputy Director Naval Operations (Irregular) and Warthog would have his own off-the-books scout plane.

Colonel John Randal and Wing Commander Ronald Gordon, *aka* "Flash Bang," were squeezed in the two tiny passenger seats in line behind the pilots. The Kingfisher had been designed to carry a single passenger, but the Razor's had been modified to add another. The aircraft was en route to the *King Duck*. Tonight Col. Randal and W/Cdr. Gordon were going to observe Lieutenant Butch "Headhunter" Hoolihan, DSO, MC, MM, RM, lead a Duck Patrol raid on one of the Italian roadhouses, called *casas di stradas*, along the coastal highway, the Via Balbia.

Col. Randal wanted to observe Frank Polanski's 47/32 Little Elephant in action, and he was allowing W/Cdr. Gordon to tag along in the interest of improving inter-service cooperation with the RAF, which up until recently had been nonexistent. And more particularly, because the Wing Commander had recommended Lt. Plum-Martin for the Distinguished Service Order for her part in originating, planning and flying OPERATION BOMBSHELL missions, which had resulted in more than one hundred Luftwaffe and Regia Aeronautica pilots being killed to date.

Airplanes can be replaced in a matter of days. To replace the loss of an experienced combat pilot with an equally experienced combat pilot requires a minimum of two years' flight training and operational flying. OPERATION BOMBSHELL missions hurt the opposition. The RAF had finally begun to recognize that fact.

W/Cdr. Gordon made a lot of friends in Raiding Forces when the Vargas Girl-looking Royal Marine pilot received her gong—she was wildly popular, highly respected and a superb pilot.

Lt. Plum-Martin was one of the most-decorated aviators England had produced in the war to date. Even so, she was not allowed to wear RAF wings. Women were only authorized Air Transport Wings.

Regulations were regulations—she had won the medals but had decided to follow Col. Randal's example and never wore them.

"Prepare to land," Lt. Plum-Martin said over her shoulder. "*King Duck* in sight."

The floatplane splashed down and taxied to the ungainly LCT. A team of RNPS sailors swarmed all over the small craft, attaching cables for the crane to hoist it aboard as the pilots and passengers scrambled up the ladder to the deck of the ship.

Skipper Warthog Finley ordered the LCT underway the instant the Kingfisher was recovered on board. The sun went down flaming scarlet, swallowed up by the turquoise Mediterranean. Night fell, and it was pitch-dark almost immediately.

After two hours, the *King Duck* hove to. RNPS sailors swung into action preparing to launch Duck Patrol's DUKWs. Skipper Finley ran a taut ship. He carried out drills every waking minute of the day and even after the evening meal—drills late into the night.

At this point the *King Duck* was approximately four hundred miles behind the enemy lines—three miles off the beach where Duck Patrol planned to land.

Lt. Hoolihan came up on the bridge. He briefed the mission: "We are launching in ten minutes, sir. You and the Wing Commander will be riding in Frank's DUKW. Tonight is planned to be a quick in and out. We will land a light patrol consisting of two gun jeeps and the Little Elephant mounted in a DUKW.

"The gun jeeps will be unloaded by two crane DUKWs. Frank will transition his gun DUKW into wheel drive. Then, in company of the two jeeps, proceed inland to the Via Balbia approximately five hundred yards off the beach.

"Once on the highway, the patrol will make a left-hand turn and proceed down the hardball for a mile to the objective—a *casa di strada* that we hope will not be expecting company.

"Immediately upon arrival, Frank will shell the roadhouse. The gun jeeps will shoot up any enemy vehicles or other targets of opportunity that happen to be on the objective. Then our patrol will do an about-face, return to the pick-up point—seeding the road with camel chip mines as we go—reload the two gun jeeps and exfiltrate back to the *King Duck.*

"Questions?"

There were no questions.

"In that case," Lt. Hoolihan said, "see you on the beach, Colonel."

"Roger that, Butch."

W/Cdr. Gordon was beginning to have reservations about the wisdom of a RAF officer, particularly one on light duty because of an injured leg, the result of a recent crash—his fifth—accompanying a Commando raid. It is one thing to roll in on a target with all guns blazing, pull out and fly away home. Tonight was going to be up close and personal.

Home was a long way off.

"Lighten up, Ronnie," Col. Randal said, sensing the pilot's apprehension as they were making their way to Frank Polanski's gun DUKW for the run ashore. "The Headhunter's one of my most trusted officers. We've served together a long time."

"Colonel," W/Cdr. Gordon said, "that is no reason at all for me to take comfort."

Col. Randal said, "You could have a point."

Skipper Finley was supervising the preparation for the launch. As usual, Warthog had the stub of a nasty-looking cigar clenched in his jaw. He was walking down the line of DUKWs inspecting each one with a critical eye. The captain of a ship underway is a king, the master of the universe.

Skipper Finley never let anyone aboard the *King Duck* ever forget it.

Lt. Hoolihan walked up as Col. Randal and W/Cdr. Gordon were preparing to climb aboard Frank Polanski's gun DUKW.

"Change of plans, sir," Lt. Hoolihan said. "When we beach, you and Wing Commander Gordon dismount your DUKW and move up to my jeep—you switch out with my driver and the Wing Commander can man the pedestal-mounted Vickers K."

"Sounds good, Butch," Col. Randal said. "Ronnie's itching to take a crack at the bad guys tonight."

Frank was sitting behind the wheel of the gun DUKW. The former U.S. Marine Corps heavy weapons man had the identical twin to Skipper Finley's stub of a cigar stuck in his jaw. When Col. Randal and W/Cdr. Gordon climbed in, he immediately began a briefing on the Cannone da 47/32.

"This gun was primarily designed as an anti-tank weapon," Frank said. "However, it is also intended for close support—don't think what the Italians had in mind was as close as we use it, Colonel."

Col. Randal said. "Probably not."

"The advantage this weapon provides is that, in addition to its armor-piercing round—which will penetrate all known enemy armor up to a German Mark III—it also has a high-explosive round, which is what we're going to use on the roadhouse tonight.

"You will be impressed, gentlemen—I guarantee."

"That's what we're here for," Col. Randal said, "to be impressed."

Frank ran down the Little Elephant's nomenclature. "This gun is 47mm, weighs six hundred ten pounds, has a muzzle velocity of two thousand sixty-seven feet per second with a maximum range of seven thousand yards—but like I pointed out, tonight we will be firing at minimum range."

"How close shall that be?" W/Cdr. Gordon asked.

"I like to try to stick the barrel in the front door," Frank said. "HE point-blank takes the fight out of everybody inside on the first round."

"He's joking, Wing Commander," Col. Randal said. "But it'll be close."

"Let's hope," W/Cdr. Gordon said, "we do not require any of the armor-piercing rounds."

"If we do," Col. Randal said, "the enemy tanks will be mounted on wheeled tank carrier transports—the single most strategic target in Afrika Korps.

"Rommel only has a limited number of carriers and the word is if we can knock 'em all out, the war in the desert is over."

"Now that sounds like information I should have been aware of before now," W/Cdr. Gordon said. "Communication between the RAF and our ground forces is turning out to be worse than previously thought."

Col. Randal withheld comment.

Skipper Finley appeared at the DUKW. "Ready to go ashore, Frank?"

"Roger, Skipper."

Skipper Finley reached in his pocket and produced a much-traveled flask that had sailed the seven seas. "Chill in the air, nothin' beats a nip a' brandy—hair a' the dog. Gentlemen?"

He handed the flask to Col. Randal.

"I want you to know I'm proud of you for sinking the U-Boat, Captain," Col. Randal said, taking a shot and passing the flask to W/Cdr. Gordon. The *King Duck* is really whipped into tip-top fighting shape."

Not many people had ever told Warthog Finley they were proud of him. Being a hero was a new experience. Living up to it was taking some getting used to.

"Take good care of the Colonel for me, Frank," Skipper Finley ordered, retrieving his flask.

"Aye, aye, Skipper,"

Up front Lt. Hoolihan's DUKW began rolling down the ramp. Then the rest of the column began slowly moving forward to launch. As usual, Col. Randal experienced a "this is insane" moment as they drove off the LCT into the sea. He turned to check on W/Cdr. Gordon.

The pilot's face had turned a pale shade of green.

Frank loved driving the DUKW. There was a big grin on his face as the amphibious truck dipped and bobbed, snaking along at the tail end of the convoy closing the three-mile distance to shore.

Trying to take his mind off the idea that the DUKW might sink—it seemed to him that it most likely would, W/Cdr. Gordon asked, "How did a U.S. Marine end up in Raiding Forces?"

"I was outta the Corps at the time, after serving a burst of six down south in the Banana Wars. The Colonel and I met when I was advising a low-life shifta warlord in Abyssinia," Frank said. "My boss brought up his army to threaten Colonel Randal, who had his own guerrilla outfit called Force N.

"My employer saw the colonel as a competitor," Frank said.

"We outmanned Force N by about five to one at the time, so eliminating the competition shoulda been easy.

"Only my guy decided to pay a call on Colonel Randal before the fight commenced. Liked to look his next victim in the eye before the bloodbath—man had an attitude."

"What happened?" W/Cdr. Gordon asked.

"The colonel shot him," Frank said. "I switched sides."

Up ahead, Lt. Hoolihan's DUKW beached. The crane DUKW in trail behind it came ashore and immediately started lifting the gun jeep out of the back. The third DUKW in the column landed. The second crane DUKW came in right behind it and repeated the process.

Utilizing one crane per jeep dramatically speeded up the landing process. The two gun jeeps were ready to roll out by the time the DUKW armed with the Little Elephant beached.

"OK," Col. Randal said, as he was climbing out, "let's see what you've got, Frank."

"You're going to love this, Colonel," Frank said. "Sit back, relax and enjoy the show."

As Col. Randal and W/Cdr. Gordon were getting into Lt. Hoolihan's jeep, the Headhunter asked the RAF pilot, "Are you are familiar with the Vickers K, sir?"

"Oh, yes."

"Excellent," Lt. Hoolihan said. "Let's roll, then. Remember, Colonel, we have to avoid driving into any patches of soft sand Frank's DUKW will not be able to negotiate across."

"Roger."

Col. Randal let out the clutch and eased off the beach in four-wheel drive. The moon was still up but sinking fast, and visibility was as good as it was going to get tonight. He was relaxed but clicked on—very aware.

Lt. Hoolihan was walking ahead of the jeep, guiding it to the Via Balbia, which was approximately five hundred yards away. The Headhunter was not taking chances about the soft sand. The Royal Marine was leading from the front—Col. Randal noted.

As he drove, Col. Randal finger-touch-checked his personal weapons—he had already done it several times on the trip ashore. Tonight he was carrying one of his U.S. 1911 Model Colt .38 Supers, a 9mm Browning P-35, a .22 High Standard with silencer, Fairbairn Fighting knife, and the Beretta 9mm MAB-38A submachine gun. He had his 45mm shoulder-fired Brixia mortar with forty rounds in a pack in the back of the jeep. He was not expecting to need them—this was a quick, arrive unexpected, under cover of darkness, shoot up the roadhouse with the 47/32 cannon and away home—but why take a chance?

Lt. Hoolihan held up his hand to stop. Then he disappeared into the dark. By the time Col. Randal had stuck one of Waldo Treywick's thin cigars between his teeth, the Headhunter was back.

"Road in sight," Lt. Hoolihan said, climbing in his seat, adjusting the handles on his twin Vickers K MGs mounted on the hood. "Ready, Wing Commander?"

"Ready!"

Col. Randal noticed that the pilot seemed less tense now that the prospect of action was at hand—tonight the RAF officer was out of his element but he was game. Good for him.

"OK, sir," Lt. Hoolihan said, "showtime."

The jeep rolled up on the hardball. Col. Randal shifted out of four-wheel drive. The lime green hands on his Rolex showed straight up 0200 hours. The *casa di strada* was approximately a mile ahead. Now the moon was down and pitch-dark was settling in.

Col. Randal flipped on the cat's eye headlights—designed to look like German blackout running lights. The other two vehicles behind him did the same. If anyone was awake at the roadhouse at this time of night they would think Duck Patrol was a friendly convoy arriving late.

That happened all the time.

Visibility was limited to the much-restricted cat's eye beam. Col. Randal resisted the impulse to speed up and get the fight started. He knew where the roadhouse was located but he did not know who or what was there.

The scheme of maneuver called for Col. Randal to pull off on the left-hand seaside shoulder of the road upon arrival and for the second gun jeep to pull off on the right desert-side shoulder, while Frank moved up between them online and commenced fire with the Little Elephant 47/32 cannon as soon as it came to bear. With any luck, Duck Patrol would be out of the target area in less than one minute—headed back to the crane DUKWs waiting on the beach to load up and exfiltrate back to the *King Duck*.

The plan called for the roadhouse to be a smoking ruin, reduced to rubble.

"Stand ready, Wing Commander," Col. Randal said over his shoulder.

Lt. Hoolihan was leaning forward over his pair of Vickers K .303 caliber MGs, trying to see past the glow of the headlamps. Up ahead, a red tail reflector glinted as the light struck it. Col. Randal immediately pulled over as planned and the second jeep pulled right.

The big DUKW rolled up and all three vehicles eased forward online until the dim shape of the roadhouse could be made out through the dark.

Duck Patrol was very close—almost in the parking lot. Three cars were parked outside the building. Cars meant officers were inside. German? Italian? It was impossible to tell, but only senior officers were authorized command cars.

"What's the bursting radius of Frank's gun, Butch?" Col. Randal asked.

W/Cdr. Gordon said, "Little bloody late to be asking, is it not?"

"Fifty yards, sir," Lt. Hoolihan said.

Uh-oh.

KAAAAABOOOM—BLAAAAAM!

Shrapnel screamed, some of it whizzing back over their heads. The muzzle blast was deafening. The sky turned a golden white from the discharge of the cannon and the instantaneous explosion of the high-explosive shell detonating.

Night vision was destroyed.

KAAAAABOOM BLAAAAAM! KAAAAABOOM BLAAAAAM! KAAAAABOOM BLAAAAAM! KAAAAABOOM BLAAAAAM!

Frank's gun team was working fast.

Not only were the Raiders night blind, but everyone in Duck Patrol was virtually deaf because their ears were ringing so loudly.

As promised, the *casa di strada* was reduced to a pile of rubble. Frank had not exaggerated. The Little Elephant was very impressive.

What was not part of the plan was that the Italian AB-41 armored car escorting a convoy of trucks driving down the Via Balbia behind Duck Patrol would open fire with its high-velocity 20mm anti-tank gun. While the 20mm round would not penetrate any known armored vehicle in the world, it was sure death on thin-skinned vehicles like gun jeeps or DUKWs.

The shell screamed by overhead, down the road into the night. When it did, it struck a fuel carrier parked in the middle of a large Axis convoy that was laagered for the night a quarter of a mile past the *casa di strada* that, until now, had gone undetected.

The ten-ton tanker went up in a ball of fire. The Italians in the laager, who had been awakened by Frank's five rapid cannon rounds and were wondering what was happening, now acquired a target—the AB-41 armored car—and they opened with what appeared to the men of Duck Patrol to be one million automatic weapons.

Tracer fire illuminated part of the enemy convoy parked down the road. It was made up of a number of captured British trucks, adding to the confusion. The AB-41 shifted its attention to what the car commander believed was a large force of enemy vehicles and commenced firing with both its 20mm anti-tank gun and its 8mm coaxial MG.

Duck Patrol was in a bad spot—caught in the cross-fire between two Italian convoys that were under the impression they were fighting for their life. While there were not actually one million automatic weapons firing at the Raiders, there had to be at least a million tracers crackling overhead from both directions, which had a detrimental effect on morale.

The only Duck Patrol weapons able to shift to fire on the Italians to the rear were the twin Vickers K pedestal-mounted MGs on the jeeps and those on the back of the DUKW.

W/Cdr. Gordon got his pair around and let off the first burst. The second gun jeep gunner opened almost simultaneously. The hail of .303 caliber rounds ricocheted off the AB-41, streaking straight up into the sky. The MG rounds caused no damage, but the tracers did attract the attention of the Italian armored car gunner.

Frank was desperately trying to muscle the big, ungainly DUKW around. He was backing and turning, fighting the wheel hard not to run off the road and get stuck in the sand off the shoulders. Finally, he managed the maneuver—but not before the AB-41 got off a round—knocking out the second of Duck Patrol's jeeps.

The Little Elephant fired a 47mm HE shell, which was not the round of choice for armored fighting vehicles but was what Frank had up the spout at the time. However, the result was spectacular. The AB-41 blew up and flipped on its side. Secondary explosions from the ammunition onboard started cooking off.

Typically, Italian armored cars traveled in pairs when pulling convoy escort duty. If there were a second AB-41 along tonight, it chose not to intervene and risk the same fate as its mate.

Now the enemy truckers traveling behind the AB-41 got into the fight. Rattled by the sight of their escort exploding, they misjudged the location of Frank's DUKW and engaged the source of all the MG rounds coming at them from farther down the Via Balbia. The battle escalated—the two Italian convoys fighting it out with Duck Patrol still caught in the middle.

Lt. Hoolihan hopped out of his seat and ran to check on the knocked-out jeep. Col. Randal engaged the laagered convoy past the smoking rubble of the roadhouse with his pair of Vickers Ks while W/Cdr. Gordon sprayed the trucks to their rear.

Not anticipating a full-scale war and always conscious of weight when driving off the beach to the Via Balbia, Frank had only brought the six 47 mm rounds. The cannon was out of action.

The Little Elephant's DUKW's machine gunners joined the fight.

Col. Randal was squeezing off crisp, short bursts from his pair of Vickers Ks when there was a rattling that sounded like hailstones striking the front of the jeep. The motor cut out. Without a moment's hesitation, he immediately unlocked his pair of MGs from their mount, threw them over his shoulder and shouted to W/Cdr. Gordon, "Bail out, Ronnie—head for the DUKW."

The Wing Commander jumped out the back of the jeep and limped alongside Col. Randal to the amphibious truck.

"Get ready to roll, Frank," Col. Randal ordered. "Both gun jeeps are knocked out."

"Which way we going, Colonel?"

"Hard left to the water," Col. Randal ordered, tossing the Vickers Ks in the back of the DUKW. "We'll put out to sea, run back up the coast and pick up the two cranes."

"Can do, Colonel."

Lt. Hoolihan was at the gun jeep when Col. Randal returned to retrieve the pedestal-mounted Vickers Ks. He had the three men from the blown-up jeep and the jeep's MGs with him.

Incredibly, no one had been killed, but all three Raiders were wounded. The AB-41's high velocity, armor-piercing 20mm round had sliced completely through the jeep, throwing off razor-sharp steel splinters in its path.

Frank turned the DUKW around again as Col. Randal placed an incendiary grenade on the hood of the command jeep. Every jeep kept one strapped to the steering column to disable the vehicle in case of emergency. He did not pull the pin.

The three wounded raiders were helped into the back of the DUKW as the firefight raged.

"Drive for the water, Butch," Col. Randal ordered, jacking a 45mm round into his Brixia. He slung his Beretta 9mm submachine gun across his chest. "I'll provide rear security."

The volume of firing continued with no decrease in intensity. Tracers were crisscrossing overhead and off to the right. Occasionally, a truck would catch fire.

The only good thing was, since they were truckers and not combat infantrymen, Col. Randal did not expect anyone on the enemy side to fix bayonets and initiate a ground attack.

"I am not leaving without you, sir," Lt. Hoolihan said.

"You've got your orders," Col. Randal said. "Move out, Butch."

"Colonel . . ."

"Don't let that DUKW get stuck in the sand," Col. Randal said. He raised the stubby little mortar to his shoulder and fired it back over the burning AB-41 armored car at the laagered convoy down the road. The result was a satisfying *BOOOOM* when the 45mm round detonated against the side of a truck.

The gas tank of the truck he hit exploded, sounding like a five hundred-pound bomb.

Lucky shot—he was not aiming at it.

"Get going."

"Yes, sir."

The DUKW rolled off the Via Balbia into the dunes between the hard-topped road and the beach, with Lt. Hoolihan walking out front guiding it.

Col. Randal kept up a steady drumbeat of mortar rounds on both convoys, shifting back and forth between the two with every other round. No one likes being mortared, no matter how small the mortar round may be. His goal was to keep heads down.

The truckers were not likely to maneuver against each other—catching him in the middle. But there was no guarantee on that.

When Col. Randal was down to his last mortar round, he pulled the pin on the No. 76 Special Incendiary grenade sitting on the hood of the jeep, turned and started for the beach. When he reached the first grassy sand dune, he turned and fired the Brixia one-handed into the side of the fuel storage tank standing beside the ruin of the *casa di strada*. It went up in a massive fireball.

The blue-on-blue battle raged on as he made his way down to the beach.

When Col. Randal reached the DUKW, he pitched his gear in the back. So much for sitting back relaxed and watching the show.

"Let's get the hell out of Dodge."

CHAPTER EIGHT

NEW MIST-O-MATIC

COLONEL JOHN RANDAL WAS SITTING out by the private pool on the third-floor suite he shared with Major the Lady Jane Seaborn at RFHQ. The sun was coming up. He had flown in from the *King Duck* about a half hour earlier.

Lady Jane came out in a white, fluffy robe, not a stick of makeup, golden tan, mahogany hair swirling in the morning breeze—drop-dead gorgeous. She was carrying a tray with steaming cups of tea.

"I ran into Ronnie having breakfast when I went down to the mess," Lady Jane said. "He informed me you were up to your typical heroics last night. Did Duck Patrol encounter more than it bargained for?"

Col. Randal said, "We did."

"Expect the unexpected," Lady Jane said, quoting from Raiding Forces' "Rules for Raiding."

"Now, how," Col. Randal said, "am I supposed to do that?"

"You wrote the rules," Lady Jane laughed.

"True—but I modified that one."

"John, may I ask you a personal question?"

"Sure—fire away."

"Why is it that you strike me as not taking this latest Afrika Korps offensive seriously?" Lady Jane said. "You seem disinterested."

"What makes you say that?"

"You order almost every person you come in contact with to take time off or go on leave. Raiding Forces is on alert to deploy, we are already desperately under strength, and yet you are authorizing even more people to be away," Lady Jane said. "Why, John?"

"We're not having this conversation," Col. Randal said. "OK?"

"My lips are sealed," Lady Jane said, noting he did not use the word "classified"—which meant what she was about to hear was an opinion.

"Rommel holds Benghazi," Col. Randal said. "Let's say he kicked off from there—not exactly sure where this counterattack started from—but let's give him the benefit of the doubt. How far east is Tobruk?"

"Two hundred thirty miles," Lady Jane said, "more or less."

"Tanks hit a maintenance wall at approximately two hundred fifty," Col. Randal said, "and that's if they're in perfect running order when they start out. Rommel's aren't—his saw hard service in CRUSADER."

"Maintenance 'wall,'" Lady Jane said. "How do you know so much about tanks?"

"That's what happened at Calais," Col. Randal said. "The 10th Panzer Division ground to a halt outside the town, broken down after having raced three hundred miles across France."

Lady Jane said, "But you destroyed the last . . ."

"The panzers sure didn't stop because my Swamp Fox Force people blew up a bridge," Col. Randal said. "German engineers could have spanned that stream in a few hours."

"Fascinating," Lady Jane said. "Rommel might reach Tobruk, possibly even capture it, but that will be as far as his tanks are able to travel without a lengthy pause for maintenance?"

"That's right," Col. Randal said.

"Why, then," Lady Jane asked, "is there such a flap at GHQ over Rommel's counterattack?"

"I have no idea," Col. Randal said.

King came out to the pool carrying a phone with the cord trailing, "The general is on the line for you, Chief."

"Colonel Randal, sir."

"Colonel," James "Baldie" Taylor said, "Dudley believes you cannot afford to wait until your convoy of gun jeeps arrives from Oasis X to carry out the operation I briefed you on. You do not even have the luxury to wait for the civilian trucks Sammy Sansom located to transport your men to the target area—we are out of time.

"Your mission needs to be executed, at least in part, by daylight tomorrow—come up with a plan."

"Roger that, sir."

"What did Jim want?" Lady Jane asked.

"We're ordered to have the initial phase of Teddy's deception in place by tomorrow morning," Col. Randal said. "The military situation is . . . 'deteriorating rapidly.'"

"Extraordinary," Lady Jane said. "Rommel is running his tanks into the ground and our side is panicking."

"My thought exactly," Col. Randal said.

"Teddy has to be five hundred miles from here," Lady Jane said. "By dawn?"

"That's what the man said." Col. Randal ordered, "King, have Karen, Pam and the wing commander report to me as soon as possible—if not sooner."

"On the way."

"Better have Ensign Hamilton up, too," Col. Randal said. "He's going to be stage managing this extravaganza."

"Anyone else, Chief?

"That's it for now—you sit in when they arrive."

When King had departed, Lady Jane said, "Our Command is so spooked—awkward. And more than a little disquieting."

"If GHQ had any guts," Col. Randal said, "they'd let Rommel run free, unopposed. Then when his tanks hit the end of their string—kill him."

Lady Jane said, "Agreed."

Within minutes, Lieutenant Pamala Plum-Martin and Lieutenant Karen Montgomery arrived wearing their swimsuits and legwarmers. King had pulled them out of Rocky's exercise class (Lady Jane was sitting it out today to spend the morning with Col. Randal). Wing Commander Ronald Gordon came in right after them. Ensign Teddy Hamilton arrived last.

Col. Randal said, "Raiding Forces has been ordered to execute Ensign Hamilton's deception operation to start at Beginning Morning Nautical Twilight tomorrow.

"Pam, can you airdrop enough supplies to keep us going until a ground convoy can reach the target?"

"Depends," Lt. Plum-Martin said, "on what we have to transport."

"Arab tents, mainly," Ens. Hamilton said. "A few other small handheld implements to make tank tracks, smoke pots and some inflatable tanks."

"Arab tents?" Col. Randal asked.

"It is not really possible to hide anything in the desert, sir," Ens. Hamilton said. "You can only make an object *look* like something else.

"Also, it is important for us to think like our enemy—Rommel. He makes cars look like trucks and trucks look like tanks, and he hides his tanks in Arab tents.

"We set up our own tents, then make artificial tank tracks leading up to each one. When the enemy aerial reconnaissance sees it from the air—hey, presto—Mr. Desert Fox will believe a brigade of British armor has miraculously appeared on his flank because that is *exactly* what he would do—hide his panzers in Arab tents."

Col. Randal said, "Makes sense."

The Vargas Girl-looking Royal Marine said, "To deliver the materials and drop the parachutists will require more than our Hudson—you will be dropping every available man, correct?"

"Negative," Col. Randal said. "Plan for no more than twenty jumpers."

"In that case, John," Lt. Plum-Martin said, "we should be able to accomplish our mission with two more Hudsons for the initial drop—possibly another after Teddy shows me exactly what it is we will have to fly in on follow-up drops."

"Can you make that happen, Wing Commander?" Col. Randal asked.

"I take it this is a high priority mission?" W/Cdr. Gordon asked.

"Field Marshal Auchinleck personally authorized it," Lady Jane said.

"Hudsons are high in demand by VIPs but are relatively low-priority RAF combat support aircraft," W/Cdr. Gordon said. "I am reasonably confident there shall be no problem securing the use of two of them on a limited, short-term basis.

"You are going to have to find pilots," W/Cdr. Gordon said. "Those are in critically short supply."

"Are you certified to fly a Hudson, Ronnie?" Col. Randal asked.

"I am, Colonel."

"Then Pam can fly one and Earthquake McGoon the other—make it happen."

"My pleasure."

"Karen," Col. Randal said, "can you have parachutes ready for the drop tonight?"

"Yes, sir."

"Do you have enough chutes available to airdrop supplies, etc., until we can get our ground convoy on the scene? And we're going to need to initiate an OPERATION LIMELIGHT-type mission simultaneously."

"In that case, we shall need to make arrangements for more of the decommissioned parachutes mothballed at RAF Habbaniya to be flown to RFHQ, John."

"Am I permitted to inquire," W/Cdr. Gordon asked, "what an 'OPERATION LIMELIGHT-type mission' might be?"

"We drop parachutes weighted down by blocks of ice in enemy territory," Col. Randal said. "The ice melts, the bad guys—or in this case, the local Arabs—will find empty parachutes, steal the silk and report the chutes to the Germans or Italians for a reward.

"Gives the other side something to think about—where did the jumpers disappear to?"

"That is brilliant," W/Cdr. Gordon said. "RAF will order the decommissioned parachutes you require flown to RFHQ immediately. Simple enough to stage a training exercise for the flying school students at Habbaniya by having them fly a real transport mission."

"All right then," Col. Randal said. "Let's do this, people."

DUSTY FROM HIS DESERT TRAVELS, ex-Lieutenant Billy Jack Jaxx arrived at RFHQ. He immediately reported to Colonel John Randal in his suite. He found him in his small briefing area, studying the map.

"You made it, Jack," Col. Randal said. "Just in time."

"Not exactly, sir," ex-Lt. Jaxx said. "I came on ahead when we received the alert for a new mission. The rest of the convoy is about a day behind."

"Glad you did," Col. Randal said. "Some of us will be making a jump later tonight. The plan is to set up a diversion—dummy tanks. Try to get Rommel to take his eyes off the ball.

"You can take a few days off for R&R or come with us—your call."

"I'll be jumping in with you, Colonel," ex-Lt. Jaxx said.

"Hit the shower, get some rest," Col. Randal said. "We'll have lunch in Cairo with Jane."

"Yes, sir—I'd like that."

"By the way, you're a free man, Jack—pardoned by the Texas governor," Col. Randal said, tossing him the copy of the *Austin Statesman* newspaper. "How's it feel to be called a hero?"

"Not like I thought it would, sir."

"That's a fact."

As ex-Lt. Jaxx was leaving, King came in, shutting the door behind him. That had never happened before. Col. Randal clicked on without knowing why.

"This might not be the time, Chief," King said. "I would like to discuss something not pertaining to current operations."

"Go ahead."

"When you have me take my post and fail to order me to shut the door, I can hear every word said in this room," King said.

Col. Randal stuck one of Waldo's cigars between his teeth, "I know that."

"What I thought," the Merc said. "Anyway, Chief, strictly off the record—I'm a Swiss national with some familiarity with international banking. I may have a solution to Captain McKoy and Waldo's gold predicament."

"Really?"

"Request your permission to discuss the subject with them," King said.

"Who do you need in this conversation?"

"The captain," King said, "Waldo, Lady Seaborn and you."

"In that case," Col. Randal said, "let's do it—get 'em up here. Have the Marine duty officer station one of the girls at the door. I'll inform Jane her presence is requested."

When the Merc returned with Captain "Geronimo" Joe McKoy and Waldo, Col. Randal and Major the Lady Jane Seaborn were sitting in the living area. The men came in and took their seats. The door was firmly shut behind them.

"OK," Col. Randal said, "lay it out, King."

"As I understand it, Captain McKoy," the Merc said, "you and Waldo are in possession of a number of gold bars stored in the U.S. Consulate in Kenya."

Capt. McKoy looked at the soldier of fortune with narrowed eyes. "Maybe so, maybe no."

"You are faced with a dilemma," King said. "U.S. citizens are not allowed to own gold—FDR confiscated all of it in civilian hands in 1939. You may be rich, but there is no way to spend your money.

"To complicate the problem, you have no sure method of transporting your gold to someplace completely safe from the Nazis."

"If a man had himself a bunch a' gold," Capt. McKoy said, "that would be a serious concern all right—between a rock and a hard spot."

"For the sake of argument," King said, "if I were an American with a large stash of gold bars, what I would do is *sell* them to a Swiss bank. That way, I would have my money in hand; if I banked the gold, I would have to worry about the Germans crossing the border into Switzerland and nationalizing the banks."

"Can you do that?" Capt. McKoy asked. "Sell gold to a Swiss bank rather than deposit it?"

"You can," King said. "The trick is, make the arrangements through a third party, which allows you to remain anonymous. Then, when the bankers are standing by ready, deliver the gold to the bank. A branch bank will work fine—there is even one in Nairobi.

"Immediately upon arrival, your shipment of gold will be inventoried. Total value can be established after each bar is inspected—the bank has to verify they are not buying bars of gold-painted lead.

"Then, while you or your representative is physically present, the money agreed to will be wire-transferred to the bank or banks of your choice anywhere in the world.

"That part will require finesse," King said. "You want to avoid tax consequences."

Lady Jane said, "Leave that to me. The Seaborn family has legal counsel here in Cairo."

"How much would a bank be willing to pay us?" Waldo asked.

"The current market rate for gold is $30 per ounce," King said. "Every country in the world wants hard assets during time of war. The only asset more desirable is diamonds because the stones are portable.

"Swiss banks have a catalog of clients who will snap up all the gold they can buy at a premium to the market rate—because almost no one is selling."

Capt. McKoy and Waldo glanced at each other.

"What do you get out of this, King?" Capt. McKoy asked.

"I pick the bank."

"Fair enough—make 'em kick you some back."

King smiled.

Col. Randal said, "How much gold do you men have in that basement?"

"Twenty-three five hundred-pound crates," Capt. McKoy said, sounding embarrassed, "we made a big haul, John."

"Over five million dollars, U.S.," Lady Jane said, momentarily stunned.

"Not countin'," Capt. McKoy said, "them sacks a' gold coins."

"Yeah," Waldo said. "There's eleven of 'em double-bagged—about the size of sandbags. How do we work that out?"

"Gold coins have a numismatic value to collectors—possibly worth more than your boxes of bars," Lady Jane said, her green eyes sparkling with delight.

"You two are rich as sultans!"

"There's been a lot a' slips betwix' the cup and the lip," Capt. McKoy said.

"Lady Jane, would you consider ramrodding the bank buyout and wire transfer deal accordin' to the plan King laid out? Use your lawyer to be our straw man—kinda like the sound of that anonymous part. Get him to review the papers, handle our side a' the negotiations and all?"

"Oh, yes."

"Thank you, ma'am—feelin' a lot better knowin' you're in the deal," Waldo said. "International finance ain't my normal forté."

"Negotiating with bankers," Lady Jane said, "is like hunting man-eating lions, Mr. Treywick."

"The most important rule a' huntin' bad cat," Waldo said, "is don't get yourself ate."

"Exactly."

Capt. McKoy looked King dead in the eye, "It don't take a genius to spot a goat in a flock a' sheep. We sell 'em coins, you're in for a cut from our side too—you're our man, King."

The Merc said, "Affirmative."

"No wonder," Lady Jane laughed, "you chose to pass on returning to Abyssinia to be knighted by the Emperor, Mr. Treywick."

"Sounded like a trap," Capt. McKoy said. "Smelled like a trap—we figured it was a trap."

Waldo said, "New-mist-o-matic?"

"CHIEF," KING CALLED FROM HIS DESK at the door to the suite, "a code word RED INDIAN message is on the way up marked 'By Hand of Officer Only.'"

Colonel John Randal looked up from the table where he was cleaning his pistols when Lieutenant Mandy Paige dashed in with the flimsy.

"Phantom asked me to deliver this, John, since I happened to be in the Operations Room when it came in."

Col. Randal read:

> INTELLIGENCE INDICATES AXIS RAIL SYSTEM NOW UTILIZING RED INDIAN FOR COMMAND & CONTROL OF TRAIN TRAFFIC STOP INITIATE OPERATIONS TO SECURE STOP EXPEDITE EXPEDITE STOP 17F

17F was Commander Ian Fleming—personal assistant to the chief of Naval Intelligence.

"King," Col. Randal ordered, "have Captain Stirling and Lieutenant Jaxx report to me ASAP.

"Get Teddy up here too—hold him at your desk until I call for him."

"On the way, Chief."

"You want me to leave, John?" Lt. Mandy asked, clearly not wanting to.

"You can stay," Col. Randal said, knowing full well the girl had a long history of worming herself into any project she wanted to. The best way to deal with Lt. Mandy was to include her from the start.

"This is a RED INDIAN—you've been partially read into the missions. What we're getting ready to discuss is classified and you won't talk about it with anyone not present—let me hear a wilco, Mandy."

"Understand and will comply," Lt. Mandy flashed a beautiful, white-toothed smile—she liked being part of the team.

King came in with Captain "Pyro" Percy Stirling and ex-Lieutenant Billy Jack Jaxx.

Col. Randal said. "Percy, I don't believe you've met Mandy Paige."

"The pleasure is mine, Mandy," said Capt. Stirling. The 17/21 Lancers, the "Death or Glory Boys," could be exceedingly charming when they chose.

"Your reputation has certainly preceded you, *Pyro,*" Lt. Mandy said.

"As has yours," Capt. Stirling said. "The word is you are quite the gun moll."

Ex-Lt. Jaxx said, "Mandy specializes in the Texas heart shot—don't turn your back on her."

Lt. Mandy said, "Kill those Japs, Billy Jack."

Capt. Stirling looked confused.

Ex-Lt. Jaxx said, "Inside joke—I'll explain later, sir."

"Raiding Forces has been alerted for a RED INDIAN mission," Col. Randal said, getting down to business. "Percy, you're not cleared to know any more about the nature of RED INDIAN code name missions than the name—understood?"

"Sir!"

"Jack serves as my raid planner and assistant team leader for RED INDIANS. King is on the team, as are the Lovat Scouts Fenwick and Ferguson, plus the Ranger Patrol Phantom Team," Col. Randal said. "Mandy, well . . . she gathers intelligence, serves as liaison and performs other unspecified duties that arise. She was my personal assistant during the siege of Habbaniya—and that says everything you need to know about her ability."

"Impressive," Capt. Stirling said.

"For our next RED INDIAN we have not been given a specific target—only a class of target," Col. Randal said. "Capture certain materials that are to be found in Italian rail stations. Percy, since you are the world's leading expert on enemy rail in Libya," Col. Randal said, "I need you to recommend a target."

"You require a station that is isolated," Capt. Stirling said. "One you can attack with a small team, spend time searching undisturbed, then disappear back into the desert with the booty you went there to obtain, I presume, sir?"

"That's the idea."

"I have precisely the target, Colonel," Capt. Stirling said. "A small coaling station with a turnstile and a water storage tank located in the middle of nowhere—and I do mean remote.

"It looks like something out of an American Wild West movie. Less than a dozen Italian railroaders man the station. No roads in or out—no enemy forces within a hundred miles or more. My Railroad Wrecking Crew never bothered to attack it because we concentrate on blowing the rails or bridges, not hitting fixed targets.

"A couple of months ago we did cut the phone lines and ambush the work crew that came on their handcart to make repairs."

"Perfect," Col. Randal said. "King, ask Ensign Hamilton in."

Capt. Stirling was pointing out the location of the train station on the map to Col. Randal, ex-Lt. Jaxx and Lt. Mandy when King and The Great Teddy entered. The target was not more than two hundred miles from where Raiding Forces was planning to set up the dummy armored brigade diversion. However, in the desert without motor transport that is a long distance.

"Mandy," Col. Randal said, "contact the Long Range Desert Group and see if they have anything going near our RED INDIAN. If so, we need them to extract our team after we jump in and conduct our raid—you handle the coordination."

"Yes, sir."

"Ensign Hamilton" Col. Randal said, "Raiding Forces has been alerted to conduct a mission that is so classified that you are not cleared to know its code word identifier—which, nevertheless, is RED INDIAN."

"Sir," Ens. Hamilton said, "I have a Most Secret Clearance—required in order to work at the places I do when I am not in school."

"Yeah, well, this is 'need to know,'" Col. Randal said, "and you don't have the need . . . so forget what you know."

"Yes, sir."

"What I want from you," Col. Randal said, "is a plan to make what we are getting ready to do not look like what we did."

"Colonel," Ens. Hamilton said, "I shall require a little more information than that, sir."

"We're going to conduct a raid on an isolated railroad coaling station," Col. Randal said. "Kill everyone present, recover certain materials that may be located on the premises. And we don't want anyone to know we were ever there."

"Then you need to go big, sir," Ens. Hamilton said. "Stage an airplane crashing into the station with two five hundred-pound bombs on board—something like that. You want the opposition to be so overwhelmed by the magnitude of the destruction that they never even consider any other possibility about what happened."

"We don't have an airplane to crash," Col. Randal said.

"In that case, sir, do you know when the train will come by?"

"We have train schedules," Capt. Stirling said. "Italians are superb railroad operators—take pride in their work. Mussolini may have fouled up everything else but he makes the trains run on time.

"We blow them up right on schedule."

"In that case, Colonel," Ens. Hamilton said, "time your raid before a train arrives. When it does, set charges to cut the track so the engine derails and crashes into the station. Place additional explosive charges inside the building so that when the derailed train hits it, everything blows sky high."

"Kid," Col. Randal said, "I can see you haven't lost a step since Habbaniya—the bad guys will never figure that one out."

"Naturally," Capt. Stirling said, "you will require my services to cut the track."

"Well, that gives me pause," Col. Randal said. "But you're right—we do.

"Jack, make a plan. Mandy, let me know the instant you hear from the LRDG. Ensign Hamilton—like your style, stud."

While Col. Randal was wrapping up his orders, Lt. Mandy was examining Ens. Hamilton's military identification card—she wanted to see how his photo turned out.

"Teddy, how did you gain *two* years in age from the time you left Habbaniya?"

Col. Randal stuck one of Waldo's thin cigars between his teeth. "Ensign, did you fail to mention an additional year you stacked on top of the one you admitted to adding when we had our little talk?"

"Yes, sir," Ens. Hamilton said. "You have to be eighteen to be admitted to bars."

"No one checks an officer's ID at a bar," Col. Randal said. "Not one wearing the OBE."

"Like you always say, sir," Ens. Hamilton said, not the least bit discomfited by getting caught red-handed in another lie about his true age, "why take a chance?"

Col. Randal said, "Good answer, Ted."

CHAPTER NINE

ARAB TENTS

CAPTAIN TAYLOR CORRIGAN, SQUADRON COMMANDER of the Wing, and Colonel John Randal were inspecting the trucks that Major A. W. "Sammy" Sansom, Cheif of Cairo Field Security, had provided—most likely stolen. Men were working like galley slaves loading all the provisions that Major the Lady Jane Seaborn and Ensign Teddy Hamilton had procured to establish the brigade-sized dummy tank diversion on the right flank—the Great Sand Sea side—of Rommel's counterattack.

"Go hard," Col. Randal said to Capt. Corrigan. "Run down the edge of the Sand Sea but stay on the good going. If a truck breaks down, leave it. I want you there in two days or less."

"Colonel," Capt. Corrigan said, "rest easy, sir. These Sudanese drivers of Major Merritt's are the most experienced long-haul men in the business. I have already instructed them we shall be running 'round the clock until we arrive."

"Outstanding," Col. Randal said. "I'll see you when you get there. Oh, by the way . . ."

He reached inside his pocket and produced a pair of British Crown rank insignia. "Pin these on, Taylor—long overdue, Major."

"Thank you, sir," the Horse Guards officer said. Raiding Forces did not stand on formality. Promotions came straight from Col. Randal without fanfare and at a time and place of his choosing, which made the event personal between the two of them. Major Taylor Corrigan, for one, liked it that way.

"Pull out the minute you're loaded."

"Yes, sir."

Lieutenant Mandy Paige drove up in a jeep. Col. Randal climbed in the passenger seat. She proceeded to a remote section of the auxiliary RAF strip that was serving as the departure airfield, where the three Hudsons were being loaded. A ring of shotgun-toting Military Police were cordoning off the aircraft.

Two of the three planes would be airdropping the Arab tents, inflatable dummy tanks, compressed air tanks, smoke pots, etc. Every machine gun Raiding Forces possessed was being rigged for the drop—the idea was to make Rommel believe a British armored brigade was lying in wait.

And that meant the Luftwaffe and/or the Regia Aeronautica would be paying a visit—in force. Raiding Forces was planning to fight back with everything they had when the enemy air arrived.

The Hudson, piloted by Lieutenant Pamala Plum-Martin, would be dropping the jumpers. She was in the cockpit, going through her preflight inspection. Wing Commander Ronald Gordon and Earthquake McGoon were doing the same in their airplanes.

A team of RAF loadmasters was working under the supervision of Lieutenant Karen Montgomery, the Raiding Forces Chief Parachute Rigger, to get all the bundles rigged. The Hudsons would be dropping wing bundles and door bundles—meaning the materials would be on pallets and shoved out the door by "door kickers" with their parachute's static lines hooked up to the steel cable running the length of the fuselage. Raiders not going on the mission would be serving as the kickers.

Armed with a clipboard and checklist, Ens. Hamilton was inventorying the loads as he moved from plane to plane.

Ex-Lieutenant Billy Jack Jaxx was supervising preparation of the jump aircraft. He was busy inspecting the cables, taping the edges of the exit door, etc. Col. Randal would be the jumpmaster with Jack Cool as his assistant.

Lt. Mandy said, "Y Patrol of the LRDG is operating approximately fifty miles south of your RED INDIAN target, John. The patrol leader has been signaled to divert and set up a drop zone. When you jump, the patrol will be laagered a mile east of the objective. At 0230 hours, they will mark the DZ with a lighted letter Y."

Col. Randal said, "Good job, Mandy."

The main party would be dropping blind without the aid of a Pathfinder Team or ground reception party. Not that it mattered. For Ens. Hamilton's purposes, one patch of the desert was as good as another.

The fact that, with the exception of the small RED INDIAN party, this was not an actual combat operation did nothing to lessen the sense of urgency of the people working at the airstrip. Raiding Forces was a precision military team by this stage—highly trained, combat experienced, used to conducting missions that came up unexpectedly with a short time fuse. Everyone pitched in—everyone did their part.

Raiders were turning up at RFHQ, forgoing part of their leave to come help with mission prep. They all volunteered to go on the operation—even some who were recovering from wounds. A couple of men had gone absent without leave from the hospital.

Captain "Geronimo" Joe McKoy and Waldo Treywick were at the airfield, critically observing every phase of the preparations. The two did not hesitate to lend a hand when it came time to muscle a bundle aboard an aircraft. Teamwork was thick on the ground.

When Lt. Mandy rolled up with Col. Randal aboard, Capt. McKoy strolled over to the jeep. "John, me and Waldo want to jump in with your team—that OK by you?"

"Fine," Col. Randal said, accepting one of Waldo's thin cigars when the ex-ivory poacher walked up. "The target is a remote railway station. The mission is classified. You're not authorized to make entry into the building—is that understood?"

"I don't think I want to be anywhere near that train depot," Capt. McKoy said. "Not with Jack Cool and Pyro Percy rigging enough Composition B to blow the Hoover Dam to kingdom come."

"Me and Joe want to see the show," Waldo said, "from a nice safe distance—say about a mile."

"Good plan, Mr. Treywick," Col. Randal said. "I'll probably be right there with you."

Lt. Mandy drove over to the aircraft where Ens. Hamilton was at work. "The Great Teddy" was leaving nothing to chance. He personally inspected each item loaded and checked it off his list.

"You have enough magic gear," Col. Randal asked, "to pull this off?"

"No, sir," Ens. Hamilton said. "We barely have what it takes to get started. Have to improvise until the ground convoy arrives."

"Major Corrigan said he can be there in two days," Col. Randal said. "You keep the charade going until then, Ensign."

"Yes, sir," The Great Teddy said, secretly thrilled that Col. Randal addressed him as Ensign—not that he would ever let anyone know.

For his part, Col. Randal noted that his tough, battle-hardened Raiders were treating the new, *very* junior officer as part of the unit. While the men would not be wanting to follow him in bayonet charges anytime soon, it was a given that Ensign Hamilton knew what he was doing when it came to the military art of camouflage and deception.

Raiding Forces respected talent.

Besides, The Great Teddy was already a living legend—inventor of the wildly popular camel chip and horse apple contact mines.

James "Baldie" Taylor drove up at the wheel of a jeep. Without getting out, he asked, "Everything going according to schedule?"

"What schedule?" Col. Randal said.

"The one you are making up as you go," Jim said.

"Yes, sir."

"Lady Seaborn informed me you were reading Rommel's book," Jim said. "Learn anything?"

"He likes to penetrate the opposition's Main Line of Resistance," Col. Randal said. "Pour through, drive deep to cause maximum disruption, then divert predesignated troops to swing around and roll up both flanks—has a high opinion of his own leadership ability."

Capt. McKoy wandered over in time to hear Col. Randal's answer.

"His current intentions certainly appear to fit the pattern," Jim said. "The Desert Fox definitely has our forces back on their heels and our high command rattled."

"What's your take, Captain?" Col. Randal asked, curling his finger around Waldo's thin cigar. "You checked the book out and gave it to me."

"Rommel ain't psychologically geared to fightin' goin' backwards," Capt. McKoy said. "He's an attack man—this excitement ain't nothin' more than a temper tantrum that ain't goin' nowhere, John."

"What leads you to that conclusion?" Jim asked. "If true, you would be the only person in Middle East Command to believe that."

"Probably the Field Marshal didn't like havin' to pull back to reconsolidate after CRUSADER—he lost a lot a' men and tanks with nothin' to show for it," Capt. McKoy said. "Made him look bad—to hisself.

"Right now he's just like a rattlesnake rattlin' his tail after he ain't got no juice left to bite with."

"Interesting take on the subject, Captain," Jim said. His prewar military intelligence specialty for MI-6 was evaluating enemy and friendly forces.

He did not quite have Rommel figured out at this point—the Desert Fox was an enigma. Jim intended to read his *Infantry Attacks.*

"I understand you have your RED INDIAN target selected, Colonel."

"We do," Col. Randal said.

"Pencil me in on the manifest to jump with your team," Jim said.

"General," Col. Randal said, "you're not authorized to go on this one..."

"Who told you that?"

"You did, sir."

"Forget what I said, Colonel—bring Rommel's book along. I can spend my time reading it while we sit around waiting for enemy air to show up to bomb The Great Teddy's magic circus into the stone ages."

As she was driving Col. Randal back to RFHQ, Lt. Mandy said, "I thought this was supposed to be nothing more than a camping trip in the desert, John. Set up a few of Teddy's inflatables—create one of his illusions."

"It is," Col. Randal said. "You don't think we'll be anywhere near those Arab tents or dummy tanks when the enemy air arrives?"

"John, do try to stay out of trouble," Lt. Mandy said. "You have a history of reckless behavior."

Lieutenant Butch "Headhunter" Hoolihan was standing outside of RFHQ when Col. Randal returned from the departure airfield.

"I was hoping to find replacements for the two jeeps we lost, sir," Lt. Hoolihan said when Lt. Mandy pulled up. "None to be had."

"Right after we take off you can have this one, Butch," Col. Randal said. "Sergeant Rawlings will be here any time. He should be able to fix you up with one more runner. Billy Jack says the Desert Patrol jeeps are on their last legs."

"I will take what I can," Lt. Hoolihan said. "Not any immediate rush, sir. Warthog put the *King Duck* in dry dock for maintenance and repairs. Duck Patrol will not be going on operations anytime soon."

"Now that you've had time to think about it, Butch," Col. Randal said, "what's your thought on the Little Elephant's performance?"

"Frank loves the cannon, sir," Lt. Hoolihan said. "Being able to drive straight out to sea in the DUKW was a life-saver. Made extracting back to the *King Duck* easy . . . but under normal circumstances we would have had to abandon our gun jeeps—no problem last night since they had both already been blown up."

"You're right about that," Col. Randal said.

"Personally, I think the jury is still out, Colonel," Lt. Hoolihan said. "The COW 37mm is approximately two-thirds lighter, it can be mounted on a jeep—which makes it more nimble, and at the point-blank range we engage from, it does almost as much damage."

"Keep experimenting—you'll work out the tactics," Col. Randal said.

"Right now, Butch, what I want is you on leave starting immediately—take a break. Notify the Operations Room where you'll be staying. Check in by phone once a day."

"Thanks, Colonel," Lt. Hoolihan said. "My lads can use time off."

"Don't worry about your jeeps," Col. Randal said. "Word is we're getting all new ones."

"Outstanding, sir," Lt. Hoolihan said.

"Mandy," Col. Randal said, "drive back to the airstrip. If we don't intervene, Pam will spend all day going over the Hudson. Bring her back here—eight hours of sleep before flying tonight.

"If she gives you any trouble, tell her I said, 'That's an order.'"

"Want me to post a guard in front of Pam's bedroom door?" Lt. Mandy said. "Lock her in her room like you threatened at Habbaniya?"

"Do what you have to do."

EVERYONE AT RFHQ GATHERED OUTSIDE to watch the convoy from Oasis X straggle into the compound. Ex-Sergeant Hank W. Rawlston was in the lead jeep chewing on the stub of a nasty cigar and looking thoroughly disgusted. Desert Patrol was a sad sight.

Vehicles towing vehicles were being towed themselves. Constant operations in harsh desert conditions without the downtime required to maintain the lightweight jeeps had proven too much for them. Jeeps can go almost anywhere, and they packed as much firepower as the average RAF fighter, but they needed time in the shop between missions. Desert Patrol gun jeeps had been bombed and strafed, had run over thermos mines and crashed driving cross-country at night—without being able to stand down for repairs for the duration of CRUSADER.

Desert Patrol had been badly misused—expected to raid long past the time it was intended to operate in the field. And, it had performed a mission it was not suited for—one that could have been better carried out by conventional armored car patrols.

OPERATION CRUSADER may have gone down in the books as a victory, but that was debatable. True, Rommel had failed to capture Tobruk, which was the basis for the claim. After a long, extended attempt, he had pulled back to his start point for no gain at the end of a very confused battle. The Desert Fox had outrun his ability to resupply the fuel he needed to keep attacking. Afrika Korps had lost virtually all of its tanks.

But then, so had Eighth Army.

Colonel John Randal did not look on the battle as a win. Desert Patrol was going to have to stand down to be completely reorganized. It needed new vehicles and new troops to replace the men who had been killed, sidelined with wounds or transferred back to their original units. Many of the latter group had chosen to leave, suffering burnout from operating behind enemy lines for extended periods of time.

Col. Randal could get more jeeps. Raiding Forces was never going to be able to replace the men lost with equally qualified desert operators—and he knew it.

"Sergeant Rawlston," Col. Randal said, "tell your people I want them working hard days and partying just as hard nights for the next two weeks. Let 'em off early to get into Cairo.

"Patch up as many of the jeeps as you can. Keep the rest for parts. Write off the entire inventory—total loss."

"Can do—that's a plan, Colonel."

"Start desert-izing the new jeeps as soon as they begin arriving—we need to get Desert Patrol back on operations as soon as possible."

"Yes, sir."

"How long's it going to take?"

"Colonel, to get the job done in any reasonable time—say three weeks—we're going to need outside help. My boys originally got Desert Patrol's gun jeeps configured in small batches as we got 'em in when you expanded the number of patrols," ex-Sergeant Rawlston said.

"This project's a little too much for my crew to handle all at once without support."

"OK," Col. Randal said. "Let me see what I can do, Sergeant."

"I'll tell the boys what you said, Colonel," ex-Sgt. Rawlston said, "about the partying."

"You do that," Col. Randal said. "Ice cold beer is waiting for your troops in the motor pool—I'll drop by and have one later."

AT 1600 HOURS COLONEL JOHN RANDAL issued two Operations Orders. The first was held in the RFHQ Operations Room for everyone going on the mission—Raiders, door kickers, pilots, aircrew, Major Clive Adair, Major the Lady Jane Seaborn and her Marines chosen to man the Operations Room, Captain "Pyro" Percy Stirling, ex-Lieutenant Billy Jack Jaxx, Lieutenant Mandy Paige, Jim, Captain "Geronimo" Joe McKoy, Ensign Teddy Hamilton, Waldo and Major Jeb Pelham-Davies, DSO, MC.

The second order was going to be held immediately upon conclusion of the first in the third-floor suite for the RED INDIAN Team.

"Situation," Col. Randal said to the crowd in the Operations Room.

"Afrika Korps has attacked east of the Gazala Line and reoccupied Benghazi. British Forces have been caught off guard and are falling back. Field Marshal Auchinleck is preparing a massive counterattack with an infusion of Grant tanks that have recently arrived from the U.S." (This was an intentional falsehood in the event anyone going on the mission was captured and interrogated—there were no Grant tanks.)

"Mission: Raiding Forces has been tasked with setting up a deception on the edge of the Great Sand Sea south of the Afrika Korps' right flank.

"Execution: A twenty-man team of Raiding Forces under the command of Major Jeb Pelham-Davies—promoted today, so congratulations are in order—will drop tonight at zero-two-thirty hours. The plan is to organize a diversion consisting of inflatable tanks and Arab tents with fake tank tracks leading up to them. The idea is to deceive enemy pilots into believing that a brigade of British tanks has magically sprouted up to threaten the Afrika Korps' right.

"Major Pelham-Davies will be advised by Ensign Teddy Hamilton of Habbaniya fame—you'll note the Ensign is wearing the Order of the British Empire on his blouse for his work during the siege. I can testify 'The Great Teddy' is a master at the art of military deception. He is also a world-class liar, having falsified his age on his admission forms to Eton and Sandhurst by not one but two years, because you have to be over eighteen to get into bars—who the hell knows his real age? Don't ask."

There was stunned silence as the crowd digested that unexpected piece of intelligence information, then everyone in the room (with the exception of Lady Jane) was on their feet laughing and cheering. Ensign Hamilton had the right stuff.

When everyone had regained their seats, Col. Randal said, "In addition, Major Adair will be responsible for setting up a radio deception to go with the phony tanks. His Phantom operators will simulate radio traffic that would normally be expected from a British armored brigade.

"Major Corrigan, also promoted this day, will travel overland to arrive at the objective on day two with a convoy of forty trucks containing more deception material.

"Simultaneously," Col. Randal said, "another operation will be taking place approximately two hundred miles east of the drop zone. That mission is classified. The troops involved will be linking up with the main party on the second day, transported by Y-Patrol of the Long Range Desert Group.

"Concept of the Operation: A twenty-man advance party of Raiding Forces will drop tonight to set up a phantom armored brigade. Ensign Hamilton will supervise the construction with the materials that will be air-dropped with the advance party—if Ted says *frog*, you jump.

"Major Adair will initiate the radio deception.

"Major Corrigan, traveling overland with a forty-truck convoy containing more deception materials, will be reaching the main party sometime on day two.

"Raiding Forces will maintain the deception until such time as ordered by GHQ to stand down.

"This concludes my briefing," Col. Randal said. "What are your questions?"

This mission was so crazy no one even knew what to ask—there were no questions.

Following the order in the Operations Room, a second "frag" order (a fragment of a full OP Order) was issued in the small map area of Col. Randal's suite for the team going on the RED INDIAN mission. Present were Jim Taylor, Capt. Stirling, Capt. McKoy, ex-Lt. Jaxx, Lieutenant Pamala Plum-Martin, Lovat Scouts Munro Ferguson and Lionel Fenwick, the two Ranger Patrol Phantom operators McQueen and Masterson (who had been schooled in specific RED INDIAN material to search for), Lt. Mandy and Waldo.

Lady Jane sat in because, well, she wanted to.

What had originally been planned as a small raiding party had ballooned to ten men due to all the strap hangers who wanted to tag along.

"Mission: We have been assigned a *RED INDIAN* target," Col. Randal said. (No one present in the room, including Jim and Col. Randal, knew all the details of a RED INDIAN—that was classified Ultra Secret—a security classification so high that Jim was the only person in the room even cleared to hear the code word.)

"Execution: The RED INDIAN Team will drop tonight on a DZ set up by Y-Patrol of the LRDG at grid coordinates AZ783296. The party will be broken down into three elements. Assault Team: Myself, Lieutenant Jaxx, King and Phantom operators—McQueen and Masterson.

"Demolitions Team: Captain Stirling and Lovat Scouts Fenwick and Ferguson.

"Support Team: General Taylor, Captain McKoy and Mr. Treywick.

"Concept of the Operation: The RED INDIAN Team will drop, and travel on foot to the objective, which will be approximately one mile distance.

"The Assault Team will take down a small rail depot expected to be manned by no more than eight Italian railroad men. Once the objective is secured, McQueen and Masterson will conduct a search of the premises while Lieutenant Jaxx, King and I place demolitions inside the building.

"Demolitions Team: Captain Stirling—with Fenwick and Ferguson providing security—will place a small charge on the railroad track with the idea to cut it so that the train scheduled to arrive at zero-five-thirty hours will derail and crash into the depot. The resulting crash and command detonated explosion inside the depot is intended to erase any sign of our presence.

"The Support Team will stand by, ready to go to the assistance of either the Assault Team or the Demolitions Team in the event it should become necessary.

"Following successful completion of the mission—to include observing the target to confirm the train derailment—the RED INDIAN Team will withdraw to the objective rally point where Y-Patrol will be laagered. Upon arriving, we will be transported to the location where Ensign Hamilton is conducting his deception.

"This mission never happened," Col. Randal said. "We were never there.

"Questions?"

SQUADRON LEADER PADDY WILCOX, DSO, OBE, MC, DFC, arrived at RFHQ shortly after the briefings wearing his trademark black eye patch over one perfectly good eye. The pilot had been away flying for SOE. He threw the mother of all temper tantrums after Wing Commander Ronald Gordon and Lieutenant Pamala Plum-Martin briefed him on the air plan.

It called for the Vargas Girl-looking Royal Marine pilot to fly to the first drop zone (DZ) in formation with the other two Hudsons, then continue on to the Y-Patrol DZ alone to drop the RED INDIAN Team. Which meant she would have to make part of the trip out and the entire long return flight home alone.

Raiding Forces Standard Operating Procedure (SOP) for Air Operations, which S/Ldr. Wilcox had laid down, called for aircraft to always fly in pairs on over-desert flights. The only reason Lt. Plum-Martin had agreed to violate SOP, being MI-6, is she knew how extremely high-priority RED INDIAN missions were.

S/Ldr. Wilcox was MI-6 himself. He was not about to allow Lt. Plum Martin to fly solo. Period.

Finally, after getting an earful from S/Ldr. Wilcox, whom he outranked, W/Cdr. Gordon got on the blower to his boss. Within the hour, the Air Vice Marshal commanding the Desert Air Force's personal Hudson arrived at the auxiliary airstrip Raiding Forces was using. It would become the fourth ship in the flight, which would allow the planes to fly in pairs after the initial drop.

After more wrangling, S/Ldr. Wilcox reluctantly consented to allow the Air Vice Marshal's personal pilot to fly the mission as his co-pilot, but insisted on bringing his own navigator.

Now, with the moving parts in place, all that remained was for the mission to get underway.

As the sun went down, Colonel John Randal was lying on his parachute next to Lt. Plum-Martin's Hudson with the RED INDIAN Team thinking, *The waiting is always the hardest part.*

CHAPTER TEN

TRAINS RUN ON TIME

THE RED LIGHT CAME ON IN THE HUDSON. The Red Indian team stirred. They were stiff. The Raiders had been doing a lot of flying.

Colonel John Randal said, "Ten minutes."

Everyone on board knew what the red light indicated; however, protocol called for the jumpmaster to give the command. So he did.

For the one hundredth time tonight, Col. Randal touch-checked every piece of his gear. Everything was right where it was the previous ninety-nine times he checked. Then he stood up and made his way forward to the cockpit.

Lieutenant Pamala Plum-Martin was in the pilot's seat with her ex-LRDG navigator sitting in the co-pilot's chair. "Hi, John—we should be coming in sight of the DZ any moment now. Have a nice flight?"

"Slept the whole way."

"There it is," Lt. Plum-Martin said.

Ahead in the night a tiny pinpoint glowed faintly. Lt. Plum-Martin had extraordinary eyesight—Col. Randal knew because *he* had extraordinary eyesight.

"Nice job, Corporal," Col. Randal said to the navigator. He knew how difficult desert navigation was, especially at night.

"Coming on six minutes," Lt. Plum-Martin said. "Good luck, John—see you soon, love."

"Make sure you get this crate home, Pam."

Col. Randal made his way back to the tail, and with ex-Lieutenant Billy Jack Jaxx helping him, opened the door. Reaching up and gripping the inside edges with his white boots (Raiding Forces never polished their field boots—all the time in the desert had sandblasted them almost snow white) on either side of the door, he arched out and looked ahead.

The force of the wind tore at his face, distorting it and blurring his vision. Col. Randal always liked the feel—hanging outside of an aircraft thundering toward a point up ahead where he and a team of heavily-armed men were going to jump out with bad intent. Only, he was always a little anxious about heights—that last was classified.

Looking back, he could see the other Hudson tucked in tight formation, flying in trail. Except for the crew, it was empty, having dropped its bundles at the first DZ. It would have been nice to split the RED INDIAN Team into two sticks and jumped both aircraft. The lead plane would not have been so crowded, and it would have put everyone on the ground quicker in a tighter pattern. However, since it was the Air Vice Marshal's personal plane, no one had considered the possibility of dropping paratroopers from it. There were no static line cables in place when it arrived at the departure airfield and no time to rig them.

Col. Randal swung back inside, glanced at the lime green hands on the Rolex Lady Jane had given him and issued the command everyone had been anticipating for the entire trip. "SIX MINUTES!"

The men struggled to their feet. As they were getting up, the ex-LRDG navigator made his way to the far end of the tail. He would retrieve the static lines after the jump and close the door of the aircraft.

"HOOK UP!"

The sound of metal on metal filled the cabin as snap links were clamped on the cable, pulled down tight shut, safety pins inserted and the static line rattled back and forth to make sure everything was firmly set and the snap link was running freely on the cable.

Tension was always high at this point, but the RED INDIAN team was made up of seasoned professionals, so tonight—not as much.

"CHECK YOUR EQUIPMENT!"

Every jumper ran his hands over all his equipment, then traced the yellow static line of the man in front of him to make sure it ran out of the parachute pack and over his shoulder without any kinks or snags. Col. Randal turned around so ex-Lt. Jaxx, who would be following him out the door, could check his.

"OK, sir."

Col. Randal turned to the door and arched himself outside once again. A burning Y was clearly visible off the right toe of his raiding boot. No other light was visible as far as the eye could see in any direction. A quick glance back at the trailing plane, then he swung back inside. He checked his watch.

"ONE MINUTE!"

"SOUND OFF FOR EQUIPMENT CHECK!"

Starting from the back of the stick, "OK, OK, OK. . . . ."

Col. Randal reached out and braced his left arm across the door. These men had lightning fast reflexes. He was not taking any chances on anyone going before he gave the command.

"CLOSE ON THE DOOR!"

Silently counting in his head, Col. Randal reached the magic number just as the green light flashed on. He slapped his hands on the outside of the door, knees bent in a crouch, looked over his shoulder and shouted, "GO!"

Then with a mighty leap, he exited the aircraft—feet and knees together, head down, chin on his chest—and in an instant he was being tossed around by the prop blast. Col. Randal had his eyes open. Everything seemed to be going in slow motion. From his peripheral vision he could see ex-Lt. Jaxx coming out the door in a perfect body position; at the same time he was watching the fuselage of the Hudson slide past like a giant shark.

There was the rustling of silk then the X-chute was open and he was floating almost in a dream state. Down below he could see the burning Y. He was drifting straight toward it.

The night was very quiet.

No need to pull a slip. There was very little breeze. Coming in almost straight down, slightly to the right, Col. Randal got his feet and knees together again and pulled his elbows in with forearms closed tight in front of his face. Glancing down, he saw the ground blur. His toes touched down, he prepared for a right front Parachute Landing Fall (PLF) and then he was rolling—hitting his five points of contact.

The ground was soft and Col. Randal barely felt the fall. He was on his feet immediately, feeling the rush of adrenalin that is always the hallmark of a successful jump from an aircraft in flight.

An LRDG patrolman arrived and was collapsing his canopy before Col. Randal could hammer the quick release on his chest with his fist.

Ex-Lt. Jaxx came in silent as a butterfly, followed by King, Jim and the rest of the RED INDIAN team.

LRDG men came up lugging the wing bundles that Lt. Plum-Martin had dropped. The bundles contained the explosives for the train station. All of them had been retrieved—which is always a concern when air dropping vital equipment needed for a clandestine mission. It can be a bad thing if you are unable to find the bundles or locate only some of them.

So far, so good.

The idea of jumping out of an airplane in the dark of night with a team of handpicked men to carry out a small-scale pin-prick raid against an unsuspecting target seems easy enough to the uninitiated. It's not.

What could possibly go wrong? Almost everything.

Col. Randal coordinated with Captain Teasdale Brown-Brown in command of Y-Patrol. The Y stood for Yeomanry Patrol, meaning the officers and men had been recruited from county cavalry regiments like the Lancelot Lancers.

Within the LRDG, Y-Patrol tended to be looked upon as a bunch of aristocratic snobs. That did not bother them in the least. The Yeomanry *were* a clannish patrol, even though they came from different regiments.

"When I fire a single green flare," Col. Randal said, "send up the truck with the explosives on board."

"Sir!"

"In the event I fire two green flares, bring up all your 30-cwt Chevrolets immediately, ready to engage with your organic machine guns," Col. Randal said.

"Don't worry—the likelihood of that happening is virtually nonexistent—but stand ready in any case."

"You can count on us, Colonel," Capt. Brown-Brown said. "The lads have been on deep desert reconnaissance operations for the last ninety days. Not a shot fired in anger. I, for one, would welcome the opportunity of a beat up on your target if the opportunity presents itself."

"We're going to hope it doesn't," Col. Randal said.

Ex-Lt. Jaxx reported, being careful not to use the mission identifier RED INDIAN, which was classified. "Team assembled and prepared to move out, sir."

"Let's do this," Col. Randal ordered. "King, lead out."

RED INDIAN TEAM PATROLLED TO THE OBJECTIVE. The night was still but chilly. It was quiet. The moon was down, but the sky was salted with a million stars.

Night time in the desert is the best time.

The order of march was Assault Team, Demolitions Team, then Support Team. Colonel John Randal followed King, with ex-Lieutenant Billy Jack Jaxx right behind him. The patrol moved as silently as a pride of panthers—which they were.

King halted. Col. Randal moved up next to him. The Merc pointed. It was barely possible to make out the silhouette of the train station. The building was blacked out. The time was 0450 hours.

The train was supposed to arrive at 0530 hours.

Captain "Geronimo" Joe McKoy moved forward, picking up Captain "Pyro" Percy Stirling as he came.

Speaking in a soft voice just above a whisper, Col. Randal said, "This is the Objective Rally Point. Capt. McKoy, set up your Security Team here."

"Roger, John—we'll come get you if you need us."

"Capt. Stirling," Col. Randal said, "take your Demo Team and move out."

"Traveling now, sir."

There was a soft rustling as the patrol split into sections and began the choreographed series of movements that would put everyone in the right place at the right time—which was running short. RED INDIAN Team was going to have to work fast. It had a schedule to keep.

The Assault Team was broken down into two sections. Attack element: Col. Randal, ex-Lt. Jaxx and King. Search element: Phantom operators McQueen and Masterson. There was no timetable for the assault to begin. It would commence the instant they were in place.

Col. Randal was clicked on and had been from the moment the Assault Team had moved out from the LRDG perimeter. He was very aware. Sounds seemed distorted. Movement felt like it was taking place in slow motion—floating.

As usual, Col. Randal had the sensation he was looking down on the patrol—observing it from above rather than leading it—he had never told anyone about this sensation.

Tonight he was armed, as usual, with his 9mm MAB-38A submachine gun and had his 45mm Brixia shoulder-fired mortar slung over his shoulder. There were three fat 45mm rounds tucked in a canvas bandoleer laced to the stock of the weapon. Lieutenant Karen Montgomery, the Chief Rigger, had made it for him.

If three rounds did not get the job done tonight, they were in a lot of trouble.

The plan of attack was as simple as it gets, which complied with Raiding Forces' Rules to "Keep It Short and Simple." Col. Randal, King and ex-Lt. Jaxx would make the initial entry. The trio would shoot everyone inside the building. Then the two Phantom operators would come in and everyone would break out flashlights to search for the RED INDIAN materials. Code books, keys, and any other written documents. But *not* any signals devices—they were to be left behind.

No one on the team understood the prohibition against confiscating physical equipment, but orders were orders. There had to be some reason. No one told them what it was.

The hope was that the front door would be left open to let air in while the railroad men slept. The Raiders padded silently up to the building, coming in from the rear, then flowing around to the front, but discovered the door was shut.

To compound the problem, the door was thick wood—not going to be able to kick it down. Not with people inside who would wake up and shoot back. When King turned the knob, it was locked.

Raiding Forces' Rules stipulated, "It's Good to Have a Plan B." And that is a military fact. This contingency had been planned for.

Silently, the Attack element split into three smaller sections. King and one Phantom operator slipped back around the side on the far end of the building while ex-Lt. Jaxx and the other Phantom operator took up position on the near end of the building—with strict orders not to peek around the corner until Col. Randal gave the OK.

Col. Randal dropped back approximately fifteen yards. He swapped the submachine gun for the shoulder-fired mortar and plopped a fat 45mm round into the chamber. The stubby weapon came to his shoulder easily. He fired immediately.

KABOOOM!

The detonation sounded unnaturally loud in the still desert air—the door disintegrated.

As quickly as Col. Randal could reload, he put a second round through the opening. The instant it exploded, he shouted, "Jack and King, move out!"

Ex-Lt. Jaxx and King charged back around to the front of the depot and made entry, firing their Beretta 9mm submachine guns as they came through the door. Col. Randal moved forward, entered the building with a Colt .38 Super in one hand and a flashlight in the other. A quick glance confirmed all six of the Italians inside appeared to be dead—one was faking it.

Holding his pistol down by his side without aiming, Col. Randal shot the man twice as he stepped over him. He called out the door, "Search party."

The two Phantom operators came in, flashlights blazing, and the search began. As the men worked, Col. Randal walked outside and fired a single green flare back in the direction of Y-Patrol.

Within a matter of seconds, a Chevrolet truck appeared out of the dark and the explosives in the bed were carried inside. It took several trips. Capt. Stirling arrived with Lovat Scouts Fenwick and Ferguson, having placed all his demolitions on the track. The rails made a slight curve with an almost imperceptible downhill slope to the depot—the perfect set-up.

Capt. Stirling affixed the detonator to the explosives in the station and ran the electrical cable out the front door. Then he walked the spool back to where the Support Team was waiting in the Objective Rally Point and hooked it up to the ten-cap blasting machine.

Everything was going like clockwork—a textbook surgical strike.

TOOOOOT! TOOOOOT!

Everyone in the building froze—the train—*and* it was twenty-minutes early. So much for Mussolini making the railroads run on time.

CRAAAACK!

The pressure cap on Capt. Stirling's charge detonated as the leading wheel of the engine ran over the blasting cap, cutting the track and derailing the train as planned. The placing of the demolitions was textbook perfect.

Metal began screaming.

"Run for it!" Col. Randal shouted.

There was a mad rush for the door as everyone tried to get out at the same time. The metal was screeching louder, sounding like something out of a Saturday matinee horror movie, only worse—a pack of tyrannosaurus-rex-sized screaming banshees coming to kill them.

The shrieking was terrifying.

"Haul ass!" ex-Lt. Jaxx shouted at the LRDG men in the truck as he ran by. The patrolmen bailed out of the Chevrolet and sprinted after the Raiders, although they could have just as easily driven, not having any idea why—questions not being on at the moment.

The screeching—shrieking—surreal screaming of tearing metal was painful to the ears. It kept getting louder and seemed alive—but mortally wounded. Like a giant, supernatural beast in its death throes.

Out of the dark the locomotive loomed, plowing through the sand, then tumbling into the depot—exactly as planned—just twenty minutes too soon. It nearly took out the Attack element and the LRDG men, who were fleeing for their lives around the far end of the station, running as hard as they could.

At the ORP, Capt. Stirling pushed down the plunger on the blasting machine when the engine hit the building, as ordered, detonating one hundred pounds of Composition B.

The resulting explosion blew the running Raiders and LRDG men completely off their feet. To a man, they thought they were dead. Waves of pain from being slammed into the ground confirmed they were not—*yet.* But the night was not over.

Behind them the sound of screeching, screaming metal intensified—getting louder and louder as the train continued to derail. The boxcars were crashing crazily into the inferno created by the Composition B. And now the men learned that this was an ammunition train, a fact previously unknown. The cars were loaded primarily with artillery and panzer shells for Afrika Korps with a few cars of small-arms ammunition.

The artillery rounds began cooking off when the railcars crashed, followed by a brilliant, spontaneous explosion. As the follow-on cars derailed, they continued to pile up. Then they blew up—one after the other.

The small-arms ammunition was crackling insanely as it cooked off.

Night turned to day in a spectacular pyrotechnics display. Shrapnel whined overhead, though some of the larger pieces made only a loud, tumbling, heart-stopping whisper—you could hear it coming, flying overhead, and going. Some pieces the size of pianos were thudding into the ground all around in the dark, which did nothing for anyone's morale.

The boxcars kept rolling into the cut metal, screeching as they derailed and exploded. Remarkably, none of the Raiders or LRDG patrolmen were injured, but they were all shaken. Everyone managed to make it to the ORP where Col. Randal found the Support Team and the Demolitions Team members to be almost as stunned by the turn of events as his Attack Team men were.

Even Capt. Stirling, who had seen his share of unexpected big-time fireworks up close and personal, seemed dazed.

Railcars continued to crash, catch fire and explode. Those that had already blown up were on fire. The rail line looked like a long burning snake—with secondary blasts rippling down its length.

At last, when everyone had recovered their wits, an inventory revealed not a single piece of RED INDIAN material had made it to the ORP. Every item collected had been left behind in the stampede to safety.

To add insult to injury, the 30-cwt Chevrolet was knocked out. It could be seen burning. Col. Randal, the Attack Team and dismounted

LRDG attachments had to trudge back to the Y-Patrol laager where they found everyone thoroughly enjoying the show.

Except to argue about who had been the most scared, Raiding Forces' personnel did not have much to say.

The RED INDIAN mission was a total bust.

For their part, the LRDG people, who did not know there *was* a RED INDIAN mission, were ecstatic. They had seen more action in ten minutes tonight than they had seen in the last ten months.

Several members of Y-Patrol were now considering volunteering for Raiding Forces.

WHEN Y-PATROL DROVE INTO Major Jeb Pelham-Davies' perimeter after dark the next day, Ensign Teddy Hamilton, *aka* "The Great Teddy," asked Colonel John Randal first thing: "How did the plan to wreck the train work out, sir?"

"Just swell."

CHAPTER ELEVEN

SHOT PLACEMENT

WHEN THE SUN CAME UP, Colonel John Randal could see all the work that had been done to create the illusion that a British armored brigade had arrived on the edge of the Great Sand Sea, threatening Afrika Korps' right flank. Arab tents dotted the landscape. There were tank tracks leading up to them, which represented hard labor on the stony ground. Many of the tents had what appeared to be the barrels of tanks' main guns peeking out. Other tanks were poorly camouflaged under netting. Most tents had cooking fires going—typical Tommies, brewing up.

All in all, it was about the worst camouflaged British armored brigade in the history of tank warfare. Col. Randal realized that was a good thing. If the idea is to fool enemy air reconnaissance, then you want the enemy pilots to see what it is they think you are hiding from them.

The location of Ensign Teddy Hamilton's deception appeared to have been chosen at random—one patch of desert seeming to be about as good as any other. In fact, the spot had been selected with great care. First off, it was on the very edge of the "good going," which was the scrub brush, hard ground—a strip approximately fifty miles wide and 1,500 miles long between the Mediterranean and the Sand Sea where all the fighting took place. Far enough out that Afrika Korps would likely never have any reason to venture near.

It was sited on a seldom-used desert track, which meant the camouflaged tanks could have arrived by wheeled tank carrier—a vital aspect of "The Great Teddy's" deception plan since it meant he only had to create fake tank tracks for a short distance leading up to the Arab tents. And the track could be used as a landing strip if it became necessary to evacuate anyone who became sick or wounded.

Also, the site was located within twenty miles of a small Italian fort. Later in the afternoon, a half hour before sunset, the two Hudsons were going to return and lay down an airborne carpet of parachutes weighted with blocks of ice in plain sight of the fort. Parachutists landing, it was hoped, would guarantee a hysterical response from the Italians to their higher headquarters.

Major Clive Adair had his Phantom operators open for business. They were set up a safe distance from the tents so as not to be caught in the crossfire when battle commenced. They were busy sending messages back and forth to each other. And their team located at RFHQ was simulating the radio traffic that would be expected from an armored brigade's higher HQ. The Germans had an excellent (bordering on phenomenal) radio intercept capability. It was a safe bet they would be monitoring the signals.

The Phantom operators were mimicking the sloppy communications procedures that haunted British operations.

Major Taylor Corrigan's twenty-man element was spread out in one-man positions hiding under camouflage netting throughout the position, but taking great care not to be too close to any of the Arab tents with the fake tank tracks leading up to them—which, it was hoped, would be bombed sooner or later. Each man had a Vickers K machine gun and five spare ammunition drums in addition to his individual weapon. Most of the men also had Bren guns captured during the invasion of Persia.

If and when the Regia Aeronautica or the Luftwaffe showed up, the plan was for the Raiders to fight back with everything they had.

Ens. Hamilton gave Col. Randal a tour. On the ground it did not appear the position could fool anyone. However, The Great Teddy's deception only had to fool enemy pilots.

No one, meaning Arab nomads or a reconnaissance patrol from the Italian fort (which was highly unlikely—the Italians were not known to venture outside the walls) was going to be allowed to approach within a mile.

Lovat Scouts armed with tripod-mounted, scoped Boys .55 caliber Anti-Tank rifles had set up a perimeter, screening the site to discourage visitors.

Captain "Pyro" Percy Stirling was busy setting out smoke pots and other pyrotechnic devices that he was wiring to a central control panel where Ens. Hamilton could orchestrate all manner of simulated explosions and fake anti-aircraft fire.

"Looks like you have a plan, Ensign," Col. Randal said. "Think it'll work?"

"Yes, sir," Ens. Hamilton said. "The illusion will only get better when Major Pelham-Davies arrives. We shall turn his trucks into tanks, set up the additional tents he will be bringing with him to make it look like the brigade is building up—might even deceive the Nazis into believing we have a division."

"If you get all our trucks shot up, Ted," Col. Randal said, "we won't have any way to get the hell out of Dodge in the event Afrika Korps decides to send a ground force to attack us."

"I shall place five trucks in deep concealment out of the line of fire, sir," Ens. Hamilton said, "in case we have to bug out."

Col. Randal said, "Good plan."

MAJOR TAYLOR CORRIGAN ARRIVED WITH HIS CONVOY, consisting of thirty civilian trucks of mixed brands and models. He also brought with him six of the SDF jeeps. The unloading of supplies began immediately.

While everyone worked on making improvements to the deception, Colonel John Randal crouched under a camouflage net with Major Jeb Pelham-Davies and Maj. Corrigan to conduct a commander's call.

"As you know," Col. Randal said, "Desert Patrol has to do a major reorganization. To that end, we're getting in fifty volunteers from the U.S. in a few days.

"Terry is recovering, but he won't be available for duty for a couple of months. When Zorro returns, he's informed me he doesn't want to resume command of Desert Patrol—his idea is to run the Lounge Lizards full-time.

"Major Black has been offered his own armored car regiment, so he will be leaving Raiding Forces.

"What I'm thinking is to have Captain McCloud assume command of the Wing when he gets back. Taylor, I'd like you to take over Sea Squadron, and Jeb, I want you at Desert Patrol—you two switch jobs."

"I like it, sir," Maj. Corrigan said.

"Likewise," Maj. Pelham-Davies said. "Taylor and I can benefit professionally from the change, sir. I've been wanting a chance to spend time in the field on extended gun jeep patrol."

"Sea duty sounds attractive to me, sir," Maj. Corrigan said, "provided I am not expected to spend much time on the bloody *King Duck*."

"ENEMY AIRCRAFT ELEVEN O'CLOCK," ex-Lieutenant Billy Jack Jaxx sang out from his position on a slight rise where he was standing air guard.

Col. Randal ran out from under the netting in time to see a bi-wing Italian Imam Ro.37 reconnaissance airplane make a slow circuit of the tent city. Then the Italian pilot rolled in for a closer look. Just because it was a reconnaissance airplane did not mean it lacked teeth—two forward-firing 7.7mm machine guns and four 100-pound bombs.

There was a mad dash all over the area for Raiders to take up their fighting positions. No one had expected the bad guys to show up this fast. They did not know that the speed of the Regia Aeronautica's response had been assisted, in no small part, by Colonel Dudley Clarke broadcasting their exact location in the certain knowledge the German Listening Service would pick it up.

The A-Force commander operated on the principle that the only reason to conduct a deception was to get the enemy to *do* something. And the best way to accomplish that was to tell him where and what it was you wanted him to do. No sense making the other side guess—they might get it wrong.

The little airplane seemed to single out ex-Lt. Jaxx as its target. It toggled a pair of bombs that fell wide and detonated, causing no damage, but they were LOUD! Then the pilot came in for the kill, firing his pair of 7.7mm machine guns.

While everyone watched in horror, the MG bullets stitched the desert floor, kicking up a double line of tufts straight toward ex-Lt. Jaxx, who was standing his ground. He muscled the big drum-fed Vickers K machine gun to his shoulder, took dead aim and blasted the airplane out of the sky. His first burst spider-webbed the windscreen, killing the pilot. Jack Cool.

The Ro.37 crashed headfirst into the ground, with its tail sticking up in the air like an upside down wine glass—right in the middle of their position.

Everything happened so fast that no one else even got off a round. Men all around the perimeter were cheering, pumping their weapons in the air and waving their hats.

They did not have long to celebrate. A pair of Macchi C-200s armed with twin 12.7mm (.50 caliber) machine guns and 100-pound bombs arrived within minutes. They streaked over, observed the funeral pyre of their reconnaissance element smoldering on the ground, and the fight was on.

Tracers crisscrossed the sky. More than eighty Vickers K machine guns or Bren automatic rifles manned by Raiding Forces and the SDF truck drivers, plus the Lewis guns dismounted from the LRDG trucks, were firing on the enemy air, and all were loaded with tracer ammunition every other round, interspaced with incendiary and armor piercing to make it look like three times the number of guns actually firing—normally tracers are loaded one round in six.

"Guns," the RNPS ace gunner who had volunteered for Desert Patrol because he had been on multiple ships sunk by U-boats and did not believe there would be "any submarines in the Great Sand Sea," had his twin 20mm Oerlikons mounted on a pedestal in the back of a Chevrolet truck—the only weapon to remain mounted on a vehicle. He hit one of the Macchis on its second pass. It flew off, trailing smoke.

Col. Randal immediately whipped out the compass he carried around his neck on a cord, tucked into the breast pocket of his bush jacket, and took an azimuth on the plane.

"King—two-seven-zero," he called out. "You and Jack take a jeep, go get the pilot."

Captain "Geronimo" Joe McKoy ran over, "I need a Bren gun, John. This Vickers K don't let me get on target fast enough—can't swing through my bird."

"Take mine, Captain," Col. Randal said. "Here he comes."

Col. Randal had abandoned his Vickers K in favor of his beautifully balanced Beretta MAB-38A submachine gun. He was not hoping for a shoot-down, but 9mm hits could cause enough damage for a plane to have to return to base—all he wanted.

The surviving Macchi made another pass, but by now everyone was getting into the rhythm of shooting at fast-moving attack aircraft, and the pilot flew into a maelstrom of automatic weapons fire. His plane flamed. He pulled straight up, trailing smoke, in an attempt to gain enough altitude so his parachute would deploy.

The pilot rolled the Macchi over on its back and was trying to bail out of the cockpit when the plane exploded.

Meanwhile, Ensign Teddy Hamilton was shouting orders to Raiders and SDF men who were standing by to set off smoke pots and other pyrotechnic devices on command when they were not firing at incoming enemy aircraft.

Some of the devices were command detonated. Those could be set off from a switchboard system Captain "Pyro" Percy Stirling had set up. The Great Teddy wanted to create the illusion that there was a huge British armored force in place. The plan was to have a lot of different things going on all at once. And that was definitely happening.

Then all was quiet. The sky was brilliant blue. It was hot.

Men were hurriedly reloading magazines. Everyone shifted position. Raiding Forces and the SDF were ready—well, almost. No one had anticipated a fight this intense.

The Ford truck where Guns had his twin 20mm Oerlikons mounted was moved to a new location. All the trucks from the convoy driven by the SDF drivers, now disguised as tanks, were shifted to new positions to include the five Ens. Hamilton had hidden with the jeeps. Y-Patrol decided it had business elsewhere and departed the area for parts unknown.

The LRDG had seen enough action for one day.

Waldo handed Col. Randal one of his thin cigars. He stuck it between his front teeth as he surveyed the frenzied activity taking place all around.

"Now, that's what I call a turkey shoot," Capt. McKoy said, cramming rounds into the Bren's magazine.

Waldo said, "Them turkeys was shootin' back, Joe."

"Here they come, boys," Capt. McKoy shouted, as he was in the process of slamming the freshly-topped off magazine into his Bren automatic rifle. Like the gunfighter he was, he kept his head up, scanning the horizon while reloading—never taking his eyes off the business of looking for who or what to shoot next.

Just off the deck, a second pair of Macchi fighters screamed in at zero altitude, blowing up giant swirling dust devils in their wake. The pilots engaged immediately.

Both Macchis were gunning for the Arab tents where they had reason to believe the tanks were concealed. That was fortunate. The 12.7mm MGs they carried were devastating in the ground attack mode and nobody wanted to get shot with one.

A terrific barrage of return fire greeted the intruders.

Col. Randal emptied his submachine gun at the pair as they thundered past.

The low-level run against highly trained, extremely motivated men armed to the teeth with Vickers K machine guns and Bren automatic rifles was not the wisest choice the Italian aviators could have made. Both planes took hits on the flyover.

Gun's twin 20mm Oerlikon was going *POCKA, POCKA, POCKA.* Tracers the size of flaming onions chased the two intruders as they egressed.

One Macchi banked away, trailing smoke—flying back in the direction from which it had come. The other—either because it had been hit or the pilot misjudged his altitude—bounced off the desert floor, tumbled, and exploded on the far side of the perimeter. It almost took out ex-Lt. Jaxx and King's jeep as they were returning with the captured Italian pilot the two had been chasing.

Maj. Corrigan shouted orders for everyone to spread out even farther. "Do not bunch up. They *will* be coming back."

Capt. Stirling rounded up a detail of four SDF men and went around putting out more smoke pots and small explosive devices.

One of the tents was on fire. They let it burn. With all the smoke, crashed aircraft, trucks disguised as tanks, and Arab tents scattered around the perimeter, it was beginning to take on the appearance of a genuine armored column under attack—even from up close on the ground.

The first round of the fight went to Raiding Forces and the SDF.

An hour went by before the next wave of enemy aircraft returned. This time the Luftwaffe decided to show the Regia Aeronautica how it was done. A flight of four JU-87 Stukas appeared overhead, high in the sky—so far up they looked like little black dots.

Col. Randal knew from experience gained during his Swamp Fox Force days in France that the price of poker was getting ready to go up. Stukas were pinpoint dive bombers. When attacking tanks—like the Germans thought they were doing today—they were armed with a pair of 1,000-kilogram tank-busting *panzerbombe cylindriseche.* He did the math. Nearly 18,000 pounds of bombs was coming straight at them—fast.

"Guns," Col. Randal shouted over to the RNPS ace gunner, "don't fire until all four planes are committed to their attack."

That was a wasted order. Guns was a veteran of more high-level Stuka dive-bombing runs at sea than he could remember. That's where he earned his nickname—shooting them down. The RNPS sailor-turned-Raiding Forces Commando had no intention of giving away his position until the Nazis were in a vertical position where they could not do anything about it.

The JU-87s dived down almost straight. The Stukas were terror weapons. Each one carried a dive siren, and they were screaming. If the Germans were hoping to scare the troops on the ground, it was working.

"Uh-oh!" ex-Lt. Jaxx said.

The captured Italian pilot looked up, saw the Stukas, and panicked. He jumped out of the jeep and crawled under it. His bad day had taken a turn for the worse.

"You think that's gonna' work, dumbass?" Waldo said to the Italian, never taking his eyes off the Stukas.

"We didn't have any a' those kinda buzzards in Abyssinia, Colonel."

"Lucky us," Col. Randal said.

When the flight was screaming down in line formation, one following the other, noses pointed straight at their target—the Arab tents—Col. Randal raised his Vickers K, having switched back to it the minute the JU-87s arrived, and loosed off a burst. The Vickers K had such a high cyclic rate that it was not possible to fire the school solution burst of six. One touch of the trigger and ten to twelve rounds were on the way in an instant.

That was the signal. Every man present opened immediately. A blizzard of tracers streaked skyward. Guns was working his Oerlikon. . . *POKKA, POKKA, POKKA . . .*

The German pilots paid not the least bit of attention to the intense wall of fire they had to fly through, though they had to be shocked by it. Down they came, dive sirens screaming louder the lower they flew. Little black dots turned into great big black dots that became really ugly airplanes.

The Nazi flying lead toggled his pair of bombs when he was low enough. It seemed possible to reach up and touch his aircraft. Then the pilot pulled up, barely avoiding crashing into the ground, which is a hazard all dive bombers face when pressing home their attacks—fixating on the target. When the Stuka pulled out of the dive, tracers converged on its exposed belly.

The JU-87 started trailing smoke, but the pilot managed to regain altitude and made a long, circling turn northwest, back toward his base.

The second Stuka pilot misjudged, got his nose over too far and flew into the ground, almost catching up with the leader's bombs. It slammed into one of the Arab tents. Over 8,500 pounds of bombs exploding almost simultaneously right in the middle of the perimeter knocked most of the Raiders off their feet.

The thunderclap of the detonation felt like a body slam. The sound was incredibly loud. It did not seem possible a noise could be that loud. For a moment, Col. Randal found it hard to breathe.

The other two Stukas dropped their bombs. They both hit tents, causing no real damage except to blow two of The Great Teddy's inflatables to smithereens. Still, another 8,500-plus pounds of aerial bombs landing inside the tent city was nothing to celebrate.

A fusillade of tracers fired by angry Raiders chased the last two Stukas as they completed their bombing run, pulled out of their dives, turned and headed for home.

Round two also went to Raiding Forces—but not decisively. The troops were not as jubilant as before. The Raiders were mentally digging in for a prolonged fight.

"Gettin' shot at don't make a man smart," Capt. McKoy said, "but it sure does make you introspective."

"You got that right, Joe," Waldo said.

"Affirmative," ex-Lt. Jaxx said.

"You reckon we got ole' Rommel fooled, John?" Capt. McKoy asked.

"I don't know."

AN HOUR BEFORE SUNSET, THE TWO HUDSONS flew over, making a low-level pass, rocking their wings as they went by. Squadron Leader Paddy Wilcox and Lieutenant Pamala Plum-Martin were flying lead with Wing Commander Ronnie Gordon, *aka* "Flash Bang" Gordon, piloting the trail plane in line astern.

The aircraft were en route to make the fake airborne drop within sight of the Italian fort twenty miles west of the tent city perimeter. Onboard the two planes were blocks of ice strapped to the unserviceable parachutes from RAF Habbaniya—worn out chutes would work fine for this mission.

Door kickers would put them out. The blocks of ice would be heavy enough to cause the canopies to deploy. The Italians would see parachutists descending. The blocks of ice would melt overnight and the next morning, if anyone from the fort went out to check, they would find only empty parachutes—provided desert nomads had not already stolen them.

The Vargas Girl-looking Royal Marine flying in the lead Hudson's left seat said, "Looks like a full-blown war zone, Paddy."

"That *was* the purpose of the exercise," Sqn. Ldr. Wilcox said. "Quite the deception, what!"

"Let's not mention," Lt. Plum-Martin said, "all those bomb craters, crashed airplanes and burning trucks to Lady Jane."

"Wilco."

THERE HAD NOT BEEN A THIRD ROUND. Raiding Forces and the SDF troopers made camp for the night. Incredibly, no one had been killed or wounded seriously, though everyone felt battered from the bomb blasts. After pulling weapons maintenance, there was not a lot to do when the evening meal was finished. So naturally, what happened was inevitable—around the command post campfire, the stories started. The first liar never had a chance.

Captain "Geronimo" Joe McKoy said, "There's always been a hot debate over which is the best stopper—.45 ACP or 9mm. Now the .45 makes a bigger hole and its proponents claim that's the deciding factor right there.

"On the other side, the 9mm men argue you can carry more rounds in your magazine because the bullet is smaller, gets deeper penetration with less recoil, which means that you can shoot more accurately—shot placement, they say, being the most important aspect of all when it comes to shootin' bad guys."

"Now, from my own personal experience," Capt. McKoy said, "having carried and used 'em both in close encounters—I can tell you that the story you can knock a man down with a .45 if you hit him in the little finger just ain't true boys—it's a myth.

"Shot placement is the thing that counts. The *size* of the bullet hole not being nearly as important as the *where* the bullet hole is.

"To prove my point, I knowed a man saved himself from a grizzly bear that was chasing him and his wife by firing one single well-placed round from his wife's puny little .25 pocket pistol she always carried in her purse—judicious shot placement."

"The couple was out hiking and got chased by a great big grizzly. The man shouted at his wife to chunk him her purse. He caught it in mid-stride, pulled out the .25, kneecapped his wife with one shot—and made it out of there alive.

"You see, boys," Capt. McKoy said, "when you're gettin' chased by a grizzly, it ain't necessary to outrun the bear—you just have to outrun your huntin' buddy."

After the laughter died down, ex-Lieutenant Billy Jack Jaxx said, "Mr. Treywick, I've always wanted to hear the story about how Miss UCLA factored into a battle plan you and the Colonel concocted when you were behind the lines in Abyssinia."

"So have I," King said.

"Well," Waldo said, "on the first day when the colonel jumped in, only he was a major then, a brigadier a little after that—the only radio he had got smashed into a million pieces when its parachute malfunctioned. We had to raise us an army, with no communications to the outside world to send us guns and money. So, we had to do it from scratch on pure guts and know-how.

"To befriend those miserable shifta trash who populated the countryside, we had to, as the colonel said, 'win their hearts and minds,' which is hard to do with indigenous lowlifes that ain't got one and the other is the size of a pea," Waldo said.

"So, there was me, Butch Hoolihan, Rita and Lana, a handful of untrained recruits, their wives, slaves, servants and some camp followers—that was our rag-tag army to start with. So the colonel decided what we'd do is shoot bad cat—meaning man-eaters—at ever' village we come to. The idea was that it would endear us to the local big shot. The deal was—which we cut out front—he'd let us recruit some-a' his men to join our army if we killed the man-eatin' lion in the neighborhood.

"We did, though that was about the worst plan in history. Raidin' Forces ain't seen no combat yet as dangerous as tacklin' them big hungry kitty cats who had grown used to feastin' on all the dead bodies left layin' around the countryside by the Italians. Sometimes those Abyssinian lions hunted people in packs in broad daylight.

"And to tell the truth, the colonel, well, he didn't display no real aptitude at lion huntin', at least not right at first—how he got that scar on his face. Hand-to-hand combat with a monster cat that nearly munched him," Waldo said.

"What happened was, about the second village we come to, I cut a deal with the local big shot to the effect that if we took care of his bad cat problem he'd let us recruit some-a' his men. So we went out and capped 'em.

"The cats was dead, problem solved—Mr. Big Shot, well, he changed his mind about us doin' any recruitin.' Besides, he had been eyeballin' some-a' our weapons, animals and Rita and Lana. What was we goin' to do about it?

"'Go away,' the Big Shot said. Oh—and leave all them things mentioned above behind. If not, he'd rub us out at sunrise the next mornin' with his army—which was about ten times the size a' our little troop a' men, boys and camp followers—meanin' women a' low morals," Waldo said.

"Now this turn of events put us in a bad spot. The colonel said, and he was right, if we let ourselves get rolled by this dirtbag, word would soon get around and our days was numbered. In Abyssinia, where the national sport is murder, ain't nothin' more guaranteed than if you show any sign a' weakness to a shifta bandit you done committed slow-motion suicide.

"Bottom line, we was done for, either way it went."

"Sounds worse than the Alamo," ex-Lt. Jaxx said. "What'd you do, Mr. Treywick?"

"The colonel didn't appear to have noticed the odds stacked against us—said we was goin' to attack *them*," Waldo said.

"And that's when he told me and Butch the story about Miss UCLA—his good-lookin' high school teacher. We made us a battle plan then and there off her homework assignment to write a report on *The Man Who Would Be King*."

"Rudyard Kipling," Ensign Teddy Hamilton said. "I read it."

"That's the one, all right," Waldo said.

"Worked like a charm. We wiped out the entire village, burned it to the ground, took the men we wanted for our guerrilla army, the choicest women, all the weapons worth havin' and all the mules—the colonel shot Mr. Big Shot.

"So, gentlemen," Waldo said, "the lesson learned here tonight is, everybody needs to get as much education as you can. You never know when it might come in handy.

"Ask Joe—that correspondence course he took titled 'The Problem is the Solution' has done saved us a couple-a' times."

"Wiped 'em out," ex-Lt. Jaxx said, "just like that?"

"In less time than it took to tell you the story," Waldo said. "Thanks, Miss UCLA."

"That the way it went down, Colonel?" Lt. Jaxx asked. "Outnumbered ten to one?"

"Close enough," Col. Randal said.

"Ted, this ain't your first rodeo," Capt. McKoy said. "Let's hear about the job you pulled in OPERATION CRUSADER."

"My part did not play out the way it was planned, Captain," Ens. Hamilton said.

"The army had completed a railhead at the front when CRUSADER broke out. It was a strategic installation, and Field Marshal Auchinleck did not want anything bad to happen to it.

"I was assigned to Captain Styles to work on military deception. He is the premier *camoufler* in the Eight Army. The captain came up with a plan—camouflage the real installation and build a decoy railhead somewhere else safe for the bad guys to bomb to their hearts' content.

"And that is exactly what we did. Only not enough building materials were to be had so we were forced to construct the railhead to three-quarter scale. Captain Styles said the enemy pilots would never notice the size differential. We had an army of laborers working 'round the clock. When completed, our decoy site was an amazing thing of beauty.

"A fake railroad was put down leading to it—we just laid the rails on the ground—but looking down out of an airplane there was no way to know.

"Bomb away, bad guys."

"And, *that* is exactly what they did," Ens. Hamilton said. "The captain and I left for a few hours to pick up additional foodstuffs and supplies. When we returned the place had been the target of a major air raid. All the worker's trucks had been damaged or destroyed—our sleeping tents had been strafed. Everything was a complete shambles.

"Except for the decoy railhead—it was completely untouched. But the station had been bombed—with a *wooden* bomb."

No one saw that coming.

The tough, battle-hardened crew around the fire laughed. At least one or two people present were thinking it would have been nice if the bombs dropped today had been made out of wood.

"I can confirm Ensign Hamilton's story, gents," James "Baldie" Taylor said. "Dudley Clarke has a photo of the wooden bomb hanging in his office at A-Force."

Ens. Hamilton did not know it, but he was coming close to being fully accepted into Raiding Forces. The Great Teddy had passed the major hurdles: 1) he had attended all the requisite schools; 2) he was a master at his military specialty—deception; 3) he had shown bravery today, continuing to perform his duty under fire in full view of everyone present; 4) he could tell a good story.

"So, Captain," ex-Lt. Jaxx asked, "how does that *the problem is the solution* deal Mr. Treywick was talking about, work?"

"All you have to do," Capt. McKoy said, "is when you have yourself a problem, say it out loud while you think in your mind—'the problem is the solution.' The answer will jump right out at you."

"Really?"

"Let's give 'er a try," Capt. McKoy said. "The entire bad guy air force tried to rub us out—that's the problem.

"See Jack—your answer pops right out!"

"I'm not getting it," ex-Lt. Jaxx said. "Nothing's popping out."

"I do," Ens. Hamilton said.

"OK, Ensign," Capt. McKoy said, "fire away—let's hear it."

"The problem is Axis Air Force pilots tried to wipe us off the face of the earth," Ens. Hamilton said. "The solution—'shoot the bastards down.'"

Dead silence around the fire.

"There you go," Waldo said. "Works every time."

"That's a little harsh, Ted," Col. Randal said, "considering you invited 'em here."

Ex-Lt. Jaxx said, "I was overthinking."

CHAPTER TWELVE

ART OF WAR

ONE OF THE PHANTOM OPERATORS ARRIVED at the Command Post and handed Colonel John Randal a flimsy. It was a Frogspawn Code Word message.

> PAM EN ROUTE TO YOUR LOCATION STOP MARK AIRSTRIP AT 2300 HRS STOP BRANDY--PARKER REQUIRE IMMEDIATE ASSISTANCE STOP BRING TWO--THREE MEN FOR BACKUP STOP SIGNED J STOP

Col. Randal glanced at his Rolex. The lime green hands read 1905 hours.

"Jack, you and King saddle up, we're being extracted for another mission. General, you were always planning to go out on the first plane—this'll be it.

"Taylor, set up a party to mark the airstrip at 2300 hours. Pam will be flying in to pick us up.

"Jeb, get all six jeeps ready to roll—how many 37mm COWs came out with the supply convoy, Taylor?"

"Five, sir," Major Taylor Corrigan said. "I wanted to be prepared in the event we came under attack from mobile ground elements."

"Mount 'em on the jeeps with all the machine guns you can," Col. Randal ordered Major Jeb Pelham-Davies. "Be ready to roll out in thirty minutes.

"Anyone feel up to a moonlight ride, report to Jeb to reserve a seat on one of the jeeps."

"What you got up your sleeve, John?" Captain "Geronimo" Joe McKoy asked.

"I think we ought to drive over and pay that Italian fort a visit," Col. Randal said. "What say you, Captain?"

"Sounds like a plan," Capt. McKoy said. "You know how I like plans, John."

"Ensign Hamilton," Col. Randal said, "give me a rundown on the 'sonic deception' device you brought along."

"Acting on Captain Styles' suggestion, sir," Ensign Teddy Hamilton said, "Colonel Clarke asked Lady Seaborn to arrange for a Cairo movie company—Studio Misr—to use their audio equipment to record the sounds of tanks on the move. Then the recording was pressed on a record—awesome sound effect, sir."

"We never had the opportunity to use it during OPERATION CRUSADER. How's it work?" Col. Randal asked.

"We can hook up the record player to the battery of a truck or jeep, sir," Ens. Hamilton said. "There is an amplifier that enhances the sound to ten times what an actual tank makes, sir. The idea is to play it within hearing distance of the enemy to make them believe armored forces are on the move."

"Put it on Captain McKoy's jeep," Col. Randal said.

"Does that mean I can come along, Colonel?"

"On one condition," Col. Randal said. "Your word of honor as an officer you will never tell Jane—ever. Even under torture."

"You have my word, sir."

"In that case, get the lead out, Ensign," Col. Randal ordered. "We're rolling in two-zero."

The perimeter exploded into a frenzy of activity. Col. Randal called Maj. Corrigan aside. "Taylor, I'm going to leave Jeb in charge after I fly out tonight. You're the far more experienced desert hand—he needs the work before he takes over Desert Patrol, with you helping advise him."

"I understand, sir."

"Be discreet."

"Yes, sir," Maj. Corrigan said. "Who are you planning to have advise me when I take command of Sea Squadron?"

"Oh," Col. Randal said, "Admiral Ransom should be able to handle that job."

"I am confident the Razor can, sir," Maj. Corrigan said, sounding apprehensive. "I hear his bite is worse than his bark."

Col. Randal said, "It absolutely is."

"SITUATION," COLONEL JOHN RANDAL said to the group of men going on the hasty mission to attack the fort. "The bad guys are twenty miles that way. We're here."

No one laughed. They were used to Col. Randal's modified frag orders—knew he used them to lower tension. However, everyone relaxed even though they realized what he was doing was a leadership trick.

Everyone, that is, except Ensign Teddy Hamilton. He was shivering with anticipation. Tonight was to be his first combat patrol.

"You only get one first mission," Captain "Geronimo" Joe McKoy whispered to him. "The idea is to be around to go on a second. Stick to me like glue tonight, young ensign."

"Mission," Col. Randal said. "We're going to ride over, Ensign Hamilton will serenade the Italians with the sounds of tanks maneuvering, then we'll fire the 37mm COWs at maximum range to mimic tank guns, shift position and repeat. We'll do that several times, strafe the place with our machine guns and come home.

"Time is short—questions?"

"Typical shoot and scoot," Capt. McKoy said.

"Roger that."

The six SDF jeeps were bristling with weapons hastily mounted anywhere one would fit. All the Lovat Scouts with their Boys .55s were aboard. Everyone was looking for payback for the intensity of the day's air raids—not that the Raiders had failed to give more than they had taken. They were after *extra* payback.

James "Baldie" Taylor, ex-Lieutenant Billy Jack Jaxx and King led out to locate the fort in the dark and establish an ORP. Col. Randal would ride in another vehicle and switch to their jeep at the ORP. In the event that time expired before the mission was completed, the command jeep would break away and race back to rendezvous with Lieutenant Pamala Plum-Martin at the airstrip.

The other five jeep's crews were made up of all volunteers, many of whom had never worked with each other in a patrol or as part of the same jeep team before. At the last minute, the truck with the mounted pair of 20mms was added to the patrol.

"Guns," Col. Randal said, "I'll ride with you to the ORP. Go easy on the 20mm tonight—you'll likely need all the ammo you can get when the sun comes up."

"Aye, aye, sir," Guns said. "Like that woman said in the Civil War plantation movie Lady Jane showed at RFHQ, 'tomorrow is another day.'

"I plan to be ready, Colonel."

"You do that."

The moonlight ride to the ORP was uneventful. Once there, an 81mm mortar was set up. Col. Randal briefed Major Jeb Pelham-Davies, who would be commanding the maneuver element, and the six jeep drivers one last time. He repeated their instructions, which were to disperse with a fifty-yard interval between jeeps, drive slowly past where the fort was—somewhere out there in the dark—firing at it once per pass with their 37mm Coventry Ordnance Works (COW) anti-tank weapons. Then circle around, drive back to their start point and repeat the process to give the impression of a long, armored column constantly in motion. Machine gunners were to fire on the fort from time to time; however, they were at the limit of their maximum effective range so the MG fire was mostly for show.

Ens. Hamilton had the hood up on Capt. McKoy's jeep, while the ex-Arizona Ranger held a flashlight so he could see to hook up the sonic sound equipment to the battery.

"Move out, Jeb," Col. Randal ordered Maj. Pelham-Davies and his vehicle commanders who were gathered around his jeep. "Commence fire as soon as we illuminate the fort. Make three full passes."

There was a mad scramble as the Raiders made ready to begin their operation. Ens. Hamilton reported, "Sonic equipment ready, sir."

"Do it," Col. Randal ordered, sticking one of Waldo's custom-rolled cigars between his front teeth. "Make us proud, Ted."

An awful, herky-jerky screeching blared from Ens. Hamilton's phonograph, shattering the tranquility of the night. The sound a tank makes is not a pretty melody—unless you happen to be a tanker.

"Horrible," Waldo said, putting his hands over his ears. "How would you like to be waking up to that noise thinkin' it was comin' after ya'.

"We coulda used somethin' like this in Abyssinia—wouldn't-a' had to fight all them battles. No self-respectin' shifta woulda hung around long enough to see what was goin' to happen next."

"Sounds like the mating call of a wild boar dinosaur," Capt. McKoy said. "Too bad ole' Hawthorne ain't along tonight . . . 'at's what I call some serious psychological warfare."

"Anybody bring any cotton?" ex-Lt. Jaxx asked.

"Fire mission," Col. Randal ordered the mortar team. "One round of illumination."

There was a loud *THUUUMP.*

After a short wait, a cracking sound came from high up in the distance. The canopy on a parachute flare popped open. The flare ignited, creating a cheese-yellow light that flickered as the burning flare swayed under its little parachute. In the distance the fort could be seen in the mellow light produced by the flare.

The stop-start, herky-jerky screeching from the phonograph was unrelenting. Off to the left of the ORP, the first 37mm COW fired . . . *KAAABOOOM!* The high-pitched Vickers machine guns screamed, sounding different at a distance than they did from up close, where the high cyclic rate made only a hissing sound. The tracers were arching high in the sky and burning out about the time they reached the ground around the fort.

POKKA, POKKA . . . Guns was peppering the target while following his orders to conserve ammunition.

"Jack," Col. Randal said, "you and King join the column. Fire 'em up. Synchronize your watches—I want you back here in three-zero."

The Merc and ex-Lt. Jaxx hopped in their jeep and roared off to get in on the action.

Capt. McKoy said, "Ensign Hamilton, that record can play itself. How'd you like to man the Vickers K on the jeep—engage from here."

"Sir!"

"Make sure not to hit our boys when they roll by."

As Ens. Hamilton was climbing in the back of the jeep to bring the pedestal-mounted machine guns into action, Col. Randal ordered the mortar crew, "Fire mission—HE on the deck."

In the distance, tracers were arching into the fort, and 37mm rounds were detonating intermittently. Not much damage was being inflicted—except to the morale of the Italians inside. The Blackshirts had to be living their worst nightmare.

The HE 81mm mortar round landed twenty yards short of the fort with a flat *CRUUUMP!*

The next round was a direct hit on the roof of the building. Then the flare drifted down to lay burning next to the fort before fizzling out in the sand. The mortar men fired another illumination round—while their orders were to conserve the HE because they might need it tomorrow, the crew was instructed to keep the fort illuminated continuously.

The crew consisted of the team of former mortar instructors attached to Ranger Patrol, and they were professionals. The idea was to shake up the Italians—not destroy the fort. The *CRUUUUUMPH* of the 81's HE rounds impacting was definitely doing that.

The Raiders manning the COWs, not being trained artillerymen and used to firing on targets at point-blank range, were not as accurate. The .37mm rounds were impacting all around the fort with the occasional lucky hit. That was fine. The effect was what counted.

Col. Randal was well satisfied with the performance. He knew that if he were inside the building in the middle of nowhere he would have believed he was under attack by a large tank force and about to be overrun. And, he would have gotten on the phone, reported exactly that and demanded reinforcements.

What Col. Randal also knew was that there were no significant Afrika Korps combat formations within one hundred miles to come to the fort's assistance. With a major counterattack in progress, Rommel was not about to be peeling off any of his assault troops to come to the aid of a lonely Italian outpost of no strategic value.

Col. Randal almost felt sorry for the Blackshirts. Everyone in the position had to think they were about to die. What the defenders did not know was he did not want them dead. He needed at least some of them left alive to keep sending out hysterical messages begging for help.

If there were any question in Rommel's mind that a major British tank force was on his flank, tonight should settle it—there was.

To be perfectly honest, Col. Randal had not expected The Great Teddy's diversion to produce anywhere near the results it had. The ferocity of the Regia Aeronautica and the Luftwaffe's air attack on the decoy tanks today came as a surprise—he had not really expected the enemy to bite.

Tonight's melodrama was icing on the cake. The battle raged. However, it was strictly a one-sided affair. The Italians were hunkered down, not fighting back. Which was how Col. Randal liked his battles to come off.

The way it worked in Raiding Forces was, if they fired one million rounds at the bad guys, that was a good day—or in this case, night. If the bad guys fired one round back at them—that was a bad day.

Ex-Lt. Jaxx and King drove up right on time. Jim threw his gear in the back of the jeep and climbed aboard.

"Captain McKoy," Col. Randal said, "will you inform Major Pelham-Davies upon his return that I have departed the area."

"Roger that, John," Capt. McKoy said. "I'll see you when I see you."

"As soon as you get back to RFHQ," Col. Randal said, "you and Mr. Treywick are released to go to the States—take care of your business."

"In that case," Capt. McKoy said, "could be some time before we meet up."

"Have a good trip."

THE HUDSON FLEW IN AND LANDED on the abandoned track a short distance from "The Great Teddy's" decoy tank brigade perimeter. Major Taylor Corrigan had the runway illuminated by lights from the SDF trucks lined on both sides of it. Ex-Lieutenant Billy Jack Jaxx drove up as the airplane touched down.

Colonel John Randal stepped out of the jeep and slung his gear over one shoulder. He shouted to Maj. Corrigan over the noise of the Hudson's engines, "If I'm not back by the time you return to RFHQ, you and Jeb go ahead and carry out your change of commands."

"Yes, sir."

Col. Randal, James "Baldie" Taylor, ex-Lt. Jaxx and King trotted out to the airplane. It had wheeled around and was racing its engines, preparing for takeoff. The four men threw their gear in the rear door and climbed aboard.

Lieutenant Pamala Plum-Martin began taxiing as soon as the door slammed shut. Clearly, the Vargas Girl-looking Royal Marine was on a tight schedule.

Jim and King stretched out on the canvas bench seats in the back while ex-Lt. Jaxx went up to the cockpit to talk to Lt. Plum-Martin.

Major the Lady Jane Seaborn, dressed in tailored battle dress uniform (BDU), mahogany hair in a French twist, was sitting in one of the theatre chairs on the front row when Col. Randal moved forward.

He had not been expecting to find her on board.

Lady Jane gave him one of her patented heart attack smiles, which had the usual life-shortening effect. "Have you been enjoying yourself deceiving the Desert Fox, John?"

"Teddy," Col. Randal said, "is a genius."

"While it is not clear if your little charade has had anything to do with it," Lady Jane said, "Afrika Korps appears to have halted on the Gazala Line right where Dudley Clarke wanted it to."

"Really?"

"Exactly as you predicted," Lady Jane said, "the German counterattack was a fake charge."

"Well," Col. Randal said, "figuring that out didn't take a crystal ball."

"The attack petrified the armchair commando set at Grey Pillars," Lady Jane said. "Simply the word 'Rommel' gives the lads at GHQ the vapors."

"The campaign in the desert is not only a war of logistics—it's a maintenance war," Col. Randal said. "Tanks need a lot of it.

"Can't attack all the time, Jane—not even the legendary Desert Fox."

"After our conversation about maintenance walls and then the Afrika Korps' sudden halt at the Gazala Line," Lady Jane said, "I have concluded that Rommel does not grasp one simple fact all horsewomen know—ride your horse into the ground, you never win a steeplechase."

"Captain McKoy thinks the same thing," Col. Randal said.

"Sun Tzu said," Lady Jane said, "tactics without strategy is the noise before defeat."

"*You* are reading *Art of War*?"

"Captain McKoy gave me a copy."

"So, why are you here, Lady Major?"

"Brandy and Parker are engaged in a highly-classified mission for R. J.," Lady Jane said. "You do not possess the 'need to know' the details—do not ask. The plan is for the four of you to parachute in to help the girls bring it to resolution."

Col. Randal said, "The general's headed back to Cairo."

"You, Jack and King, then," Lady Jane said. "Brandy will brief the mission, meaning the parts you are cleared for, on the drop zone."

"Pam could have told us that much," Col. Randal said. "Why are you onboard, Jane?"

"Missed you," Lady Jane said, "actually."

"I was only gone overnight."

"What difference does that make?"

Col. Randal did not have an answer. He was in way over his head with drop-dead gorgeous Lady Jane Seaborn.

He'd missed her too.

CHAPTER THIRTEEN

SMITH AND JONES

COLONEL JOHN RANDAL, EX-LIEUTENANT Billy Jack Jaxx and King were standing in the tail of the Hudson. The wind was howling in the door, which was open and lashed down. The red light was on.

Major the Lady Jane Seaborn walked back to stand next to James "Baldie" Taylor. The MI-6/SOE Special Operations Chief Middle East was going to retrieve the static lines after the three parachutists exited the aircraft.

Lady Jane was there to give Col. Randal a last kiss. Ordinarily, Lady Jane did not indulge in public displays of affection, but lately she had relaxed her standards. "We will be back in exactly four hours to pick you up. Be safe, John—lunch at the Gezira Club tomorrow."

Col. Randal gave her a wink, then arched himself outside the aircraft to make a final jumpmaster check. The trailing Hudson, flown by Wing Commander Ronnie Gordon, was bobbing off the port side of the tail of the jump aircraft. The RAF liaison officer to Raiding Forces was getting in a lot of flying time for a man who was supposed to be on light duty from his latest in a long series of crashes—the reason for his sometimes nickname "Flash Bang."

It was not that W/Cdr. Gordon was a bad pilot. He just got shot down a lot.

In the near distance up ahead, to the left of the nose of the Hudson, Col. Randal could see a burning letter "L" on the ground. It was the correct authentication signal. The light marked the spot where he wanted all three jumpers to land in as tight a formation as possible.

"Close on the door."

Ex-Lt. Jaxx and King pressed forward until all three Raiders were touching. When the L was one finger off the toe of his never-polished, sun- and sand-blasted, canvas-topped raiding boot, Col. Randal said, "Let's go."

The prop blast from the Hudson's powerful engine grabbed him like a giant, invisible hand. The sensation felt like he came to a screeching halt in mid-air, then was sent tumbling—which is an addictive experience. At least it was now that he had done it as many times as he had. Col. Randal never told anyone that he liked hitting the prop blast, which did not make any sense—being apprehensive about heights as he was.

The chute cracked open, then there was only silence—absolute silence. Col. Randal looked down at the burning L between his boots. No need to pull a slip. He was coming straight down, right on the marker.

Then Col. Randal was swiveling to make a right front PLF. He landed in soft sand, indicating the DZ was in the edge of the Sand Sea. There was so little breeze, his X-type parachute drifted down, collapsed, and landed on top of him.

As jumps went, this was one of the nicest he had ever made.

Brandy Seaborn was there immediately, helping him out from under the canopy. She said, "Hello, handsome."

"Well, hello to you too, Mrs. Seaborn," Col. Randal said. "Is that a pistol in your pocket or are you just happy to see me?"

"It's a Beretta, John," Brandy laughed. "You gave it to me—I am sooooo glad to see you."

Brandy put her arms around his neck and placed her forehead against Col. Randal's. "Mmmmm—you smell like gunpowder, love."

"You have no idea what the last eighteen hours have been like," Col. Randal said. "If anyone ever asks you to be a decoy, don't do it."

Ex-Lt. Jaxx and King were down, recovering their parachutes. Captain Penelope "Legs" Honeycutt-Parker and two SDF troopers were assisting them. Not that they needed much assistance.

Col. Randal noticed there were two men in khaki observing what was taking place. Their facial features were obscured by Arab kaffiyeh scarves wrapped around their faces. Four of Major Jack Merritt's armed SDF troopers were providing security. And that was it.

The SDF men took the parachute bags and placed them in the back of the two jeeps parked by the burning L.

Brandy made the introductions, "John, I would like you to meet Mr. Smith and Mr. Jones."

Col. Randal did not believe those were their real names. No one offered to shake hands. He did not care for either of them on sight.

"Mr. Smith has decided to work for British Intelligence. Mr. Jones is his . . . friend."

"I see," Col. Randal said. Which meant he did not have a clue what was going on. However, he instinctively understood that "friend" had connotations outside the normal meaning of the word.

Ex-Lt. Jaxx and King had separated themselves slightly from the conversation, which gave them a better angle to kill Mr. Smith and/or Mr. Jones should the need arise. Col. Randal was clicked on.

"Here is what is going to happen," Brandy said. "A small, uninhabited oasis is approximately two miles south of where we are standing. Three Chevrolet trucks are parked there. Five Nazi Brandenburger Commandos are with the vehicles.

"John, I need you, Jack and King to go over there and shoot them."

"Noisy," Col. Randal asked, "or quietly?"

"Either way," the golden girl said. "I simply require them dead."

Mr. Smith, speaking with a European accent Col. Randal was unable to place, said, "The Brandenburg Regiment is the finest special operations unit in the Wehrmacht. Do not let their reputation concern you. Germans are helpless in the desert like babies—the swine are unable to perform even simple tasks."

Col. Randal said, "Then why don't you go do it?"

"I have certain skills," Mr. Smith said. "They do not include wet operations—your reputation precedes you, Colonel."

"Are they going to be expecting trouble?" Col. Randal asked.

"No," Mr. Smith said. "I left the Brandenburgers with a full bottle of Schnapps. Not that they did not have an adequate supply of their own. The fools have been drunk most of our journey."

"On your return, John," Brandy said, "your team, Parker and I will move to a strip of hard ground where Pam can land and pick us up.

"Mr. Smith and Mr. Jones will take one of the Chevrolets and drive to Tripoli. The other two trucks will be driven to Cairo by the SDF men with the jeeps."

"What about the bodies?" Col. Randal asked. "We'll be leaving fingerprints, Brandy."

Capt. Honeycutt-Parker said, "Let the buzzards have them."

COLONEL JOHN RANDAL, EX-LIEUTENANT Billy Jack Jaxx and King moved out on the azimuth Mr. Smith provided. The moon was out and the footing firm, though they were in sand. The Raiders made good time.

Col. Randal did not, however, follow the azimuth for more than a half mile. He made a hard right turn and moved off another half mile before turning back toward the oasis on a new heading. Why take a chance—Mr. Smith may not have been telling the truth.

The Brandenburgers could be lying in ambush somewhere on the line of march he had recommended. Col. Randal was having a difficult time believing the German Commandos were as helpless as claimed. The men he had encountered from the Brandenburg Regiment (an outfit wholly controlled by the Abwehr and made up of some of the most ruthless operators on the planet) had not fit that description.

Then again, he had read classified intelligence reports that indicated German Special Forces did not perform up to their normal standards when operating in the isolated desert environment of the Middle East.

In the distance was a small glow.

"Check it out, King," Col. Randal ordered.

Without a word the Merc disappeared in the dark. He was gone for approximately fifteen minutes according to the lime green hands on Col. Randal's Rolex. It seemed like a lot longer than that.

"Who do you think Smith and Jones are, sir?" ex-Lt. Jaxx whispered as they waited.

"I have no idea," Col. Randal said. Actually he thought he knew the identity of one of them—Lazzlo Almasy. The famous Hungarian desert explorer turned Nazi super phantom, bane to British Intelligence in Middle East Command. The man who regularly transported Abwehr spies across 1,500 miles of the trackless Great Sand Sea from Tripoli to Cairo.

"Mrs. Seaborn and 'Legs' Parker are awfully brave to be out here in the middle of the desert meeting Nazis with only four SDF men as security," ex-Lt. Jaxx said.

"Yes, they are," Col. Randal said.

King arrived.

"The set-up is exactly as Mr. Smith described, Chief. The only difference, there was one man standing guard."

"*Was?*"

"He is not standing guard any longer."

"All right, then," Col. Randal said, "let's do this. King, take point."

They checked their firearms—9mm MAB-38A submachine guns—the weapon of choice of Raiding Forces. Then King stepped off, moving like a big hunting cat.

The night was cool, perfectly still and eerily quiet. The sand muffled their boots. All three of them were competent in the art of silent movement.

Up ahead, the glow turned into a flickering fire, then the shadows of trucks could be seen. The three Raiders patrolled in single file on high alert.

The Merc led them into the perimeter of the trucks, then froze as they stepped to the edge of the circle of light from the fire. At that point, Col. Randal and ex-Lt. Jaxx moved up beside him on line.

Around the fire could been seen the bundles of four sleeping figures wrapped in blankets. A radio tuned to a Berlin station was playing Lili Marlene. There was more than the one empty bottle of Schnapps littering the ground.

Col. Randal raised his 9mm MAB-38A. When he saw out of his peripheral vision that ex-Lt. Jaxx and King had also raised their weapons, he fired a crisp burst into the nearest figure.

Ex-Lt. Jaxx and King were in action almost simultaneously. The three submachine guns sounded unnaturally loud. The Nazis never knew what hit them. None of the Brandenburgers even had a chance to make it out of his blanket.

It was all over in less than three seconds.

"Never fight fair," ex-Lt. Jaxx said as they moved forward to make sure everyone was dead. It was not one of Raiding Forces' Rules, but it might as well have been. The concept was hammered home on a regular basis in the unit.

A search turned up five 9mm MP-28 submachine guns, known to be favored by the Brandenburg Regiment. The Germans had five 9mm Walther P-38 pistols as well.

"Bring the weapons," Col. Randal said. "Time to go."

"That was cold," ex-Lt. Jaxx said. "We just shot four sleeping drunks, sir."

"Well, you're the little boy who told me he dropped a bundle of dynamite sticks down the chimney of a hideout on a gang of outlaws one night while serving a warrant with the sheriff," Col. Randal said.

"True," ex-Lt. Jaxx said. "But they were waiting inside with Thompson submachine guns and BARs stolen from a National Guard Armory in Waxahachie, Colonel."

"What did you want me to do, Jack?" Col. Randal asked. "Wake 'em up before we shot 'em?"

"Negative, sir."

As the three were nearing the site of the burning L, Col. Randal asked King, "Were you able to recognize Mr. Smith's accent?"

"Hungarian."

COLONEL JOHN RANDAL AND MAJOR the Lady Jane Seaborn were sitting behind a potted palm in the back of the Gezira Club. Lady Jane was entertaining him with stories about the people in the room. He was very relaxed, which was the effect she always had on him when they were together.

"See the slim brunette woman at the bar surrounded by admirers?" Lady Jane asked. "Do you find her beautiful?"

Col. Randal peeked out from under one of the low-hanging palm leafs to get a better view. "Attractive . . ."

"Christine Granville," Lady Jane said. "Recently returned from an extraordinarily hazardous mission in Europe for SOE. It is said she is unbelievably brave—claims to be a former Miss Poland."

"Really?"

"She is like catnip to men—they become addicted to her," Lady Jane said. "At least two have committed—or at least attempted to commit—suicide over her. It is said she has the morals of an alley cat."

"Catnip, huh?"

"SOE in England has no use for Christine for some reason," Lady Jane said. "She claims Brigadier Gubbins only wants to sleep with her—not assign her another mission.

"MI-5—meaning R. J., is suspicious that Christine may not have British best interests at heart," Lady Jane said. "Even SOE, as incompetent as the Cairo office is, are leery of her.

"On the other hand, the expatriate Polish community considers her a national hero."

"Don't tell me you're planning to recruit Miss Catnip for your Royal Marines," Col. Randal said.

"No," Lady Jane laughed. "Dudley Clarke already beat me to it. He is setting up a miniature A-Force version of RFHQ and stocking it with women called "Dudley's Duchesses."

"You're making that up," Col. Randal said.

"Not true," Lady Jane said. "I believe Dudley is jealous of you, John."

"Why me?" Col. Randal said. "You're the one who keeps bringing all the good-looking girls on board, Jane."

Lady Jane laughed and flashed her fabled heart attack smile. "You brought your slave girls Rita and Lana from Abyssinia, Mandy from RAF Habbaniya. And, you imported me from England."

"Ahhh . . ."

"Dudley has led a tumultuous love life," Lady Jane said. "Two head-over-heels affairs, one right after the other, with women he intended to marry. Jilted—each time.

"One of his lovers literally left him waiting at the station in Bulgaria after he made a long train trip across Europe to marry her before the war.

"A female friend was on hand to greet him when he arrived. She explained his fiancée was running late. And then disappeared with the suitcase full of money Dudley had smuggled into the country for his intended—who never showed."

Col. Randal said, "That's the worst story I've ever heard."

"Agreed," Lady Jane said. "Dudley is a man who loves beautiful women. While they enjoy his company, women do not fall for him. They never see him as more than a friend."

"Left the man standing at the station and stole his money," Col. Randal said. "Damn!"

"Christine is his newest Duchess," Lady Jane said.

Col. Randal said, "I don't believe she was ever Miss Poland."

COMMANDER IAN FLEMING, RNVR, straight off a plane out from the UK, walked into the restaurant. The maître d' pointed toward the palm. As he made his way to the back of the room, the debonair Naval Intelligence officer waved to his brother, Peter, who was having a drink at the bar with Captain David Stirling.

Cmdr. Fleming walked up to the table where Colonel John Randal and Major the Lady Jane Seaborn were sitting.

He said, "GOLDEN FLEECE."

It was the second-most secret code word in the British Empire (neither Col. Randal nor Lady Jane was cleared to know how high its security classification actually was). Number two in priority only to CROMWELL, which would announce that the Nazi invasion of England was in progress—if that ever happened.

Col. Randal said, "I guess that means no dessert."

CHAPTER FOURTEEN

BLACK CAT OR LUCKY LADY

COMMANDER IAN FLEMING WAITED until they arrived back at RFHQ and were in the privacy of Colonel John Randal's and Major the Lady Jane Seaborn's third-floor suite to begin his briefing. James "Baldie" Taylor was waiting when they came in.

"Singapore is about to fall," Cmdr. Fleming said. "The Japs landed in Malaya six weeks ago. Lieutenant General Arthur Percival did not seem concerned or do much about it. He estimated it would take up to a year for the Nips to make their way through the 'impenetrable' jungle. Besides, British Forces outnumbered the Japanese three to one.

"Additionally, the 8th Australian Division arrived, increasing the numerical advantage for our side even more. The Aussie division commander is on record saying, 'One Australian is equal to ten of the little yellow bastards.'

"According to Field Marshal Percival 'the Japanese all wear glasses, which make them poor soldiers. If they have bad eyesight and cannot shoot straight . . . well, that makes them even worse pilots. Not to worry—Singapore is the Gibraltar of the Far East.'"

Cmdr. Fleming opened an elegant silver case and took out one of his custom-blended cigarettes with three gold rings on the tip.

"The Japanese Air Force swept in, blew the RAF's Brewster Buffalos out of the sky, sank the battleships *Prince of Wales* and the *Repulse* and now have achieved air superiority over the fortress.

"Nipponese infantry, mounted on bicycles, launched a lighting attack down the only hard-topped track, and the impenetrable jungle proved not to be so impenetrable. You see, all the big guns in Singapore were pointed the wrong way—out to sea."

Jim said, "True to form, the wily Japs failed to cooperate with Percival's plan. They chose not to land right in front of the coastal artillery batteries where he wanted them to. Came in the back door, kept coming—swarming over, around or through any obstacle.

"Now the Japanese are ensconced on the outskirts of the city," Cmdr. Fleming said.

"Percival is the archetypical Colonel Blimp-type officer who has led our army from defeat to defeat starting day one of the war," Jim said. "The general is so stupid he needs to be in an institution. And he will be soon enough—a POW camp."

"The Japanese intent is to *humiliate* Europeans," Cmdr. Fleming said. "The Land of the Rising Sun is not a signatory to the Geneva Convention, so the Nips have no moral constraints. They have proven to be astonishingly savage."

Jim said, "We have a confirmed report that they captured a military hospital, bayoneted over four hundred Australian patients plus all the doctors and nurses. It is said they have raped every woman the length of the peninsula—possibly an exaggeration—or not.

"The fools took photos, then had local Chinese chemists develop the pictures—because Japan has been at war with China since 1937, SOE has copies."

Cmdr. Fleming said, "I brought a few along with me, which I shall show you in private, Colonel, unless you have an interest in gang rape snuff photos, Lady Jane."

"Gang rape," Lady Jane said, "has always been one of my favorite genres of pornography, Ian."

"In conclusion," Cmdr. Fleming said, regretting the weak attempt at humor, "our navy is sunk."

"The air force has been shot down. There is no central command structure functioning in Singapore. Soldiers are deserting their posts—estimates run as high as a third of the army being absent at any given time.

"Chaos reigns in the city and there is rioting in the streets.

"Am I painting a sufficiently bleak picture of the situation? Singapore will be the biggest military defeat in the history of the British Empire—over eighty thousand Commonwealth troops are going in the bag and there is nothing we can do about it."

Col. Randal said, "You traveled all the way out to Egypt to tell me a war story?"

"Actually," Cmdr. Fleming said, "yes."

"Why are you here, Ian?" Lady Jane asked, not happy. She knew people living in Singapore. It was supposed to be the safest place in the British Empire.

Lady Jane also knew this was not a social call.

"The Far East Combined Bureau," Cmdr. Fleming said, "Bletchley Park's super-secret cryptographic outpost in Singapore. Twenty-four people—eighteen men, six women stationed in the city. Not a single one can be allowed to fall into Japanese hands.

"Colonel Randal, your mission, conveyed verbally to me by the Prime Minister, is to fly to Singapore and evacuate the Bureau personnel. In the event your assignment cannot be accomplished with absolute certainty—eliminate any possibility of their capture at all costs."

"You mean," Col. Randal said, "kill them?"

Cmdr. Fleming said, "Dead men tell no tales."

"MANDY," COLONEL JOHN RANDAL ORDERED. "Have Major Sansom locate Mud Cat Ray and deliver him to RFHQ most immediate."

"Anything else, John?"

"Find Billy Jack, Roy and King and have them report to me," Col. Randal said. "What's Pam's ETA?"

Lieutenant Mandy Paige said, "She and Wing Commander Gordon landed thirty minutes ago with the last of the Raiding Forces personnel being flown back from what the Raiders are calling 'Teddy's Turkey Shoot.'"

"Have Pam report here too," Col. Randal said. "Be discreet—the Wing Commander is not on the 'need to know' list."

"Understood."

"Is Jim still here?"

"He is in the bedroom he maintains, John," Lt. Mandy said.

"Ask him to come see me at his earliest convenience," Col. Randal said. "Then I need you to stay on the desk in King's place."

"Yes, sir," Lt. Mandy said. "John, surely you are not alerted for another mission?"

Col. Randal said, "I'm taking a vacation."

Red arrived. The Flying Clipper Girl, who was also in the employ of MI-6, said, "John, I have been tasked with making the arrangements for your air travel.

"Pam will fly you and your party to RAF Habbaniya. From there you will transfer from the Hudson to a BOAC Flying Clipper that has been diverted for this mission because it has the range to fly to the Port of Chennai.

"Upon arrival in India, you will transfer to a Catalina which will fly your team on to Singapore. Once there, the PBY will have to refuel while you go ashore and recover the Bureau personnel for the immediate return trip.

"I shall travel with you as far as the Port of Chennai—afraid you have to make the final leg of the outbound journey to Singapore on your own, John."

"I can do that," Col. Randal said.

"When your party arrives back from Singapore, everyone will board the Flying Clipper for the return flight to RAF Habbaniya. At that point, the Bureau personnel will continue on to the UK while we fly here to RFHQ.

"How many people do you anticipate taking with you?" Red asked.

"Three," Col. Randal said.

"Works perfectly," Red said. "The outbound flight shall be virtually empty while the return will be close to capacity.

"Any questions, John?"

"How's Terry doing?"

"He is doing well," Red said. "The doctor says Terry should be able to perform light duty in about three weeks."

"I was hoping to have him released to RFHQ to take charge here while I'm gone," Col. Randal said. "Pretty light duty—he could do it from bed."

"Probably not on, John," Red said, her Clipper Girl-cool cracking a bit. "Terry was gravely injured—loves to say 'it's always darkest before pitch-black.'"

Col. Randal said, "He almost made it to full fade out."

James "Baldie" Taylor arrived, looking casual in loafers, slacks and a knit shirt.

"You needed to see me, Colonel?"

Col. Randal said, "Anything about Singapore I need to know, General?"

"Afraid I have not been out there in years," Jim said. "Colonel, I have to confess to being stunned by the implosion of our army. The British Empire is spiraling out of control—the loss of Singapore will make Pearl Harbor seem like a sideshow in comparison."

Col. Randal said, "I'd appreciate it if you would get with Fleming, go over his plan with a microscope to see if he's got all the bases covered. He's not an operations man."

"Do it right now," Jim said.

"The *need* for your mission I do not understand—those cryptanalysts should have been evacuated long before now," he said.

"The *why,* I understand loud and clear—those signals people cannot be captured. The Japs would need about thirty seconds to crack the lot of them. Cruelest torturers in the world—the Nazis are rank amateurs in comparison."

Lieutenant Roy Kidd and ex-Lieutenant Billy Jack Jaxx walked in as Jim was leaving.

"Roy says there was only one last high-altitude bombing attack after we departed the area, sir," ex-Lt. Jaxx said. "I thought Teddy's decoy operation was supposed to be a camping trip, not the Gunfight at the OK Corral."

"That's the way I had it figured too, Jack," Col. Randal said.

"Same here, sir," Lt. Kidd said. "What a shootout—can't believe we got away with none of our people getting anything more than a few scratches."

"I'm flying out this afternoon for Singapore," Col. Randal said, changing the subject. "You two studs are coming with me."

Ex-Lt. Jaxx and Lt. Kidd perked up.

"This is a quick in and out," Col. Randal said. "You'll be briefed later, but the main idea is we have to bring out a team of two dozen radio operators with high-security clearances before the town falls."

"Singapore about to be overrun?" ex-Lt. Jaxx said. "What happened? All the BBC nightly news stories we've been listening to night after night while on patrol talk about it being the 'Gibraltar of the Far East'."

"Roger that, sir," Lt. Kidd said, "We can defend Singapore from the 'Yellow Peril' for a thousand years or until hell freezes over—whichever comes first."

"I don't think the Japanese were listening to the BBC," Col. Randal said.

King walked in as they were talking. Col. Randal said to the Merc, "We're flying to Singapore in a few hours."

"How long are we planning to stay, Chief?"

"Less than an hour," Col. Randal said, "if I have anything to say about it. Dress for success, just in case."

"Affirmative."

"Roy and Jack are going," Col. Randal said. "On the trip out it's just the four of us, an empty plane with a full crew of Clipper Girls—enjoy yourselves, gentlemen."

Ex-Lt. Jaxx said, "Sounds like my kind of mission, sir."

"Affirmative," Lt. Kidd said.

"Our destination is classified," Col. Randal said as they were leaving. "Anyone asks, we're flying to RAF Habbaniya—mission undisclosed."

Five minutes after they left, Lieutenant Pamala Plum-Martin arrived, still wearing her flight suit. "You asked to see me, John?"

"You'll be flying a small team to RAF Habbaniya later today. Get with Red to brief you on the details."

"Will you be leading the team?" Lt. Plum-Martin asked. "You need a break, John."

"So do you, Pam," Col. Randal said. "You've been flying 'round the clock—two weeks off as soon as you touch down back here from Habbaniya. That's an order—no flying.

"Yes, sir," the Vargas Girl-looking Royal Marine pilot said. "Whatever this mission is, be safe, John—I should not want anything to happen to you."

"All I'll be doing, Pam," Col. Randal said, "is evacuating a party of civilians from Singapore, who all hold high intelligence clearances."

The Royal Marine officer was a longtime MI-6 operative. Col. Randal knew he was not fooling her. Why would Naval Intelligence be flying him halfway around the world to evacuate a party of people they could put on an airplane if all was well?

Lieutenant Plum-Martin left immediately.

"Sammy's here, John," Lt. Mandy announced.

Major Sammy Sansom, Chief of Cairo Field Security walked in with Acting Provisional Sub-Lieutenant Skipper Mud Cat Ray, OBE, RNPS.

Col. Randal said, "Skipper, as I remember it, after OPERATION LOUNGE LIZARD you were planning to go out to Singapore—what happened?"

"That's right, Colonel, I was," Skipper Ray said. "Only Wino wanted to go too, so we flipped for it. I lost. Sure worked out good for me—command of a trawler.

"You gave me the best ship I ever sailed on."

"Any idea where to find Wino in Singapore?" Col. Randal asked.

"If he's not on his tug," Skipper Ray said, "my guess is you'd find Wino drinking himself blind in the Black Cat or the Lucky Lady—they're on Lavender Street—girlie bars. That's where I'd be if I was him."

Maj. Sansom gave Col. Randal a look.

"Would you mind waiting outside, Skipper," Maj. Sansom said. "I need a word in private with the colonel on another subject."

"Aye, aye, sir," Skipper Ray said. "Want to thank you again, Colonel, for springing me outta prison."

"Don't kill anybody else," Col. Randal said, "unless it's absolutely necessary."

"You got my word."

As soon as they were alone, Maj. Sansom said, "Nice work, Colonel, taking out the Brandenburgers for Mrs. Seaborn and Captain Honeycutt-Parker. Those ladies made a major recruitment for our side and we could not risk any possibility of witnesses getting back to Tripoli who might compromise it."

"I see," Col. Randal said, which meant he did not.

"Problem is," Maj. Sansom said, "our brand-new double agent had already dropped off two highly-trained Abwehr operatives before Mrs. Seaborn and Captain Honeycutt-Parker caught up to him.

"Now we have two German spies on the loose in Cairo I have to track down."

"You're good at that," Col. Randal said.

"I could use your help."

"I'm flying out this afternoon," Col. Randal said.

"That's fine," Maj. Sansom said. "What I need is for you to let me borrow Rita and Lana to dance at the Kit-Kat Club again. It's a sure bet those two spies will turn up there sooner or later. German agents always do.

"Moe, the manager, has been badgering me to talk to you about letting them come back before this came up anyway," Maj. Sansom said.

"Your slave girls are so popular he will lift the ban on you coming to the club if you do."

"They're not my slaves," Col. Randal said.

"That is not what the girls say."

"If you need Rita and Lana," Col. Randal said, "and they agree—OK by me."

"Colonel," Maj. Sansom said, "this situation is so grave that we have been giving serious thought to enlisting Rocky to dance at the Kit-Kat until we round up these two enemy agents."

"Rocky?" Col. Randal said. "Let me know, Major. I might want to catch her show."

Lt. Mandy came in after Maj. Sansom left.

"Did Sammy tell you about the two Nazi spies in Cairo, John?"

"Yes, he did."

"R. J. wants to saturate the Kit-Kat Club with counterintelligence people because enemy agents go there to try to make local contacts they can use. In addition, about half the dancers are Hungarians or Egyptians not always loyal to our side. Some are willing to help Germany—particularly the Hungarians."

Col. Randal said, "He wants Rita and Lana back at the club."

"I am thinking about dancing too," Lt. Mandy said. "Don't tell my mother."

"Mandy," Col. Randal said, "if I catch you dancing at the Kit-Kat . . ."

"OK, John," Lt. Mandy laughed. "Just a thought."

Jim came running up the stairs, "Colonel, who are you taking with you to Singapore?"

"Jack, Roy and King," Col. Randal said.

"You cannot depart," Jim said, "until I get back from Major Twitterington's office. It should not take long."

Then Jim ran back down the stairs without explanation.

"Mandy," Col. Randal asked, "you ever hear of a Major Twitterington?"

"Before the war, King Farouk was afraid someone would poison him," Lt. Mandy said. "He hired Professor Twitterington to make sure his food was not poisoned. So the professor hired local women to taste the king's food before every meal. Those in the know call him 'Twitters the Taster.'

"Nowadays the professor is a major. He used to be employed by R. J. to look for messages written in secret ink. Now he works for A-Force as a forger."

"That's some story, Mandy."

"Stranger than fiction," Lt. Mandy laughed. "But then, we *are* used to that, right John?"

Sergeant Major Mike "March or Die" Mikkalis arrived. "You needed to see me, Colonel?"

"I'm flying out and not exactly sure when I'll be back—probably not long," Col. Randal said. "Captain McCloud may arrive with a group of Americans who have volunteered for Raiding Forces before I return.

"If that happens, you take charge of getting the troops desert-qualified until Mad Dog is medically released for full duty—then he'll take over."

"Rough," the baby-blue-eyed former French Legionnaire asked, "or easy?"

"These men will all be U.S. Paratroopers," Col. Randal said. "I need as many of them as we can get to make the cut—weed out any who don't. But keep in mind, we need replacements."

"My pleasure, sir."

MAJOR THE LADY JANE SEABORN was in her bedroom reclining on the bed with a sketch pad. She was a talented artist, though she only drew for her own amusement.

Colonel John Randal walked in. "What're you drawing, Jane?"

"Operational wings," Lady Jane said. "Jock Lewis asked me to help him design them for the Special Air Service. I made a tracing from a cartouche in the Great Pyramid that is almost perfect."

Col. Randal said, "What are operational wings?"

"Something to do with how many patrols an SAS man has gone on," Lady Jane said. "Sounds like something out of Baden-Powell's Scouting for Boys.

"I thought we might redesign our parachute wings using the same ancient Egyptian pattern, only with different colors."

"Yeah, I like 'em," Col. Randal said, studying her drawing. "Let's do it."

"SAS is going to use Cambridge blue as the background on theirs," Lady Jane said, flipping the page. "I was thinking ours could be violet—my favorite color."

She showed him her drawing of a pair of the wings with violet thread."

"No," Col. Randal said, "I don't think so."

"What color would *you* prefer, John?"

"Light infantry green."

"Love it," Lady Jane said. "Matches my eyes."

Col. Randal said, "I didn't know that."

THE HUDSON WAS SITTING WITH ITS MOTOR ticking over. The team traveling out to Singapore was on board, along with Commander Ian Fleming and Red—they would be traveling as far as India. The plane was waiting for James "Baldie" Taylor to arrive before taking off for RAF Habbaniya.

When Jim came aboard, he passed out pigskin leather folders containing credentials for Colonel John Randal, Lieutenant Roy Kidd, ex-Lieutenant Billy Jack Jaxx and King.

TO: ALL MILITARY/CIVIL OFFICERS.

THE BEARER OF THIS DOCUMENT IS ON SPECIAL ASSIGNMENT. RENDER ANY ASSISTANCE REQUESTED WITHOUT QUESTION. UNDER NO CIRCUMSTANCE IMPEDE THIS OFFICER IN THE PERFORMANCE OF HIS DUTIES. THERE ARE NO LIMITATIONS TO THIS ORDER.

SIGNED
ALAN BROOKE
FIELD MARSHAL
CHIEF OF THE IMPERIAL GENERAL STAFF

"Naturally, these are forgeries," Jim said. "No one in Singapore will know the difference. Your mission is so vital that Colonel Clarke and I debated the merits of having the signature line signed by the Prime Minister."

"Wow," ex-Lt. Jaxx said. "A get-out-of-jail-free card."

"That is exactly what it is," Jim said. "Do not hesitate to produce it if and when needed. You are authorized the use of deadly force should anyone fail to comply."

Col. Randal said, "General, I don't have an officer to command Raiding Forces while I'm gone. Would you consider stepping in?"

"Glad to," Jim said. "Admiral Ransom should be back in the next few days. Between the two of us, we should be able to manage."

"I'm confident you can, sir," Col. Randal said.

Jim said, "When you arrive, your contact will be Lieutenant Colonel Valentine Killery—SOE's man in Singapore. He has been ordered to have your party standing by assembled, ready to board the Catalina for the return trip.

"Fly in, extract the Far East Combined Bureau people, come home—we have other business that requires your attention, Colonel."

"My plan exactly, General."

As Jim stood up to depart the aircraft he said, "Good luck."

CHAPTER FIFTEEN

SINGAPORE TEA

LIEUTENANT PAMALA PLUM-MARTIN landed the Hudson at RAF Base Habbaniya, the site of the four-day siege by the Iraqi Army during the short-lived Anglo/Iraq War conducted by rebel officers of the Golden Square. Everyone on both sides (meaning the politicians) was doing their best to erase it from the history books.

The Iraqis did not want to advertise their humiliating military performance against the badly outnumbered British, and the British needed Iraqi oil and air bases to conduct the war against the Nazis. Both parties did their best to act like it had never happened.

Very few decorations were awarded to the defenders of RAF Habbaniya, and one of those was given to a man who had been recommended for court martial for dereliction of duty.

Except for experiencing a small number of air raids after the siege had already ended, the base was back to being a sleepy backwater. The big war had moved on. A truck was waiting to transfer Colonel John Randal's party up the escarpment to Lake Habbaniyah, where the group was to board the Flying Clipper for the flight to India.

Because there were some unhappy Iraqi generals who blamed Col. Randal for the loss of a large number of gold bars they had looted from their own government and the shootout in the lobby of the British Overseas Airways Corporation (BOAC) when he rescued Red from the rebels, it was deemed advisable for him to remain incognito.

He kept his Ray-Ban sunglasses on at all times and wore his green Commando beret instead of the cut-down Australian bush hat he had worn during the battle.

Col. Randal boarded the Flying Clipper immediately upon arrival.

When the crew arrived, ex-Lieutenant Billy Jack Jaxx, Lieutenant Roy Kidd and King sported the looks of kids in a candy shop. There were a dozen Clipper Girls plus Red to serve four passengers. The stewardesses, not having been briefed on the nature of the flight, understandably believed them to be VIPs—Commandos on some dangerous mission right out of a movie. Had to be to rate travel on a Flying Clipper reserved strictly for them.

The girls were impressed.

Normally, to qualify for a seat, a passenger needed to have a title, hold flag rank, or be an ambassador-level civil servant.

Having spent time hanging out with Major Sir Terry "Zorro" Stone in Cairo, ex-Lt. Jaxx had previously met several of the stewardesses. King knew a few too. Apparently Clipper Girls preferred men with a hard edge. The party started as soon as the giant airplane was airborne.

Col. Randal took up residence in the small, plush compartment that he and Major the Lady Jane Seaborn normally occupied when they traveled together. He lay down on one of the two lounges and went straight to sleep.

When he woke up, Red was there with a meal fit for a king. She reclined in the lounge next to him and they chatted for a while. The two had known each other since before OPERATION LOUNGE LIZARD, the raid on Rio Bonita, but this was the first time they had ever spent any considerable time alone talking. Col. Randal decided he liked her a lot.

Beneath Red's cool "Keep Calm and Carry On" Clipper Girl exterior beat the heart of a hell-raiser.

Col. Randal drifted back off to sleep—he had a lot of catching up to do—having been on continuous operations for longer than he could remember.

The missions all blurred together after a while, and Col. Randal had not realized how exhausted he was. He knew it is never a good idea for any commander of combat troops to be running on pure adrenalin for any extended length of time. Much less the commander of a special operations unit that operated exclusively behind enemy lines and lived by its wits. Except for meals, he pretty much slept the entire 2,500-mile flight.

The Flying Skipper splashed down in the Port of Chennai, India.

As the Clipper Girls waved good-bye, Col. Randal and his team deplaned and immediately boarded a Catalina for the final leg of the flight to Singapore. It was another long flight.

When the seaplane landed, a cutter manned by a pair of Royal Navy ratings was standing by to take them ashore. Lieutenant Colonel Valentine Killery, the SOE man in Singapore, was on board.

The plan was for the Catalina to refuel, then stand by to take the Bureau personnel on board for the return flight. Singapore appeared to be in flames. Long-range artillery was coming in and detonating. Fuel tanks were burning. Enemy aircraft could be seen dropping bombs over the town.

Singapore reminded Col. Randal of his arrival in Calais, only on a larger scale.

Behind them, the Catalina exploded in a massive orange fireball—a Japanese A6M Type O fighter swooped down and took out their way home in a single pass.

Ex-Lt. Jaxx said, "Uh-oh!"

King said, "So much for the Japs being bad pilots."

Lt. Kidd asked, "Do we have a Plan B?"

"Negative. Yours was the final plane expected in," Lt. Col. Killery said. "The last ship has either sailed or been sunk. Take a look at all the wrecks around the harbor."

Col. Randal said, "Colonel, are you aware of the full extent of my orders?"

Lt. Col. Killery said, "I can surmise."

"When we come ashore," Col. Randal said, "Jack, you and Roy will stay with the cutter. Colonel, you stand by with them, ready to help us move the Bureau personnel down to the dock."

"We cannot possibly fit twenty-four people plus your team in this cutter," Lt. Col. Killery said. "And if we did, where would you go? It's two thousand miles to India."

"That is a problem," Col. Randal said.

When the cutter pulled up to the dock, the scene on shore was something out of a psychotic nightmare or a Saturday matinee about the fall of Rome. The animals, at least the ones that did not eat people, had been released from the zoo to fend for themselves. When Col. Randal came up on to the street, a giraffe galloped by, drunken Australian soldiers were smashing the windows of store fronts with empty beer bottles, a naked Eurasian woman trotted past, artillery exploded close by.

"How long will it take you to assemble the Bureau people?"

"Everyone is waiting in a warehouse half a block from here," Lt. Col. Killery said. "I have a detail of six Royal Marines guarding them."

"How do I find Lavender Street?" Col. Randal asked.

"*This* is Lavender Street."

"Which way to the Black Cat or the Lucky Lady?"

Lt. Col. Killery looked at Col. Randal as if he had lost his mind. "Three blocks up the street you will find the Lucky Lady on the right side. The Black Cat is three doors down."

Col. Randal said, "Let's go, King."

The two set off through the swirling mass of humanity and animals running wild in the street. People did not appear to be afraid—they had all simply gone mad. A giant Indian Sikh in uniform with a turban was standing on a corner waving a curved sword at anyone who ventured near.

King shot him.

The Lucky Lady came into sight. It was the typical Far Eastern brothel masquerading as a bar, identifiable by a huge lighted sign out front and the words in English, "Girls, Girls, Girls." Inside, patrons could buy a watered-down drink called "Singapore tea" for the girls, some of whom were quite beautiful.

When Col. Randal and King entered, the place was dark and mostly empty except for a dozen or so bored-looking Singapore Tea Girls. They had no cause for concern. The fall of the city held no terrors for them. Their clientele would simply switch from drunk Europeans to drunk Japanese—life would go on—business as usual.

With all the disorder in the street, the Lucky Lady was like the calm in the eye of a hurricane. The madam was a Malaysian woman of a certain age, smelling of cheap perfume. She greeted them at the door.

Col. Randal said, "Where can I find 'Wino' Muldoon?"

The madam pointed to a far back corner of the dark room, "He there."

Mike "Wino" Muldoon was sitting at a table with three girls in slit silk skirts. The girls were sipping Singapore tea—Wino was drinking rum. There were a couple of empty bottles on the table.

"Go away," Col. Randal said to the girls. The Tea Girls scattered like a covey of quail.

Wino looked up, bleary-eyed, "Who the bloody hell do . . . wait, I know you. You're the Mad Major. What are you doing in scenic downtown Singapore?"

"Warthog and Mud Cat sent me," Col. Randal said. "I have a mission for you."

"Warthog and Mud Cat . . ."

"They work for Raiding Forces full-time now," Col. Randal said. "Command ships—Royal Navy Volunteer Reserve—we've got one waiting for you.

"Do I have to wear a sailor suit?"

"I believe you asked me that once before, Wino."

"That's right," Wino said, "I did . . . or maybe it was Mud Cat."

"The problem is," Col. Randal said, "we have to get out of Singapore first—your tugboat still afloat?"

"I got the *Big Toot II* hid in a jungle lagoon up a slough about twenty miles from here," Wino said. "She's victualed, topped off and ready to sail. Been sitting here debating heading up there, casting off and setting sail for far shores—only there's still a lot a' booze to be drunk and I can't talk any of these girls into going with me."

"Do you have a crew?"

"Oh, yeah," Wino said. "They're down at the Black Cat—I do my drinking alone, except for . . ."

"Let's go," Col. Randal said. "You hang around much longer you'll be drinking sake."

"Yes, sir, Major Randal, sir," Wino said. "Ain't never developed a taste for that evil juice."

"*Colonel* Randal," King said.

"Mad Colonel—don't have the same snap," Wino said, staggering to his feet.

"What's the plan?"

"I have no idea," Col. Randal said. "Counting on you for that, Wino."

COLONEL JOHN RANDAL ARRIVED BACK at the dock where Lieutenant Colonel Valentine Killery, ex-Lieutenant Billy Jack Jaxx and Lieutenant Roy Kidd were waiting. He and King were in the *Big Toot II's* whaleboat full of drunken tugboat sailors. There were two Singapore Tea Girls in slit silk dresses; the crew had brought them along from the Black Cat. The sailors refused to leave the girls behind.

"What in the world?" Lt. Col. Killery said.

"We need three more cutters, whaleboats or other small launches," Col. Randal said, stepping ashore. We're going to get our passengers."

Lt. Kidd and ex-Lt. Jaxx took the two sailors from the cutter that had brought them ashore. They searched the dock area. Small craft of all kinds were abandoned everywhere because they were worthless for escape. The sailors picked out three, loaded extra cans of fuel, which they took off other abandoned boats, and were back within thirty minutes.

By then Col. Randal and Lt. Col. Killery had departed for the warehouse where the Far East Bureau personnel were waiting.

The Royal Marines guarding the building allowed them inside, then quickly shut the door. In the warehouse were twenty-four civilian personnel scared out of their wits. Col. Randal noted the Marines were all armed with Thompson submachine guns and handled them like they knew how to use them.

Lt. Col. Killery had everyone gather around.

"This is Colonel Randal. You may have heard of some of his exploits—the Prime Minister personally hand-picked him to fly out to Singapore to escort you back to the UK."

Col. Randal said, "The Catalina that was to fly us to India was destroyed by a Jap A6M Zero shortly after we landed."

A moan came from the group and some of the people began to cry. They knew the fate that awaited them if captured. A report had come in that morning, confirmed by their own intercepts, that the Japanese had wrapped two hundred prisoners in barbed wire, poured gasoline on them, then lit the fuel off.

The intelligence report stated the Japanese laughed as the flaming prisoners ran around screaming—human torches.

"However, there is a fallback plan," Col. Randal said. "We have a ship hidden twenty miles up the coast from here. What is going to happen next is we are going to depart here for the dock. Once there, you will be broken down into parties and board small boats for the trip along the coast to where the ship is located.

"Do everything I tell you and we can all make it out of here," Col. Randal said. "Cross me and I'm authorized to shoot any member of the Bureau I deem a threat to the group. My job is to get you home safe—I'm not about to let anything or anyone stand in the way of making that happen.

"Is that clear?"

"Clear," the group said in unison, sounding hopeful but not entirely convinced—the shooting people part not being lost on anyone.

"I didn't hear you."

"CLEAR!"

"All right, then," Col. Randal said. "I can tell we're going to get along just fine."

Lt. Col. Killery said, "Leave all of your luggage here except for stout shoes or jackets to wear at night. We will be departing this building in ten minutes."

"If anyone is in possession of any classified material, I want it right now."

As the group was going through their luggage, Col. Randal had a quiet word with the corporal in charge of the Royal Marine security detail. He showed him the forged order in the pigskin credentials case. "Escort the party to the dock when we move out. Instruct your men that in the event anyone attempts to break away from the group for any reason—shoot 'em."

"Sir!"

"Inform your Marines," Col. Randal said, "I'll be taking them out with us—you're working for me now."

"Yes, sir!"

NIGHT FELL. In the tropics, when the sun goes down it gets dark fast. There is very little in between day and night. The little convoy of boats cast off and headed along the shore, traveling a half mile out to sea. No one, meaning any Japanese who had cut through the jungle to the coast, could see them.

Behind them, Singapore had all its searchlights sweeping the sky in a forlorn hope of shooting down Nip aircraft that flew over from time to time indeterminately unloading strings of bombs. The Japanese were not launching a coordinated, all-out air attack. Their air raids were intended merely to harass and terrorize.

Lt. Col. Killery was in the lead whaler with Col. Randal and Mike "Wino" Muldoon.

He said, "General Percival is planning to surrender the city tomorrow. He and Piggy Heath have been arguing about the timing for days now."

"Piggy Heath," Col. Randal said. "The general who commanded the 5th Indian Division in Abyssinia—had several car crashes—one into a camel?"

"That would be Piggy," Lt. Col. Killery said. "He has date-of-rank as a lieutenant general on Percival by a few days but is subordinate—been at each other's throats since he arrived. The two never could come to any agreement on what tactics to use to defend against the Japs—so nothing much was ever done.

"The Nips' strategy of combining speed with savagery seemed to paralyze the two generals' brains.

"A lot of good men are going to pay for their clash of egos and inability to adjust to the Japs' tactics. There's no way we should have lost this bloody thing."

"A timid commander kills more of his men than a reckless commander," Col. Randal said, quoting Sun Tzu, as he glanced back at the searchlights over Singapore. The swaying beams reminded him of a Hollywood premiere.

Only Singapore was not a movie.

After two hours, Wino turned in toward shore. They beached next to a stream; the *Big Toot II* was concealed not far away.

"We got the tug anchored about a quarter-mile upstream," Wino said. "Wait here, Colonel, while I take my boys up there to get her. We can load the passengers on board from the beach."

"Roger," Col. Randal said.

Time stood still after the tugboat crew departed. The dense jungle grew almost down to the water. It seemed dark and ominous—unless you had spent as much time in a jungle as Col. Randal had. To him the jungle was a safety buffer—there was zero likelihood any Japanese military unit of any size would force their way through it when their objective was Singapore.

The whaleboat arrived.

Wino said, "There be lights on the *Toot*—somebody's on board and it ain't anybody we know."

So much for the jungle being a safe buffer. A Japanese recon patrol must have worked its way down the watercourse to investigate the possibility of a larger force being able to reach the beach in order to use it as a high speed avenue of approach to march on Singapore.

"How many men?" Col. Randal asked.

"Hard to say," Wino said. "We saw the lights up ahead through the jungle and immediately cut the motor on the whaler. Watched a while, but we couldn't tell much."

Col. Randal called a council of war. "Wino, put your crew in the whaler. I'll be on board with you.

"Jack, Roy and King, follow in the cutter with four Marines—Corporal, you pick the three men you want to come with us."

"Yes, sir."

"Colonel Killery," Col. Randal said, "you stay here with the rest of the party and two Marines. Wait for the tug.

"You might not want to mention the fact that Japs are aboard it at the moment—you understand your orders if we do not return?"

"I do, Colonel."

"Wino," Col. Randal said, "let's ease up to the *Big Toot* and see if we can't sort this out."

The whaler cast off with four of the tug men rowing. The night was hot—one hundred percent humidity. The knowledge that the enemy was aboard the tugboat, their only way out of Malaysia, did not make the trip any more enjoyable.

The whaler was idling through a teeming jungle that was emitting all kinds of strange sounds that no one could identify. It was like a flashback for Col. Randal—to when he was on patrol sneaking up on a known encampment of Huk bandits. The sounds were reassuring—no one was out there moving around in the dark. If there had been, the jungle would have been dead quiet.

Col. Randal saw the lights at the same time Wino cut the motor and pulled the whaler up against the bank. He climbed out and walked back to the trailing boat. "I'll make a quick recon—stay here."

The ground was soft but not muddy. Col. Randal eased his way through the nipa palms. The trees were thirty feet tall. There was not a lot of underbrush in the way of ground palms.

After traveling about fifty yards, he arrived at the bank of the lagoon. Col. Randal could see the tug anchored and tied off to the bank on the far side, approximately one hundred yards across the water. There was a string of light bulbs burning, but he could detect no movement.

When he returned to the boats, he called everyone together on the bank. "Lights are on, but no one is moving around. You have any liquor stashed on the tug, Wino?"

"Tug men can't function without their daily ration of rum, Colonel—you know that."

"What could I have possibly been thinking?" Col. Randal said. "The Japs may have discovered the booze—with any luck they're passed out drunk."

"On the other hand, they might have heard your motor the first time you came up here and are waiting in ambush."

"That ain't good," Wino said.

"We're going to proceed on the second possibility," Col. Randal said. "Roy, take the corporal and his Marines . . . move around through the jungle skirting the lagoon and come up on the tug from landside.

"Jack, you, King and I will swim across the lagoon, climb up the crash tires mounted on the side of the tug—take out everyone onboard with our silenced High Standard .22s.

"Roy, if you hear firing, come on board quick and back us up."

"Yes, sir."

"Wino," Col. Randal said, "you wait here. King will swim back to bring you forward after we take down the tug."

"What if I hear gunfire?" Wino asked.

"Wait one hour," Col. Randal said. "We either win this right now here tonight or the people back on the beach are done for."

"Done for?"

"I gave Killery strict orders to shoot the civilians if we're not back by sunrise." Col. Randal said. "Don't ask me why—it's classified. I'm only telling you so you'll understand why there's firing from the beach if you're not back by daybreak."

"I'll be hoping there ain't any bloody firing," Wino said. "In either direction."

"If you fail to hear from me in one hour, Wino," Col. Randal said, "pick up Colonel Killery and the two Marines. After that, you're on your own—this never happened."

"I can see you ain't mellowed none, Colonel," Wino said, "from our Gold Coast pirate days."

"Move out, Roy," Col. Randal ordered. "I'll give you a twenty-minute head start."

The wait seemed like twenty hours. When the lime green hands on Col. Randal's Rolex watch finally showed the time had expired, he said, "Follow me."

The three Raiders crept through the nipa palm trees to the edge of the lagoon. The tug was still lit up. As before, there was no sign of movement on deck.

"Think you can swim that far, Jack?" Col. Randal whispered as he checked the action on his .22 caliber High Standard to make sure a round was in the chamber.

"I've been practicing with Lady Jane and Rocky's crew mornings," ex-Lt. Jaxx said softly as he was checking his pistol. "I'm always dead last on the swims, but it's a two-mile race. This lagoon's a snap, sir."

"That's good to know," Col. Randal said. "I thought you'd given up on working out with the girls after the first one nearly killed you."

"Rocky said I could have her," ex-Lt. Jaxx said, "if I could catch her, sir."

"Rocky said that?"

"Affirmative."

King said, "No wonder you keep going through all that torture every morning—thought you were crazy."

"I am," ex-Lt. Jaxx said. "Rocky has a way of doing that."

"You need to figure out some way to cheat, Jack," Col. Randal said. "OK—let's do this."

COLONEL JOHN RANDAL, ex-Lieutenant Billy Jack Jaxx and King slipped into the water. The three began to silently breaststroke their way toward the *Big Toot II*, heads up—eyes on the target.

Even the water felt warm.

Nothing was moving on the boat. That seemed strange. Someone had turned the lights on.

Col. Randal did not really believe they were going to find the Japs passed out drunk.

In no time the three Raiders were up against the side of the tug holding on to the old truck tires Wino had mounted on the sides to act as crash bumpers. Ex-Lt. Jaxx was on the left—he would be responsible for clearing the bow (or the mug deck, as tugboat men called it). Col. Randal was in the middle and he was going to be responsible for clearing the mid-ship area, while King, on the right, was tasked with securing the stern.

Acting as one, the Raiders began climbing. Before they could reach the deck, firing broke out from the far side—Thompson submachine guns and Lt. Kidd's distinctive ZK-383.

There was no return fire.

By the time Col. Randal swung over the top, Lt. Kidd was there standing on the far side of the tug waiting for them. Without any warning, a

Japanese soldier armed with a gleaming samurai sword sprinted up the ladder from below, bursting out on the deck. He was screaming "*BANZAI!*"

Col. Randal commenced firing instantly, working the trigger on the High Standard Military Model D as fast as he could, stitching the Jap—but the tiny .22 caliber rounds were having no noticeable effect. King was firing also. Then ex-Lt. Jaxx opened the instant he had a clear shot.

The one-man banzai charge was not slowing—while things seemed to be taking place in slow motion, the attack was happening in the blink of an eye. It was like a bad dream—the Japanese swordsman would not go down.

Then Lt. Kidd engaged from the shore with his ZK-383—a finely made Czechoslovakian weapon that literally spewed 9mm rounds, almost cutting the Japanese in half. The Nip fell dead at Col. Randal's feet, still clutching his samurai sword in both hands.

Ex-Lt. Jaxx said, "That was intense."

Col. Randal changed the empty magazine on his High Standard and swapped it for his Colt .38 Super—silence not being an issue now.

"Colonel," Lt. Kidd said, "I think you're going want to take a look at what we found over here."

"Let's finish clearing the tug first, Roy," Col. Randal said. Backed up by ex-Lt. Jaxx, he started down below. King and Lt. Kidd followed, weapons at the ready.

It was deserted. There were empty bottles rolling on the deck. The Japanese had discovered the *Big Toot II's* rum.

They had not passed out drunk.

"OK, Roy," Col. Randal said, "what is it you want to show me?"

"We killed five bad guys, sir," Lt. Kidd said. "They were having bayonet practice."

"Bayonet practice?"

"Yes, sir," Lt. Kidd said. "That's what I need you to see."

Col. Randal followed him off the tug to the bank of the lagoon. There were five dead Japanese soldiers sprawled on the ground. The Royal Marines were standing over them fingering their Thompson submachine guns.

Tied to the trunks of trees were two dead Malaysian natives—they looked like pincushions.

"I think," Lt. Kidd said, "I could really hate Japs—they were laughing when we came upon them, sir."

"I already do," ex-Lt. Jaxx said.

"King," Col. Randal said, "go tell Wino it's time to get the hell out of Dodge."

CHAPTER SIXTEEN

KILL MERLIN

THE BIG TOOT II WAS HELL in a very small place. The tugboat had been steaming for four days, dodging Japanese submarines, surface craft, enemy air, and hoping to come across a friendly ship. Only they never saw any enemy submarines, surface craft or airplanes—and not a single friendly ship or plane.

Colonel John Randal wondered if maybe everyone had been killed, sunk or had shot each other down and the tugboat was the last ship on the planet. You begin to think things like that when there are over forty people crammed in a small tugboat that had never been designed to carry passengers or make long voyages. And with the rations running out, the water going fast—sanitation out of control, the people onboard the *Big Toot II* were living a slow-motion nightmare.

The ocean was big and empty.

Most of the passengers had been seasick the entire voyage. More than a few of them were so bad off it was thought possible they might die. The crew was in particular distress; not a drop of liquor to be had since they left Singapore. The Japs had drunk it all. Some of the tugboat's crew was prostrate, suffering symptoms of advanced alcohol withdrawal.

The *Big Toot II* plowed steadily on and the tropical sun beat down.

Wino was steering for Sri Lanka. Steaming at ten knots, they should make it in six days, which meant they had two more days of sailing left—but the tug would be running on fumes by that time. The *Big Toot II* was sending out distress signals more or less nonstop, but there had been no response. Col. Randal had the radio operator continually transmit the letters GF—the agreed-upon emergency signal prior to the mission—meaning GOLDEN FLEECE.

At this point in the odyssey, some on board would welcome the sight of a Japanese destroyer flying a Rising Sun flag.

Ex-Lieutenant Billy Jack Jaxx sang out, "Aircraft eleven 'o clock—looks like a Catalina PBY."

The plane could just as easily be a Japanese flying boat—all they could see was a speck on the crystal blue horizon.

"If that's an enemy aircraft," Col. Randal ordered his Raiders and the Marines, "when it lands, on my command, open fire—concentrating on the cockpit. Give it everything you've got.

"Then you ram it, Wino."

"You lubbers get forward, cut those tires away from the mug deck," Wino shouted to his crew. Those tug crewmen who were able to stand stumbled forward and went to work slashing the ropes.

"When I hit that Jap plane, I plan to cut it in half," Wino said. "Machine-gun the survivors in the water, Colonel."

In thirty years as a sailor, this was his worst voyage—and Wino wanted payback.

"I don't think that's going to be necessary," Col. Randal said. He had spotted a red-over-green set of flares fired from the aircraft—the traditional Commando signal of success. The colors were not a coincidence.

Someone knew who they were.

"Consolidated PBY Catalina," ex-Lt. Jaxx said. "Air-Sea rescue, sir."

As word got around, people began streaming up from below. The passengers were screaming, crying and cheering when the big, beautiful PBY rescue airplane touched down in the ocean. Some were doing all three at the same time.

A large, motorized rubber raft was launched from the Catalina. It came alongside. A U.S. Navy lieutenant in khakis and a billed officer's hat boarded the tug.

He reported to Col. Randal, "Sir, Lieutenant Jackson—your receiver must be malfunctioning. We can hear your GF call, but you have not been acknowledging our response."

"Anything's possible on the *Big Toot,* Lieutenant," Col. Randal said. "She's not designed for open-sea sailing. This has been a rough trip."

Lt. Jackson said, "There's a Royal Navy Commander Fleming with some God-high security clearance who has been driving us crazy to find you. I'm to contact him immediately with a report on the status of your mission—what is your mission, sir?"

"That's classified," Col. Randal said. "You can inform the commander I have *all* the packages he sent me to collect—make sure you say *all.*"

"Yes, sir," Lt. Jackson said. "I'm to begin transferring your people immediately. How many will that be?"

"Twenty-four civilians, ten military, the crew of the tug," Col. Randal said, "and two Singapore Tea Girls."

"Colonel, the PBY can't take off with that many people on board," Lt. Jackson said.

Wino said, "You ain't taking my bloody crew anywhere, Mr. U.S. Navy. We're sailing the *Toot* to Sri Lanka—we made it this far—we're going all the way.

"Send over every drop of rum you got on that airplane of yours and some rations, sonny. We don't need that much food."

Lt. Jackson said, "We don't have any rum, sir. Just a small flask of alcohol for medicinal purposes."

"Get that medicine over here and be quick about it," Wino ordered. "We have sick men onboard—meaning me."

"Yes, sir," Lt. Jackson said. "There's a Royal Navy destroyer en route to arrive within the hour. It will escort you the rest of the way to port. Maybe they have rum on board, Skipper."

"Royal Navy, you can bet they do," Wino said. "Hardest-drinking sailors on the seven seas."

As they were talking, the first load of passengers was already making the transition to the Catalina PBY. It took four trips to transfer everyone.

Before he climbed aboard with the last group to cross, Col. Randal said, "We'll probably be gone by the time you arrive in Sri Lanka, Wino. Pay off your crew—Colonel Killery will pick up the tab—and arrange to sell your tug courtesy of an organization that does not officially exist."

"Same deal as last time, Colonel?" Wino asked. "I made out like a bandit on that one."

"Same deal—Colonel Killery has orders to escort you on board the first airplane to my headquarters when you hit port," Col. Randal said.

Wino said, "Tell Mud Cat and Warthog I can hardly wait to get the old Gold Coast firm back together again."

"I'll do that."

COLONEL JOHN RANDAL was not prepared for the reaction to the operation when he arrived back in Cairo. He thought it was no big deal. His team traveled to Singapore and did what it had to do to accomplish the mission.

That was not how anyone else saw things.

The extraction of the Far East Combined Bureau was classified. But that did not mean a lot of very important people did not know about it—including the Prime Minister of Great Britain and the President of the United States. When Col. Randal, Lieutenant Roy Kidd, ex-Lieutenant Billy-Jack Jaxx and King flew back to Cairo aboard the Raiding Forces Hudson piloted by Lieutenant Pamala Plum-Martin, they were immediately whisked to Field Marshal Claude Auchinleck's private residence for a secret awards ceremony.

As FM Auchinleck presented Col. Randal with the Order of the British Empire, he said, "We are not really sure of what to do with you, Colonel—the OBE may not be the appropriate decoration for this particular action, but it's the only one anyone can think of at this point in time. Consider it an interim award until we can sort it out.

"Congratulations on a most important mission nicely done."

When FM Auchinleck presented the Military Cross to Lt. Roy Kidd, he said, "So, you are Raiding Forces' premier truck killer. I understand there will be a slightly more public ceremony in the future, during which I shall be presenting you with an extraordinarily rare honor for a lieutenant, award of the Distinguished Service Order.

The Field Marshal came to Lt. Jaxx, "What to say, Texas—you keep running up the score. This makes your fourth MC and I have been informed you will be receiving a fifth for shooting down an enemy airplane in what has been described to me as a 'single combat.' What do they feed you cowboys?"

King received another fat envelope.

Major the Lady Jane Seaborn got Col. Randal.

When the two were ensconced behind a palm in the Gezira Club, she said, "I have never been so worried in my life—do not ever do anything like that to me again, John."

"All we . . ."

James "Baldie" Taylor arrived at their table.

"Promise I will not take up much time—three quick points, then I shall be gone, Lady Seaborn."

"You better be," Lady Jane said, flashing a watered-down version of her heart attack smile—it did not sound like she was joking.

"First, knowing you, Colonel," Jim said, "you probably do not realize what a magnificent feat you pulled off. When we heard your Catalina had been destroyed, it sent shock waves from Cairo to London to Washington.

"Percival was not being straightforward about how dire the situation was in Singapore or we would have extracted those Bureau people much sooner. Their capture would have been catastrophic to the war effort.

"Even their death would have been a major blow—some of the operators you brought out possess certain knowledge and skills that are virtually irreplaceable.

"Second," Jim said, "a couple of developments have been percolating here while you were gone. I shall give you a brief outline, and Lady Seaborn can fill you in on certain other details after I leave.

"Captain Alfred Seebohm," Jim said, "621 Radio Intercept Company—Rommel's genius radio interceptor. As you are aware, Mrs. Seaborn and Captain Honeycutt-Parker have been assigned to track the unit down.

"Nothing short of another GOLDEN FLEECE has a higher priority," Jim said. "Is that clear?"

"Crystal," Col. Randal said.

"Lastly," Jim said, "you know, on the night that you, King and Lieutenant Jaxx jumped in to assist them, Mrs. Seaborn and Captain Honeycutt-Parker made contact with an Abwehr agent tasked with transporting spies across the Great Sand Sea to Egypt?"

"I do," Col. Randal said, "no one has ever briefed me on the details."

"By the time they caught up to the Nazi, whose identity you are not cleared to know—before your team arrived on the scene—the two agents he was delivering had already departed for Cairo. Now we have a massive manhunt underway to run them to ground."

"I'm up to speed on the two spies, General," Col. Randal said. "Mandy filled me in before I left."

"Good," Jim said. "Starting immediately, Colonel, I am ordering you to take two weeks' leave for rest and recreation. However, in the event something comes up where you could aid in the capture of those two German spies—R. J. and I would take it as a personal favor if you participate."

"Count me in," Col. Randal said.

After Jim had departed, Lady Jane said, "The only spy hunting you will be doing is at our private pool at Mena House."

Col. Randal said, "Fine by me."

"I am quite aware you want to see Rocky's show at the Kit-Kat," Lady Jane said. "If you cooperate, I might let you off for good behavior a few hours one night to take it in."

Hoping to change the subject, Col. Randal said, "Mandy told me she wanted to go undercover as a dancer."

"Mandy claimed you threatened her life if she did," Lady Jane laughed. "Half of my Marines have been temporarily seconded to counterintelligence to dance at the Kit-Kat—I volunteered, but R. J. said I was too well-known in Cairo."

"You're kidding," Col. Randal said.

"Thought it might be fun, actually," Lady Jane giggled. "For King and Empire."

"What's such a big deal about two more spies in Cairo?" Col. Randal asked. "There's probably half a dozen in this restaurant right now."

"These particular Abwehr agents are thought to be highly trained professionals," Lady Jane said. "Field Marshal Auchinleck is concerned they will discover the plans for his next offensive—happened to him once before in Norway."

"So," Col. Randal said, "what's the part you're supposed to brief me in on?"

"The Rommel legend," Lady Jane said. "It has spiraled out of control. The troops are convinced he is a military genius with something close to superhuman powers—we cannot beat him.

"The Desert Fox fable has become so widespread, fistfights break out in bars if anyone disparages him."

"Really?"

"After CRUSADER, our troops are convinced Rommel must have a crystal ball that tells him all our plans, since he knows them *before* they do.

"The Desert Fox cult has become so rampant, Field Marshal Auchinleck sent out a message to all commands to be read to the men; it said Rommel was simply another enemy commander—aggressive—but no mastermind."

"How did that work out?"

"Achieved the opposite intended effect, naturally," Lady Jane said. "Once a myth takes flight, people seldom bother with facts. Besides, the Desert Fox does have a wizard with a crystal ball—Captain Alfred Seebohm of the 621st Radio Intercept Company.

"British field commanders simply cannot be convinced of the need for radio security," Lady Jane said. "Our units seldom bother with using call signs. Officers simply use each other's names. Often as not, they transmit in the clear.

"Long distance messages are sent in Morse Code. As you know, every operator has a unique typing pattern called a 'fingerprint,'" Lady Jane said.

"Since our senior commanders *never* rotate teletypists from one division or corps to another, the 621st recognizes the sender the instant they transmit. That gives away the British order of battle, which provides the Germans with a tremendous tactical advantage—completely takes away our element of surprise."

Col. Randal said, "Auchinleck's generals' outdated tactics, our inferior tanks, the RAF refusing to provide close air support, combined with a lack of signals security, that's how Rommel does it—we're beating ourselves."

"Agreed," Lady Jane said. "Now you know why it is vital for Raiding Forces to take down Seebohm's 621st—kill Merlin, explode the Desert Fox's magic crystal ball."

"Rommel's no superhero," Col. Randal said. "I'm not even convinced he's all that great of a combat commander. Every desert campaign ends with him having lost nearly all of his tanks."

"When Brandy and Parker locate the 621st and you eliminate his magician," Lady Jane said. "we shall find out."

"Roger that," Col. Randal said.

COLONEL JOHN RANDAL said, "What makes you so sure I'm interested in Rocky's show at the Kit-Kat?"

"I would be concerned," Major the Lady Jane Seaborn said, "if you were *disinterested*."

CHAPTER SEVENTEEN

SOLID GOLD

COLONEL JOHN RANDAl was stretched out by the private pool to the suite that Major the Lady Jane Seaborn kept at the exclusive Mena House Hotel. The Great Pyramid was just a few hundred yards away.

Lady Jane and Lieutenant Mandy Paige, in matching black French-cut swimsuits, were sitting at the end of the pool at a glass-topped table getting manicures done by a pair of Egyptian girls from the hotel's salon.

Rita Hayworth and Lana Turner, the slave girls Col. Randal had liberated in Abyssinia, were floating on rafts.

Col. Randal was having a nice day.

One of Lady Jane's Royal Marines walked out wearing shorts and a crop top—she was on duty at the door since King was on semi-leave, checking in several times a day to see if his services were required.

"Captain Reupart to see you, Colonel."

"Send him out, Stephanie," Col. Randal said.

Captain Roy "Mad Dog" Reupart was the Raiding Forces Training Officer when he was not leading desert patrols. He was recovering from an injury suffered during the CRUSADER Operation. Capt. Reupart had been with Raiding Forces since they went through No. 1 British Parachute School—he had trained the Raiders, then volunteered to join the unit. In Col. Randal's opinion, Mad Dog was the best trainer of troops in the army.
"Pull up a chair, Roy," Col. Randal said.

"Yes, sir."

"We received a cable stating that Captain McCloud will be arriving tomorrow with the fifty-man contingent of U.S. Paratroop volunteers that we've been expecting for Raiding Forces," Col. Randal said. "I need them qualified for Desert Patrol as soon as possible—you up to that?"

"Yes, sir." Capt. Reupart said. "You know, Colonel, my wish is to reconstitute my patrol and return to active patrolling."

"I do," Col. Randal said. "And, you can—only you're more valuable to me right now as a trainer."

"Thank you, sir," Capt. Reupart said. "Is there anything different about this batch of volunteers I should take into consideration?"

"I've been thinking about that," Col. Randal said. "These men will be in U.S. uniform—not replacements for the American Volunteer Group."

"You want them to operate as a unit, sir?"

"Negative," Col. Randal said. "At least not until they have five or six months under their belts spent on operations. I understand there'll be three officers in the group and six NCOs. What I want you to do is evaluate the leaders and give me a private report from time to time."

"Can do, Colonel."

"Since Travis handpicked these volunteers, I expect they'll be good men. Weed out any you feel won't be a good fit," Col. Randal said. "We have to reorganize, so be prepared to advise our Desert Patrol Leaders who need replacements about how individuals in the group perform during your training—they'll be asking."

"Yes, sir—right man, right job."

"Sergeant Rawlston believes Americans make the best jeep drivers because they grew up driving. Factor that in when you make your recommendations."

"I agree with Sergeant Rawlston's assessment, sir," Capt. Reupart said. "We shall make a point to identify the best drivers."

"Perfect."

"With your permission, Colonel," Capt. Reupart said, "I would like to borrow a few of the Blue Patrol ex-Foreign Legion men for the initial phase of the training—getting acclimated to the desert."

"Pick anyone you like—Sergeant Major Mikkalis has already been notified to assist, at least on a temporary basis," Col. Randal said.

"I'm going to need a replacement Blue Patrol leader. Has to speak French and be able to handle the toughest soldiers we've got—any thoughts?"

"Not at the moment, Colonel."

"Come with me to meet the troopship when it arrives tomorrow," Col. Randal said. "Get the new men settled in at RFHQ, then start your training program the next day."

Soon after Sgt. Reupart departed, Brandy arrived wearing a snow-white swimsuit. She waved at Col. Randal. The golden girl took Lt. Mandy's place at the glass-topped table. One of the manicurists started working on her nails while she and Lady Jane chatted.

Lt. Mandy came over and stretched out on the lounge next to Col. Randal.

"Guess what?"

"OK—what?"

"Y-Service has intercepted several Afrika Korps radio communiqués to its outlying posts advising them to be on the lookout for Auto Gyro helicopters."

"Really?"

"Fabulous idea, John," Lt. Mandy said. "My first radio deception worked like a dream—R. J. is impressed. Love you."

"I guess that lets Rocky off the hook?" Col. Randal said.

"Actually, no," Lt. Mandy said. "Intelligence is complicated. Rocky may have realized we were testing her. No harm, from her point of view, if a few remote Italian outposts are placed on the lookout for phantom helicopters if it solidifies our confidence in her."

Col. Randal said, "I can see how that might be."

"On the other hand," Lt. Mandy laughed, "Captain Merryweather is having Teddy—he's back at Eton—make recordings of Royal Navy helicopters that are in the experimental stage for use on submarines. Colonel Clarke is having the recordings flown here on a priority basis.

"Dudley wants you to order our patrols to play them through loudspeakers outside remote Italian outposts at night—something he calls 'sonic deception.' The idea is to drive the bad guys crazy."

"We can do that," Col. Randal said.

Lt. Mandy said, "Remember I told you about the two Abwehr spies on the loose in Cairo?"

"I do."

"They went straight to the Kit-Kat Club," Lt. Mandy giggled. "Exactly the way Sammy Sansom predicted. He was in the club, saw two men at a table and one of them was lighting a cigarette with a fifty-pound note—turned out to be the Nazis. Sammy is a brilliant counterintelligence operator.

"Somehow he struck up a friendship with the spies. Like something out of the movies."

"No kidding," Col. Randal said. Now he would not be going to see Rocky dance. Oh well.

"Classified—we did not have this conversation, John," Mandy said. "*You* do not have a need to know."

"Roger."

"On a different subject, strictly off the record . . . another conversation we never had, Lady Jane cried her eyes out when we learned your Catalina had been destroyed in the harbor at Singapore," Lt. Mandy said.

"That's not good."

"Brandy was inconsolable. Rita and Lana teared up too," Lt. Mandy said. "No one thought the girls even knew how to cry."

"What about you, Mandy—shed any tears?"

"Just for show, John," Lt. Mandy laughed. "I knew you would have an ace up your sleeve."

Rita and Lana were summoned to have their nails done. Lady Jane and Lt. Mandy took their places on the rafts. Brandy came over and stretched out next to Col. Randal.

He always enjoyed talking to her; they were close friends.

"Gave us a real scare, handsome," Brandy said, rubbing some oil on one of her perfect, golden legs.

"Sounded worse than it was," Col. Randal said.

"Not what Billy Jack says."

"You can't believe him."

"King backed his story up."

"Well," Col. Randal said, "the trip did have its moments—*Big Toot II* was not a luxury cruise liner."

"John, the surrender of Singapore is the single most humiliating defeat in the entire history of the British Empire," Brandy said. "The Prime Minister stated publicly that our troops failed to fight—is that true?"

"Strictly between us," Col. Randal said, "I told Jane there was no way Singapore, with over eighty thousand troops, could have been taken by a force of twenty thousand Japanese—attacking down the length of Malaya through a jungle.

"The odds were all in our favor and there was plenty of time to prepare defenses. The word is, Percival refused to allow any earthworks to be constructed on the land side because it would 'be bad for morale.'"

"Seriously?" Brandy said.

"You can't make this stuff up," Col. Randal said.

"With your experience operating in the jungle against the Huks," Brandy said, "surely you must have thoughts on why we lost, John."

Col. Randal said, "Bad leadership."

"Exactly what Father says," Brandy said. "He believes Percival should have been able to whip the Japanese after their long, overland-approach march through the jungle, 'with eighty thousand Boy Scouts.'"

"Is the Razor back from England?"

"Flew in this morning."

"If you see him before I do, tell him I have another skipper for him," Col. Randal said. "'Wino' Muldoon."

"John, you *do* know colorful people."

"I know you, Brandy," Col. Randal said. "You're solid gold."

"Yes, I am," Brandy laughed, oiling the other equally perfect leg. "Now, to business—as you are aware, Parker and I are on a mission to hunt down Captain Alfred Seebohm and his 621st Radio Intercept Company."

"Do you have a plan?"

"Not at the moment," Brandy said. "Parker organized a small operations center at RFHQ for us to work out of. We shall be collecting signals intelligence from our Y-Service in an attempt to pinpoint the 621st location long enough for you to deal with it. But that poses a challenge.

"Seebohm is the acknowledged master of signals intelligence—he will never make a stupid mistake that gives away his position. My guess is the 621st shall be constantly relocating to throw us off the trail."

"You can bank on it," Col. Randal said.

"Everyone slips up, Seebohm will too . . . eventually," Brandy said. "When we do gain actionable intelligence on the 621st, Raiding Forces is going to have to react fast. That means a team of Raiders constantly on standby with transport aircraft, gun jeeps or whatever else you need ready to swing into action."

"We're going to require outside support, Brandy," Col. Randal said. "All our aircraft, with the exception of the Hudson, and most of our equipment, other than the gun jeeps, consists of obsolete hand-me-downs no one else has any use for. Even our jeeps are total wrecks after CRUSADER.

"We don't have what it takes for a high-speed, low-drag assignment like yours."

"I met with Field Marshal Auchinleck to discuss the mission," Brandy said. "He agreed to provide us with a blank check. In his mind, eliminating the 621st is the highest priority mission in Middle East Command—even higher than GOLDEN FLEECE.

"Questions, John?"

Col. Randal asked, "Is there a requirement to take Seebohm prisoner?"

"We prefer alive in order to interrogate him," Brandy said. "Dead is fine."

"Who am I working for?"

"Me," Brandy said, and for once she was not laughing. "Are you OK with that, John?"

"I am." Col. Randal asked, "Does the operation have a name?"

"Not yet."

"Does now," Col. Randal said. "OPERATION SOLID GOLD."

MAJOR SIR TERRY "ZORRO" STONE arrived poolside with Red. He was still shaky, recovering from his wound. Doctor Stephen Milam had cleared him for "extreme" light duty.

Major the Lady Jane Seaborn said, "We have spare swimsuits in the guest bedroom, Red."

Brandy said, "Hi Terry, you are looking much better," as she got up off the lounge and slipped into the shallow end of the pool.

Rita and Lana twittered like canaries. Generally ambivalent to men, they thought Maj. Stone looked like movie star Errol Flynn.

While Red disappeared into the suite to change, Maj. Stone pulled up a chair next to Colonel John Randal.

"Keeping extraordinarily high-quality female company as usual, old stick," Maj. Stone said. "How does one keep one's concentration around this pool?"

"Who said anything about concentrating?" Col. Randal said. "Especially since Jane has a hard time getting Rita and Lana to keep their tops on."

"I understand the girls are stars at the Kit-Kat," Maj. Stone said. "Now that I am up and around, I intend to make it a point to drop in to catch Rocky's next show. Word is it's something one has to experience at least once in a lifetime—see Rome, and die.

"Rocky may not be dancing anymore," Col. Randal said.

"Just the luck," Maj. Stone said.

"What are you doing here, Terry? Light duty means resting at RFHQ or the hotel of your choice in Cairo. I need you to recover as soon as possible. A major reorganization is in the works."

"Precisely what I wanted to talk to you about, old stick," Maj. Stone said. "Like we discussed earlier, I prefer to focus on commanding the regiment.

"Father is recruiting—sending new men to parachute training and then to Special Warfare Training Center. However, our county is sparsely populated, and he only has a small pool of men to draw from. He wired me that there were twenty-two brand new, fully-trained Lancers en route to Egypt as we speak."

"I can appreciate that, Terry," Col. Randal said.

"Why don't we work it this way—we'll *attach* the Lounge Lizards to Desert Patrol—not *assign* them. That way you can be promoted to Lieutenant Colonel but still be under the administrative control of Desert Patrol."

"An elegant solution," Maj. Stone said. "The Duke shall be pleased. However, be advised that he is going to want to keep the Americans we currently have assigned. Hands across the sea and all that."

"No problem," Col. Randal said. "A contingent of fifty new U.S. Paratroop volunteers will be arriving tomorrow. Get with Mad Dog—pick out all you need."

Red came outside in a green swimsuit that looked like it had been painted on. The Clipper Girl was a stunner. Unlike most redheads, she was tanned almost chocolate brown—no freckles.

"I shall go inside for a nap on your couch," Maj. Stone said. "In my weakened condition, it's probably wise to take the scenery out here in small doses."

"Roger that," Col. Randal said.

"R. J. AND A COLONEL FELLERS TO SEE YOU, COLONEL."

"Send 'em out, Stephanie."

Colonel John Randal knew Brigadier Raymond J. Maunsell, who seldom dressed in uniform and liked to be called "R. J.," quite well. Major the Lady Jane Seaborn had mentioned Colonel Bonner Fellers, the United States Army attaché in Cairo, several times. He had never met him.

The two senior officers pulled up chairs and sat down.

"John, let me introduce you to Bonner Fellers," R. J. said.

Col. Fellers said, "Your reputation has preceded you, Colonel."

"So has yours," Col. Randal said.

Lady Jane had said everyone liked and respected the American. He had been all over the battlefield observing OPERATION CRUSADER in a civilian private-purchase automobile.

Jim had mentioned that Col. Fellers sent daily dispatches back to his boss, Lieutenant General George C. Marshall, Army Chief of Staff, and that President Roosevelt ordered copies, which he called his "Little Fellers," to be hand-carried to his office as soon as they arrived so that he could personally read each one.

R. J. said, "As we discussed, John, I have been working out the details for your transfer back to the U.S. Army. Here is what we have arrived at—you transfer in grade of full colonel. Is that satisfactory with you?"

"It is."

"You will continue in command of the Strategic Raiding Forces, provided there is an assurance from you to expand it to include an equal-sized contingent of U.S. to British troops. Colonel Donovan, director of the U.S. Office of Coordinator of Information, will supply you with the personnel from Airborne Command at Ft. Benning."

"I like that."

"James Taylor will serve as the Special Operations liaison between COI and MEHQ. Your chain-of-command will remain unchanged. Is that acceptable?"

"It is," Col. Randal said, wondering what his chain-of-command *was* exactly. That had never been made clear to him.

Raiding Forces was simply assigned high-priority missions as they came up and otherwise left alone to fight the war as they saw fit, concentrating on hitting strategic targets like enemy wheeled truck transport and fuel depots, killing Axis pilots where they congregated, shutting down enemy rail lines, etc.

"Now for the icing on the cake," R. J. said. "Bonner, would you care to explain?"

Col. Fellers said, "The U.S. Army is going through a massive expansion. The plan, which is classified, is to raise one hundred divisions.

"Unfortunately, we face shortages of everything—during the Louisiana Maneuvers, our troops used logs to represent anti-tank weapons, wooden rifles to teach drill and ceremonies. We do not have enough tanks for our own armored divisions being formed, much less enough to continue supplying armored vehicles to Russia and Great Britain at our current pace.

"The powers that be in Washington intend to send Air Corps and support units to Egypt, which the Chief of Staff tends to view as a strategic backwater, but no ground combat troops—the General Staff want to invade Fortress Europe across the Channel first thing."

"Good luck," Col. Randal said.

"My sentiments exactly," Col. Fellers said. "It could take years before we're ready to attempt a complex operation of such magnitude—the brass are not listening to me on the subject.

"All that said, the thinking in high places is that the United States Army could benefit from having a token combat unit in Egypt as a demonstration of our support for our British allies.

"If you agree to the terms R. J. has laid out," Col. Fellers said, "a regiment of parachute infantry will be dispatched to your command by the first available transport."

"You want to assign a PIR to Raiding Forces?"

"Affirmative."

"So," Col. Randal said, "what am I supposed to do with it, exactly?"

Col. Fellers looked him dead in the eye, "Whatever you want—no strings attached. It's a token gesture. There will not be any other ground troops assigned to this theatre of operations. You will be the senior U.S. ground commander in Egypt."

"What say you, John?" R. J. asked.

"Parachute infantry is useless in the desert without wheeled transport," Col. Randal said. "To be of any value, the regiment needs one jeep for every three men, one three-quarter-ton truck per platoon, and half-dozen two-and-a-half-ton trucks per battalion."

"Consider it done," Col. Fellers said, a little too quickly. Col. Randal felt the faint ding of an alarm bell go off, but he could not understand why.

"Do we have a deal?"

"We have to work out the details of the American Volunteer Group transfer back to the U.S. Army also," Col. Randal said. "I need to be able to promote experienced leaders."

"As the commander of an independent regiment, you are authorized to promote anyone up to the rank of major," Col. Fellers said.

Col. Randal glanced at R. J., who gave him an almost imperceptible nod.

"We have a deal."

EX-LIEUTENANT BILLY JACK JAXX ARRIVED at the pool. Colonel John Randal waved him over to where he and Major the Lady Jane Seaborn were sunning on the lounges.

"Sorry to interrupt your leave," Col. Randal said. "I have a mission for you."

Ex-Lt. Jaxx looked around the pool, "I wish you'd interrupted a little earlier, sir."

Lady Jane laughed.

"Brandy Seaborn is involved in a highly-classified mission. I'll let her brief you on the details," Col. Randal said.

"The short version is, we need to set up a Quick Reaction Force to respond to a specific target that is highly mobile and prone to relocate frequently.

"I want you to be my deputy commander. Select the team, which will be on standby—ready to deploy at a moment's notice," Col. Randal said.

"Pam will be tasked to fly the mission."

"In the event I'm not available when the operation launches, you lead it."

"Yes, sir."

"Field Marshal Auchinleck believes this mission is the most important in the Middle East Command's theatre of operations—keep that in mind, Jack, at all times.

"Brandy is overall commander, we report to her—which means you do when I'm not here."

"You want me to work for Mrs. Seaborn?" ex-Lt. Jaxx said, looking at Brandy floating on a raft in the pool.

"Affirmative."

"Wow!"

MAJOR SAMMY SANSOM ARRIVED. Stephanie, the Royal Marine, escorted him out to the pool. The Chief of Cairo Field Security came over to where Colonel John Randal and Major the Lady Jane Seaborn were sunning.

Maj. Sansom said, "Lady Seaborn, could you give us a moment?"

"Certainly," Lady Jane said, getting up and slipping into the pool.

Lieutenant Mandy Paige strolled over and stretched out in Lady Jane's place on the lounge.

"I will cut straight to the chase, Colonel," Maj. Sansom said. "Mrs. Seaborn and 'Legs' Parker intercepted a high-value enemy desert expert out of Tripoli whose mission has been to deliver Abwehr agents to cities in Egypt. Unfortunately, as you already know, the two agents the Nazi was delivering on this trip had already departed for Cairo before the women caught up to him on the last leg of what the Abwehr calls OPERATION KONDOR.

"The two spies were soon discovered in the Kit-Kat, attempting to make social contacts with the patrons in hopes of using them, with or without their knowledge. The idiots recruited me.

"Both men are staying on a houseboat moored on the Nile next door to Hekmet Fahmey's—the feature dancer at the club.

"The Jewish Intelligence Agency, the Haganah, sent in a female agent who slept with one or both of the Nazis, then searched their houseboat after they were asleep. She found a long-range transmitter concealed in a cabinet. We believe there is a second radio, delivered by a disaffected Egyptian army officer named Anwar Sadat, hidden on Hekmet's houseboat.

"After the club closes tonight, I have promised to take the two Kondor spies to meet with a group of anti-British Arab League revolutionaries.

"We need you to show up at the Kit-Kat, Colonel, pick up Hekmet and take her to dinner on a floating restaurant while Mandy and a team of my people clandestinely search her houseboat for the second radio."

Col. Randal said. "Haven't we tried that before?"

"Yes, we have," Maj. Sansom said. "Only this time, don't sleep with the target, and for God's sake don't shoot her."

THE KIT-KAT WAS PULSATING when Colonel John Randal arrived, crowded with wealthy Egyptians, civilian merchants of half-dozen nationalities, officers from the best regiments on leave from the desert and the usual complement of "gabardine swine" from MEHQ.

Mo, the manager of the club, made a big show of having one of his staff carry a table up to the very edge of the dance floor for Col. Randal, giving him the best seat in the house. Another member of the Kit-Kat staff produced a white tablecloth while the first came back with a pair of chairs. A waiter arrived with a magnum of champagne.

The show was in full swing—Rita and Lana were doing a dance that would have gotten them arrested at the Muthaiga Country Club in Kenya—which was thought to be impossible.

Rocky appeared at the table and sat down. Col. Randal signaled a waiter, who arrived with a second glass, popped the cork on the bottle of bubbly, and poured the champagne.

To say that Col. Randal was the center of attention in the smoke-filled room—second only to Rita and Lana—would have been a major understatement.

"Here is what is going to take place, John," Rocky said in her sexy Norwegian accent. "The Royal Marine dancers, Rita, Lana, and I will flirt with you outrageously tonight. Ignore us at first. Even though we come and sit at your table, do not talk to us.

"When Hekmet dances, make full eye contact with her, but never smile. Do not make any overt gesture to invite her to your table. Let her make the first move.

"Dancers cannot stand rejection. They are fiercely competitive when it comes to men. The first time Hekmet comes to sit at your table, give her champagne but do not talk to her—watch the girl performing.

"Then when the Raiding Forces girls come to your table the next time, flirt with us and laugh. Give us champagne. Hekmet will be jealous. She is used to being the center of attention.

"In the dressing room, Hekmet will inquire who you are and we shall say that you are a great hero and a magnificent lover but you have a paramour—Lady Jane. All this will make you irresistible to her.

"Most of the girls make dinner dates for after the show. Do not ask. Make Hekmet invite you—she will.

"You suggest the place Lady Jane told you about—it's her favorite."

Rocky leaned across the table and kissed Col. Randal on the cheek, then she was gone as Rita and Lana finished their dance to the sound of pounding drums and crashing symbols.

Col. Randal looked around the darkened, smoke-filled room. King was sitting at the bar. Ex-Lieutenant Billy Jack Jaxx was at another table, chatting up a Hungarian dancer.

Major Sammy Sansom, wearing an off-white linen suit, was at a table with a couple of men. He appeared to be drunk.

Rita and Lana shimmied up to Col. Randal's table, ringing and clapping their finger cymbals. They rubbed up against him like cats. The girls were clearly trying to steal the show from the next performer.

Dancers have been known to do that.

Rita and Lana finally sat down at the table and the waiter appeared with two more glasses. Since the two Zar priestesses had vowed never to speak to him except in a life-or-death emergency, that made ignoring them—per Rocky's instructions—a snap.

After drinking their champagne, the girls gave him big beautiful smiles, then vanished into the crowd on their way to the dressing room.

The rest of the night proceeded exactly according to script. Major Sir Terry "Zorro" Stone was right—Rocky's show was the Eighth Wonder of the World.

The feature dancer, Hekmet Fahmey, turned out to be about ten times more beautiful than Col. Randal had counted on. Golden complexion that rivaled Brandy's, dark hair, exotic green eyes—a lot like Lady Jane's. Exuded sex.

At 0200 hours the two of them found themselves alone on the roof of one of the more expensive Nile River restaurants in a private, open-topped pavilion formed by curtains. Ten million stars were gleaming in the sky.

Col. Randal and Hekmet were reclining on couches opposite each other, sipping more champagne. There was electricity in the air. He was pretty sure that she was a witch—or possibly Cleopatra reincarnated.

Nothing good could possibly come from this.

Major the Lady Jane Seaborn arrived unannounced and unexpected, in the best tradition of Raiding Forces, storming through the curtain that served as the entrance. She grabbed the bottle of champagne that was icing down in a tall, three-legged bucket and threw it at Col. Randal, while screaming at Hekmet in three different languages.

The dancer was so shocked she appeared paralyzed.

Col. Randal certainly was—this had not been part of the plan.

"I should kill you," Lady Jane shrieked at Hekmet, as she reached for the ivory-gripped Colt .38 Super at her waist.

"Jane," Col. Randal yelled, getting tangled up in the table alongside the couch as he was trying to get up. "Don't . . .

"Stay out of this, John," Lady Jane shouted, fumbling for the pistol. "You piece of *frogspawn!*"

Uh-oh!

Col. Randal jumped up, knocking over the table, grabbed Lady Jane and threw her over his shoulder. He tossed a roll of money to Hekmet, "Pay the bill, call a cab—I'll get Jane out of here before she does shoot you."

Then he went down the stairs, taking them two at a time with Jane hanging over his shoulder. Col. Randal ran out of the restaurant and across the gangplank to the shore, where he found Lady Jane's Rolls-Royce parked, with King leaning against the side of the car.

Without a word, King opened the back door and stood aside as Col. Randal threw Lady Jane on the back seat. She was laughing so hard that tears were streaming down her cheeks.

King ran around, climbed in behind the wheel and floored the Rolls as Col. Randal jumped in the back.

"Jane, what the hell?"

"You should have seen the look on your face," Lady Jane said, laughing harder. "Great fun."

"Not for me," Col. Randal said. "Was this on from the start?"

"Yes, it was," Lady Jane said. "How were *you* planning to conclude the evening's festivities, John?"

Col. Randal decided that was a question for another time. "I was simply following my orders—someone should have informed me."

"We wanted to keep it real," Lady Jane said, laughing so hard she started to hiccup.

"Real," Col. Randal said. "You nearly nailed me with that champagne bottle—I thought you were about to shoot Hekmet."

"Possibly have done her a favor if I had," Lady Jane said.

"Mandy found the second radio."

CHAPTER EIGHTEEN

U.S. 71ST AIRBORNE DIVISION

COLONEL JOHN RANDAL AND MAJOR the Lady Jane Seaborn were on the dock when the ship carrying ex-Captain Travis McCloud and fifty U.S. Paratroop volunteers for Raiding Forces arrived. A convoy of gun jeeps was waiting to transport the men to RFHQ. Any infusion of new troops was always an exciting time.

Every patrol, with the single exception of Lieutenant Roy Kidd's Scout Patrol, needed replacements. The plan was to make the new troops feel part of Raiding Forces from the minute they arrived. Captain Mike "Mad Dog" Reupart, who was still on light duty, had orders to get them desert-qualified in the shortest amount of time possible—a "gentleman's course," where the idea was to teach—not harass. Then the patrol leaders would be allowed to make their selections.

Any man who did not measure up would be quietly removed from the program or dropped from the patrol they were assigned to in the event they did not perform up to standard. Since these men were all triple volunteers—volunteered for the army, volunteered for Jump School and volunteered for hazardous service with Raiding Forces—and then hand-picked by ex-Capt. McCloud, Col. Randal was not expecting much of a loss rate.

Lady Jane was almost beside herself with anticipation. She had adopted Raiding Forces as her personal pet project when the unit was in its infancy, struggling to learn how to conduct its first pinprick raids against the French Coast. Even though she'd been offered other, much more prestigious assignments, she had steadfastly stayed with the Raiders from Seaborn House to the Gold Coast, then to Abyssinia and Egypt.

Now, with the United States in the war, Raiding Forces was going to be the recipient of the first contingent of American fighting men in U.S. uniform to deploy to the Middle East Command's theatre of operations.

Colonel Dudley Clarke and a gaggle of photographers, including a film crew, were on hand to record the arrival. Normally troop movements are classified. However, this one was a major event, a turning point in the war—America was swinging into action.

Except it wasn't.

These fifty U.S. paratroopers would be the only American combat troops to serve in Egypt until the arrival of the independent airborne regiment Col. Randal had been promised. And that would be *all* the U.S. Army's fighting men coming to Egypt.

There was, however, no need for the Germans to be let in on that particular piece of information. Ex-Capt. McCloud's men would be billed as the advance party of a massive U.S. Army troop movement to Middle East Command. Photos would appear in newspapers worldwide. Col. Clarke had always wanted a parachute battalion for his deception operations, and now he was going to turn these fifty jumpers into one in a very public way.

The A-Force commander had already obtained Col. Randal's OK to allow the new Raiding Forces volunteers to make daily demonstration jumps in sight of Cairo, before or after their training. Real live jumpers were going to be a lot better than the pseudo parachutists made out of duffel bags filled with sand that A-Force had been using for deception most of the last year—actual paratroopers could be dropped closer to town.

The Middle East Command's band was standing by. Field Marshal Claude Auchinleck arrived in his staff car to take part in the deception.

Ex-Capt. McCloud was followed down the gangplank by the volunteers, carrying their duffle bags over one shoulder, wearing their overseas caps with the round parachute patch stitched on the left side at a jaunty angle and their pants blousing into brown, spit-shined Cochran jump boots. The band started blaring "Stars and Stripes Forever." Dockworkers and spectators who had gathered around when they heard "the Yanks were coming" began cheering. Sailors on other ships ran to the rails to see what was happening and joined in the celebration. Soon, ship's captains all over the harbor were tooting their horns and ordering their fire hoses sprayed in salute.

Col. Clarke said to one of his cameramen, "Get a shot of those jump boots."

Ex-Capt. McCloud called the volunteers into formation—three ranks.

"Capt. McCloud and fifty U.S. volunteers reporting for duty, sir!"

Col. Randal returned his salute, then he and Lady Jane, accompanied by ex-Capt. McCloud, did a slow walk-through inspection. This was mainly for show, a mark of respect, and would most likely be the last formation these men would hold for a long time—Raiding Forces not being known for standing on ceremony. The troops had a hard time keeping their eyes locked to the front when Lady Jane came by.

More than a few were wondering what they had gotten themselves into.

Col. Randal reported to FM Auchinleck—he took up a position to his left with Lady Jane as ex-Capt. McCloud marched the U.S. contingent of Raiding Forces past him. The Field Marshal took the salute.

As soon as everyone was aboard the jeeps, the convoy was away to RFHQ. Col. Randal and Lady Jane were in the lead gun jeep with the colonel at the wheel. The moment the convoy pulled out of sight, on signal from Col. Clarke, a banner on poles went up.

The cameras zoomed in.

"WELCOME U.S. 71st AIRBORNE DIVISION"

There *was* no U.S. 71st Airborne Division.

CAPTAIN "GERONIMO" JOE MCKOY and Waldo Treywick were waiting at RFHQ. The pair had returned from their real estate tour of West Coast properties the night before. They had spent the entire morning supervising the chefs from the exclusive Bradford Hotel in the gentle art of cooking Bar-B-Q.

None of the Bradford chefs had ever even heard of Bar-B-Q, but they soon got into the spirit of a new culinary adventure. The sauce was a complete mystery, but Capt. McKoy gladly shared his "secret" recipe, which he confessed "would be a lot better if we had us about a half-a' fifth a' tequila to throw in it"—but alas, there was no tequila to be had in Cairo.

Capt. McKoy also decided that the new U.S. volunteers might like to have "a batch-a' hush-puppies." This idea caused a certain amount of angst among the cook staff. The Bradford men were willing to slaughter two steers for the feast but drew the line at cooking puppies. They relented when the ex-Arizona Ranger explained the ingredients consisted primarily of cornmeal—not little dogs.

Problem was, once the chefs prepared the hush-puppies, they ate most of them.

They all agreed the Bar-B-Q went down especially well with Egyptian Stella Beer. There were cases of the green bottles—sporting the yellow label with its distinctive blue star—on ice, waiting for the festivities to begin. Word was, if you drank enough Stella Beer you could go blind.

When the convoy arrived, it was greeted by a party of fifty Raiders under the supervision of Sergeant Mike "March or Die" Mikkalis. The Raiding Forces men shouldered the paratrooper's duffel bags and carried them into the barracks (a converted horse stable) that had been reserved for the new arrivals. Inside were bunk beds that were made up and waiting—like you would find in a luxury hotel.

The idea was to welcome the Americans—make them feel a part of the team from the start.

As the troops were getting settled in, Major Jeb Pelham-Davies was showing the three officers, Captain Duke Slater, Lieutenant Richard "Dynamite Dick" Coogan and Lieutenant Dan Morgan, to the transient officer-quarters building. Enough rooms were available so that every officer in Raiding Forces had his own, though they were seldom at RFHQ to occupy them.

"How did your trip go?" Col. Randal asked Capt. McKoy.

"John," Capt. McKoy said, "people are flat giving land *away* on the West Coast. They're in a panic—what's bein' called the 'Jap Flap.' Sorta a reverse Oklahoma Land Rush. I ain't never seen anything like it."

"Why?"

"A Jap submarine lobbed a few shells ashore at one of the oil refineries and that caused a scare," Capt. McKoy said. "Then they had what everybody's calling 'The Battle of Los Angeles.' That happened while we was out there.

"Anti-aircraft guns goin' off all night long. Nobody knows what they was shootin' at but, accordin' to witnesses, it weren't no weather balloon like the Army claims. And, that was all she wrote on the price a' real estate.

"Me and Waldo bought us about ten thousand adjacent acres apiece up at Malibu. Best lookin' beachfront you ever saw makes up about ten miles of our property line.

"Scooped up another twelve thousand acres outside Hollywood in the hills for investment. We may be developers after the war—when we ain't raisin' palomino quarter horses up at Malibu."

"Land barons," Col. Randal said. "Sounds like you two did well."

"Crazy good," Capt. McKoy said. "We was buyin' prime real estate for ten cents on the dollar and gettin' the mineral rights—them Japs ain't ever gonna invade California. How would they get there?"

"They can't," Col. Randal said. "But the Japanese may take over all of China, Asia and the Philippines. I think our side has way underestimated the capabilities of the Land of the Rising Sun."

"Heard you had yourself a little Jap problem while I's gone," Capt. McKoy said. "Singapore just rolled over?"

Col. Randal said, "Didn't fight back."

"Word is," Capt. McKoy said, "the Japs are driving on Bataan. General MacArthur is holed up on Corregidor—that don't sound too good."

"No," Col. Randal said, "it doesn't."

James "Baldie" Taylor arrived with Brigadier Raymond J. Maunsell, who liked to be called R. J., and Colonel Bonner Fellers, the U.S. Army attaché to Middle East Command. Ostensibly, the three were there to be social. Vice Admiral Sir Randolph "Razor" Ransom showed up as they were parking their car.

All of Major the Lady Jane Seaborn's Royal Marines were present as well as Veronica Paige. Red had come with two of her Clipper Girl girlfriends from the flight to Singapore who may have been looking for ex-Lieutenant Billy Jack Jaxx and King. Brandy Seaborn and Captain Penelope "Legs" Honeycutt-Parker were present. Even Rikke Runborg, *aka* Rocky, was sampling the Bar-B-Q.

Col. Randal pulled aside ex-Captain Travis McCloud and ex-Lt. Jaxx.

"I'll be transferring back to the U.S. Army shortly," Col. Randal said. "As part of my inducement package, an independent Parachute Infantry Regiment is being shipped to Egypt for me to command in conjunction with Raiding Forces."

"That's terrific, sir," ex-Lt. Jaxx said.

"We'll see," Col. Randal said. "But here's the interesting part—as the commander of an independent regiment I can promote people up to the rank of major.

"What I want to do, Travis, is to promote you to major. Not sure yet in what capacity; be thinking about it. Jack, I'm promoting you to captain—youngest in the army.

"That work for you men?"

"Yes, sir!" both officers chorused.

"We need to figure out what to do with our AVG troops," Col. Randal said. "The army wants them to re-enlist. Give me recommendations on the men you endorse for promotion in the enlisted grades. I want your opinions on anyone who you believe might be a candidate for a direct commission.

"Get back to me."

"Roger, sir," ex-Capt. McCloud said. "Let's make separate lists, Jack, then compare notes—then we can talk to the other Patrol Leaders."

"Yes, sir," ex-Lt. Jaxx said.

The young Texan was a late arrival to Raiding Forces, but in the time he had been there he had made his presence felt. Now he was being elevated into the upper command echelon.

"When we do transfer," Col. Randal said, "you'll be sworn in at your new grade."

He handed each of them one of Waldo's custom-rolled cigars, and all three lit up with his battered U.S. 26th Cavalry Regiment Zippo.

"Congratulations, gentlemen."

When Col. Randal saw Lieutenant Butch "Headhunter" Hoolihan walk by, he said, "Butch, do you have a moment?"

"Yes, sir."

The two walked off a short distance. Lt. Hoolihan had been with Col. Randal from the day he had pulled him out of a club car on a train to stand guard over his private compartment while the initial concept of OPERATION TOMCAT was being briefed. The Royal Marine had been commissioned in the field, having jumped in with the three-man advance party of Force N.

Col. Randal said, "Pick your replacement, Butch—I'm sending you to Achnacarry to do a tour as an instructor at Special Warfare Training Center."

"Bloody hell, sir . . ."

"You've been on constant operations longer than anyone in Raiding Forces. You're going—is that clear, Lieutenant?"

Lt. Hoolihan was Col. Randal's most highly-prized junior officer. He had earned that status the hard way—in the field behind enemy lines under harsh and desperate conditions. It was time for him to have a break.

"Yes, sir."

"Four months," Col. Randal said. "Then come back and have any job you want. Fair?"

"Roger," Lt. Hoolihan said. "Thank you, sir—I could use a break from the *King Duck*. What a beast of a ship."

VAdm. Ransom walked over. "I understand you have another skipper for me, Colonel—Wino Muldoon?"

"Yes, sir," Col. Randal said. "He was one of the three tugboat captains on OPERATION LOUNGE LIZARD out of the Gold Coast—which you're not supposed to know anything about, Admiral."

"I know nothing about the operation at all," VAdm. Ransom lied. He knew every detail.

"I met Skipper Muldoon at the reception after Raiding Forces' Investiture ceremony at the Palace following OPERATION LOUNGE LIZARD. We shall find employment for him. Sea Squadron could stand expansion for additional operations I am contemplating.

VAdm. Ransom was now a card-carrying member of MI-6—or the Inter-Services Liaison Department (ISLD), as it was known under its cover name in Egypt. He had recently been ordered by Admiral John Godfrey, Chief of Naval Intelligence, to support GOLDEN FLEECE and RED

INDIAN missions in Middle East Command, working in conjunction with Commander Ian Fleming—though that was classified.

The Razor was the Royal Navy's Director of Operations (Irregular)—the Admiralty having recently promoted him on paper by dropping "Deputy" from his job description. VAdm. Ransom was coming up in the world of Naval Special Operations and Intelligence.

"It's my understanding that Wino captained the tug that brought you out of Singapore. Good show, Colonel. Better than you shall ever know."

"He did, sir," Col. Randal said. "I think you're going to like him."

"I am sure I will," VAdm. Ransom said. "I also understand you are to be offered command of a U.S. Army Parachute Infantry Regiment."

One of VAdm. Ransom's express assignments, given him in person by Brigadier Stewart Menzies, *aka* C, the chief of the British Secret Intelligence Service, was to make sure that Col. Randal remained in command of Raiding Forces.

R. J., Col. Clarke, Jim and Lady Jane all had identical marching orders.

"Yes, sir," Col. Randal said, "that's what I hear."

"Pray tell," the Razor said, "you shall not be leaving Raiding Forces? Command of a full regiment is a fine thing for an officer of your age, but it could not possibly render the service to the war effort you are doing now. A lot of officers are capable of commanding parachute infantry.

"Special operations commanders with your experience—irreplaceable."

"I'm not sure how the PIR will play into our current operations, sir," Col. Randal said. "My intention is to stay with Raiding Forces for the duration—if I can."

"Colonel," VAdm. Ransom said, "we are not having this conversation—I happen to be in a position to guarantee that you do."

"In that case, sir," Col. Randal said, "I'll quit worrying about being reassigned by the War Department."

It was not lost on Col. Randal that the admiral was another in a long line of people who seemed overly concerned with persuading him to keep doing exactly what he wanted to do.

R. J., Jim and Col. Fellers were hovering nearby, waiting for VAdm. Ransom and Col. Randal to finish their conversation. When the admiral departed in search of his daughter, Brandy, Jim came over and said carefully under his breath, so no one else could overhear.

"GOLDEN FLEECE."

BRIGADIER RAYMOND J. MAUNSELL, JAMES "Baldie" Taylor and Colonel Bonner Fellers were in Colonel John Randal's third-floor suite. Lieutenant Mandy Paige was on the desk out front since King was supposed to be on leave—he and ex-Lieutenant Billy Jack Jaxx were chatting up the two Clipper Girls who had come to the party with Red. Major the Lady Jane Seaborn arrived, uninvited.

Col. Fellers said, "Lady Seaborn, this is a classified briefing restricted to need to know only . . ."

Flashing her patented heart attack smile, Lady Jane said, "*I* have a need to know."

And that was that.

Jim used Lady Jane's unexpected arrival as an excuse to say, "Colonel Randal, may I have a word with you outside?"

"Yes, sir," Col. Randal said, following him out on the landing.

"As you know, Bonner Fellers is the U.S. military attaché," Jim said quietly, but apparently not caring that Lt. Mandy could hear.

"Military attaché is a polite term for military spy—Bonner's with us and we have given him unprecedented access to the intelligence side of our operations, within limits. However, we make a point of not allowing him anywhere near A-Force.

"Under no circumstances should you ever discuss Colonel Clarke with Colonel Fellers—even after your transfer to the U.S. Army. Same thing goes for GOLDEN FLEECE and/or RED INDIAN operations.

"You will be given verbal orders from the Field Marshal, who is the commander-in-chief of all U.S. Forces arriving in Middle East Command, to that effect."

"Understood, General."

When the two went back inside the suite, Col. Fellers said, "Shortly after the attack on Pearl Harbor, the Japanese Air Force caught most of MacArthur's airplanes on the ground at Clark Field in the Philippines and wiped them out. There is no excuse for it. Our Air Corps had plenty of advance warning, but General Brereton chose not to disperse the airplanes for reasons of his own—the rest is history.

"The Imperial Japanese Navy conducted an amphibious landing in the Lingayen Gulf, which we were unable to oppose for lack of an effective air force. Then, drove on Manila, captured it, routed our troops and the Philippine Army—even though we outnumbered them at least three to two—and now the Japs have us pinned on Bataan.

"Following Plan Orange, MacArthur retreated to Corregidor where he is under incessant naval, artillery and air bombardment.

"General MacArthur is acting on the belief that a relief force from the United States is being readied to bring in reinforcements as called for in Plan Orange, but that is wishful thinking now. There is not going to be any U.S. Navy relief convoy. MacArthur is on his own.

"The reason we are having this conversation today is because a combined U.K./U.S. signals intelligence team is stationed on Corregidor—identical to the one you recently brought out of Singapore.

"Colonel Randal, you are to fly to the Philippines and extract the signals people on Corregidor before the Japs conquer the fortress island. Under no circumstances are they to be allowed to fall into enemy hands—I will provide you with written orders prior to your departure to that effect."

R. J. said, "It is imperative this operation remain hush-hush, Colonel. MI-5 has reason to believe your mission to Singapore was compromised—the Japs were quite possibly lying in wait for your Catalina to land."

Col. Fellers said, "We have strong indications Rommel has a highly-placed master spy in Cairo who betrayed your mission to the Japanese in advance. Unfortunately, we have no idea who the mole might be."

"None of us," Jim said, "have any desire to chance a repeat performance of what happened to you in Singapore.

"In that case," Col. Randal said, "keep this mission a secret. No one outside this room should have a need to know any details."

"You are on leave, John," Lady Jane said, "Field Marshal Auchinleck's orders."

"I spoke to the Field Marshal," R. J. said. "Colonel Randal is cleared for the operation."

"In that case, I shall be flying out to the Philippines with the Raiding Forces team," Lady Jane said.

No one present felt like arguing with her.

CHAPTER NINETEEN

ISLAND OF DOOM

COLONEL JOHN RANDAL, UNITED STATES ARMY (he, Major Travis McCloud, and Captain Billy Jack Jaxx had taken the oath of enlistment at RFHQ), Maj. McCloud, Capt. Jaxx, Lieutenant Butch "Headhunter" Hoolihan and King were on board the Hudson flying to RAF Habbaniya. Major the Lady Jane Seaborn, Red and her two Clipper Girl girlfriends were also on the airplane, as was James "Baldie" Taylor.

Lieutenant Pamala Plum-Martin was at the stick—once again violating her orders from Col. Randal not to fly for two weeks.

Jim gathered everyone, to include the Clipper Girl crew, in the back of the plane where he briefed the mission. He did not bother using the standard five-paragraph format. Everybody knew the situation and the mission.

"When we land, you will load on a British Overseas Airlines Corporation bus to make the overland trip to Lake Habbaniyah where you will immediately board a Flying Clipper 314—I shall remain at Habbaniya. All you men in the party will be incognito, wearing zippered BOAC flight suits over your uniform.

"As soon as you are on board, the Flying Clipper will take off and fly to a lake on an island that will be known to you only as 'Mystery Island.' In the event anyone is captured later they will not be able to identify the location, which is, as the Americans say, 'Top Secret.'

"Once at Mystery Island, Colonel Randal, Captain Jaxx and King will transfer to a U.S. Navy Catalina and be flown to Corregidor, which is also known as the 'Rock,' arriving under cover of darkness. Upon arrival, they will be escorted to Malinta Tunnel, where General MacArthur's HQ is located. The signals personnel to be extracted will be assembled, waiting for you at the main tunnel entrance," Jim said.

"Get a good head count, have each individual produce his or her photo ID, then immediately re-board the Catalina for the return flight to Mystery Island. Upon landing on the lake, the Corregidor party will transfer to the Flying Clipper, which will take off for the return flight to RAF Habbaniya.

"With any luck, Colonel Randal, Captain Jaxx and King shall not be on the ground for more than an hour—but you all have a lot of flying ahead of you.

"Questions . . . no?

"In that case—Colonel Randal would like to say a few words."

Col. Randal said, "When my party departs for the Rock, Major McCloud will take command of those of you remaining behind on Mystery Island. In the event we do not make it back—or the Jap Air Force attacks and destroys the Flying Clipper before we do—McCloud, you will use the Top Secret credentials you have in your possession to secure other air or naval transport out of the combat area immediately."

Twitters the Taster had worked his magic producing counterfeit orders purporting to be from the U.S. Army Chief of Staff.

Col. Randal continued, "In the event that's not possible—the Japanese Army invades Mystery Island, for example—you will take Lady Jane and the Clipper Girls into the hills and hold out until rescued.

"Lieutenant Hoolihan is junior to you, Travis, but should escape and evading become the order of the day, he's in tactical command. Butch is the most experienced jungle fighter in Raiding Forces—that's why he's along. Is that clear?"

Maj. McCloud said, "Clear, sir."

"I don't expect any of that to happen," Col. Randal said. "But it's 'good to have a Plan B' . . . or in this case, 'C.'"

THE FLYING CLIPPER LIFTED OFF WITHIN MINUTES of Colonel John Randal's party coming aboard. Like on the flight to Singapore, the plane was virtually empty. There was the same Clipper Girl crew. The girls joked that they were getting to be old hands at flying behind enemy lines on clandestine missions.

But it was no laughing matter.

Red escorted Col. Randal and Major the Lady Jane Seaborn to one of the larger suites in the tail of the plane to accommodate visitors during the flight. This one was decorated in art deco shades of turquoise and black with gold accent. There were two divan couches and a pair of plush chairs.

Lady Jane asked Red to shut the curtains for privacy—she was not feeling sociable at the moment. In fact, she was decidedly unhappy that Col. Randal was being asked to interrupt his much-needed leave to go on a mission that could have been accomplished by someone else.

Up front, the party was on as soon as the aircraft was airborne.

One of the stewards in a starched white jacket arrived to take their dinner order. BOAC had failed to get the memo there was a war on. Aboard the Flying Clipper there was "one class travel." No concessions.

As usual, when Col. Randal was alone with Lady Jane he became super-relaxed. Sometimes they did not even talk—enjoying each other's company being enough. He had never experienced that kind of relationship before.

For her part, Lady Jane could entertain herself better than any woman he had ever met. She stretched out on her divan and took out her sketchpad. Col. Randal dozed off.

When he woke up, Lady Jane showed him what she was working on—parachute wings based on a tracing she had made of a cartouche she discovered in the Great Pyramid. This redrawn pair had "Light Infantry Green" thread as per his instructions—the color matched her eyes.

"Perfect," Col. Randal said. "The question is, now that I'm back in the U.S. Army, will I be authorized to wear 'em?"

"Absolutely," Lady Jane said, "confirmed.

"I have been researching U.S. Army uniform regulations, which are a little vague on the exact placement of qualification badges, awards and decorations. Jump Wings, designed by our friend Captain Yarbrough, are generally worn over the heart on the left side. Foreign awards and qualification badges are worn the right side of the uniform—where you will wear the Raiding Forces wings."

"I didn't know that," Col. Randal said.

Lady Jane said, "I arranged with Bonner Fellers to have orders cut authorizing you to wear your Rangers regimental insignia as a foreign decoration.

"Looks like this," she said, flipping a page to a cutaway drawing of the front of a uniform. It showed "The Rangers" regimental badge with the Raiding Forces parachute wings over it on the right breast of the blouse and the silver U.S. Jump Wings on the left.

"I like it," Col. Randal said. Lady Jane had exquisite taste. He approved of almost everything she ever suggested. On the rare occasion when he did not—he made it a point to rethink.

"Our British troops," Lady Jane said, "do the exact opposite—Raiding Forces wings over their heart and U.S. Jump Wings on the right side of their uniform. Everyone wears the Raiding Forces flash on their left shoulder."

Lady Jane took her role as patroness of Raiding Forces seriously. Being from a military family, she knew little things like patches, badges and insignia were important to the troops.

Col. Randal respected her for that—enough that he chose not to tease her about it, which took a great deal of restraint on his part since he teased her about nearly everything. Lady Jane enjoyed being teased—but not too hard.

She said, "Love your U.S. Army colonel's eagles, John."

CAPTAIN BILLY JACK JAXX CAME BACK to sit with Colonel John Randal and Major the Lady Jane Seaborn. He had fast become one of her favorites. That was a good sign—Col. Randal placed a high value on her opinion of people.

Capt. Jaxx said, "Are you sure about this promotion, Colonel?"

"I am, Jack," Col. Randal said. "Why do you ask?"

"To be honest, sir," Capt. Jaxx said, "wearing these railroad tracks, I feel like I'm going to a masquerade ball in a U.S. Army costume."

Col. Randal did not say so but he felt the same about his eagles.

"Dangerously handsome, Captain Jack," Lady Jane said, zapping him with one of her heart attack smiles. "The Tri-Delta sorority girls at the

University of Texas will be impressed. I shall send a press release to the Austin newspaper as soon as we return."

Capt. Jaxx always had difficulty remembering to breathe around Lady Jane. He was pretty sure she knew that.

"Lighten up, Jack," Col. Randal said. "I never pay attention to age—ability's all that counts. Don't forget—I'm your CO. I don't make mistakes."

"There's always a first time, sir," Capt. Jaxx said.

"Given any thought to our SOLID GOLD Reaction Force?" Col. Randal asked, sticking one of Waldo's custom-rolled cigars between his front teeth. He knew he could not smoke it—Lady Jane did not permit cigars in enclosed quarters.

"Only that we're going to need to be able to pick up and travel long distances fast on short notice," Capt. Jaxx said. "There's no telling where the 621st might turn up when it does."

"Keep in mind," Col. Randal said, "we have to make it seem like an accident—fortune of war. The idea is to never let the bad guys know we were stalking Seebohm."

Capt. Jaxx said, "That requirement complicates planning, sir. We can't drop by parachute right on Seebohm's headquarters, which is the best way to travel to a distant target, get there quick and utilize the element of surprise to the max."

"Keep working on it, Captain," Col. Randal said. "You'll think of something."

One of the glamorous Clipper Girls came to retrieve Capt. Jaxx. He was wanted back at the party.

"Leave the colonel and Lady Seaborn alone, Billy Jack—they have better things to do than talk to you."

Maj. McCloud walked back to brief Col. Randal on the volunteers that he had brought back from Ft. Benning. There had not been time before—developments had been breaking so fast.

Before he could begin, Col. Randal said, "You're a ringer, aren't you, Travis?"

"Sir?" Maj. McCloud said, caught off guard.

"You've never bothered to mention where you went to college," Col. Randal said. "What'd they offer you at Ft. Benning when you were doing your recruiting?"

"West Point, sir," Maj. McCloud said. "Class of '39."

"Kept that under your hat." Col. Randal pointed his cigar. "What'd they offer you, Travis?"

"Promotion to major—command of a battalion in the 502nd, sir."

"You turned that down?"

"Yes, sir," Maj. McCloud said. "I wanted to get back to Raiding Forces. Our army is so unprepared, my guess is it's going to do nothing but training for the better part of another year before it sees any real action."

"Knew you were a ringer," Col. Randal said. "Your bosses expected you to learn everything you could from Raiding Forces, then come back and teach it at Ft. Benning—must be real disappointed in you."

"You sent me to recruit, sir," Maj. McCloud said. "That's what I did."

"Commendable," Lady Jane said. "Command of a parachute battalion is a high honor to refuse, Travis."

"Yes, it is," Col. Randal said. "OK, run it down, Major."

"Captain Duke Slater was a company commander in the 501st, then when I came out here, he took my place at the Infantry School teaching Airborne Tactics," Maj. McCloud said. "A Virginia Military Institute man. We won the lottery when he volunteered, sir.

"Duke can do it all.

"Lieutenant Dan Morgan completed two years at Auburn, an OCS graduate—he's from Delanco, Georgia, sir. Grew up in the mountains hunting and fishing. He was the 505th's Regimental Reconnaissance Platoon Leader. They were not happy to see him go.

"Lieutenant Richard "Dynamite Dick" Coogan—his father owns a demolitions company that specializes in taking down high-rise buildings, bridges, etc. Dick grew up around explosives. The navy offered him a direct commission in the Seabees, but he turned it down to join the paratroops as a private, sir.

"He was sent to OCS at Ft. Benning. There, Dick was noticed by his instructors when his class went to the demolitions range to learn the basics of military explosives. Upon graduation, Lt. Coogan was immediately assigned to the Infantry School to teach demolitions."

"Outstanding," Col. Randal said. "How about the NCOs?"

"All held positions of responsibility," Maj. McCloud said. "Two were squad leaders in the airborne regiments, two were Black Hats at Jump School, one was an instructor on the 81mm mortar committee and one had worked for me teaching tactics at the Infantry School."

"Very good," Col. Randal said. "Tended toward recruiting instructors, I see."

"Learned that trick from you, Colonel," Maj. McCloud said. "In the military, the best command, lead or teach—I picked men I knew."

Col. Randal said, "You did well, Major."

"Probably not welcome back at Ft. Benning, sir," Maj. McCloud said. "I recruited the cream of the crop."

Col. Randal said. "That's too bad."

THE FLYING CLIPPER SPLASHED DOWN in a lake at a Top-Secret base somewhere in the Pacific. No one believed it was really called Mystery Island. Colonel John Randal, Captain Billy Jack Jaxx and King immediately transferred to a U.S. Navy Catalina and were airborne by the time the big BOAC flying boat had been towed into a cove and covered with camouflage netting topped off with palm leaves.

No party atmosphere on this flight. The Catalina was flying straight into harm's way. There was no plan B for this phase of the mission.

Col. Randal slept most of the time. Capt. Jaxx and King did the same, storing up energy for who who-knew knew-what lay ahead. Hours later, the U.S. Navy pilot came back to give a short briefing.

"We will be landing in approximately thirty minutes, sir. It's a little tricky. We have to put down on a narrow strip of water *behind* the minefield that surrounds Corregidor. And do it without the aid of landing lights.

"The island is on blackout.

"We will put you ashore, then immediately begin to take on fuel. Requires approximately a half half-hour to forty-five minutes. I'd like you back on board with the people you intend to pick up—ready for takeoff—by the time we're topped off, sir."

"Do my best," Col. Randal said.

"The Japs don't have night-fighter capability according to latest reports, sir. They do fly the occasional night bombing mission. Incoming artillery from Bataan is a regular occurrence.

"We need to make this a touch-and-go, Colonel—the less time we spend anywhere near Corregidor, the better."

Col. Randal said, "I'm familiar with the island. We only have to cover a short distance—you don't want to get the hell out of Dodge any faster than I do."

The PBY landed and taxied to one of the three piers at Army Dock, located on what was called Bottomside. The Rock also had a Topside and Middleside—not much imagination expended on names on Corregidor. Malinta Tunnel was located Bottomside—not far from the piers.

An officer carrying a shaded flashlight was waiting for Col. Randal when he stepped on the dock.

"Major Mattesion, sir. I have your party assembled, standing by here ready to load. We moved everyone down out of the tunnel when your pilot radioed the plane was coming in for landing."

"Very good," Col. Randal said.

"The general would like a word with you," Maj. Mattesion said.

"Jack," Col. Randal ordered. "You and King check IDs against our manifest and load 'em as soon as the pilot gives the all-clear to come aboard. I'll be back right after I report to General MacArthur."

Maj. Mattesion gave a running commentary on the situation on Corregidor as they walked to Malinta Tunnel.

"The tunnel was designed to house four thousand people. However, the hospital was built on top of Topside. One of the dumber things I've ever seen the military do and there's a long laundry list of really stupid things we've done out here in the four years I've been assigned to the Islands.

"The Japs bombed the hospital into rubble the first day, along with the officer's quarters and enlisted barracks. Now we have eleven thousand people crammed into a space designed for four thousand.

"Plan Orange calls for Corregidor to hold out for six months. By then, a navy relief force is supposed to arrive from the States. Problem is, there's little chance of holding out that long. No reports of the reinforcements being on the way have been confirmed.

"Have you any news?" Maj. Mattesion asked.

"Negative," Col. Randal said. "I've been on operations behind the lines in Egypt and Libya for the last two months—not up to speed on developments in this part of the world."

That was not exactly true. Col. Randal knew no convoy was coming. The briefing on Corregidor had been classified, so he used that as an excuse to justify his answer. In truth, he did not want to be the bearer of bad news.

Corregidor was to be left twisting in the breeze—the island fortress was lost.

It did not take a psychologist to recognize, even in the dark, that Maj. Mattesion was drowning in depression. It was common knowledge how the Japanese treated prisoners after the atrocities they committed following the surrender at Singapore.

Grisly stories were coming in every day from Bataan.

Col. Randal felt the sudden urge, akin to panic, to escape off the island right now—right this minute.

Malinta Tunnel ran for over eight hundred feet and sported high, arched ceilings bored into solid rock. Lights ran the length of the roof. The tunnel was damp and musky and smelled of unwashed people.

Men and women were crammed inside, lining the walls, milling around listlessly. Gloom permeated the air. Everyone was bored. There was nothing to do but wait—but for what?

The clock was ticking on impending disaster. Everyone knew it. Corregidor was a slow-motion nightmare in Technicolor.

Unlike Singapore, where the military and civilian population had seemed to go crazy, the troops in the tunnel were simply despondent. A palpable feeling of despair sucked the energy out of the air. Lethargic twenty-year-olds moved like eighty-year-old men.

Lateral tunnels ran off both sides of the main passageway. General Douglas MacArthur had his headquarters in the third lateral on the north side from the east entrance. Maj. Mattesion waited outside as Col. Randal went in alone.

Inside, the light was garish. A despondent lieutenant colonel sporting General Staff insignia was sitting at a desk. He pointed at an office and said, "The General is expecting you, sir."

Col. Randal marched in, saluted. "Colonel Randal reports, sir."

General Douglas MacArthur returned the salute with a sort of half wave. He had been a living legend during WWI, leading his troops of the 42nd Rainbow Division over the top across "No Man's Land" armed only with a swagger stick.

Now his men called him "Dugout Doug." Col. Randal understood the troops even had a derisive song by that name.

"I believe you have something for me, Colonel."

"Yes, sir," Col. Randal said, reaching for the envelope in the inside pocket of his faded khaki BDU jacket.

Gen. MacArthur opened the letter and read its contents silently. He looked like a Roman emperor carved in stone—or maybe God. The general was clearly exhausted or in the same state of depression as everyone else on the island.

He must know about the "Dugout Doug" moniker—that had to hurt.

Gen. MacArthur laid down the letter. "I had two principal staff officers during the time period when you served out here, Colonel. One was Lieutenant Colonel Dwight Eisenhower and the other was Lieutenant Colonel Bonner Fellers. The most trusted of the two by far was Bonner—my confidant.

"The President wrote me that he thinks so highly of Bonner's daily communiqués from the Middle East Command that he has them delivered to the White House as soon as they arrive. George Marshall, the chief of staff, is resentful of how much weight FDR puts on them—he advised the President they were merely one officer's observations of events and did not represent official War Department policy.

"Bonner says in this letter that you have been commanding a secret outfit—a 'Commando' unit."

"Yes, sir."

"Seems rather strange to be naming an elite raiding organization after one of your former enemy's maneuver elements," Gen. MacArthur said, picking up the oversized corncob pipe on his desk. "But then, the British do have an unorthodox way of doing things."

"That is a fact, sir," Col. Randal said.

"So you're the man who shot Smiling Jack," Gen. MacArthur said, sticking the unlit pipe in his mouth, studying Col. Randal like a hawk.

"I used to read *your* patrol reports, Colonel. Read like fiction. My intelligence people said you exaggerated them. Is that why you cut off the bandit's head and sent it to my HQ?"

"Sir . . ."

"The Huks were a great concern in those days," Gen. MacArthur said. "As you know, they're controlled by the Chinese Communists. I was afraid they were preparing to rise in open revolt.

"The Japanese invasion has put the Red's timetable on hold, but back then the Huks were troubling. You were my most successful Huk hunter."

"Sir, I had two very good NCOs," Col. Randal said. "I just did what they told me to."

"You strike me as a lucky officer," Gen. MacArthur said. "When our army eventually gets organized and we launch our counteroffensive against the Japs, I can always use lucky officers—there shall be a place for you in my command, Colonel, if you ever so desire."

"Thank you, sir," Col. Randal said, not knowing what else to say, wondering if the general was aware that there was not going to be a relief convoy, much less a counterattack—was he misinformed or in denial?

Gen. MacArthur handed a sealed envelope across the desk. "Bonner informs me you have a personal relationship with a Lady Seaborn who has access to high-level back channels. He says she possesses the ability to make something appear on President Roosevelt's desk in forty-eight hours. Is that true?"

"Possibly, sir," Col. Randal said. "Lady Jane has a wide network of contacts. The President's son, Jimmy, has a relationship with Raiding Forces—been on operations with us in the past."

"I want the President to have the opportunity to read my unvarnished assessment of the military situation here," Gen. MacArthur said. "Can I count on you and your lady to ensure that FDR receives this report via confidential courier 'Eyes Only'—no one else to have access to the contents?"

"I can do my best, sir," Col. Randal said.

"Thank you," Gen. MacArthur said, "I am afraid we did not treat you as well as we should have when you were out here before, Colonel. But that is water under the bridge now."

"Sir," Col. Randal said, "I've been expressly ordered not to evacuate anyone not listed on my manifest. However, I understand your wife and boy are with you here on the Rock—I'll be glad to escort them to safety."

"My wife is a soldier's wife. My son is a soldier's son," Gen. MacArthur said. "They will share a soldier's fate."

"Offer stands, General," Col. Randal said. "Time's short—the plane's taking off as soon as you dismiss me."

"A friendly heads-up, Colonel," Gen. MacArthur said, ignoring him.

"Eisenhower hates Fellers—jealous because I relied more heavily on Bonner's advice than his own.

"Ike can be vindictive. Fortunately, he's buried somewhere in the bowels of the War Department pushing a pencil—where, most likely, the man will never be heard from again.

"Be advised," Gen. MacArthur said, "should you two ever cross paths, Eisenhower was outraged about Smiling Jack's severed head with its mouthful of gold teeth landing on his secretary's desk.

"Ike never forgets a slight."

THE CATALINA SPLASHED DOWN ON THE LAKE at Mystery Island. The passengers were immediately transferred to the Flying Clipper. In record time, the big, luxurious flying boat was making its takeoff run on its way back to RAF Habbaniya with a lot of happy people on board.

Mission accomplished.

While everyone else celebrated, Colonel John Randal retreated to his lounge with Major the Lady Jane Seaborn.

Lady Jane asked, "How did your meeting with General MacArthur go?"

Col. Randal stretched out on one of the lounges. "The general doesn't seem to have a grasp on the immediate situation . . . or at least want to talk about it. Most of the conversation was about what had happened in the near past before the war—it was strange."

Col. Randal shut his eyes, wanting to relax like he always did when he was alone with Lady Jane. He could not get the men and women of Corregidor out of his mind.

The island of the doomed.

CHAPTER TWENTY

FIVE-SEVEN-FIVE

COLONEL JOHN RANDAL, MAJOR the Lady Jane Seaborn, all the officers of Raiding Forces and most of the men who were not on operations or training were standing on the dock waiting for a troop transport ship from the United States to land. On board the ship was the Parachute Infantry Regiment (PIR) assigned to Col. Randal. Excitement was thick on the ground.

Field Marshal Claude Auchinleck was scheduled to put in an appearance with the U.S. Military Attaché. Colonel Bonner Fellers had something come up at the last minute and was unable to accompany him.

Colonel Dudley Clarke was on hand with members of the press to record the event. He intended to make maximum use of the arrival, which he was going to exploit to the fullest, portraying the PIR as the tip of the iceberg of a massive infusion of American troops into Middle East Command.

The band was standing by.

Today marked a turning point in the history of Raiding Forces. An airborne regiment is a big organization. Change was coming—the war was picking up.

As they waited, Major Travis McCloud briefed Col. Randal on what to expect. The table of organization of a PIR called for three battalions of three companies each and a regimental staff. Officer troop strength was one colonel (Randal), four lieutenant colonels, six majors, twenty-six captains and 103 lieutenants. Enlisted troop strength was 2,029 men.

The regiment assigned to Raiding Forces was the 575th Parachute Infantry Regiment (Separate) (Special). The "Special" designation was a last minute add-on to indicate that the 575th was not intended to conduct purely conventional airborne operations.

As the ship docked, Maj. McCloud said, "Sir, the Five-Seven-Five was formed in the Panama Canal Zone. It was originally an experimental Para-Glider battalion. The regiment was carrying out jungle training and conducting patrolling operations protecting the Canal from saboteurs before it was alerted for an invasion of the Vichy French island of St. Martinique.

"When it was decided to send an airborne regiment to the Middle East, the 575th was relieved of that assignment, which was taken over by the 551 PIR."

Lady Jane said, "What a magnificent command, John."

Col. Randal was wondering how he was going to employ such a large combat formation—Raiding Forces had barely exceeded two hundred men all up when it was at its peak strength, prior to all the losses incurred during CRUSADER.

First to disembark was a squad of MPs, armed with stubby M-1897 12-gauge shotguns. They took up position at the foot of the gangplank. None of them were wearing parachute wings or jump boots, which indicated they were not a part of the 575th.

Then a young major with a clipped mustache led the troops off. The paratroopers had large duffel bags thrown over one shoulder and their weapons—primarily brand-new .30 cal. M1 Garand rifles—slung over the other. Most of the men looked like they had been sleeping in their clothes for the entire voyage and were recovering from hangovers; some were unshaven.

Other troops coming down the catwalk were being escorted by MPs. A few of those paratroopers were in handcuffs. Col. Randal had never seen a less military-looking formation of men.

"Major Everard Beauchamp reports, suh."

Col. Randal returned the salute, never taking his eyes off the troops streaming down the gangplank.

"Suh, the Five-Seven-Five has arrived."

Col. Randal did not make any response. He knew what he was looking at. Every slacker, goof-off and eight ball in Airborne Command at Ft. Benning had been reassigned to the 575th PIR prior to its deployment.

It appeared jump-qualified prisoners had been released from the brig to join the regiment.

Captain "Geronimo" Joe McKoy said, "Hot damn!"

The bandleader was so mesmerized by the sight, he never gave the signal to play.

The last stragglers came down the gangplank, being pushed by a follow-up squad of shotgun-toting MPs. As the policeman took the handcuffs off one burly paratrooper, he turned around and chased the MP back up the gangway.

There were a lot fewer jumpers present than the 2,029 called for in the table of organization and equipment (TO&E) and nowhere near the num-ber of officers allocated when 575th PIR was all ashore.

FM Auchinleck was a soldier's soldier. He realized what had happened. The Field Marshal chose to forgo a welcoming speech. He decided the wisest course of action was to return to Grey Pillars and let Col. Randal sort it out.

Even Col. Clarke was flummoxed—he was not about to plant photos of these tramps in uniform in newspapers around the world.

As the troops were climbing on to trucks for the ride to RFHQ, Col. Randal said, "OK, Major Beauchamp—let's hear it."

"Suh," Maj. Beauchamp said, "what you have here is the 2nd Battalion, 575th Parachute Infantry Regiment. Not all these men are original members, Colonel. We had substitutions made at Ft. Benning prior to deployment—a lot of our best men were transferred out. Replacements transferred in.

We're four-hundred-thirteen officers and men all up."

Col. Randal asked, "Where's the other two battalions?"

"There are no other battalions, suh," Maj. Beauchamp said.

"There never was."

MAJOR EVERARD BEAUCHAMP CALLED a formation as soon as the troops unloaded from the trucks outside the gates at RFHQ. Colonel John Randal, Major the Lady Jane Seaborn and Maj. Beauchamp made a leisurely walk-through inspection. It was possible to smell alcohol on the breath of a large number of the men. More than a few were surly, unkempt, exuding resentment—those who were not seemed embarrassed to be standing the formation with the rest.

Maj. Beauchamp was mortified.

However, Col. Randal and Lady Jane did not seem to pay any attention to the bad attitudes, lack of shaves or slovenly jump suits—which took a lot of fun out of it for the U.S. Paratroopers. What's the point of being rebellious if no one notices?

Lady Jane was a real attention-getter. Even the most unkempt troopers with the biggest chips on their shoulders were wondering about her. Inside the compound, the men could see the Royal Marines and Clipper Girls sunning around the Olympic-sized swimming pool outside RFHQ.

Not what the Five-Seven-Five expected.

The men had erected their regimental sign—a big square of canvas with large red letters painted on it from their Panama Canal Zone days before being transferred to Ft. Benning prior to deployment to Egypt.

575th PARACHUTE INFANTRY REGIMENT
JUNGLE RANGERS

The sign seemed silly, considering it was planted in sand with desert as a backdrop as far as the eye could see.

Col. Randal took out his 9mm. P-35 Browning High Power. Without a word, he took aim at the sign and commenced fire, *BLAM, BLAM, BLAM.* . . . . Then he calmly changed magazines and repeated a second string of shots.

"Major Beauchamp," Col. Randal ordered the startled commander of the Five-Seven-Five.

"Yes, suh."

"Have your officers fall out. Captain Slater will show them to their quarters. Sergeant Major Mikkalis will march the regiment to its barracks. Once they arrive, place your battalion on alert for a combat jump tonight. Then report to my office."

"Yes, suh," Maj. Beauchamp said, with a slight catch in his voice. A combat jump the first night the regiment arrived in Egypt was beyond anything he had anticipated in his wildest imagination. Training drops took longer to prepare for than the regiment was being given to get ready for a combat mission tonight.

Sergeant Major Mike "March or Die" Mikkalis called the formation to attention, "RIGHT FACE, FORWARD MARCH, EYES RIGHT . . ."

As the troops marched past the 575th PIR regimental sign, the men saw the word JUNGLE had been neatly X'd out by 9mm bullet holes.

Beautiful women, a trick-shooting colonel and not a single word from anyone about their military bearing—or lack thereof. The men of the 575th were beginning to get the impression that they were strangers in a strange land—or at least assigned to an outfit like no other.

And the troops did not even know about the upcoming combat jump yet.

Col. Randal and Lady Jane went inside the main building up to their third-floor suite. Lieutenant Mandy Paige was trailing along behind. She was trying to keep up and write down the instructions Col. Randal was dictating rapid-fire.

King was already at the security desk when they arrived.

"Major McCloud, Captain McKoy, Captain Jaxx and Captain Slater first," Col. Randal said, as he and Lady Jane went past into the suite. "Hold Major Beauchamp until I call for him."

"Roger that, Chief."

Lady Jane disappeared into her bedroom. Lt. Mandy dashed off to locate the people Col. Randal wanted to report to him. The day had taken an unexpected turn. Nothing had gone as expected.

Captain "Geronimo" Joe McKoy was the first to arrive. King sent him straight in. He found Col. Randal standing in the small briefing area of the suite, studying the wall map.

"Jungle Rangers," Capt. McKoy said. "What a hoot."

"Pick out an isolated target," Col. Randal said. "One you've already raided before. We'll drop the Five-Seven-Five on it tonight."

"Now that sounds like a plan, John," Capt. McKoy said. "I'd say we ought to hit that place with the airstrip next to it we took down about six months back—Fort No. 9."

"Good choice," Col. Randal said, locating the position on the map with his finger.

"The Italians ain't gonna put up much in the way of a fight," Capt. McKoy said. "And more important, there's no enemy in any sized force within two hundred miles to send out a rescue column."

Major Travis McCloud, Capt. Jaxx and Capt. Slater arrived.

"Travis, do you remember the first patrol you went on with Raiding Forces?" Col. Randal asked.

"How could I forget, sir?" Maj. McCloud said. "Charging an enemy fort in a fully topped-off aviation fuel tanker with explosives wired to a pressure plate on the front bumper and the fuse lit on a landmine strapped to the back."

"You and Duke were Airborne Tactics instructors," Col. Randal said. "Now's the chance to put your experience at the Infantry School to work. Plan a drop for the Five-Seven-Five on that target—Fort No. 9, for tonight. Time is tight and we're going to need a full Operations Order."

Maj. McCloud looked startled.

"Jack," Col. Randal said, "I need you to jump in with a Pathfinder team to mark the drop zone. Put together a team—select your men from the Five-Seven-Five. I want this to be an all-American operation as much as possible."

"Yes, sir!"

"You're letting *that* rabble make a combat jump, Colonel?" Maj. McCloud said. "First night off the boat—that's totally crazy, sir."

"Well, Travis," Col. Randal said, sticking one of Waldo's cigars between his front teeth. "That's why we're doing it."

"Pam's here, Chief," King called from the door.

"Send her in," Col. Randal said.

"Wilco."

"Here's the general idea," Col. Randal said, wrapping up the meeting as the Vargas Girl-looking Royal Marine pilot walked in.

"Drop the regiment, take down the objective, followed by a fifty-mile forced march to a rendezvous with a convoy of Jack Merritt's trucks.

"Questions?"

"We'll have a lot of them, Colonel," Maj. McCloud said. "Try not to venture too far from RFHQ until we get this done, sir."

"I'll be in the area," Col. Randal said. "Organize the Five-Seven-Five into two elements—a Support Element and Assault Element. Travis, you command the Assault Element.

"We'll let Major Beauchamp command the Support Element. Captain McKoy, you'll be attached to advise him—get with the major as soon as possible to provide him first-hand intelligence on the target."

"Will do, John."

"Duke, you take command of one of the assault units. I want Roy Kidd in charge of another. The concept of the operation is to let the Five-Seven-Five have a tune-up battle and get their initiation into combat over with—under the most experienced commanders we can field.

"At this point I don't know any of the new officers, so use as few of 'em as possible for key tasks—but try to find a way to make it look like we're *not* doing that."

"Understood, sir," Maj. McCloud said.

As they were leaving, Col. Randal pulled Maj. McCloud aside. "Travis, I'm thinking about putting you in command of the Five-Seven-Five after tonight—how's that sound?"

"I would like that, sir—a lot."

"Good," Col. Randal said. "Don't be surprised when we reorganize it. The battalion is of no use to us as it's configured now."

"Understood sir."

After they departed, Lieutenant Pamala Plum-Martin said, "You wanted to see me, John?"

All along, the plan had been to have the 575th PIR make a demonstration jump in full sight of Cairo the afternoon of their arrival. There were three reasons: to show the new arrivals that in Raiding Forces they could be expected to do operations on short notice, to accomplish a training mission for the new United States Army Air Force (USAAF) 37th Airlift Squadron of C-47s recently arrived in Middle East Command, and to impress the denizens of Cairo and the attendant enemy agents in the city that a major U.S. Paratroop formation was now on scene.

"Pam," Col. Randal said, "we're going to cancel the demonstration jump. As you heard, instead we're going to drop the Five-Seven-Five in this area here later tonight."

Col. Randal pointed to the map with the tip of his cigar. "Will you notify Wing Commander Gordon about the change of mission?"

"The original plan was to give the C-47 troop transport pilots a training mission," Lt. Plum-Martin said. "An actual combat drop—better yet. The U.S. Air Corps pilots will all get to brag they're veterans."

"Yes, they will," Col. Randal said.

"I shall make the arrangements with Ronnie," Lt. Plum-Martin said.

"One more thing," Col. Randal said. "We're violating the principle of reconnaissance. Do you think the Wing Commander could manage to have the RAF do a flyby—make sure Rommel hasn't parked a Panzer Division at Fort No. 9?"

"Possibly he and I can fly it," Lt. Plum-Martin said.

"I'll let you off your mandatory stand down from flying a couple of days early," Col. Randal said, "since you never paid attention to my orders anyway.

"You can drop Jack's Pathfinder team tonight."

"Thanks, John."

"Tell Mandy to have Roy Kidd report to me," Col. Randal ordered as she was leaving.

"Lieutenant Montgomery, Chief," King said. "Major Beauchamp is here as well."

"Send Karen in."

Raiding Forces' Chief Rigger walked in. She had been a civilian rigger at No. 1 Parachute School, then commissioned and transferred to Lady Jane's Royal Marines on the day the Raiders graduated.

"Karen," Col. Randal said, "we've canceled the training jump. In its place, the Five-Seven-Five will be making a combat drop tonight. That means instead of a Hollywood jump with no weapons or equipment, you'll have to rig for combat.

"Any problem?

"Negative, John," Lt. Montgomery said. "The Five-Seven-Five brought T-4 parachutes with them from Ft. Benning and they should have all their other gear as well. If not, the men can make the jump with weapons exposed the way Raiding Forces does."

"Let's do that anyway," Col. Randal said. "Might as well get the Five-Seven-Five used to the way we operate right from the start."

"U.S. Airborne doctrine," Lt. Montgomery said, "calls for dropping heavy weapons like mortars and machine guns by door or wing bundles."

"Drop the mortars in bundles," Col. Randal said. "Machine gunners need to jump with their MGs on lowering lines."

"Yes, sir," Lt. Montgomery said.

She was very capable—the highest praise a serving member could receive in Raiding Forces.

"King," Col. Randal called as Lt. Montgomery was leaving.

King stuck his head in the door.

"We need to assign someone to shadow Karen while she gets the Five-Seven-Five rigged," Col. Randal said. "There aren't any women riggers in the U.S. Army.

"Someone needs to keep an eye on her to make sure our new troopers comply with her instructions—no questions asked."

"Allow me, Chief," King said. "Flanigan can sit in here."

"Good," Col. Randal said. "Plan to jump with Jack's Pathfinders or accompany me on the main drop as part of my command party—your call."

"I can drop in with Jack," King said, "then link up with you on the DZ."

"Sounds like a plan," Col. Randal said. "Keep your eyes open this afternoon, King. I want a comprehensive report on the Five-Seven-Five—in private."

"My pleasure," King said. "Lieutenant Kidd's here."

"Send him in."

Lieutenant Roy Kidd came in, "Yes, sir?"

"Roy," Col. Randal said, "you're an American citizen serving in the Indian Army—how would you like to transfer to the U.S. Army?"

Lt. Kidd said, "Is that a possibility, sir?"

"Promotion to captain is part of the deal," Col. Randal said, "if you do."

"I'm in, Colonel."

"OK," Col. Randal said. "I'm going to use you with the Seven-Five-Seven as a company commander on a combat jump tonight—don't be thinking you're going to get a permanent slot after it's over.

"You're far and away too valuable as Scout Patrol Leader to have you running a company of paratroopers."

"Understood, sir."

"Report to Major McCloud," Col. Randal said. "He's planning the mission and commanding the assault element."

"Yes, sir."

"Have Major Beauchamp come in on your way out."

Maj. Beauchamp reported ramrod straight.

Col. Randal said, "Where you from, Major?'

"New Orleans, suh—ROTC at Louisiana State. I'm NG, Louisiana National Guard."

"You're a long way from Bourbon Street," Col. Randal said. "Did you get your men settled in?"

"Yes, suh, those pyramidal tents down on the beach make excellent barracks," Maj. Beauchamp said. "My men—or at least the ones from Panama—are used to heat. This is a drier climate. I think they'll adapt reasonably well, Colonel."

"Good—tell me about the Five-Seven-Five."

"We formed in the Canal Zone before the war started, suh, with troops shipped in fresh out of Jump School at Ft. Benning," Maj. Beauchamp said.

"The War Department was concerned the Panama Canal might be subject to attack—or at least sabotage. Originally the plan was to have a full regiment, but the army never got around to assigning the other two battalions—we're what they call a 'bastard outfit,' suh."

"Yeah," Col. Randal said, "I can see that."

"Then," Maj. Beauchamp said, "we were alerted to jump on St. Martinique and turned over our security responsibilities to the 551 PIR.

"Not long after that, suh, the Five-Seven-Five was relieved from the St. Martinique mission and ordered to Ft. Benning for immediate overseas deployment to Egypt.

"We spent the majority of our time doing jungle training or patrolling the Canal, suh," Maj. Beauchamp said, "then we switched to a crash course on fighting in built-up areas for the St. Martinique jump.

"Our CO was a West Point man and a fine training officer. He worked us hard, but they transferred him out when we arrived at Ft. Benning—bumped me up from S-3 to command."

"How would you rate the regiment?" Col. Randal asked.

"I'd say the Five-Seven-Five was a pretty good outfit, suh, or it was before the 'Airborne Mafia' click at Benning assigned every jump-qualified misfit and malcontent, to include criminals, on the post to us before the regiment shipped out."

"Here's what's about to happen," Col. Randal said. "Major McCloud is going to assume command—you'll be his XO, at least initially. Expect a complete unit reorganization—we don't do things by the book in Raiding Forces."

"That's what I hear, suh," Maj. Beauchamp said.

"Raiding Forces is a small-scale, pinprick Combined Operations outfit," Col. Randal said.

"Most of our missions are classified. I'm not exactly sure how to work a parachute infantry battalion-sized element into our current plans. One thing is a given, the Five-Seven-Five has a lot of rigorous training ahead of it—followed by an even more intensive schedule of combat operations."

"Yes, suh," Maj. Beauchamp said with a glint in his eye. "We're only a half battalion, so reorganizing shouldn't take that long. These men are ready to get at the enemy, suh."

"We have a set of rules which you'll get to know by heart," Col. Randal said. "One of them is 'Right Man, Right Job.' Our goal is to put round pegs into round holes—you'll find there's a lot of opportunities in Raiding Forces.

"Those troopers—to include officers—who don't measure up are out, is that clear?"

"Perfectly, suh."

As Maj. Beauchamp was leaving, King announced, "The general is here, Chief."

Jim walked in. "That was ugly—a half-strength battalion of yardbirds."

"You didn't think the U.S. Army was going to send us a crack parachute regiment, did you, General?" Col. Randal said.

"Claimed they were," Jim said. "One could always hope."

"I've canceled the demonstration jump for this afternoon," Col. Randal said. "We'll drop on Fort No. 9 tonight instead—a little attention-getter for the Five-Seven-Five."

"Now *that*," Jim said, "is an excellent idea."

Lady Jane came out of the bedroom after Jim had rushed off to call Col. Clarke to advise him to send over the camera crews. Kitting up for a combat jump being the absolute best material ever for what the A-Force commander desired, which was to enhance his deception that large-scale American ground forces were making their initial entry into Middle East Command.

And going straight into combat.

Lady Jane said, "I *love* the Five-Seven-Five—what a perfect little regiment."

Some of the paratroopers had been so drunk during the walk-through inspection, their buddies had to prop them up.

CHAPTER TWENTY-ONE

SOBERING UP FAST

COLONEL JOHN RANDAL ISSUED THE FIRST part of the Warning Order to the assembled paratroopers of the Five-Seven-Five. The men were sitting in portable bleachers that Major the Lady Jane Seaborn had arranged to have delivered from one of the Cairo schools and set up inside the RFHQ compound.

The drinkers in the regiment were sobering up fast.

"Situation," Col. Randal said. "You men are the first American ground combat forces to arrive in Middle East Command. This is an active theatre of operations. You have been alerted for a drop tonight at 2200 hours.

"Mission: Capture an Italian strongpoint known as Fort No. 9.

"Execution: You will be flown to the target in C-47 aircraft—drop on a DZ that will be marked by an advance party of Pathfinders. Attack and overrun the fort. Then, march overland to a pick-up point fifty miles east of the objective, where you will be met by a convoy of trucks that will return you to Raiding Forces Headquarters—a desert journey that will take approximately six days, most of it behind enemy lines."

There was absolute silence in the bleachers.

"Now," Col. Randal said, "before Major McCloud comes out and briefs you on Command and Signal and Administration and Logistics, I have a couple of comments.

"You are about to make airborne history. First combat parachute jump by the U.S. Army in WWII—I'll be leading the stick on the first C-47 over the DZ.

"Next, the 2nd Battalion is no more. Tonight you'll be jumping under your new name.

"575th Rangers, Strategic Raiding Forces."

AS MAJOR TRAVIS MCCLOUD BRIEFED the rest of the Warning Order, Colonel John Randal took Waldo Treywick around back behind the bleachers.

"Stand at attention, Mr. Treywick."

The grizzled ex-ivory poacher, soldier-of-fortune, former slave, newly-minted millionaire and California land baron looked startled but did his best imitation of snapping to. However, Waldo forgot to take the custom-rolled cigar out of his mouth.

"In the U.S. Army," Col. Randal said, reaching in his pocket, "Counterintelligence Corps officers, no matter what their rank, wear officer's U.S. insignia on both lapels of their uniform blouse or on the collars of their shirts. That way, no one ever knows what they are. Could be a private—could be a general."

Col. Randal pinned brass U.S. insignia to the lapels of Waldo's tailor-made khaki bush jacket.

"Get the picture?"

"Which one am I?"

"Be anything you want to be," Col. Randal said, handing Waldo a laminated U.S. Army military photo ID card prepared by the forger, Major Edward Twitterington, *aka* Twitters the Taster, of A-Forces Printing Section (Type X).

"These should keep you out of trouble now that America is in the war.

"On the other hand . . ."

CAPTAIN BILLY JACK JAXX CAME AROUND behind the bleachers where he had seen Colonel John Randal and Waldo Treywick disappear.

"Sir," Capt. Jaxx said. "The Five-Seven-Five has a twenty-man I&R platoon. Looks pretty good—so does their platoon leader, Lieutenant Clint Hays. Can I have 'em?"

"What?"

"The Intelligence and Reconnaissance platoon, sir," Capt. Jaxx said. "For my Pathfinder team."

"Do you need that many men?"

"Major McCloud mentioned there's two or three hangars on the airstrip at Fort No. 9," Capt. Jaxx said. "After the Pathfinders mark the DZ, sir, we can move out and secure 'em for you, sir."

"Make yourself happy, Jack," Col. Randal said. "Clear it with Major McCloud—he's drafting the plan."

"Yes, sir," Capt. Jaxx said. "Dynamite Dick wants to strap hang."

"Who?"

"Lieutenant Coogan," Capt. Jaxx said. "The new demolitions officer who came out with the last group of American Volunteers."

"That's fine," Col. Randal said, thinking his young captain was doing some talent spotting. Good for him. "Coogan can use the experience."

"Transferring to the CIC, Mr. Treywick?" Capt. Jaxx said. "I'd hate to be a Nazi spy with you and Mandy on the case."

"Ain't really a counterintelligence man full-time, Jack," Waldo said. "I'm what you might call the Raiding Forces auxiliary spook."

"Scare the hell out of people," Capt. Jaxx said, "wearing U.S. brass with no rank insignia—they'll think you're coming for 'em."

Col. Randal said, "That's the plan."

The Warning Order concluded. A mad rush ensued to clear the bleachers. There were a million things the troops had to get done to prepare for the mission.

Jumpmasters from the Five-Seven-Five (there were plenty of qualified jumpmasters on their roster) had to be briefed. Then they were to be linked up with the individual C-47 they would jumpmaster, from the 37th Airlift Squadron flying the mission. The jumpmasters had to conduct an aircraft inspection on the plane their stick would be jumping from. Maps were to be issued, ammunition drawn, weapons test-fired, radio operators had to conduct commo checks, rations, water, and on and on.

An Army Air Corps major from the 37th Airlift Squadron arrived to consult with Col. Randal. This was a big change of mission for the USAAF. Considering tonight would be a history-making event, Army Air wanted to get it right. After outlining the mission, Col. Randal passed him off to Maj. McCloud for a detailed briefing.

The men of the Five-Seven-Five were down on the beach in their tents, frantically packing and repacking their personal gear. No one wanted to forget anything. The paratroopers had trained a long time for their first combat jump, and now it was coming at them fast.

Bayonets were sharpened. Weapons given one last cleaning—no such thing as being too sure. Hand grenades were issued.

While the paratroopers worked, off-duty Raiders were wandering through the tents observing, passing out the occasional word of encouragement, and critically evaluating the U.S. Army-issue equipment. The weapon in the Five-Seven-Five inventory that attracted the most attention from the desert veterans was the M-1 rifle.

None of the Raiders had ever seen anything like it before—and they were impressed.

The Browning Automatic Rifle (BAR) was thoroughly scrutinized. The jury was out. The Raiders had a high opinion of the BAR's British counterpart—the BREN.

Everyone agreed the reserve parachutes were a nice touch.

Colonel Bonner Fellers finally put in a belated appearance. He apologized for the Five-Seven-Five. The captain of the troop transport carrying the regiment had cabled him concerning the low state of the troops before the ship docked.

Col. Fellers had been embarrassed to show up when they landed.

"It'll be fine, I'm not looking for choir boys," Col. Randal said, "Lady Jane says she loves 'em."

"She must see something I don't," Col. Fellers said. "Airborne Command at Benning really did a number on us.

"If Captain Jaxx is available, I'd like to speak to him, Colonel."

Col. Randal said to Lieutenant Mandy Paige, "Round up Roy and Jack."

Lieutenant Roy Kidd arrived first. While they waited, Col. Randal asked Col. Fellers to swear him in to the United States Army in the grade of captain.

"We can perform the ritual and draw up the paperwork later," Col. Fellers said, "Congratulations, Captain Kidd—welcome to the United States Army."

"Backdate it to the same date as Billy Jack's," Col. Randal said "Same date of rank."

When Lt. Mandy returned with Capt. Jaxx in tow, Col. Fellers said, "I received a telegram from General MacArthur yesterday—he and his family departed Corregidor for Australia by PT boat last night.

"One of his last acts before leaving the Rock was to award you, Colonel Randal, the Distinguished Service Cross and you, Captain Jaxx, the Silver Star for your 'daring rescue mission.' King is set to receive a substantial cash bonus."

"You're joking, sir," Capt. Jaxx said. "The bravest thing I did was party with the Clipper Girls."

Jack Cool.

"Whatever transpired," Col. Fellers said, "the general has spoken."

"'Smiling Jack,' the Huk bandit, was mentioned in his letter to me, Colonel. We shall have to have a conversation about that one day soon," Col. Fellers said. "I've been wanting to hear your version of events for years."

Col. Randal said, "Not much to it."

"On another matter," Col. Fellers said, "what's the status of the original American Volunteer Group personnel? I have instructions to re-enlist them as soon as possible."

Col. Randal said, "There hasn't been time to meet with the AVG men to discuss their plans. Most have been pressed into service for the drop tonight as 'stiffeners' for the Five-Seven-Five."

"Keep in mind," Col. Fellers said, "that as an incentive for re-enlistment, we will promote anyone you recommend."

"Count on, as a minimum," Col. Randal said, "advancing everyone at least one grade as part of the package. We may want to give a few people direct commissions."

"Consider it done."

BRANDY AND CAPTAIN PENELOPE "LEGS" Honeycutt-Parker were working to build a giant sand table of the objective for the Operations Order. They had both been with White Patrol when it attacked Fort No. 9. The two made sure every detail was absolutely to scale and correct.

Captain "Geronimo" Joe McKoy, who had been there as well, stopped by to inspect their work and make a suggestion or two.

What the women came up with was one of the best terrain maps of its type Col. Randal had ever seen, to include those at Achnacarry—the Special Warfare Training Center. Major Travis McCloud, who had also been on the first attack on Fort No. 9—charging the fort with Col. Randal in an aviation gas fuel truck with a landmine strapped on the rear bumper and a lit detonator, declared the sand table the equal of anything he had seen at the Infantry School.

A five-foot pointer was not available at RFHQ, so a bamboo fishing pole was pressed into service for the briefing. Brandy had a foot-long portion of the tip painted red.

A *lot* of attention was being paid to detail.

The rattle of gunfire commenced. The Five-Seven-Five were moving by platoon to an improvised range on the beach to test-fire their weapons. Sounds of the firing ratcheted up the tension in the air.

Colonel Dudley Clarke came by with a team of photographers. "Excellent idea, Colonel—clipping the regiment's name to 575th Rangers. The other side will never know what it means. I can work with that."

"Good."

James "Baldie" Taylor said, "I shall be dropping with your command element tonight, Colonel."

"Glad to have you, General."

Col. Randal and Maj. McCloud went over the Operations Order. The two spent an hour working through the plan from start to finish. No one was allowed to interrupt them—Col. Randal was scheduled to brief and he wanted to make sure he understood every last detail of the Mission Statement and Concept of the Operation. He would leave the rest up to Maj. McCloud.

Then, Col. Randal, Maj. McCloud and Major Everard Beauchamp went over the list of officers who were going to command the various support and maneuver elements. The plan called for Raiding Forces officers to command the maneuver elements, while Five-Seven-Five officers were in command of all the support elements.

Col. Randal issued the Operations Order at 1500 hours. It was a tour-de-force. With the 575th Rangers assembled in the bleachers, working without notes, he walked the Rangers through everything that was going to happen from the time the briefing ended until the troops linked up with the convoy at the Rally Point to transport them back to RFHQ following the mission.

He kept it short and simple.

The 575th Rangers would drop on the airstrip adjoining Fort No. 9. The battalion was broken down into two elements—a three-company Assault element under Maj. McCloud and a Support element consisting of the HQ company under Maj. Beauchamp. The support element contained all four of the Five-Seven-Five's 81mm mortars and all eight of the .30 cal. 1919 Browning Light MGs. On signal, the mortars would conduct a fire mission against Fort No. 9. The MGs would lay down suppressive fire.

Then, on signal from Col. Randal—three green flares—the mortars would shift their fire to the palm grove behind the fort, the MGs would cease fire and Maj. McCloud would assault the objective.

Fort No. 9 was so small only A/575 Rangers under Captain Roy Kidd would make the attack. B and C companies would lay down covering fire with their organic weapons—M1s, BARs and Thompson submachine guns. Then the two companies would shift their fire to the palm grove behind the fort on signal from Maj. McCloud—a red flare.

Once the fort was secured, the Five-Seven-Five would assemble on the DZ and immediately move out on a forced march to the ORP where they would rendezvous with a convoy of trucks under Major Jack Merritt.

Operations Orders do not get much simpler. Every man understood exactly what was expected of him. The plan that had been crafted was a simplified version of what the Infantry School called a "holding attack." The Five-Seven-Five knew it well.

As soon as Col. Randal completed the order, the officers in charge of the various elements took command of their troops and immediately moved out into the desert to conduct rehearsals. Time was limited. The Five-Seven-Five was scheduled to board a convoy to the departure airfield at 1730 hours.

VERONICA PAIGE WAS IN CHARGE OF PREPARING the manifests at the Departure Airfield. She had four tents set up, one for each company of the 575th Rangers. Royal Marines were manning typewriters as the troops filed through. The men each gave their name, rank, serial number, and chalk number when they reached a typist. The girls made the typewriters sound like machine guns.

Everywhere on the airfield, troops were on the move.

Colonel John Randal and Major the Lady Jane Seaborn arrived in a jeep with Waldo and Lieutenant Mandy Paige in the back seat. The sun was beginning to go down when they pulled up. The desert quickly started to cool.

Lieutenant Pamala Plum-Martin could be seen talking to Captain Billy Jack Jaxx and Lieutenant Richard "Dynamite Dick" Coogan. When Col. Randal walked over, she said, "Here are aerial photos of Fort No. 9 taken four hours ago, John.

"Ninth Air Force sent a photo reconnaissance plane over. They were delighted to have the opportunity to fly a recon mission in support of an Air Corps combat operation—this degree of inter-service cooperation shall not last forever."

Col. Randal glanced at the photos. The fort looked exactly the same as the last time he had seen the place, except the metal hangars were a lot worse for wear, having been shot up by Vickers K MGs and scorched with aviation fuel.

There were three trucks parked by the hangars, and the aviation fuel tanker had been replaced. No aircraft were in sight. Fort No. 9 was a remote emergency landing strip, not an active airfield.

"OK, Jack," Col. Randal said, "you're up to something?"

Capt. Jaxx said, "How about a do-over, sir—missed the first one."

"I knew you were going to be trouble tonight," Col. Randal said. "Go talk to Maj. McCloud."

"Yes, sir."

"Pam," Col. Randal asked, "will you be dropping the Pathfinders in the Hudson?"

"Negative," the Vargas Girl-looking Royal Marine said. "Ronnie acquired a C-47 for the Pathfinders. The assistant squadron commander is flying right seat for me—I get a check ride in a Dakota, dropping Jack."

"All right, I won't give the Pathfinders another thought, then," Col. Randal said. "They're in good hands."

Captain "Geronimo" Joe McKoy strolled over. He and Col. Randal stepped off a short distance for a private conversation.

"What's your impression of Major Beauchamp so far, Captain?" Col. Randal asked.

"Real Southern gentleman," Capt. McKoy said. "I think we're gonna like him, John."

"Jack intends to secure the hangars—make sure the support element doesn't fire on 'em," Col. Randal said, handing him a copy from the stack of aerial photos Lt. Plum-Martin had given him.

"Think about using these three trucks parked next to the hangars to transport the wounded, heavy equipment, parachutes and the AVG men when we pull out."

"That works," Capt. McKoy said.

"I'll have you and Mr. Treywick take charge of the AVG men for the return trip. Ride to the Rally Point in comfort," Col. Randal said.

"The rest of the Five-Seven-Five is in for a spirited desert march—King's setting the pace."

"Ain't gonna be as much as a single bullet hole in them trucks," Capt. McKoy said, "I'll guarantee you that. Plannin' on puttin' the hurt on those Ranger boys, John?"

"That is a fact."

"King'll get their attention," Capt. McKoy said. "Them Rangers'll learn to never squat with their spurs on when he gets done with 'em."

Col. Randal said, "Make sure you're on one of the trucks."

COLONEL JOHN RANDAL AND MAJOR the Lady Jane Seaborn drove around to each of the C-47 Dakota aircraft. The men were chuted up, lying on their parachutes waiting for their final jumpmaster inspection before boarding the jump aircraft. Tension was in the air. When Col. Randal and

Lady Jane arrived at each airplane, the men would attempt to struggle to their feet, but Col. Randal always ordered—"As you were."

"You men all know your job," Col. Randal said, telling every stick the same thing, hoping it was true. He was getting ready to find out. "Follow your orders, be alert."

"Let's do this."

Col. Randal and Lady Jane ended up at Chalk 1, Stick 1, which he would be jump mastering. With the exception of Jim, he did not know a single person who would be on the aircraft.

Col. Randal worked his way down the line of paratroopers who were reclining on their chutes. Each jumper had to stand up and go through a final jumpmaster inspection. He took his time. The inspections were like reading Braille—feeling with his fingers for things he could not see with his eyes.

Col. Randal could do the inspection with his eyes shut. In fact, he trained blindfolded.

The jumpmaster inspection is a personal thing between the jumper being inspected and the officer or NCO doing the inspecting. The idea being for the person undergoing inspection *not* to have any deficiencies at this late stage and for the jumpmaster to demonstrate a high degree of professionalism—thus gaining the trust of the men he was going to be in charge of on board the aircraft.

It also gave Col. Randal a chance to joke with each of the paratroopers—hoping to bring down the tension level of men who were getting ready to go into battle for the first time. At this point, it was impossible to tell the original members of the Five-Seven-Five from the men who had been let out of jail and forced to involuntarily volunteer to join the regiment before it sailed.

The immediate threat of combat has a way of forging a unified outfit out of a group of misfits that all the training missions in the world cannot accomplish.

When he finished inspecting the last man in the stick, it was almost time for Lieutenant Pamala Plum-Martin to depart with the Pathfinders. They would be taking off twenty minutes before the main body. Col.

Randal walked over to her C-47 to check on Captain Billy Jack Jaxx and the I&R platoon serving as Pathfinders.

The paratroopers were chuted up, sitting around in a semi-circle beside the Dakota, with Capt. Jaxx in the center. Facing the stick, he was reclined back on his parachute, holding court. It was apparent that although the young captain had had only a short while to work with the platoon, the men were comfortable having him in command tonight.

"Capt. Jaxx," Col. Randal said, taking pains to treat his Pathfinder commander with exaggerated courtesy in front of his troops. "Ready to go?"

It was not really a question.

Jack Cool was always ready to go.

"Yes, sir," Capt. Jaxx said. "Lieutenant Coogan and I worked out that other thing we talked about with Major McCloud."

"Good," Col. Randal said. "See you men on the DZ."

The I&R platoon chorused, "Airborne, sir!"

One element of the Five-Seven-Five was clearly already feeling like they were a part of Raiding Forces. Capt. Jaxx had worked his magic. He was that caliber of leader.

Lady Jane, Lt. Mandy and a couple of the Clipper Girls arrived in a jeep to see the Pathfinders off. Colonel Dudley Clarke was there with his photographers and film crew recording the event.

While the girls chatted up the paratroopers, Col. Randal jogged back to his stick and chuted up—he was cheating tonight. Lieutenant Karen Montgomery had packed an X-type parachute for him. The U.S. T-4 had a vicious opening shock. And the U.S. harness did not have a quick-release system—jumpers had to unbuckle the heavy canvas straps (which was impossible under some conditions, such as being wet—not likely in the desert—or being dragged by high winds—which was a real possibility).

In the future, Col. Randal planned to have the Five-Seven-Five jump British X-type chutes with quick release and U.S. reserves. Lady Jane already had it on her "To Do" list to obtain the chutes, which was not going to be easy, there being a severe shortage of British parachutes.

Jim gave him a quick jumpmaster inspection.

From the Pathfinder C-47 came a loud engine backfire that sounded like a pistol shot, followed by a high-pitched wheezing as a propeller slowly turned over and started rotating. Then the Dakota's engine broke into a full-throated roar—rough-sounding, like a Harley Davidson motorcycle.

The second engine popped, started wheezing, slowly turned over and then both engines were purring, smooth as silk, sounding powerful—straining at the leash, ready to get going.

Lt. Plum-Martin wasted no time. She sent the C-47 hurtling straight down the strip and lifted off into the night. The mission was on.

Tension on the departure airfield was at the boiling point.

Lady Jane, Lt. Mandy and the Clipper Girls arrived at Col. Randal's aircraft about the same time as Brandy and Captain Penelope "Legs" Honeycutt-Parker drove up in another jeep.

The men of the Five-Seven-Five—those who volunteered to be in the regiment in Panama and those who had been shanghaied at Ft. Benning—could not help noticing that Raiding Forces personnel, men and women, had gone to the trouble to turn out en masse on their own time to assist with the marshaling preparations and to see them off on their mission.

This was a military organization that looked out for its own.

THE RED LIGHT CAME ON TEN MINUTES OUT. Colonel John Randal made his way to the front of the C-47 to take a look out the windscreen. The 37th Airlift Squadron's CO, Lieutenant Colonel Randolph Johnson, was flying the plane. He had the best navigator in the squadron in his crew tonight.

Up ahead through the star-filled sky, nothing at all could be seen at this point. The Dakota was hurtling through space. Col. Randal had hoped to see some sign of the railroad flares the Pathfinder team would be putting out on the DZ—no joy.

"Six minutes in thirty seconds," Lt. Col. Johnson said over his shoulder, alerting Col. Randal that he was going to have to get back to the rear of the plane and start his sequence of jump commands. "Happy landing, sir. Don't worry, I'm going to drop you on target, on time—right on the money."

"I'll stand the first round at the Long Bar if you do," Col. Randal said.

He made his way down the aisle between the two rows of paratroopers in the back. The Air Corps loadmaster had the door open and the wind was howling. When Col. Randal reached the back, he turned and faced the seated jumpers, stuck both palms out and shouted, "SIX MINUTES!"

Then he braced both of his canvas-topped raiding boots against each side of the open door, reached up and with his fingertips, grasped the channel that ran around the door and arched his body outside the Dakota. Up ahead, he still could not see anything at this point. However, off to the side to the rear, tucked in tight formation, was the second C-47 in the two-ship serial.

Major Travis McCloud was on board that airplane and Col. Randal knew he would be going through the same sequence of jumpmaster tasks. Six more serials of two Dakotas each were flying behind and would be arriving over the DZ in one minute intervals—the 575th Rangers would all be put out in seven minutes.

The classic airborne carpet.

THE CONDITIONS FOR THE JUMP WERE NEAR-PERFECT. A lot can go wrong with weather in the desert. Tonight, for a change, there were no sudden cloudbursts, the winds were not excessive, and there was no sign of the dust storms that can spring up at a moment's notice. Still, Col. Randal would have felt a lot better if he could see the burning arrowhead Jack Cool was going to mark the DZ with.

"STAND UP AND HOOK UP!"

The jumpers struggled to their feet. The men unhooked the snap links from the canvas carrying handle on their reserve parachute on their chest. The yellow static line was strung over their right shoulders. They attached it to the steel cable running down the length of the roof of the C-47 and jerked down, locking it. Then came the tricky part—inserting the safety wire dangling on the string into the tiny hole at the base of the snap link. Once that was accomplished, the wire was bent down with the trigger finger—all done while trying to maintain balance in a swaying airplane.

"CHECK STATIC LINE!"

The rasping sound of metal on metal filled the compartment as the paratroopers vigorously rattled their snap links back and forth on the steel cable.

"CHECK YOUR EQUIPMENT!"

While the men checked their equipment, Col. Randal went back to the door and arched outside again to take a quick look down the length of the fuselage of the C-47 toward the DZ, hoping to see the burning arrow. Nothing.

Col. Randal was beginning to have second thoughts about this mission. This was the largest airborne operation he had ever been involved in. He did not know the troops he commanded—they didn't know him. The Five-Seven-Five had never heard a shot fired in anger.

And for all Col. Randal could tell, right now they were getting ready to drop into the middle of nowhere. The 37th Airlift Squadron was the first USAAF troop carrier unit in Egypt, they had never conducted a parachute operation before and they had virtually no experience with desert flying at night. There was no guarantee the squadron could even find Fort No. 9.

What could possibly go wrong?

"SOUND OFF FOR EQUIPMENT CHECK!"

"OK! OK! OK! . . ."

Col. Randal went back to the door and arched outside. He spotted a glimmer on the ground up ahead. Capt. Jaxx was on the DZ. It was marked.

Relief swept over him as Col. Randal swung back inside. He glanced at his Rolex.

"ONE MINUTE!"

Tension in the aircraft shot up to pressure cooker level. The troops wanted to go. The Rangers started rattling their static lines back and forth.

Col. Randal went back to the door, arched out to make a final check and could see the shape of an arrow of red burning railroad flares. There was no sign of tracers, which would indicate fighting on the ground.

"CLOSE ON THE DOOR!"

The stick shuffled forward, doing the "Airborne Shuffle," never picking up their boots to eliminate the possibility of tripping.

Col. Randal swung into position in the door, advanced his right boot until half of it was in space, knees bent, reached out and slapped his palms flat down on the outside skin of the aircraft. He could feel the rivets.

When the burning arrow was off the edge of the toe of his unpolished raiding boot, he leaned his head back inside the aircraft and shouted, "Let's go!"

Then he launched out the door in a tight body tuck—head down, hands on the ends of his reserve parachute, elbows in tight against his sides, feet and knees together. The prop blast from the C-47 tumbled him over and over. Behind him the static line was deploying his parachute.

Tonight they were jumping at one thousand feet—twice as high as a normal combat jump to reduce the possibility of jump injuries. When Col. Randal's parachute cracked open, he looked down between his boots and saw he was coming straight down, right on the tip of the burning arrow—not drifting at all.

A pair of faces on the ground were looking up at him. Col. Randal took up the prepare-to-land position, rocking his knees to make sure they were not locked, boots touching, elbows in, and put his chin on his chest and mentally geared up for his PLF. He could have made a stand-up landing, but since those were prohibited for a reason, he went limp.

Captain Billy Jack Jaxx and King grabbed him before he could make his parachute landing fall—so it was a "sort-of" stand-up landing.

Parachutes were drifting down silently on the DZ. The second serial was overhead, and jumpers were spilling out. The 575th Rangers were executing a textbook combat parachute jump far in the enemy's rear.

Major Everard Beauchamp arrived at the assembly point with Captain "Geronimo" Joe McKoy and Waldo.

Capt. McKoy said, "Ain't this really somethin'?"

CHAPTER TWENTY-TWO

SMOKE 'EM

THE SECOND SERIAL CAME OVERHEAD and began to discharge its load of Rangers. Major Travis McCloud arrived at the assembly point with his command party. Captain Roy Kidd came by with part of A Company and immediately set off to his ORP—the rest of his men had orders to follow as soon as they landed. Parachutes were descending all around.

Colonel John Randal found himself on the ground, behind enemy lines in close proximity to the objective, armed to the teeth, but without a job. At this point, he was a mere spectator. He did not like the feeling one bit, although it was quite an adrenalin rush to be observing this operation unfold all around him.

Everyone had their orders and they were rushing by, intent on carrying them out. So far, not a shot had been fired. It was unclear if the Italians in Fort No. 9 actually realized there were parachutists on the ground—they might have believed the airplanes were a flight of bombers en route to bomb Tripoli.

Or, the Blackshirts may have been paralyzed with fear—maybe they had already decamped over the back wall like the last time Raiding Forces had paid a call.

Major Everard Beauchamp was supervising the recovery of the wing-dropped bundles containing the four 81mm mortars. The Louisiana National Guard officer appeared very unruffled for being on his first combat operation a long way behind enemy lines.

With no winds of any substance to scatter the bundles, he had his battery in place and firing on Fort No. 9 in record time. Shortly after, the first mortar round went down the tube. The battery of eight M1919 .30 caliber Browning Light machine guns (LMGs) was engaging the fort as soon as they could be set up.

The firing intensified as additional LMGs engaged.

Although Maj. Beauchamp had his men in action quickly and the mortar men of the Five-Seven-Five were performing with the precision of a Swiss watch—being highly trained in the drill—unfortunately, the peacetime army did not have the luxury of much actual live firing. The 81s were not hitting a lot, but they were creating fear and despondency on the objective.

The eight .30 caliber Browning LMGs, once they found the range, were hammering the mud walls of Fort No. 9. The problem was, the walls were about two feet thick. So while the eight guns—firing approximately six hundred rounds per minute each—were splattering the building with a hailstorm of steel-jacketed rounds, they were not causing much damage.

Parachutes were still coming down as the final serial thundered overhead. As the jumpers landed, they struggled out of their harnesses, dropped their chutes where they lay and dashed off on a dead run for their Objective Rally Point.

At the ORP, Maj. McCloud had his Assault element under tight control. The Rangers had strict orders not to begin firing until given the command. He wanted to assemble as many of his men as possible prior to launching the attack on the fort. The idea was to deliver a heavy dose of concentrated fire by B and C Companies acting in support of A Company's attack.

With covering fire, it is not necessary to inflict casualties, although it's good if you do. The purpose of the exercise is to make the bad guys keep their heads down and not shoot back as the assault goes in.

To that end, it doesn't hurt to have the attacking element screaming and yelling like wild men when they attack, bayonet fixed, touching off a round every time their left foot hits the ground—carrying out walking fire.

Maj. McCloud's intent was to obtain the maximum element of shock in order to enhance the element of surprise. He was hoping the Italians were not aware he had enfiladed Fort No. 9. Having taught Airborne

Tactics at the Infantry School, Maj. McCloud knew exactly what he was doing tonight and why he was doing it.

Col. Randal decided to walk over and have a word with Maj. Beauchamp. He found him in the thick of things at the mortar battery, which was firing to beat the band. The mortarmen were really laying it down.

"Major," Col. Randal said, "I want you to start displacing your LMGs two at a time to Major McCloud—he can use them to support his attack and they'll be useless here once the signal goes up to shift your fires."

"Roger, suh."

"Also," Col. Randal ordered, "change of plans. When the time comes to shift your mortar fires, start breaking down three of your 81s. We'll be loading them on captured trucks when the Five-Seven-Five pulls out.

"Keep one 81 firing on the fort—illumination rounds only, no HE. Clear?"

"Yes, suh."

Col. Randal did not want to mention he was concerned the mortar crew might accidently drop a short round on A Company when it went in for the attack.

A Ranger ran up and saluted. "Sir, Private Komansky reports."

"Well," Col. Randal said, returning the salute. "Go ahead, Komansky—report."

"Captain Jaxx sends his compliments—the hangars are secure, sir."

"Very good."

"Jack Cool . . . I mean Captain Jaxx said to tell you there's an Italian plane parked in one of the hangars, sir," Pvt. Komansky said. "He believes it's like one your blond pilot Lieutenant Plum-what's-her-name has, sir."

"Inform Captain Jaxx," Col. Randal said, "I'll be there in zero-five."

"Yes, sir!"

Col. Randal turned to Maj. Beauchamp, who was snapping out orders to everyone in sight, rapid-fire. "Is there anyone in the Five-Seven-Five with a private pilot's license?"

"I have one, suh," Maj. Beauchamp said. "Our S-4, Captain Reacher, does as well."

"Reacher any good?"

"Oh, yes," Maj. Beauchamp said. "Wealthy family—father owns the plane, a twin engine Beechcraft I believe, suh. Had a pilot's license since he was fifteen."

"Have Captain Reacher report to me at the hangars," Col. Randal ordered. "Whatever you have him doing, find someone else to take over."

"Mackalroy," Maj. Beauchamp ordered one of his paratroopers, "locate Captain Reacher; have him report here immediately."

"Sir!"

"King," Col. Randal asked, "who's the best AVG navigator along tonight?"

"Pettigrew, Chief."

"Get him—meet me at the hangars."

"On the way."

Col. Randal and Jim walked to the hangars, where they found that Capt. Jaxx had the I&R platoon setting up a perimeter. Captain "Geronimo" Joe McKoy and Waldo were inspecting the trucks—a Chevrolet, a Ford and a Bedford—all captured from the British and reflagged with Italian colors. Now they had been captured back.

Lt. Coogan was working on the fuel tanker.

"There was no one home when we arrived, sir," Capt. Jaxx reported. "Thought you might like to see the airplane we found."

They walked into one of the hangars and turned on their hook-nosed flashlights. The little green plane was an IMAM Ro.63. The same type Raiding Forces had captured and pressed into service.

Jim said, "I can fly it out of here. No sense letting this Ro.63 go to waste."

"There's a Captain Reacher on the way to be your co-pilot," Col. Randal said. "King's rounding up Pettigrew to navigate—I'd fly to Oasis X."

"Good idea," Jim said. "I shall start my preflight, and we can be airborne straightaway. This is a great capture, Colonel."

"We're just about up, sir," Capt. Jaxx said. "I've arranged with Maj. McCloud to shift his fires on my signal—a pair of red flares."

"Move out when ready," Col. Randal said.

King arrived with Cpl. Pettigrew at about the same time a tall captain from the Five-Seven-Five walked inside the hangar—Capt. Reacher. Jim and the captain began looking over the IMAM Ro.63.

Jim ordered, "Pettigrew, plot a course to Oasis X. We are taking off in three minutes."

"Yes, sir!"

Capt. Jaxx and Lt. Coogan climbed on board the ten-ton fuel tanker. With Jack Cool at the wheel, they slowly rolled out.

As they came by, Col. Randal said, "Light 'em up, Jack."

Capt. Jaxx shouted, "Dick set charges on the bomb dump out back of the hangars, sir—a one-hour time fuse. There's about forty-five minutes left on the burn."

"Glad you mentioned it," Col. Randal said, as the ten-ton tanker truck picked up speed.

"Me too," Waldo said. "That ain't no minor news flash."

Capt. Jaxx fired his flare pistol signal to Maj. McCloud. Seeing the flare Maj. McCloud fired his flare pistol signal to Maj. Beauchamp.

Maj. Beauchamp gave the command, "Shift your fires!"

As ordered, three of the mortars immediately ceased fire while one began putting up illumination rounds over Fort No. 9. The 81mm parachute flares cracked open and began slowly floating down from the sky, creating a mellow-yellow, otherworldly glow.

Then Maj. McCloud signaled B Company and C Company to commence firing their personal weapons. M1s, Thompson SMGs and BARs opened, putting out grazing fire aimed at the palm grove behind the fort. The eight belt-fed .30 caliber M1919 Browning LMGs, having been displaced, opened simultaneously. The sound of the combined weapons was like a massive thunderstorm breaking.

M1s, being semiautomatic, put out an impressive volume of fire, making it seem like there were a lot more riflemen present than there actually were.

"Jack doing what I think, Chief?" King asked.

"Roger that," Col. Randal said, sticking one of Waldo's thin cigars between his front teeth.

Capt. McKoy strolled over, "You reckon that same tubby little Regia Aeronautica *tenente* is still in command of the fort, John? His girlfriend, if she's still around, ain't gonna like this next part one little bit if he is."

Col. Randal said, "We're getting ready to find out."

"Is Jack gonna try to blow that place up like you and Maj. McCloud did last time we was here, Colonel?" Waldo asked.

"Affirmative."

Waldo said, "Uh-oh!"

The IMAM Ro.63 roared into life. Jim taxied out of the hangar, waved out the window, then the beautiful little aircraft rolled past the mortar that was firing the illumination rounds, picked up speed and took off in an incredibly short distance. It disappeared into the night.

Col. Randal ordered, "OK—Lieutenant Hays, pull in your security. Rally on the mortars."

"Yes, sir," the Five-Seven-Five I&R platoon leader said.

Flanking Fort No. 9, Captain Roy Kidd was in command of A/575, the company tasked with making the ground attack. He had all three platoons on line, lying in the prone position.

The Rangers were becoming increasingly anxious to get going.

There had been a few bursts of MG fire from the roof of the fort when they first arrived, but that had long since died out. Capt. Kidd was pretty sure the Italians had abandoned the position. He did not share that thought with his men.

Capt. Kidd wanted his Rangers psyched up, giving it everything they had when A Company stood up and went in for the kill. The quicker they overran the objective, the better—time saves lives in the attack. The longer it takes to develop an assault, the longer the troops are exposed to enemy fire.

A lot of commanders never learn that.

Maj. McCloud fired the flares to signal attack.

"FIX BAYONETS!" Capt. Kidd shouted, "ON LINE—MOVE OUT—FOLLOW ME!"

Then he gave a loud, piercing rebel yell.

The Rangers stood up as one, screaming, and began their attack—riflemen firing a round every time their left foot hit the ground, BAR men and Thompson gunners squeezing off short, crisp bursts. The 575th Rangers went straight in—the first bayonet charge by U.S. Army Forces in the Middle East Command in WWII.

The only problem was, when the assault line reached the mud wall, the Rangers had to stop, throw grappling hooks over the top and scale the wall before continuing their history-making bayonet charge. The men discovered it can be tricky climbing up a rope in the middle of a firefight carrying an M1 rifle with a bayonet fixed.

The Rangers resumed firing immediately after making it over the wall. The sound and fury of all the automatic weapons going at once was spectacular. Most importantly, the fire was so disciplined it gave confidence to the men as they began to make their way toward the objective.

Capt. Kidd's Rangers were going in for the kill and nothing could stop them now—only there was not much to obstruct their attack. Nearly all the Italians were hiding in the palm grove, and they had no intention of resisting, much less defending the fort.

The rebel yelling picked up in intensity as the Rangers closed. If any of the Fascists were not already terrorized, they were now.

In the flickering artificial moonlight of the 81mm parachute flares, the Rangers could see the ten-ton fuel tanker rolling toward Fort No. 9 up ahead. The troops were under strict orders not to fire anywhere near it—they had been briefed on what was about to take place. A Company's assault line conducted a pause short of the main building, as planned before the final assault.

No one was prepared for what happened next.

Capt. Jaxx was at the wheel of the ten-ton fuel tanker topped off with high grade aviation gas. Lt. Coogan, *aka* "Dynamite Dick", was in the passenger seat. There was a pressure plate on the front bumper that was wired to explosives mounted on the fuel tank.

However, unlike when Col. Randal and Maj. McCloud did it the first time, there was no fuse burning on a land mine strapped to the back. Dynamite Dick was not about to ride in a truck full of highly flammable avgas that was wired to blow itself up with a fuse burning—being a highly-experienced professional, he had affixed a dead man's switch to the land mine on the rear bumper.

Lt. Coogan was holding the detonator in his hand like a grenade with the pin pulled. If he let go, there was a ten-second delay—then the truck blew. What that meant was that he and Capt. Jaxx did not have to guess how much time was left before bailing out.

However, Capt. Jaxx still could not bump into anything. There was no delay on the pressure plate charge on the front fender. When it hit something—*KAAABOOOM!*

And, a single tracer from Fort No. 9 could blow the thin-skinned tanker sky-high.

Capt. Jaxx began to pick up speed, but he was not interested in going fast. When he jumped out from behind the wheel, he wanted the tanker to continue on straight and true. Slow was better for that.

The gate came up ahead.

The trick was to get the fuel tanker truck through the gate and bail out inside the mud wall surrounding the fort—without banging into anything.

Visibility was good. However, the mellow-yellow light from the swaying parachute flares was a little spooky—sitting on a ten-ton incendiary bomb as the two officers were.

"You good to go, Dick—standing by to hit the silk?"

"Yes, sir," Lt. Coogan said. "Do this kind of thing often in Raiding Forces?"

"That's a Rodge," Capt. Jaxx lied. "Almost every day."

Jack Cool.

Actually, he was about half-petrified—whose idea was this?

Oh yeah . . . his.

The sound of the concentrated gunfire from the Ranger's assault line off to the right was deafening. The rebel yelling and blood-chilling screaming sent a shiver down the spine of everyone who heard it—on both sides. There was no let-up, even though A/575th had briefly paused the assault.

Col. Randal said, "Let's go."

He led the way—Capt. McKoy, Waldo and King walking down the road to Fort No. 9 following Capt. Jaxx and Lt. Coogan in the fuel tanker.

Up ahead, Capt. Jaxx managed to drive the truck through the gate of the fort without banging into the wall on either side—which, under normal circumstances, would have been no big deal since it was double-wide.

But riding in a ten-ton fire bomb with a detonator on the front bumper changes the difficulty factor.

Unknown to Capt. Jaxx, after Raiding Forces' last visit, the *tenente* had taken precautions to ensure that no one would ever drive a truck full of explosives into the main building of Fort No. 9 again. He had an obstruction erected.

Not having much in the way of building materials, local Arabs were hired to make bricks out of the desert sand using an ancient technique augmented with a few bags of concrete.

Then the workmen built a three foot-high wall directly in front of the garrison. This should have prevented anyone from crashing into the building. However, this was Libya and Fort No. 9 was located on the very edge of the Great Sand Sea.

There is a lot of sand in the Great Sand Sea. The wind also blows more or less constantly. No one had bothered to sweep away the sand that blew up against the wall and, over time, it had virtually disappeared—buried almost to the top.

Instead of a barrier, the sand now created a ramp.

In daylight, Capt. Jaxx and Lt. Coogan would have seen the tracks that drove around the obstruction on both sides. But in the mellow, ambient light of the parachute flares, neither man spotted the tracks or the change in elevation of the road.

That is, they did not see it until the last second before hitting it.

"BAIL OUT," Capt. Jaxx screamed, semi-hysterically.

He went out one side of the open-topped cab, and Lt. Coogan went out the other side, letting go of the dead man's switch in mid-air—which meant the fuel tanker was going to blow in ten seconds—no matter what.

The tanker continued rolling up the sand ramp and sailed about six feet in the air from momentum before nose-diving straight down into the ground on the far side, setting off the pressure-activated detonator. *KABOOOOOM!*

Incredibly, the aviation fuel tank did not explode.

The back end of the massive truck was now traveling faster than the front. The fuel tanker stood up on its nose when the pressure plate on the front bumper exploded.

Twisting like a steel tornado to the sound of screeching metal, the tanker crashed against the side of Fort No. 9, standing upright almost perpendicular and *KABOOOOOM!*

The explosives on the rear bumper detonated.

The blast created the mother of all fireballs, with the orange mushroom-shaped explosion billowing ten stories in the air. Fort No. 9 was engulfed in flames.

Also unknown to Raiding Forces was that the *tenente* had taken one other precaution to defend his outpost.

The last time Raiding Forces had arrived unexpected and unannounced, the *tenente's* men hightailed it over the back wall to the palm grove the instant the fort came under attack. To give his troops added confidence that they had the means to defend the position and not run away, the commandant had stocked almost the entire ground floor with ammunition, grenades and mortar rounds. His thinking being, if another attack occurred, it was best to have the munitions inside the garrison rather than outside.

That was a mistake.

A massive secondary explosion tore through the building, blowing up and out the roof like a volcano, causing the second and third stories to collapse. Debris rained down for a long time. It seemed like no one inside could have survived.

The Rangers ceased fire, stunned by the sight of their objective disintegrating before their eyes. No one had explained it to them like that. The Five-Seven-Five had never witnessed an explosion of such magnitude.

Capt. Jaxx was lying in the ditch on one side of the road. He called over to Lt. Coogan, who was in the ditch on the other side, "You all right, Dick?"

Lt. Coogan said, "What the hell just happened?"

Capt. Jaxx said, "I think we got 'em."

Col. Randal's command party strolled up as the A Company Rangers stormed in to search the ruins of Fort No. 9.

"Looks like them Italian boys built their obstruction a little too low and a little too close to the house to do much good," Capt. McKoy said. "Real poor preventive maintenance, lettin' that sand pile up like 'at."

Waldo said, "I ain't never seen a ten-ton truck stand up like that—made a big boom."

Col. Randal looked down at Capt. Jaxx lying semi-concussed in the ditch, "Whatever they're paying you, Jack—it ain't enough."

Capt. Jaxx said, "Anyone know how to check your blood pressure?"

The tubby little *tenente* stumbled out of the rubble, leading his pleasantly plump mistress by one hand. Two of Capt. Kidd's men immediately "captured" them at bayonet point. The Rangers prodded them over to where Col. Randal's command party was standing.

The *tenente* was not a happy camper—even though the couple's survival was a miracle. Tonight was the last straw. The commandant wanted to surrender.

He burst into tears when Col. Randal told him no.

Col. Randal needed him to be there to tell the tale when relief arrived. No sense performing a drop deep behind enemy lines if the bad guys did not have an eyewitness to explain how terrifying "the sudden appearance of the entire US Seventy-First Airborne Division" was to experience.

To make sure the *tenente* knew exactly who had attacked Fort No. 9, Col. Randal stuffed one of the cards printed by Colonel Dudley Clarke in the front pocket of his uniform. There was a large pair of US Jump Wings on one side and a message on the back: "Compliments of the US Seventy-First Airborne Division."

"HAVE YOUR BATTALION ASSEMBLE on the drop zone," Colonel John Randal ordered Major Travis McCloud.

"Yes, sir."

"Get me a good count," Col. Randal said. "Load your heavy weapons and anyone injured in the three trucks. Then move out. King will be leading the march."

"Wilco."

"Captain McKoy," Col. Randal said, "take command of the three trucks. Pick the AVG drivers you want and you'll need a navigator."

"I know just the men, John," Captain "Geronimo" Joe McKoy said. "Already briefed 'em."

“In that case, you and Waldo are cleared to roll out as soon as the trucks are loaded,” Col. Randal said. “Don’t wait for us. Keep going until you link up with Jack Merritt.”

“Can do,” Capt. McKoy said. “See you when I see you.”

“Captain Jaxx,” Col. Randal ordered, “have Lieutenant Hays and the I&R platoon fold in behind King in the line of march. You can travel with the platoon or with me. I’ll be on point with King—at least initially.”

“Roger,” Capt. Jaxx said, gingerly climbing to his feet. “I’ll be with the platoon, sir.”

“Lieutenant Coogan,” Col. Randal ordered, “inform Major McCloud as to the status of the demolitions charges you placed on the bomb dump—we don’t want to be anywhere in the area when it goes up.”

“Yes, sir.”

As King and Col. Randal walked back to the DZ, King asked, “How hard do you want me to go on the Rangers, Chief?”

Col. Randal said, “Smoke ’em.”

CHAPTER TWENTY-THREE

FUBAR

COLONEL JOHN RANDAL WAS IN HIS THIRD-FLOOR suite in the small private briefing area. A big chalkboard was set up on an easel. He was diagramming ideas for the reorganization of Raiding Forces. This was approximately his third try.

Captain "Geronimo" Joe McKoy and Waldo Treywick were sitting in chairs, critiquing his every move. The three were enjoying themselves.

They had flown in from the desert early that morning.

The Five-Seven-Five had been in for a rude awakening when it reached the rendezvous with Major Jack Merritt, fifty hard-marching miles' distance from Fort No. 9. King had followed to the letter Col. Randal's orders to "smoke 'em." The Rangers were all in when they arrived at the rally point—or they thought they were.

Instead of a convoy to transport the tired paratroopers back to RFHQ, what they found was Sergeant Major Mike "March or Die" Mikkalis and eight hard-as-nails ex-Foreign Legion Raiders from Blue Patrol, all wearing their white Legion kepis and malevolent expressions.

The sight of them standing at parade rest in the middle of nowhere when the Rangers marched in had a chilling effect on the officers and men of the Five-Seven-Five.

Sgt. Maj. Mikkalis' orders were to keep the Five-Seven-Five in the field for the next four weeks, conducting all manner of training necessary to provide the Rangers with the rudiments of desert raiding operations as it was conducted by Raiding Forces. Captain Mike "Mad Dog" Reupart would join the team of ex-Foreign Legion trainers in the next few days. He was training the fifty-man contingent of the new AVG volunteers, but Col. Randal intended to pull him off that assignment.

The Rangers were more than a little shocked to learn that their training would take place *behind* enemy lines. And from the looks of the ex-Foreign Legionnaires, they were not in for a gentle initiation to the mysteries of desert warfare.

B/575th Rangers were loaded aboard Maj. Merritt's trucks to be convoyed back to Cairo. The plan was for them to be flown to the UK to the Special Warfare Training Center located at scenic Achnacarry, Scotland.

They would undergo their desert training at a later date.

All three companies would rotate through the Commando Castle one at a time. Col. Randal wanted his U.S. troops fully indoctrinated in all aspects of the art of small-scale, pinprick raiding. The U.S. Army's training was not the equivalent of the British Commandos—he demanded only the best for the Five-Seven-Five.

The Rangers had performed above expectations in the attack on Fort No. 9. Even though they had met limited resistance, it was still a complicated mission. Putting on a parachute, flying behind enemy lines in the dark of night and jumping on an enemy target is not for the faint of heart.

The troops had held up well on the forced march, even though King had nearly marched them into the ground—to include Col. Randal, who had been regretting the "smoke 'em" order for the last twenty miles or so.

Everyone in the Five-Seven-Five agreed that the trek was worse than the combat, which is one of the justifications for hard training. The troops would rather be at the front in battle than safe in the rear, training.

The two-day "Death March"—struggling to keep up with the Merc leading it—would go down in the annals of Ranger legend.

What had looked like a rabble when the Five-Seven-Five came off the troop transport was beginning to jell into a cohesive fighting force. Col. Randal was not surprised. Troublemakers from a volunteer unit like the U.S. Paratroops often make outstanding combat soldiers—in garrison, high-spirited paratroopers become bored, one thing leads to another and they find themselves in the brig.

The problem was going to be with the officers and NCOs. Col. Randal expected to find Airborne Command had taken the opportunity to rid itself of a lot of bad apples when the Five-Seven-Five shipped out.

He intended to give everyone a fair chance. Then, those who did not measure up to Raiding Forces' standards were out—plus anyone could quit at any time. The enlisted troops who failed would be assigned to the docks to work as stevedores unloading ships—the officers would go to Grey Pillars where they could push pencils and hang out at the Long Bar to their hearts' delight.

Col. Randal had issued orders to Sgt. Maj. Mikkalis to be brutal with his evaluation of the officers. Only the best would be allowed the privilege of commanding Raiding Forces troops.

Col. Randal was quite sure that Sgt. Maj. Mikkalis and his merry band of ex-Foreign Legion sadists were going to apply the same standard to the Five-Seven-Five NCOs, only worse.

James "Baldie" Taylor and Lieutenant Pamala Plum-Martin were waiting at the rally point. The two IMAM Ro.63s were concealed under camouflage netting. Col. Randal, Capt. McKoy, Waldo, Lieutenant Richard "Dynamite Dick" Coogan and King were to be flown back to RFHQ.

Lt. Coogan was slated to marry up with Captain "Pyro" Percy Stirling in order to accompany him on a railroad busting patrol. There was a cer-tain amount of angst about what might happen when those two teamed up, given Dynamite Dick's initial showing with the ten-ton fuel truck. He had the makings of a big-bang man.

Captain Billy Jack Jaxx had elected to stay in the field to spend more time with the I&R platoon. He liked what he saw so far.

Not long after the Five-Seven-Five marched in, Captain Roy Kidd's Scout Patrol arrived at the rally point.

Col. Randal called over Capt. Jaxx and the I&R platoon leader, Lieutenant Clint Hays.

"Jack, I want you and Lieutenant Hays to accompany Roy on patrol —he's going to demonstrate his truck plinking technique."

"Outstanding, sir," Capt. Jaxx said.

"Lieutenant Hays, pick your two best riflemen to understudy Captain Kidd's Lovat Scout snipers," Col. Randal ordered. "The captain and his boys are our premier truck killers."

"Yes, sir," Lt. Hays said. "My platoon has a two-man sniper element armed with scoped M-1903s."

Col. Randal said, "The Lovat Scouts are going to show you something that works a little better than Springfield rifles at extreme long range."

"That I'm looking forward to, sir," Lt. Hays said.

"Jack, you understand," Col. Randal said, "we may have to pull you out of the field in a hurry if a SOLID GOLD, RED INDIAN or a BOMBSHELL comes up."

"Roger that, sir."

Then, Col. Randal's party had boarded the airplanes for the flight back to RFHQ.

COLONEL JOHN RANDAL SAID, "Raiding Forces" and wrote the words at the top of the chalkboard. "Let's break it down into two ground elements—Lancelot Lancers and Rangers with one seagoing element, Sea Squadron. He was still tweaking his plan.

"We'll fold Desert Patrol into the Lancers under Terry Stone. And, we'll have one reinforced gun jeep company of Rangers under Travis McCloud, which will be styled 'Ranger', with a platoon of amphibious Rangers assigned to Sea Squadron once they get back from Achnacarry."

"That should make the Rangers and the Lancers about equal in size," Captain "Geronimo" Joe McKoy said. "Five patrols each."

"Roy Kidd's Scout Patrol will be a Raiding Forces asset reporting directly to me," Col. Randal said, diagramming it separately from the other three command elements. "As will the Railroad Wrecking Crew II under Percy."

"That's a good idea," Capt. McKoy said. "What's the plan for Billy Jack?"

"He's going to form a Special Missions/Quick Reaction Team out of part of my Ranger Patrol, which needs to be renamed now that the Five-Seven-Five has arrived."

Waldo said, "Raider Patrol."

"I like that, Mr. Treywick," Col. Randal said, writing it on the board. "It will be under my direct control."

"Jack's takin' a real close look at the I&R platoon," Capt. McKoy said. "What d'you reckon he's got up his sleeve, John?"

"I don't know," Col. Randal said. "We'll find . . ."

King stuck his head in the door, "Sergeant Blackburn, Chief."

"Send him in," Col. Randal ordered.

Sergeant Rex Blackburn, the Ranger—now Raider—Patrol mortar NCO, walked in and reported, having been summoned earlier by Col. Randal.

"The Five-Seven-Five 81 mortar crews need work, Sgt. Blackburn," Col. Randal said. "Come up with a plan, pack your bags and join Sergeant Major Mikkalis in the field. The crews looked pretty good in action but couldn't hit anything."

"Yes, sir."

"You're the best in the business," Col. Randal said. "Make it happen, sergeant."

James "Baldie" Taylor arrived as Sgt. Blackburn was leaving.

Col. Randal ran through the reorganization chart with him.

Jim said, "I have one suggestion—why not call Major McCloud's gun jeep company 'Ranger Force'? That gives you the Lancelot Lancers Yeomanry Regiment and Ranger Force, which still barely totals up to two full companies of troops, but sounds like an entire brigade of desert raiders."

"We can do that," Col. Randal said. "I like it."

"Dudley is sure to love having a phantom special operations brigade to play with," Jim said. "Particularly one with the ability to carry out real live missions. He will probably try to make the Nazis believe it's a full division—giving him two pseudo parachute divisions."

Jim's suggestion gave Col. Randal an idea that solved a problem he had been trying to work through for some time—how to best employ Major Sir Terry "Zorro" Stone. Now all he was going to have to do is sell it to him.

"Sergeant Rawlston, Chief."

"You wanted to see me, Colonel?" the AVG ex-sergeant asked.

"Stand at attention, Sergeant," Col. Randal. "Lady Jane—front and center."

Drop-dead gorgeous Major the Lady Jane Seaborn came out of the bedroom with three khaki BDU jackets over her arm, which she carefully laid over the back of one of the overstuffed chairs in the living area. Then she walked up to where ex-Sergeant Hank W. Rawlston was standing at attention while holding the nasty stub of his blunt cigar against one grease-stained pants leg.

Lady Jane reached into her shoulder bag, produced a switchblade jump knife Col. Randal had never seen before and touched a button on the handle. A razor-sharp spear-point blade appeared as if by magic. She had everyone's attention.

Without a word, Lady Jane cut the chevrons off one sleeve of the sergeant's blouse, then walked around and neatly removed the other. Sgt. Rawlston was wondering what crime he had committed *now* that justified his being busted. This was not the first time it had happened.

"I'm the commander of a regiment of U.S. Army Paratroopers," Col. Randal said. "Demeaning for an officer in my position to have a mere sergeant as my chief of maintenance.

"You've been promoted to Chief Warrant Officer, skipped a grade—more fitting—provided that you re-enlist."

"Congratulations, Chief," Lady Jane said, her green eyes sparkling, as she pinned Chief Warrant Officer's insignia on his collar. "There are three new BDU jackets for you on the chair over there, all with the proper badges in place."

"Could have gotten you a direct promotion to captain, Mr. Rawlston," Col. Randal said, handing him one of Waldo's custom-rolled cigars, "but I knew you'd turn it down."

Chief Rawlston said, "Holy . . . !"

COLONEL JOHN RANDAL AND MAJOR THE LADY Jane Seaborn were sitting in the back of the Gezira Club restaurant behind a palm. Rita and Lana were at the table. The two Zar Cult priestesses caused quite a stir when the group walked in.

Due to their undercover work at the Kit-Kat Club, Rita and Lana had become local celebrities. Every man, and some of the women, in the room, knew who they were. The girls, totally aloof as they always were in public, did not appear to notice the attention.

Col. Randal was the object of much envy, as well as quite a bit of speculation, it being well-known that Rita and Lana openly referred to themselves as his slaves. The question in everyone's mind was what Lady Jane thought about her boyfriend being the owner of the hottest duo attraction at Cairo's most notorious nightclub.

Or, was there more to it behind closed doors?

Major Sir Terry "Zorro" Stone, drinking at the bar with one of his hospital nurses, joined them at the table.

Rita and Lana lost their haughty expressions, replacing them with their standard-issue magnificent smiles now that they were seated with their backs to the crowd. The pair twittered like canaries when Maj. Stone arrived. Normally ambivalent to men, the girls thought Zorro looked like their favorite movie star, Errol Flynn.

And he did.

Col. Randal said, "Jane, do you have a pen?"

When she produced one from her purse, he unfolded a paper napkin and started to diagram the new Raiding Forces Table of Organization. Maj. Stone watched skeptically.

"So, here's the deal, Terry," Col. Randal said. "We roll Desert Patrol into the Lancelot Lancers—you can consider it a new squadron and we will attach Travis McCloud with a reinforced company of Rangers as well, which will be called 'Ranger Force.'

"Now you have three gun jeep squadrons, so we'll reflag the Lounge Lizards as the Lancelot Lancer Raiding Regiment—Raiding Regiment for short."

Maj. Stone studied the diagram, "I shall have Phantom message the Duke straightaway. You can never predict how he will react—at least I have never been able to."

"What's your thought?"

"Like the name, old stick," Maj. Stone said. "An elegant solution for re-enforcing the regiment—one of your best."

"Understand," Col. Randal said, "the purpose of the exercise is to have a joint U.S./U.K. outfit. This plan will make you my Deputy Commander—not simply the Raiding Regiment's commanding officer."

"The cheese in the trap?"

"There it is."

"Fine," Maj. Stone said. "I knew you would have your way sooner or later. You never give up."

The maître d'brought a phone to the table. "Call for you, Lady Seaborn."

As she took her phone call, Maj. Stone excused himself to get back to the nurse at the bar.

Lady Jane put her hand over the mouthpiece of the phone, "Chief Rawlston is at the dock, John. He says the Five-Seven-Five jeeps have arrived—what is a SNAFU?"

"Situation Normal All *Fouled* up," Col. Randal lied.

"We have a SNAFU," Lady Jane said. "A big one."

"No kidding," Col. Randal said. "I never really expected the U.S. Army to send us one jeep for every three men in the Five-Seven-Five like Colonel Fellers promised.

"How many did we get?"

Lady Jane burst out laughing. "Eight hundred sixty-six."

"SNAFU, hell," Col. Randal said, "That's a FUBAR."

"And what," Lady Jane asked, "is a FUBAR?"

"Fouled Up Beyond All Recognition."

COLONEL JOHN RANDAL, JAMES "BALDIE" TAYLOR, Colonel Dudley Clarke, Colonel Bonner Fellers and Chief Warrant Officer Hank Rawlston were standing on the dock watching the 575th Ranger's jeeps being unloaded.

Captain "Geronimo" Joe McKoy was showing Waldo Treywick how to display his brand-new counterfeit CIC identification card. Col. Clarke had the A-Force forger "Twitters the Taster" make the ID for him.

The problem with the ID card was that Waldo was not in the U.S. Army and he did not have any rank. The A-Force forger had resolved that issue by placing a 0 in the space that said "Rank." While that would probably confuse anyone who saw it, questions might be raised.

Major the Lady Jane Seaborn, Rita and Lana were paying rapt attention to Capt. McKoy's tutorial.

"Now the thing to keep in mind, Waldo, is nobody knows what the CIC does for sure," Capt. McKoy said. "And *you* ain't gonna volunteer any information—mystery bein' a good thing for a man in your particular situation."

"Yeah," Waldo said, "loose lips could sink my ship."

"So what you do," Capt. McKoy said, "if you ever have to produce your credentials, is hold your trigger finger over the rank part down here in the corner—which, in your case, is zero. And hold the ID up at arm's length so whoever you're showing the card to can see it.

"Make it casual, while tryin' to look real sinister.

"The main thing is—a CIC man never surrenders his ID," Capt. McKoy said. "Keep it in your possession at all times—meanin' don't hand the card over for someone to inspect. Anybody asks why not, say it's against regulations. Nobody'll know if it is or it ain't."

"Got it," Waldo said.

Lady Jane was thinking she needed to have A-Force produce counterfeit SOE ID cards for Rita and Lana.

Col. Randal and Col. Fellows walked over from where the big brass had been holding their council of war on what to do with all the jeeps.

Capt. McKoy said, "What's the verdict, John?"

"Colonel Clarke is going to take responsibility for setting up a motor park at a secure site for the bulk of the jeeps," Col. Randal said.

"I need you to take charge of transporting the vehicles from the dock to the A-Force motor park."

"Sounds like a plan," Capt. McKoy said. "Anybody know why the army sent us so many?"

Col. Fellers said, "To hazard a guess, some harried Port Authority officer in the States probably received orders to ship one jeep for every three men in the 575th PIR to Egypt. He verified the TO & E of a parachute infantry regiment, then divided by three—unaware that the Five-Seven-Five is, in reality, only a half-strength battalion."

"There's always that ten percent," Capt. McKoy said, "who don't get the word."

"Army got it backwards, 's what happened," Waldo said. "Three jeeps per man.

"So, Joe . . . how's 'the problem is the solution'—like it said in that correspondence course you took back in the day—workin' on this jeep deal?"

"Good question, Waldo," Capt. McKoy said. "Ain't real sure them college professors ever envisioned somethin' like this. I'm shootin' blanks—nothin's poppin' up when I give it a try."

Lady Jane said, "Where do we find eight hundred sixty-six drivers?"

"That answer," Capt. McKoy said, "ain't comin' through either."

VICE ADMIRAL SIR RANDOLPH "RAZOR" Ransom arrived on the dock. He immediately pulled Colonel John Randal aside.

"Colonel, I am shipping out tomorrow morning on a classified operation in which Raiding Forces does not play a role. The troops involved are green and have never been in action.

"Would it be possible for you to provide one of your officers for me to take along to act as an advisor?"

"Yes, sir," Col. Randal said. "Who would you like to have, Admiral?"

"Lieutenant Hoolihan," VAdm. Ransom said. "The Headhunter is far and away the most experienced amphibious man in the Royal Marines."

"Butch is scheduled to report to Achnacarry for a tour as an instructor at the Special Warfare Training Center, Admiral, but we can push that back until you return, sir."

"I would appreciate if you would," VAdm. Ransom said.

"He's yours," Col. Randal said, "as soon as I can get him to my HQ to promote him to Captain—you two try to stay out of trouble, sir."

"Thank you, Colonel," VAdm. Ransom said. "Out-bloody-standing!"

CHAPTER TWENTY-FOUR

GOD'S TRUTH, LTD.

AS THE SUN WAS COMING UP, Brandy Seaborn and her partner-in-crime Captain Penelope "Legs" Honeycutt-Parker—the Lauren Bacall look-alike—arrived at the suite Colonel John Randal shared with Major the Lady Jane Seaborn. They were not on a social call.

"Cutting your morning exercise class, ladies?" Col. Randal asked. He had clicked on the moment the two walked in the door.

Brandy said, "We have a probable SOLID GOLD target, John."

Col. Randal said, "Show me."

"Captain Seebohm sets up the 621st with a central headquarters tent and other tents fanned out like the tentacles of an octopus—they can be a long distance apart. Each tent contains radio interception equipment—we want Seebohm, who we believe will be in the central HQ tent," Brandy said. She produced a grainy, black-and-white aerial photo as they walked over to the wall map in the small briefing area of the suite.

Normally, Brandy flirted with Col. Randal for fun. Not today . . . she was all business—strictly professional.

"We believe this is a photograph of the 621st—our target is located right about here on the map. Most likely Seebohm is eavesdropping on the 9th Australian Division surrounded at Tobruk."

Brandy was pointing to a spot about five miles from the Mediterranean coast, in the middle of nowhere.

"What's the plan?" Col. Randal asked, sticking one of Waldo's cigars between his front teeth.

"We want you to hit it," Capt. Honeycutt-Parker said. "Fast."

"The 621st is highly mobile," Brandy said. "Seebohm is here today, gone tomorrow. The good captain is not about to make it easy for us."

As he picked up the phone and dialed the Operations Room—Col. Randal ordered, "King, locate Captain McKoy. Have him report up here."

"Roger, Chief," the Merc responded through the open door from the desk in front of the suite. He knew what that tone meant.

Col. Randal dialed the Operations Room duty desk again. The Royal Marine Duty Officer in the Operations Room answered the phone.

"Stephanie," Col. Randal said, "recall Duck Patrol—expedite."

"Yes, sir."

He put down the phone, "Parker, would you go find Pam?"

"On the way, John."

"The problem, Brandy," Col. Randal said, "Raiding Forces is on total stand down. Sea Squadron has its entire fleet in dry dock, to include both of Randy's MAS boats. Your father and Butch flew out on a Catalina this morning for parts unknown.

"So I don't even have a Duck Patrol leader—and they are the only way to reach your SOLID GOLD target with enough firepower for the job."

Captain "Geronimo" Joe McKoy walked in, having been found downstairs at breakfast.

"You lookin' for me, John?"

"Brandy has a potential SOLID GOLD target," Col. Randal said, tapping the map. "The Headhunter is committed to another mission. I need you to take charge of Duck Patrol—or at least as many of its people as we can find on short notice, minus Frank's gun DUKW.

"Head up that way, go ashore, drive overland to the objective and put eyes on the target. If the 621st is still in place, then under cover of darkness I'll drop in with a team and we'll take it out."

"How am I supposed to get Duck Patrol from here to there?" Capt. McKoy asked. "We ain't got any sea transport."

"That is a problem," Col. Randal said.

"Leave it to me," Brandy said. "I shall have Field Marshal Auchinleck commandeer a trawler. You can combat load the DUKWs on board by crane."

"Find us a ship, Brandy," Capt. McKoy said. "Warthog'll supply the crew—he ain't gonna wanna be left out of this."

Col. Randal said, "Get it done."

"Duck Patrol sails tonight, John," Capt. McKoy said, "if we have to hijack us a boat."

"I know you will, Captain."

As the others were leaving, Lieutenant Pamala Plum-Martin came in, wearing her workout togs and leg warmers with a towel around her neck. The snow-blonde Royal Marine pilot was glistening.

"I was planning to come see you after our swim," Lt. Plum-Martin said.

"About what, Pam?" Col. Randal asked. The two had served together for a long time. They were comfortable around each other—he trusted her with his life, frequently.

"Ronnie found a BOMBSHELL target," Lt. Plum-Martin said. "Air Intelligence identified a small, isolated beachfront hotel. Several squadrons of Luftwaffe pilots reportedly use it as their BOQ. They operate off satellite airfields in the area."

"That *is* a good target," Col. Randal said. "Only we don't have any Raiders. Everyone's on leave. Show me anyway."

The Vargas Girl-looking Royal Marine pointed to the map with a scarlet-tipped nail.

Col. Randal said, "Exactly the target we're always looking for.

"King, can you come in here?"

The Merc studied the map coordinate Col. Randal indicated with the tip of his unlit cigar.

"Most likely an exclusive resort hotel for wealthy Egyptians to take their mistresses before the war," King said. "Discreetly located all alone on the coast—private."

"Contact Mr. Zargo," Col. Randal said. "See if he can confirm that German pilots are billeted there."

"Roger," King said. "Make a great target if they are."

"It would," Col. Randal said. "Unfortunately, the only people we have to raid it would be you, me and Mandy."

"Recommend," King said, "we not mention that to Mandy, Chief."

"Pam," Col. Randal said, "I need you to have Billy Jack and the new Five-Seven-Five officer, Lieutenant Hays, extracted from Scout Patrol. They're needed here fast."

"Do my best, John."

"Send another pilot, you stand by ready at RFHQ. No telling what could happen next," Col. Randal said.

"Brandy's evaluating a possible SOLID GOLD target, which will take priority over anything else. Check in with her. Stay up to speed on the status of the mission."

"Wilco," Lt. Plum-Martin said. "Things always heat up when Raiding Forces is least able to carry them out—like the 'Gunfight at the Blue Duck.'"

"Let's not think about it," Col. Randal said. The situation was eerily similar—irresistible target, Raiders all on leave. He got shot.

"Pam," Col. Randal said, "have Rocky stop by before she leads the morning swim."

"Will do."

Twenty minutes later Rikke Runborg padded in, wearing her bathing suit. "Yes, John?"

"Terry Stone is getting ready to tell me he's fit enough to return to full duty," Col. Randal said. "I'm not taking his word for it."

"Oh?"

"When Zorro can make it through one of your workouts," Col. Randal said, "you let me know. Then he's cleared—good to go."

"As you wish," Rocky said. "Sir Terry was gravely injured, John. My classes consist of vigorous, high-intensity ballet warm-up calisthenics, light-weight, high-repetition resistance training with Indian clubs—plus the swim—will possibly take time for him to achieve our level of fitness."

Col. Randal said, "That's what I think too."

After Rocky had gone to lead the morning two-mile swim, King said, "I thought Major Stone was a friend of yours, Chief."

"He's always wanted to get to know Miss Runborg better," Col. Randal said. "I'm giving him the opportunity."

"Zorro always likes to say 'it's always darkest before pitch-black,'" King said. "He is about to find out how true that is."

James "Baldie" Taylor and Commander Ian Fleming arrived. King showed them into the suite. Col. Randal clicked on immediately. He was beginning to feel whipsawed.

He knew Cmdr. Fleming did not travel out from London to Egypt without reason. In the past, his arrival had always resulted in Raiding Forces being tasked to execute a high-value mission.

What Col. Randal did *not* know was that ever since the Kriegsmarine had added a fourth rotor to their Enigma encoding machine, Bletchley Park was no longer able to read any of the German Navy's communications—that source had gone dark.

Unrelated to the additional rotor being added, but at approximately the same time, the Nazi U-boat war had gone into overdrive. Submarines were taking an even heavier toll on Allied shipping than ever before.

Great Britain was being strangled.

And the truly frightening part was that there were never more than six U-Boats operating against British sea lanes at any one time. What if the Kriegsmarine deployed more?

Cmdr. Fleming said, "GOLDEN FLEECE."

Another thing Col. Randal was not cleared to know was that GOLDEN FLEECE was the second-highest priority code word in British military lexicon. Right behind CROMWELL, which would signal the German invasion of England—if it ever came.

What Col. Randal *did* know was that when he heard GOLDEN FLEECE, he was to drop everything he was doing and immediately execute the mission that followed—with alacrity.

He recognized that Jim was uncharacteristically grim this morning, which gave him something else to think about.

"There is a tiny island—a cay, actually, located ten miles off Crete," Cmdr. Fleming said. "Only a flyspeck on the map and does not even have a name. The place is isolated, uninhabited and completely treeless. You can stand in the middle and see across it in all directions.

"The Kriegsmarine has a B-Dienst radio station located on the island," Cmdr. Fleming said.

"Raiding Forces is alerted to raid the station tonight with your RED INDIAN Team. Kill or capture the German signalmen and recover all pertinent signals equipment and documents of intelligence value," Cmdr. Fleming said.

"Naturally, no fingerprints. A Royal Navy destroyer will be standing by off shore to shell the station at sunrise the morning after the operation to cover up any signs of your raid."

Lady Jane and Lt. Mandy came in from their swim, drying their hair with towels, breezed past and went straight out to the private pool.

"Hello, Ian," Lady Jane said as they disappeared outside to sunbathe.

"War is hell," Cmdr. Fleming said.

"Yes, it is," Col. Randal said, picking up the phone and dialing the Operations Room. "Stephanie, find my Lovat Scouts Fenwick and Ferguson. And my Phantom team."

The Royal Marine said, "The Scouts are somewhere in the desert hunting ibex, Colonel—I shall attempt to locate the Phantom operators for you, sir."

"We have a situation," Col. Randal said, putting the phone back in its cradle. "I don't have a RED INDIAN Team."

"Explain," Cmdr. Fleming said, taking out one of his custom-blended cigarettes with the three gold rings on the end and tapping it on his elegant, sterling silver case.

"Raiding Forces is on stand down after CRUSADER," Col. Randal said. "When everyone comes back from leave and the hospital, we'll be at fifty percent strength—maybe less.

"Captain Jaxx is on patrol with Captain Kidd—we are attempting to have him flown back now, but no word on that yet. RED INDIAN Team members Fenwick and Ferguson are away on a hunting trip. We're trying to locate the Phantom operators you trained to search for GOLDEN FLEECE material.

"In addition," Col. Randal said, "Raiding Forces has been alerted for two other missions—one Field Marshal Auchinleck personally feels is a higher local priority than GOLDEN FLEECE."

Cmdr. Fleming's veneer of suave gentility vanished in a flash, his eyes narrowed. He snarled, "Nothing has a higher priority than GOLDEN FLEECE."

"Tell that to the Field Marshal," Col. Randal said.

"I brought a navy signals intelligence officer with me who is parachute qualified," Cmdr. Fleming said. "He can identify the Nazi equipment we require—put together a team to capture the GOLDEN FLEECE target, Colonel, and do it now.

"After all, you *do* have an entire regiment of American parachutists to draw from."

The atmosphere in the room was tense. Having suffered the appalling losses Raiding Forces had taken in CRUSADER, Col. Randal was in no mood for some rear echelon armchair commando to be picking targets for his men to risk their necks on. Not without good cause—made clear.

"Tell him," Col. Randal said.

Jim said, "The Five-Seven-Five is a regiment in name only—totally green, trained in *jungle* warfare in Panama. They are in the field now for a month's acclimation and to learn how to operate in the desert environment.

"No help there, Commander."

Cmdr. Fleming said, "I had no idea."

"Everyone take a deep breath," Jim said. "Colonel, you try to scrape together a raiding party—there are believed to be only a half-dozen German signalmen on the objective. We can arrange for you to have anything you want in the way of support—ships, aircraft, etc. Raiding Forces, *has* to accomplish this mission.

"There is no higher priority."

"For the record, Colonel," Cmdr. Fleming said, "I am acting on the express orders of the Prime Minister, which is a conversation the two of us have had before."

Jim said, "Put me on the manifest for the raid if that helps."

"Great," Col. Randal said. "That means our team will consist of you, me, King and Mandy—maybe we can augment it with Rita and Lana if I can get them to take the night off from dancing at the Kit-Kat."

Cmdr. Fleming turned pale. It was beginning to sink in that there was a legitimate reason for Col. Randal's reluctance to take on a new mission. Normally, he was the most can-do of all the army officers Naval Intelligence worked with.

"Here's what I need for starters," Col. Randal said. "Two Dakotas—and they have to be wheels up in the next thirty minutes to pick up the 575th Rangers I&R platoon. Pam will brief the pilots.

"No Dakotas, no mission—is that clear?"

"Perfectly," Cmdr. Fleming said. "What else do you require?"

"I'll get back to you on that," Col. Randal said. "Now, if you two gentlemen will excuse me . . ."

As they were leaving, Col. Randal ordered, "King, I need Pam."

"On the way, Chief."

Lady Jane came in from the pool where she had been listening in on the conversation from concealment beside a crack in the sliding door—all those spy schools she attended had taught her tricks nice girls were not supposed to know. Mandy followed her inside.

Concerned by what she overheard, Lady Jane placed a call to Brandy, who ran upstairs to the suite. Lt. Plum-Martin arrived back from the swim. The Royal Marine was dressed but had her wet, snow-blonde hair swept back.

Col. Randal briefed the women on developments. Raiding Forces had three high-priority missions. There were virtually no troops available. Most of his officers were absent or not fit for duty. Sea Squadron had its ships in dry dock.

In the best of times, three simultaneous special operations would strain Raiding Forces' resources. These were not the best of times.

Lady Jane asked, "What are your intentions, John?"

"Drive on," Col. Randal said. "Hit the targets."

COLONEL JOHN RANDAL TOOK A CALL from the Operations Room. "Captain McCoy phoned, sir—Duck Patrol is standing by to sail. The captain says he was only able to assemble half of the patrol's complement of troops," Stephanie said. "Warthog Finley is on board to skipper a trawler Brandy borrowed from the Royal Navy Patrol Service. Wino Muldoon is along as an observer.

"Frank is at the dock with his gun DUKW awaiting instructions, as per your orders."

"Thanks, Stephanie," Col. Randal said, hanging up.

Almost immediately the phone rang again, "Sir, the plane with Billy Jack and Clint Hays will be landing in five minutes. Roy Kidd is with them as well."

"Have them report to me," Col. Randal said, "the minute they get here."

Apparently, acting on his own initiative, Captain Roy Kidd had decided to turn over Scout Patrol to his assistant patrol leader and make himself available for whatever was taking place at RFHQ.

His decision gave Col. Randal the last piece of the puzzle he needed to finalize his plans.

COLONEL JOHN RANDAL HUDDLED with Captain Billy Jack Jaxx, Captain Roy Kidd and Lieutenant Clint Hays in his suite as soon as they reported in.

"Raiding Forces has been alerted for three Top Secret missions. We do not have enough personnel available to handle them. To augment our troop strength, the I&R platoon is being flown here to RFHQ. Expected to arrive in the next three hours.

"When they do, Jack, I want you and Lieutenant Hays—plus five Rangers you handpick for Team A—to be prepared to conduct a parachute drop on a target later tonight. I will lead the team—the general will be coming along, as well as a Royal Navy intelligence officer.

"Roy, your mission is to link up with Frank Polanski—Team B. You two—plus a Phantom operator, a navigator and the Little Elephant's gunner—will take the gun DUKW, launch three miles off shore and land right about here on this beach," Col. Randal pointed to the map.

"Drive inland to the Via Balbia, then motor east for approximately a mile and attack the hotel located here," Col. Randal indicated the target.

"Timing is not an issue. Initiate your attack as soon as you arrive. Fire up the hotel. No one gets out alive—clear?"

"Yes, sir."

"Then turn north and head into the desert on an azimuth of 185 degrees. Somewhere on your line of march, you will be met by one of Mr. Zargo's men—a man known to you as Club. You've worked with him before?"

Capt. Kidd said, "I have."

"We have no idea how the DUKW is going to perform in the desert. If the truck can't negotiate the terrain, cache it and you will be picked up by either Raiding Forces or a patrol from the LRDG.

"Questions?"

"A one-DUKW raid?"

"Small-scale."

"Roger that," Capt. Kidd said. "I like it, sir."

"Following the drop by Team A and the subsequent capture of a classified German target," Col. Randal said, "Team A will board a Walrus amphibian, be flown back here to RFHQ where it will transfer to a C-47, fly to another DZ, jump in, re-enforce Captain McKoy and Duck Patrol, which is designated Team C tonight, and assist them in carrying out a raid on another classified target.

"Upon conclusion of Team C's mission, Pam is going to extract Jack, Roy, the general and myself in the Hudson for return to RFHQ. Duck Patrol will return to Oasis X, traveling overland.

"Lieutenant Hays," Col. Randal said, "you'll accompany Capt. McKoy as he patrols back to X, hitting targets of opportunity along the way.

"Questions?"

"Sir," Lt. Hays asked, "is service with Raiding Forces always like getting swept up in a tornado?"

"Actually, Clint," Col. Randal said, "the Five-Seven-Five arrived during a lull in our operations."

Capt. Jaxx said, "That's a definite Rodge."

Jack Cool.

MAJOR SIR TERRY "ZORRO" STONE ARRIVED at Colonel John Randal's suite. He WAS not expected. Normally laid back, he did not seem his normal self today.

Maj. Stone said, "R. J. and Jim are on the way. When they arrive—I was never here. Understand, old stick?"

Col. Randal clicked on, "Roger."

"There is a major counterintelligence flap at Grey Pillars," Maj. Stone said. "An intense spy hunt is underway—no one is above suspicion."

"Mandy mentioned it," Col. Randal said.

"When R. J. and Jim arrive," Maj. Stone said, "they are going to ask you questions—act surprised, but under no circumstances get angry or lose your temper."

"I can do that."

"One other thing," Maj. Stone said, as he was turning to leave. "The Duke likes your idea about the name change and reorganization of the Lancelot Lancers, old stick—sent me a message that he would be nominating you for the next King's Birthday Honors List."

"What's that mean?"

"Almost anything."

A half hour later, King stuck his head in the door, "R. J. and the general are on the way up, Chief."

The two officers arrived and entered the suite. R. J. shut the door firmly behind them.

Jim said, "Colonel, I realize this is not the best time, but there is no good time for what we are here to talk to you about."

Col. Randal said, "What might that be?"

R. J. said, "We have a Nazi mole embedded somewhere at the highest echelon of Middle East Command. We have knowledge that Rommel is receiving information that can only come from a highly-placed source with unfettered access to the top echelon of GHQ. The spy's reports include assessments of our top commanders, tactics and equipment. While not flattering, the information is breathtakingly accurate."

"Do you suspect Rocky?" Col. Randal asked, sticking one of Waldo's cigars between his teeth.

"No," Jim said. "Ever since you allowed Rocky to move into RFHQ she has been reclusive—rarely leaves the compound unless you or Lady Jane are with her.

"We know she has no way to transmit the volume of information to the Germans we are investigating, even if she were in possession of it. If Rocky is a Russian spy—they are our allies, we have no concerns if Stalin knows our intentions."

"I see," Col. Randal said, which meant he did not have a clue.

R. J. said, "Nothing we discuss today is to *EVER* leave this room—on your word as an officer."

"It won't, Brigadier."

"Lady Jane," R. J. said, "has unrestricted access to Field Marshal Auchinleck and all the senior officers at Grey Pillars. At any time has she ever indicated to you any political connection that might cause you to believe she is sympathetic to or has ever had any association with either the Nazi or Fascist Parties?"

"Are you crazy?" Col. Randal said.

Jim said, "Colonel, this will be a lot easier for all of us if you simply answer the questions to the best of your ability. We are all three friends, but this transcends friendship—nothing personal."

Col. Randal said, "Yes."

"Explain," R. J. said.

"Jane's husband, Mallory, took her to a political club for members of the Six Hundred and high government military and political people—weekends in the country," Col. Randal said. "God's Truth, Ltd., I believe it was called.

"Mallory was flirting with the idea of being a Fascist—thought it would advance his navy career."

"Is Lady Jane political?" R. J. asked.

"No," Col. Randal said. "Jane has zero interest in politics."

"Is it true," R. J. asked, "you once accused her of sleeping with you at the behest of the British Secret Service because you are a Special Forces officer?" R. J. asked.

"Yes."

"Were you joking or did you have a reason?"

"Both," Col. Randal said.

"What was her response?"

"'Only at first.'"

Despite being professional intelligence officers, R. J. and Jim were unable to contain their amusement.

"And what was your motive for the question?" R. J. asked.

"I never understood," Col. Randal said, "why Jane was attracted to me in the first place—still don't."

"Do you have any reason to suspect Lady Seaborn is not a loyal British subject?" Jim asked.

"No."

"We were never here," R. J. said. "We never had this conversation."

Col. Randal said, "Yes, we did."

CHAPTER TWENTY-FIVE

DONKEY MEAT

TEN RANGERS HANDPICKED from the I&R platoon were assembled out front of RFHQ. Five would be assigned to Captain "Geronimo" Joe McKoy's Team C. Five would be assigned to Colonel John Randal's Team A.

The dusty Rangers flown in from the desert where they had been undergoing hard training under Blue Patrol's ex-Foreign Legionnaires were sitting on the ground, leaning back on their packs, waiting to see what happened next. They did not have long to wait. Col. Randal and Lieutenant Mandy Paige came outside to brief the troops.

One of the Rangers called, "ATTENTION!"

Col. Randal ordered, "As you were.

"You men have been selected for a Top Secret mission. Raiding Forces is conducting three raids tonight. Your team leaders will brief you when you're assigned to your team.

"The action is going to be short-range," Col. Randal said. "We have Thompson submachine guns for those of you who prefer them for close, fast work during the hours of darkness."

There was a murmur from the Rangers—this was getting interesting.

"Lieutenant Paige is here to give you a security briefing," Col. Randal said. "Listen up. This is no drill."

Lt. Mandy stepped out in front of the Rangers dressed in her off-duty uniform of blue jean cut-offs, peewee cowgirl boots and a great tan. There was very little chance the troops would not "listen up."

"Tonight, you Rangers are about to participate in a clandestine mission of national importance," Lt. Mandy said.

"Acting in my capacity as the Raiding Forces Counterintelligence Officer . . ."

Col. Randal had to resist a smile—Raiding Forces didn't have a counterintelligence officer.

" . . . I need to brief you on the security ramifications of participating in strategic special operations," Lt. Mandy said. "Raiding Forces has rules. One is 'Keep it Short and Simple.'

"So I will," Lt. Mandy said. "What you are about to do tonight never happened. Are we clear?"

"Yes, ma'am," the Rangers chorused.

"You are not authorized to tell your Ranger buddies. No war stories. No bragging in bars. Is that clear?

"Clear!"

"An organization so secret even its initials are classified," Lt. Mandy said, "has requisitioned a former leper colony in Beirut. Nowadays the place is called a 'mental institution'—staffed by the lepers.

"Anyone deemed a security threat," Lt. Mandy said, "for example, a Ranger who talks in his sleep about a classified Raiding Forces operation, will find himself institutionalized there for the duration—is *that* clear?"

"HELL YES!"

"Did I go too fast for anyone?"

"HELL NO!"

"Have a nice night, boys."

COLONEL JOHN RANDAL DROVE MAJOR the Lady Jane Seaborn to the dock in a jeep as the sun was beginning to sink into the desert, putting on a spectacular light show.

"I've been wondering," Col. Randal asked, "What made you think the Rangers were the 'perfect little regiment' when they first arrived?"

"Their jump boots," Lady Jane said. "Even the scruffiest Ranger's boots were polished bright enough for me to put my eye liner on in the reflection off their toe."

Brandy Seaborn, Captain Penelope "Legs" Honeycutt-Parker and Lieutenant Mandy Paige were waiting when they arrived. They wanted to see for themselves that the SOLID GOLD mission was being supported to the fullest extent.

James "Baldie" Taylor and Commander Ian Fleming were present, but were making a point of staying out of the way—strictly observing.

Lady Jane brought an ice chest full of Coca Colas to the five Rangers picked for Duck Patrol. She passed them out. The troops sat on the dock eating Italian rations they had scrounged from Fort No. 9 and drinking the Cokes.

The Rangers were Lady Jane's new pet project.

Captain "Geronimo" Joe McKoy strolled over with Waldo. "You boys like Italian cookin'?" Capt. McKoy asked.

"Yes, sir. Beats K-rations."

"Know what's in them cans?" Waldo said. "Donkey meat."

Several of the Rangers became physically ill, right then and there.

"The most important rule to remember when eatin' captured enemy rations," Waldo said, "is know what you're eatin."

Capt. McKoy sipped one of Lady Jane's Cokes while he waited for the gagging men to recover. Then he assigned each Ranger to a veteran Duck Patrol Sea Squadron operator. Exactly the way it was taught at the Special Warfare Training Center. The buddy system—new troops married up with old hands.

Duck Patrol (minus), Team C for tonight's operation, was augmented with Col. Randal's two phantom operators. Their assignment, which was classified, was to lead the search for German signals equipment once the 621st was overrun. The raid was a hasty mission—not much time for detailed planning.

Skipper Mud Cat Ray turned up to tag along on the mission. He was without a ship because his trawler, *Pirate's Dream,* was in dry dock. That meant all three of the Gold Coast tugboat captains were together again, ready to put to sea for the first time since the raid on the Portuguese Protectorate, Rio Bonita.

Captain Roy Kidd and Frank Polanski could be seen on board the ship with a map spread out over the hood of the Little Elephant's gun truck,

Team B. Col. Randal walked up the gangplank to listen in on their conversation about their BOMBSHELL target. Capt. Kidd and Frank had an interesting night ahead of them.

Capt. Kidd asked, "Once we complete our mission, Colonel, are we cleared to hit targets of opportunity as we work our way back to Oasis X?"

"You can," Col. Randal said. "Keep in mind, we don't know how the DUKW is going to perform in the desert—I'd be careful about chancing what might turn into a running gunfight."

"Point taken, sir."

"You ready, Frank?"

"Affirmative."

"Happy hunting."

It was time for Skipper Finley to cast off. The Rangers and their Duck Patrol counterparts came on board. Col. Randal had a final word with Capt. McKoy, took a long last look around at all the preparations going on board the ship, then walked back down to the dock.

Capt. McKoy called over the rail, "See you when I see you, John."

The raid was on.

COLONEL JOHN RANDAL WAS LYING BACK on his parachute at the Raiding Forces departure airfield. He was surrounded by the Team A stick of Chalk 1 that would be jumping on the small island ten miles off Crete. Five minutes ago, he had concluded his final Frag Order.

The plan called for him to jump on the nameless island with Team A, consisting of Captain Billy Jack Jaxx, James "Baldie" Taylor, Lieutenant Clint Hays, King, five Rangers and a Royal Navy Volunteer Reserve lieutenant who was a signals intelligence specialist. The team would immediately storm the German radio station, which was located in a tent. Then, once the mission was completed, Team A would board a pair of Walrus amphibious aircraft to fly back to RFHQ.

Good plans are easy to understand. The only part that anyone was having any difficulty getting a handle on was the fact that Team A would be jumping with no reserve parachutes tonight. The Rangers were having serious reservations. None of them had ever jumped without a reserve.

The reason for not using the reserves was due to the extremely short length of the DZ. The jumpers had to get down fast in order to avoid ending up in the Mediterranean. Team A would be jumping *below* five hundred feet.

A reserve parachute was useless at that low level. There was a good chance of jump casualties tonight. That was the reason the Rangers were included on the team—Col. Randal was taking his replacements with him.

He did not mention that fact in the Frag Order.

Team A was jumping British X-type parachutes. The Rangers had never jumped them before. Captain Roy "Mad Dog" Reupart, a former instructor at No. 1 British Parachute School, spent an hour familiarizing the men with the quick release system.

Compared to the U.S. Airborne Forces' harness that had to be unbuckled one buckle at a time or cut off with a jump knife, the British system was light-years ahead as far as practicality on combat jumps. The Rangers loved the system—pull the safety clip, hammer the release on your chest with your fist and the parachute fell to the ground. The Americans could not understand why the Five-Seven-Five had never had quick releases before now.

No one seemed to care what parachute they jumped, as long as it opened, but Col. Randal knew the Rangers would care once they experienced how soft the X-type parachute deployed. The U.S. Army's T-4 had a vicious opening shock that created something called "riser burn" on jumper's necks. The X-type chute did not do that.

An engine popped on one of the Dakotas of the 267 "Pegasus" Squadron, Royal Air Force, being piloted tonight by Squadron Leader Paddy Wilcox, and the wheezing sound of a prop turning over could be heard.

Col. Randal ordered, "On your feet."

There were two chalks—six jumpers in one stick, five in the other. He would be the jumpmaster on the lead aircraft. Capt. Jaxx would jumpmaster the second.

Col. Randal and Capt. Jaxx performed final jumpmaster inspections—not that they were needed. Both officers had already done one thirty minutes previous, but there is no such thing as being too sure on a mission like this.

Even though it was pitch-dark, everyone who could get away from RFHQ and a lot of Raiders who had been in Cairo had returned to be on hand to see them off. No words were spoken, but as the two sticks marched past, everyone in the crowd started clapping.

Major the Lady Jane Seaborn was standing by the door to Col. Randal's chalk.

She kissed him on the cheek, "Be safe, John."

Stick 1 helped each other up and into the door at the tail of the C-47—it was pretty high, and then the last man—Col. Randal—had to be pulled up. Everyone was armed to the teeth. The three Rangers in Col. Randal's stick had traded their M1 Garand rifles for Thompson submachine guns, opting for the additional firepower.

Almost as soon as the door was closed and bolted shut, the C-47 began to taxi. Stick 1 consisted of Col. Randal, King, three Rangers and one very anxious Royal Navy Reserve Officer—a recent graduate of No. 1 British Parachute School. Tonight would be his first operational jump since earning his parachute wings.

Shortly after takeoff, Col. Randal went down the aisle of the aircraft to talk to the four new men.

"Here's what's going to happen. The instant you exit the door, take up a tight tuck in a good prepare-to-land position—elbows in hard, chin down and *DO NOT* lock your knees. Your canopy will deploy, you will make one swing and be on the ground—like the swing landing trainer in Jump School.

"You're not supposed to hit all Five Points of Contact at the same time, but that's exactly what's going to happen. Don't be surprised—jump up, drop your harness, lock and load, stand fast and I'll roll up the stick.

"No shouting, AIRBORNE!"

The Rangers were raring to go. The RNVR signals intelligence officer did not seem as enthusiastic.

Col. Randal had a quiet word with King, who would be the last man in the stick—the pusher. Then he went back to his place on the end of the bench seat running down the side of the Dakota next to the door, sat down and went to sleep.

His eyes came open. The red light flashed on. Col. Randal stood up, "TEN MINUTES."

Col. Randal shuffled up to the cockpit. The C-47 seemed to be skimming across the waves. Sqn. Ldr. Wilcox was in the command pilot's seat. He was not wearing his trademark black eye patch tonight—he had it on but it was pulled up.

Up ahead was the tiny island.

"Two hundred fifty feet, Paddy," Col. Randal said. "Try hard not to make it any lower."

"Wilco," S/Ldr. Wilcox said. "Good luck, Colonel."

Col. Randal shuffled back and started the series of jump commands as soon as he returned to the tail of the plane. The loadmaster had opened the door and the wind was howling.

"STAND UP!"

"HOOK UP!

"CHECK STATIC LINE!"

Tonight the jump commands were condensed. There was no reason to check equipment or sound off—they were all jumping.

Col. Randal arched his body outside the door doing his jumpmaster check. He could see the trailing C-47 bobbing and swaying behind. Up ahead, the island was approaching fast. He could see water all the way around it—the beach on the far side of the DZ was coming up fast too.

Col. Randal swung back inside, "CLOSE ON THE DOOR."

The Rangers were not rattling their static lines tonight. The lack of reserves may have dampened their enthusiasm for false bravado. As ordered, they crowded up as close together as they could get, right behind Col. Randal. The idea was to land in as tight a cluster as possible.

The shore flashed under the Dakota. Col. Randal ordered, "Let's go."

He leapt out as vigorously as he could, the X-type parachute popped open with a satisfying crack, then *WHAAAAM!*

It felt like he bounced a couple of times. Col. Randal experienced pain the entire length of his body—actually hit the five points of contact on his left side all at the same time. While he was pretty sure he was going to live, breathing was a problem.

Col. Randal considered the idea of lying there for a while to rest.

All members of Team A from both aircraft were down by the time he struggled to his feet and hit the quick release on his chest, dropping the parachute—which took less than ten seconds.

Col. Randal began moving in the direction of flight, rolling up the stick.

Capt. Jaxx appeared out of the dark, looking none the worse for wear. King was also undamaged. The Merc was with Lt. Hays, the Rangers, Jim and the RNVR officer. Nearly everyone else was banged up, but pressed on—shaking it off. Col. Randal was impressed with how quickly the new Rangers had assembled.

Team A left their parachutes where they lay. The destroyer would land a party of Royal Marines at first light to police up the tiny cay and retrieve them. Nothing was going to be left behind on the island to indicate that there had been a raid on the B-Dienst radio station.

With everyone assembled, King led out, moving swiftly. He could see in the dark like a cat. Capt. Jaxx was right behind him, followed by Col. Randal, Lt. Hays, the navy signals officer, Jim, then the Rangers.

The night was cool. There was a half-moon glowing. It was perfectly quiet.

Within minutes, Team A was at the pyramidal tent that housed the Nazis. King and Capt. Jaxx immediately made entry without pause as the Rangers shook themselves out into a loose firing line . . . Thompson submachine guns at the ready, standing by for developments.

Col. Randal went into the tent with his MAB-38A submachine gun shouldered, with Jim right behind.

The Germans were asleep—at least they had been before Capt. Jaxx and King made entry. Apparently, low-flying airplanes were no cause for alarm. By the time Col. Randal arrived, all six radiomen were in their bunks with their hands in the air, scared stiff.

The bright light from Capt. Jaxx and King's hooked-nose flashlights shining in their eyes and the Merc shouting in German that if a single man moved a muscle "British Commandos are going to kill you all" had a paralyzing effect on the Nazis.

The RNVR signals intelligence officer immediately began his search for GOLDEN FLEECE material.

Col. Randal went outside and fired red over green flares—the signal of success.

Within minutes, a cutter from the destroyer standing offshore landed on the beach, and Commander Ian Fleming stepped out, accompanied by four 9mm Lanchester Mk1 submachine-gun-toting Royal Marines. Another cutter pulled in beside it.

The RNVR signals intelligence officer came out of the tent. Col. Randal heard him inform Jim and Cmdr. Fleming, "No joy—not tonight."

Cmdr. Fleming did not look happy.

ACTING PROVISIONAL SUB-LIEUTENANT SKIPPER Warthog Finley had his borrowed trawler hove to three miles off the shore. Captain Roy Kidd, Frank Polanski, the Phantom radio operator, the loader for the Little Elephant and an ex-LRDG navigator were sitting in the gun DUKW. It was being lowered over the side of the trawler by the deck crane.

A DUKW crane launch from the deck of a ship is one of the most harrowing experiences Raiding Forces Sea Squadron personnel had to endure—at least for the Raiders in the DUKW.

A Ferris wheel ride at an amusement park is a cheap thrill. Being swung out over the Mediterranean in the dark of night, then lowered down the side of a ship in a two-and-a-half-ton amphibious truck and plopped in the sea behind enemy lines—that's a real thrill.

Not to worry. Skipper Finley's crew had trained to perform the drill until they could do it in their sleep. The DUKW splashed down as light as a rubber ducky in a bathtub.

Frank cranked up the engine and headed for shore. Skipper Finley immediately got the trawler underway, headed up the coast to drop off Captain "Geronimo" Joe McKoy and the remaining men of Duck Patrol.

The gun DUKW was on its own, sailing on a private enterprise. Capt. Kidd liked it that way. He was comfortable operating behind the lines. However, tonight was a first—Raiding Forces had never sent a lone vehicle on a mission all by itself.

Capt. Kidd was going to raid the remote hotel BOMBSHELL target that Air Intelligence had identified as a Luftwaffe hostel. The Nazis had requisitioned it for pilots to stay in while they were operating from the desert airstrips in the immediate area –flying mostly against Tobruk. Then the gun truck was to make its way overland to Oasis X.

Some people might consider their assignment a suicide mission. No one on the DUKW thought so. Raiding Forces did not do suicide missions.

ACTING PROVISIONAL SUB-LIEUTENANT Skipper Warthog Finley made way as soon as the DUKW was clear of the trawler. The plan was for him to sail up the coastline well out to sea and drop off Duck Patrol. The second mission was more complicated for the sailors from the purely technical standpoint of seamanship. The crew would have to launch four DUKWs with gun jeeps in the back and one DUKW with a crane mounted.

The five DUKWs would make their way ashore. The crane DUKW was along to unload all four gun jeeps. Then all five DUKWs would motor back to the trawler and be retrieved by its crane.

Then Skipper Finley would make a mad dash back in the direction of Alexandria at full speed to reach the safety of the RAF air umbrella before daybreak. By any measure of seamanship, it was a tall order.

Captain "Geronimo" Joe McKoy and Waldo Treywick were sitting in the gun jeep in the bed of the first DUKW launched over the side by the deck crane. The RNPS coxswain circled while the other four amphibious trucks were lowered into the water. Capt. McKoy was anxious to get going, but the unloading operation could not be hurried.

Duck Patrol had to land on a deserted beach, unload the four gun jeeps from the DUKWs, and then drive inland approximately five miles to the grid coordinates where Brandy Seaborn believed the 621st Radio Intercept Company was set up—the idea being to find, fix and finish the Desert Fox's crystal ball reader.

If the SOLID GOLD target was there, Capt. McKoy's Phantom operator was to signal Colonel John Randal (who would be airborne en route to their location) the mission was a green light. Team A would drop in and kill or capture Captain Alfred Seebohm with Duck Patrol in support.

There was nothing simple about this plan.

Finally, all four DUKWs were successfully launched, bobbing and weaving their way toward the beach. They made it to shore undetected, and the process of unloading the gun jeeps began immediately.

When the last gun jeep was on the ground, Capt. McKoy drove inland while the DUKWs went back into the water to return to the trawler. It did not take long for Duck Patrol to travel four of the five miles to the objective.

Waldo dismounted and with one of the Rangers backing him up, disappeared into the dark. As they moved out, the ex-ivory poacher said, "Sonny boy, you better be silent as a ghost."

"Don't worry—I'm from Kentucky, Mr. Treywick," the Ranger whispered back. "Grew up in the hills hiding out from revenuers sneaking around looking for my granddaddy's still—ain't nobody gonna hear me I don't want 'em to."

The two quickly traveled across the desert to where the target was reported to be—and there it was. A single tent. Seebohm's HQ—the SOLID GOLD target would be somewhere behind it in the distance.

When the recon party returned to Duck Patrol, Waldo said, "Right on the money Joe—SOLID GOLD."

Capt. McKoy ordered the Phantom operator, "Contact Colonel Randal—target in sight."

The plan was for Duck Patrol, with Col. Randal's Team A onboard, to advance to within a mile of the tent Waldo had located. A small party armed with silenced weapons would advance on the target and take it out as quietly as possible.

Then Duck Patrol, with Team A on board, would come on line and drive in the direction where they hoped Seebohm's HQ tent would be located. When they found it, the Raiders would engage with every weapon the patrol had.

It was not much of a plan.

Waldo got behind the wheel of Capt. McKoy's command jeep and slowly drove in the direction of the 621st Radio Intercept Company. He was going to keep it under observation until Team A arrived.

Capt. McKoy climbed in the passenger seat on another jeep and led the three remaining Duck Patrol gun jeeps two miles west to a likely spot and stood by to set up a DZ for Team A.

After what seemed like a lifetime, but which was in fact less than thirty minutes, the Phantom operator said, "Five minutes out."

Capt. McKoy pitched out a red railroad flare. The other two jeeps did the same.

Up in the Hudson, piloted by Lieutenant Pamala-Plum Martin, Col. Randal was arched out the door looking for the Initial Point (IP) when he saw the three flares on the ground.

The Vargas Girl-looking Royal Marine pilot saw them too. She was in high spirits. Captain Roy Kidd had radioed "BOMBSHELL MISSION ACCOMPLISHED."

Col. Randal swung back inside and shouted at his stick, "CLOSE ON THE DOOR."

Then he turned back to the door, put the toe of his right canvas-topped raiding boot halfway over the edge of nothingness. Knees bent in a crouch, he reached out and slapped his hands, palm down, outside on the skin of the Hudson on both sides of the door.

Col. Randal was not doing all that great. The pain from his first jump earlier had started to kick in. And he was beginning to feel fairly stiff. Fortunately, this jump was going to be at eight hundred feet, which should result in a much softer landing.

When the flare was just off the toe of his boot, Col. Randal shouted, "GO."

He jumped as hard as he could, but somehow got it wrong. In his mind he was counting "One thousand, two thousand, three thousand . . ." the way Airborne Command taught at Ft. Benning. The parachute was supposed to be open by "four thousand."

When that happened, the jumper was supposed grab the risers and look up to "CHECK CANOPY" to make sure it had deployed properly and that there were no blown panels. British paratroopers did not do that. Since they did not jump reserves, there was not much they could do in the event their chute had malfunctioned.

When Col. Randal reached "four thousand," nothing had happened. He looked up and saw that the X-type parachute had not deployed. It was a streamer—what U.S. Paratroopers called a Roman Candle.

Col. Randal immediately began the drill. He leaned back, reached down, grabbed the handle of his reserve parachute, yanked it as hard as possible and thought he had ripped it completely off when the handle tore free in his hand—not a reassuring feeling. Again, nothing happened!

Then Col. Randal remembered he had to deploy the reserve chute by hand, which he started doing as fast as he could. The white silk canopy spilled out and blew back against his legs. This was officially not good.

He reached down, grabbed the silk parachute, gathered it up and tossed it out away from his body. The wind caught the canopy and the reserve popped open. When that happened, the main chute deployed too. Now Col. Randal was coming down under two parachutes, but by this time he was extremely low to the ground.

With two chutes pulling in different directions there was no way to attempt a parachute landing fall. He crashed flat on his back. *WHAAAM!*

On this jump he did not hit a single one of the five points of contact. Col. Randal did not immediately jump up and dust himself off in the approved Airborne manner. He was in a lot of pain.

Both parachutes drifted down and covered him like a shroud. He was not having a good night.

Captain Billy Jack Jaxx ran over.

"You OK, Colonel?" Capt. Jaxx asked as Col. Randal struggled to his feet and hit the quick release, dropping his harness.

"Just swell," Col. Randal said, through gritted teeth.

"You're supposed to drop the handle after popping your reserve, sir." Capt. Jaxx said, noting that the Colonel was still holding his.

"Not a chance, Jack," Col. Randal said. "I pulled this one so hard it's got my finger grooves bent in it."

"Sir," Capt. Jaxx said, "reserve handles are made out of solid steel."

Col. Randal said, "Yeah."

CHAPTER TWENTY-SIX

PAIN

COLONEL JOHN RANDAL WAS SITTING on the steps in the shallow end of the private pool of the suite he shared with Major the Lady Jane Seaborn—back from the desert. It was an hour before sunrise. He was hoping soaking in the water would make some of the pain go away. It would be fair to say his morale was low.

When Duck Patrol linked up with Waldo immediately after Team A jumped in, he reported the 621st Radio Intercept Company was gone. The Germans had struck the tent he had under observation, loaded it on a truck and driven off in the dark.

No SOLID GOLD.

Duck Patrol set off across the desert to raid targets of opportunity on their way back to Oasis X. The Rangers went with Captain "Geronimo" Joe McKoy to acquire actual patrolling experience. They would be dropped off to link up with the rest of the Five-Seven-Five later to continue their training.

Col. Randal, James "Baldie" Taylor, Captain Billy Jack Jaxx and King had been picked up by Lieutenant Pamala Plum-Martin and flown back to RFHQ in the Hudson. Except for the report of the successful BOMBSHELL mission, it had been a long, frustrating night.

Lady Jane came out and slipped into the pool beside him. Golden tan, her mahogany hair swept back—drop-dead gorgeous. She put her arm around his shoulder with her scarlet nails splayed on his chest. That felt good.

"Do you know how Prime Minister Churchill defines success, John?" Lady Jane asked.

"I have no idea."

"He said it is 'going from failure to failure with no loss of enthusiasm.'"

Col. Randal said, "Well, that would be us."

Lady Jane said, "I inherited my title at birth. It set me apart from the other children. My family was so enormously wealthy and famous I was like a little twig trying to grow up under the shadow of a giant oak tree. Until the night you appeared, my life was spent trying to conform to what others expected of me.

"You allow me to be myself," Lady Jane said. "I love you, John."

She kissed him on the cheek.

Col. Randal wondered if Lady Jane was the Nazi spy.

To be continued in *Raiding Rommel* –
book XI in the Raiding Forces Series

The Raiding Forces series continues…all the way to VE Day.

To be on our notification list for the next book,
contact phil@philward.com

THE RAIDING FORCES SERIES CONTINUES...

ALL THE WAY TO VE DAY

If you have feedback or questions, please contact author
Phil Ward at phil@philward.com.

Visit the Raiding Forces series website and sign up
for the e-mail list at http://www.philward.com

Visit the Raiding Forces series Facebook page at
https://www.facebook.com/raidingforces

Get a glimpse of what happens next by reading the first chapter of Book XI, *Raiding Rommel*

CHAPTER ONE

SNAFU

COLONEL JOHN RANDAL WAS SITTING in the empty bar of the Continental Hotel on the north end of Colbert Street in Vichy French Diego Suarez, Madagascar—the third largest natural harbor in the world. He was alone at a table with his back to the wall sitting in a huge bamboo chair with a clamshell fan back that went up three feet over the top of his head. The chairs were designed so that four of them could be pulled in close together to form a discrete private booth.

It was that kind of place.

Col. Randal was reading a brochure he had picked up in the lobby of the hotel when he checked in. Madagascar, *aka* the Red Island because of its scarlet-colored dust, was the fourth largest island on earth. It was like a tiny continent surrounded by the Indian Ocean. Originally settled by Asians, then the Bantus from East Afrika. Nowadays it was a Vichy French colony run by expatriate French citizens.

The locals were called Malagasy.

Top Secret intelligence reports indicated the Japanese were eyeing the island to use for a submarine base. U.S. code breakers, having cracked the Japanese diplomatic code called 'Purple', had recently learned Berlin was urging Tokyo to occupy Madagascar.

Hitler wanted Tojo to interrupt the British Eighth Army's sea lanes prior to Rommel's next offensive. It was hoped by the Nazis they would then be able to prevent British Forces from receiving new tanks from the U.S. Then the Desert Fox could drive the Allies out of Libya and Egypt, capture the Suez Canal and knock England out of the war—information not in the pamphlet or known to Col. Randal.

Except for the part about Rommel trying to capture the Suez Canal—he knew all about that first hand.

According to the guide, Madagascar was a mysterious place where it was difficult to separate fact from fiction. For example, at one time it may have been a pirate enclave that declared itself its own nation called Libertaria—or maybe not. Col. Randal thought a thing like that should not be so hard to pin down since it allegedly took place only about a hundred years ago.

The island had two hundred fifty species of birds—forty-four percent only found there.

It was home to the Panther Chameleon—the size of a housecat, the orange-red Tomato Frog, the Giraffe-Necked Weevil, which had a long neck, and the Satanic Leaf-Tailed Gecko.

Ten of the island's mammals could not be found anywhere else in the world.

There was a three foot tall, three-toed bipedal humanoid creature with a bad attitude and long claws called the Kalanoro. Only no one had ever actually killed, captured or even photographed one because the animal's toes were backward so hunters went the wrong way when they tracked it.

And there was a tree that ate people.

A beach was located not far from the hotel where the local French girls went topless—Col. Randal imagined they were as elusive as the Kalanoro.

King was at the bar having a drink while talking to the bored bartender—tourism having taken a sharp decline since the start of the war. Captain "Geronimo" Joe McKoy, Waldo Treywick and Acting Provisional Sub-Lieutenant Skipper Warthog Finley, DSO, OBE, RNPS were off somewhere chartering a fishing boat.

Col. Randal and his party were hiding in plain sight. He was wearing an oversized Hawaiian shirt that concealed a pair of 1911 Colt .38 Supers, his High Standard Military Model D .22 w/silencer in a chest holster—a faded pair of blue jeans and his old cowboy boots that were so soft they could be rolled up in a ball. He did not have any idea why he was in Diego Suarez.

The United States was not at war with Vichy France.

The British were not at war with them either, at least officially. However, it had been deemed advisable no one on the mission to Madagascar have a British passport—everyone carried U.S. visas except King, who was Swiss.

The United Kingdom *had* sunk the French fleet at Oran, invaded the French colonies of Lebanon and Syria and was now more than a little annoyed with the collaborationist Petain Regime because his Vichy Government had 'invited' the Japanese to occupy the French colony Vietnam.

Indochina gave the Japs a springboard to Malaya, which led to their being able to attack Singapore from the rear inflicting the most embarrassing defeat on the British Empire in its storied history. The U.S. was not exactly pleased with the Vichy government either. Part of the Japanese fleet that invaded the Philippines had staged in Cam Ranh Bay.

No one, to include the French Colonial Army, wanted to see the Rising Sun flag flying over Madagascar. In Saigon, French officers were being required to salute Japanese privates—which was intended to be demeaning. However, it was difficult to predict what the local Vichy politicians might do.

Anything was possible.

Col. Randal had no knowledge of French plans or intentions regarding the Japanese.

What he did know was that tomorrow morning at sunrise 5 Commando was going to conduct an amphibious assault, storm ashore and attack the port of Diego Suarez right about where he was sitting—OPERATION IRONCLAD.

Col. Randal's orders were to, "Meet an agent or agents known to you."

TWO FRENCH WOMEN DRIFTED INTO the Colonial Hotel's bar in their swimsuits—wearing their tops. Diego Suarez had a relaxed dress code, being a beach town in a French Colony. Swimwear was acceptable attire almost anywhere.

The ladies went to the bar and ordered drinks.

Captain "Geronimo" Joe McKoy came in with Waldo Treywick. They went to the bar and ordered drinks.

Rikke Runborg walked in wearing her swimsuit—she was extremely fit—which caused the droopy-eyed bartender to perk up. Rocky rippled over to Colonel John Randal's table against the wall and sat down in one of the large clamshell-backed bamboo chairs.

Rocky's arrival cleared up the question of who the 'agent or agent's known to you' was going to be. She was the last person he would have ever expected to be entrusted with a secret mission in a foreign land.

Rocky was a Nazi spy—or had been—and might be the Russian agent Marina Lee who stole the British battle plans and gave them to the Wehrmacht resulting in the loss of Norway early in the war. Nowadays she was a double agent working for the Secret Intelligence Service MI-6 out of Cairo. It was said she was Field Marshal Irwin Rommel's most trusted spy. Rocky had convinced the Desert Fox to leave Afrika and fly to Italy to celebrate his birthday the day before OPERATION CRUSADER kicked off.

Some in MI-6 believed Rocky to be the single most valuable intelligence asset the Middle East Command possessed. Which would make risking her on a dangerous mission in a backwater like Madagascar seem like a crazy idea. On the other hand, there were those in Counterintelligence MI-5 who believed Rocky was a triple agent—meaning she was still working for the Germans.

Or possibly the Russians… or maybe the Germans *and* the Russians. And that made sending her on a mission even crazier.

Col. Randal could not have been more surprised if one of the bipedal, three-toed Kalanoro had walked in.

The bartender came over to take Rocky's drink order. King went to the jukebox, studied the menu of songs, selected several and dropped coins in the slot. Soon a wild throbbing big band jungle song heavy on the drums was blaring.

It was believed the hotel rooms might be bugged. In the event the bar was too, no listening device ever invented was going to be able to record with that noise booming.

Rocky pulled the other two chairs in close leaving a small crack for Col. Randal to peek through to keep an eye on the door.

"Hello, John," she said in her sexy Norwegian accent.

"Hello to you, Rocky," Col. Randal said. "Enjoying yourself at the beach?"

"I was by the pool on the roof," Rocky said, "to observe when you checked in."

That sounded like pretty good spy craft to Col. Randal—not that he knew much about the subject.

The bartender brought Rocky her drink. He acted like he might like to hang around and join the conversation. She had that effect on men.

Hair the color of ice, big white teeth, and a fabulous tan, she tended to suck the oxygen out of a room. For the first time Col. Randal noticed her eyes were the color of ice too.

He let Rocky go first. So she did.

"Percy Mather, a well-connected, highly-thought-of French business man who has lived here for many years, is SOE's man in Madagascar," Rocky said. "Our mission is to bring him out before British Commando's come calling tomorrow morning. Or—it was.

"Unhappily, our assignment has turned into what you Americans call a SNAFU— Lady Jane taught me the expression. She thinks it funny."

"I see," Col. Randal said, which meant he did not have a clue what she was talking about.

"SOE has chartered a sixty-foot dhow called the *Lindi* equipped with a long range radio and sonar. It has been charting the coastline in the invasion area. The crew has done excellent work with the mapping. They determined that an island marked on the chart is actually a mile and a half from where it really is, which could have caused the Royal Navy invasion fleet to run aground," Rocky said.

"That," Col. Randal said, "would not have been good."

"For the preponderance of their duties, the *Lindi's* crew is incompetent or cowards, possibly both," Rocky said.

"The dhow rendezvoused with Percy two nights ago on an isolated beach and brought him a bottle of knockout drops. SOE's orders were for him to throw a party tonight for all the senior military and political leadership and place the drops in the punch bowl. It was hoped everyone in attendance would wake up twelve hours later to find 5 Commando patrolling the streets of Diego Suarez," Rocky said.

"This is where the SNAFU occurred. The agent from the *Lindi* who delivered the knockout drops mentioned that the effect only lasted three minutes—enough time for a spy to get away in an emergency.

"Percy asked for a clarification since that information did not match the original plan for the drops to work for twelve hours. Another rendezvous was scheduled for the next night—last night. The *Lindi* failed to appear.

"Percy had no way to hand over the secret intelligence documents he had brought with him. He could not confirm how long the knockout drops would last. So after a long fruitless wait, he cut the phone cable that ran along the coast road knocking out all landline communications between Diego Suarez and the rest of the island, then returned to the Continental Hotel."

"Sounds like a good piece of work," Col. Randal said.

"Regrettably," Rocky said, "when he arrived back here, Percy was arrested by the Centre d' Information Gouvernementel—the Vichy Colonial Secret Police—CIE. The CIE found all the notes and sketches he was carrying. He was turned over to the army who threw him in a prison cell and offered the services of a priest.

"Percy is scheduled to be put in front of a firing squad at dawn.

"Would you agree," Rocky said, "the situation has deteriorated into what you refer to as a FUBAR?"

COLONEL JOHN RANDAL LOOKED OUT through the crack between the two empty chairs. Captain "Geronimo" Joe McKoy and Waldo were dancing with the two French women over by the jukebox. Acting Provisional Sub-Lieutenant Skipper Warthog Finley was sitting at the end of the bar nursing a beer. He established eye contact with Col. Randal and made a slashing motion across his throat.

Not going to be any boat off the island.

"Now," Col. Randal thought, "We have a FUBAR."

AN UNSHAVED MAN IN A RUMPLED WHITE tropical suit came into the bar, headed to straight to the bar, ordered a drink and threw it down in one gulp then ordered a refill.

Rocky saw him pass by the crack between the two chairs screening their table. She pushed one of them back to get a better look at the newcomer. The two locked eyes. Without hesitation she waved for him to join their table.

The man in the suit threw down the second drink, ordered a third, then strolled over to where Colonel John Randal and Rocky were sitting.

"John," Rocky said, "allow me to introduce you to Percy Mather."

Col. Randal said, "I thought you were getting shot in a few hours."

"That may still be on," SOE's man in Madagascar said. "The Vichy military commandant in Diego Suarez decided to play it safe—keep all his options open. I am out on 'house arrest' as long as I agree to stay confined to the Continental Hotel—the bartender is CIE, as are the desk clerks."

"Do the authorities know the Commandos are coming?" Col. Randal asked.

"Not as far as I am aware," Percy said. "Suspect something is up—no idea what."

"We will rescue you," Rocky said.

"Maybe not," Col. Randal said. "There's no boat available to take us off the island."

"Correct," Percy said. "The few fishing boats in Diego Suarez have been impounded by the navy to prevent the locals from using them for potential anti-Vichy resistance activities."

"We need to be away before morning," Rocky said. "Surely there is some craft available for the right price."

"I had a list of the ships operating out of Diego Suarez but it was confiscated. I believe I can recall it from memory," Percy said, "The converted liner *Bougainville,* packed with guns and welded on armor plate, rated an auxiliary cruiser, the *D'Entrecasteaux*—an anti-submarine sloop, and two submarines—the *Benveziers and the Le Heros.*"

"Any others?" Rocky said.

"There is one small steamer," Percy said. "The SS *Wartenfels* arrived here in March after a mad dash for Portuguese East Afrika where she had been interned since the beginning of the war."

Col. Randal clicked on, "A Nazi ship?"

"German flagged," Percy said. "There is speculation a Kriegsmarine wireless team is onboard monitoring British merchant traffic in the Mozambique Channel. I have never been able to confirm the report."

"Give me a minute," Col. Randal said.

He stood up, walked over to the bar and stood next to Acting Provisional Sub-Lieutenant Skipper Warthog Finley—but ignoring him.

"Would you take the lady at my table whatever she is drinking," Col. Randal said to the bartender.

The bartender mixed the drink and rushed to deliver it to Rocky.

Col. Randal stood staring straight ahead at the mirror not looking at his reflection but watching Captain "Geronimo" Joe McKoy and Waldo behind him cutting the rug with the two French women. Whatever wild improvised dance they were doing he was pretty sure it did not have a name.

Col. Randal said, "Ever hear of a ship out of Portuguese East Afrika called the called the SS *Wartenfels*?"

"I have," Skipper Finley said, taking a sip of the beer from the bottle he was drinking. "German freighter. The Portuguese have the ship interned. Me and Wino moved her to a new berth for the port authorities one time before you showed up and ruined our reputations as honest hard-working tugboat men."

"The *Wartenfels*," Col. Randal said, "is docked here in Diego Suarez."

"Colonel," Skipper Finley said, "that tramp steamer is our ticket out 'a here. Take down her crew, leave me a couple 'a men for the engine room and I can sail us to meet the Royal Navy or all the way back to Egypt if we need to."

Col. Randal said, "Get your bags packed."

"I ain't had time to unpack."

Col. Randal turned to go, glanced at King, then over to the bartender still at the table talking to Rocky and nodded.

The Merc stared back with no visible expression.

RIKKE RUNBORG LEFT FIRST, RETURNING to the pool on the roof. Colonel John Randal went up to his room. Percy Mather had another drink then went to his room, put on his swimming trunks and walked up to the pool to nap in the sun—he had not slept well in jail. Acting Provisional Sub-Lieutenant Skipper Warthog Finley finished his drink and wandered upstairs to the pool area where Percy pointed out the location of the SS *Wartenfels,* which was clearly visible from the roof of the hotel. Captain "Geronimo" Joe McKoy and Waldo Treywick hung out with the French women for an hour then went to their rooms.

King stayed in the empty bar.

AT 2300 HOURS COL. RANDAL REACHED THE PIER where the SS *Wartenfels* was docked. He thought he was the first one there.

Rocky arrived. She was no longer wearing her swimsuit but a dark blouse and a pair of black slacks tucked into soft suede, rubber-soled half boots. The .32 Sauer Model 13 Col. Randal had given her was in her purse. When she moved she was as silent as a butterfly and almost invisible in the dark. Clearly the former ballet dancer was a professional.

The two decided to stroll down the dock to do a walk-by of the SS *Wartenfels.* No one else was in sight except a couf men up the pier night-fishing—Capt. McKoy and Waldo.

It was dark. There were no lights on the wharf. Madagascar was not on blackout since the colony was not at war, it was just no one had ever gotten around to installing any.

"Evening," Capt. McKoy said when Col. Randal and Rocky walked by."Catching anything?" Col. Randal asked.

"Not a nibble," Waldo said. It would probably have helped if they had put bait on their hooks. The SS *Wartenfels* was moored not more than ten feet away.

Tramp steamer was a good description. The ship was a rust bucket. A dim light was glowing in the wheelhouse on the bridge and the sultry sound of Lil' Marlene was drifting out of what was most likely the radio shack. That would make at least two people standing watch on the upper deck. Percy Mather had said that nights, the bulk of the crew was most often to be found in one of the local bars or bordellos.

The gangplank was unguarded. Long, boring duty interned in Portuguese East Afrika for over two years and now stationed on the remote tip on the north end of Madagascar had lolled the German crew into a false sense of security.

That was good.

Col. Randal and Rocky continued on past to the end. They faked gazing out at the ocean for a while then turned to go back. Skipper Finley was standing on the jetty next to the SS *Wartenfels* talking to someone onboard. He knew the crew from when his tugboat, the *King Kong*, had moved the ship to a new berth in Portuguese East Afrika.

The two fishermen had called it a night. They were waiting when Col. Randal and Rocky walked ashore. King and Percy were there as well.

Percy said, "Quite the commotion at the Continental as we were surreptitiously effecting our departure out the back door. The relief shift found the bartender dead in the wine cellar. Man apparently slipped, fell down the stairs and broke his neck."

"That's too bad," Col. Randal said.

Skipper Finley walked up, "Talked to the cook who'd come out on deck to smoke a cigarette. There's five men onboard. The captain's drinking in his cabin, the radio operator, a skeleton crew of two men in the engine room to keep the steam up and the cook—everyone else is out on the town.

Col. Randal said, "King, team up with Skipper Finley. You've got the ship's captain – lead out first. Captain McKoy, you and Mr. Treywick go below and seize the two sailors in the engine room, we want 'em alive.

"I'll take the radio operator.

"King, once the captain's secure, deal with the cook."

"Mr. Treywick, loan your silenced High Standard .22 to Percy. That Fritz Special 38/44 of yours won't be heard from the bowls of the ship if you have to use it. Try not to —we need the stokers in one piece to do their job.

"Percy, you and Rocky stand by ready at the gangway. Don't let anyone on or off the ship."

"Questions?" Col. Randal said. "Let's do this."

King and Skipper Finley started up the pier. Col. Randal was right behind them. Then came Capt. McKoy and Waldo. Rocky and Percy waited a few moments to give them a head start then they strolled up the dock.

There was no one at the gangway when King and Skipper Finley stepped on board the SS *Wartenfels*. However, the cook, a chain smoker, had come out on deck to have another cigarette. King shot him three times with his silenced .22 High Standard Military Model D.

Skipper Finley led the way to the captain's cabin.

Right behind them came Col. Randal who stepped over the body of the cook and followed the two up the stairs to the upper deck.

Capt. McKoy and Waldo came aboard and saw the dead cook lying in their path with a glowing cigarette still in his lips.

"They claim," Capt. McKoy said, "Smokin' can be hazardous to your health."

Waldo said, "Killed him."

They went below, pistols at the ready.

On the upper deck Skipper Finley pointed to an open door. King stepped into the lead. He went in and found the ship's captain passed out drunk on his bunk. They tied him up, shut the door and went to the bridge to make ready the SS *Wartenfels* to get underway.

When King and Skipper Finley disappeared into the captain's cabin, Col. Randal moved on past and walked toward the open door where the music was coming from— Glenn Miller's 'In the Mood', as popular in Berlin as London or New York.

Col. Randal stepped into the radio room. There was a sailor sitting in a chair in front of a bank of radios. Next to the radios was a 9mm Luger P-08. While Col. Randal was trying to get out "*Hande Hoch*," the Nazi lunged for the pistol.

WHIIIIICH, WHIIIIICH.

The silenced .22 did not make a sound any louder than a match striking.

Col. Randal rolled the dead German out of the chair. Next to the Luger was what he was looking for—a wooden box. When he opened it, inside was a typewriter device. He had no idea what the machine did exactly—only that it was something the Navy Intelligence Division, Royal Navy, would go to any length to get their hands on.

Even that knowledge was more than Col. Randal was cleared to know.

Capt. McKoy and Waldo made their way down to the engine room. They slipped inside and found two sailors on duty. The Germans wisely surrendered.

"You boys must be married men," Capt. McKoy said as he indicated with the barrel of his Colt .38 Super pistol for them to start shoveling coal. "Made yourself a good decision."

The SS *Wartenfels* slipped the dock and made her way out of the harbor. It required some tricky navigation because the trip was a long, circuitous voyage around the north end of the island. Fortunately, Percy was a skilled yachtsman and knew his way into and out of Diego Suarez.

No one paid the slightest attention.

The ship was German flagged and could come and go as she pleased. No sane French naval officer would dare to interfere with a Kriegsmarine vessel under way. Everyone in Diego Suarez knew there was a long distance radio aboard. The story about her being a merchant steamer was a fig leaf—the SS *Wartenfels* was a spy ship.

Once they were out of the harbor and could feel the swell of the open seas, everyone started to breathe a little easier. As soon as he could be spared from the bridge, Percy went to the engine room and tuned to a radio frequency Col. Randal supplied. Then the Frenchman began to transmit the mission identifier, *Shortcake Harvester* and the code word *Golden Fleece.*

Col. Randal was beginning to get the idea Percy Mather was a skilled and resourceful SOE operative.

An acknowledgement came back right away.

Percy transmitted a brief message explaining the *Shortcake Harvester* team was aboard a captured enemy ship en route to attempt to rendezvous with the Royal Navy.

The comeback was to report to the commander of Force H, Rear Admiral Edward Syfret, for instructions. It included the necessary radio frequency to make contact with the flagship of the Royal Navy's invasion fleet.

"Percy," Col. Randal said, "none of this never happened."

ABOUT THE AUTHOR

PHIL WARD is a decorated combat veteran commissioned at age nineteen. A former instructor at the Army Ranger School, he has had a lifelong interest in small unit tactics and special operations. He lives in Texas, on a mountain overlooking Lake Austin.

Other books in the Raiding Forces Series:

Those Who Dare

Dead Eagles

Blood Wings

Roman Candle

Guerrilla Command

Necessary Force

Desert Patrol

Private Army

Africa 1941

www.ingramcontent.com/pod-product-compliance
Lightning Source LLC
Chambersburg PA
CBHW070836020826
48982CB00020B/1366/J

* 9 7 8 0 9 9 6 8 1 6 6 6 3 *